DIAMOND CITY

ASTRID COLE

Hardback: 979-8-9881469-0-2
Paperback: 979-8-9881469-1-9
eBook: 979-8-9881469-2-6

Cover design by Kira Rubenthaler and James T. Egan, Bookfly Design
Book design by Mike Corrao, Mayfly Design
Editing by Emily Lawrence

Library of Congress Catalog Number: 2023906701

AUTHOR'S NOTE

Diamond City is an adult novel that touches on mature themes that include but are not limited to sex, drugs, rape, and suicide. For a full list of warnings, please visit my website at astridcolebooks.com.

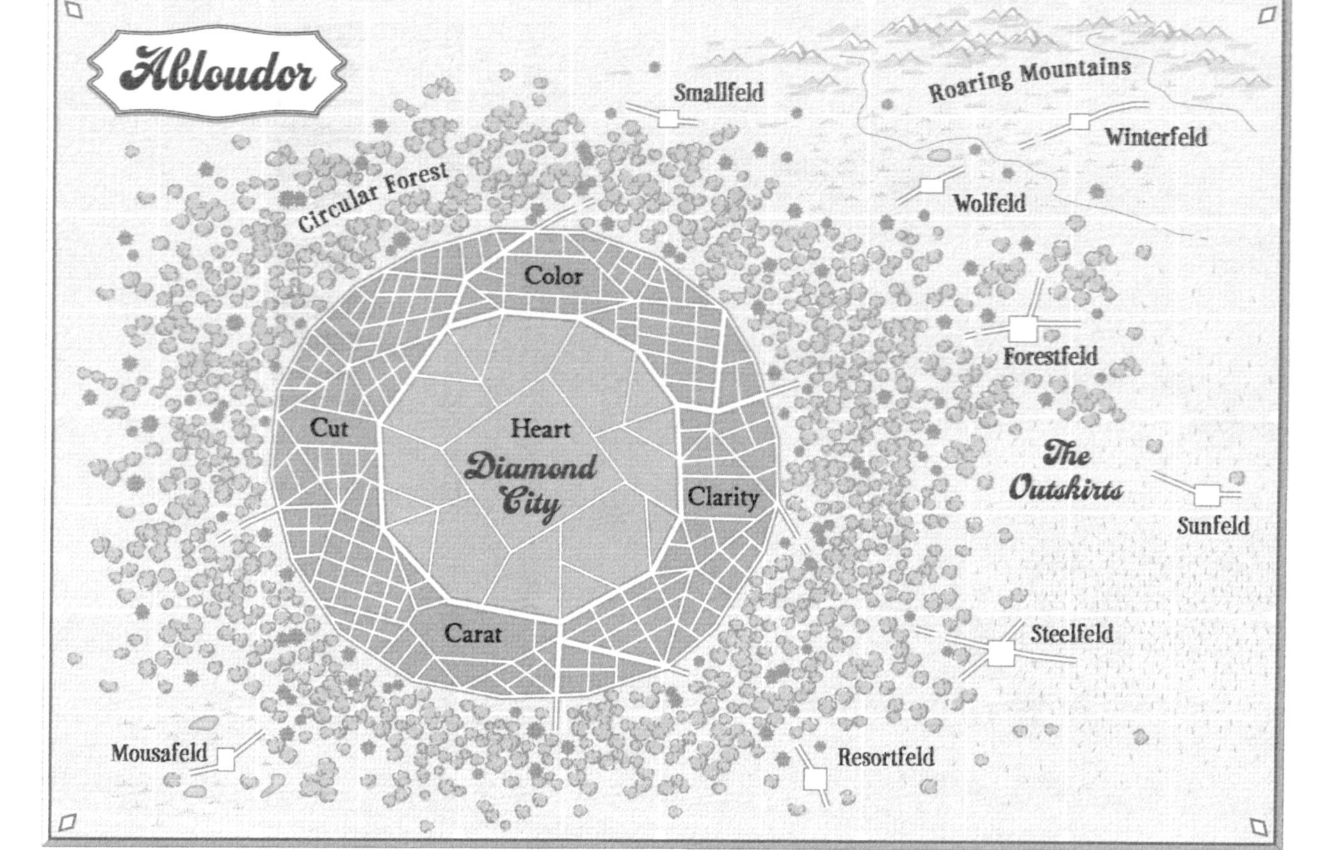

Abloudor
Smallfeld
Roaring Mountains
Winterfeld
Circular Forest
Wolfeld
Color
Forestfeld
Cut
Heart
Diamond City
The Outskirts
Clarity
Sunfeld
Carat
Steelfeld
Mousafeld
Resortfeld

DIAMOND CITY CALENDAR

1 - Month of Birth

2 - Month of Love

3 - Month of Loyalty

4 - Month of Shine

5 - Month of Purity

6 - Month of Light

7 - Month of Flare

8 - Month of Innocence

9 - Month of Courage

10 - Month of Strength

11 - Month of Energy

12 - Month of Faith

To Aris,

For all the laughs and conversations as we brainstormed
this. You're the greatest.

CHAPTER 1

The Cell Collector

Sage wanted to marry Louis Kilstrong, the most handsome man in Diamond City. If his beautiful clear eyes and curly hair wasn't enough to make every woman (and man) swoon, he was the prince to boot. He lived in Heart, the glorious capital, where buildings looked like castles and the spires were the tallest anyone had ever seen. After so many years of war, fighting, and serving pizza, Sage had the right to dream she'd live there one day, didn't she?

Her roommate, Samson, would say that she shouldn't be taking anything for granted, that so many people in Diamond City broke their backs just to survive day-to-day life. Even in the Cut District, where businesses thrived and tourists took weeks to visit as many attractions as possible, there were foreclosure signs here and there. Just the other day, the bubble tea shop across the street from Sage's apartment had vacated. Strange, because the place had always been busy, although there were rumors of family theft and money laundering.

Maybe so, and maybe Sage did have to be more thankful for the pizza restaurant she managed to keep afloat, but she wanted something exciting at this point in her life. Posters of Louis, castles, and clouds weren't enough. Her nieces understood what it was like to live with longing, for their crushes in school were on the unattainable list, too. But at least they had day-to-day contact with their love interests, while Sage was so far away from hers. She had never even met Louis, prince and heir to the Diamond City throne.

The Allseer was like an emperor, the almighty ruler, who took orders from no one and wrote his own laws. There was a council in place to help him along, but the Allseer wasn't known for compromising and consultations. He cherished his position of power like a bag of jewels and made sure his next-in-line, Louis, was off-limits to the public and confined to the palace, with authorized visitors only.

That's why, tonight, Sage was on a mission. If she wanted a shot at palace life, then she had to hunt down the "Cell Destroyer." Lame name, but he was no joke if he was picking off the city's most powerful soldiers. To celebrate, he visited bars and downed a few drinks. Tonight, he was at Travel the Diamond.

Sage looked up at the sign with a diamond sticking out of a daiquiri glass like a large ice cube. Travel the Diamond featured drinks from other districts, too, but most customers were here for Cupid's Arrow, one of the strongest liquors in the market. It stupefied drinkers like lovesick puppies; some couldn't handle the burn and rushed to the hospital for medical attention. That's why bartenders diluted it for specialty drinks, and people who thought they could resist it signed waivers to keep them from suing. The only ones brave enough to do that were washed-out, ex-soldiers who were retired from the military and didn't have much to live for anymore. Regulars knew their places.

The people inside were loud and giddy, enjoying their escapes from everyday life. Despite the Allseer's tight reign, they cherished the progress their city fostered. New technology, like vending machines with holographic displays; medical advances, like fully functional prosthetics; and the freedom to travel any of the four districts in Diamond City inspired many to get off their asses. People no longer had to bypass border security to visit their relatives, and that in itself was a lot to be thankful for. In the old days, the four districts had been at war with each other, competing for dominance and complete supremacy. That's why the Allseer had to be tough if he wanted to command and earn respect from everyone.

As Sage got closer to the double doors, she took a breath, redid her bun because the frizz was everywhere, and threw her hood up. At this bar, security was lazy about checking people's IDs and patting them down. Without a glance at her face, they let her right through.

It was warm, comforting, and low-key. It was the perfect night for a swig of diluted Cupid's Arrow, perhaps with a serving of deep-fried onion rings, but Sage had work to do. She already knew it was going to be easy because she found her target at the bar just as expected. Tall, brooding, dark, and hooded: the tell-tale signs of someone who was up to no good. Maybe it was a little bit too obvious, but the Cell Destroyer was confident enough to ward off any attempts at capture by the Allseer's forces. Hell, if he was going around killing Enhanced, the Allseer's most powerful fighters, then he had every right to sit there and sip all the booze he could put away.

Sage walked right up to an open seat beside the Cell Destroyer. She wasn't as wary or as careful as she should have been, but she was equally confident with her abilities and even more eager to state, "How do you do it? Everyone in the Allseer's circles wants to know. Enhanced are invincible. Some even say they're immortal. The Allseer's toy soldiers who aren't supposed to break. So . . . how do you kill them?"

The Cell Destroyer's curls of hair hid his eyes but not his hooked nose and stubby chin. He had no stubble, so he saw to his appearance regularly. That said a lot about his lifestyle in Diamond City, where only upper class socialites cared for shiny, perfect faces. And that was as much as he was willing to reveal to a stranger who already suspected who he might be. That's why he didn't turn his head or look at her as he said, "And how would you know I do anything, my lady?"

"The Private Guard," Sage said honestly. "They work for the Allseer, and they're concerned because someone's been picking off their strongest soldiers." She had pictures and reports as evidence on her phone and showed them to the Cell Destroyer.

All the victims looked like dried-up mummies who had been extracted from their sarcophagi. Like someone had stuck a vacuum cleaner in them and just sucked every sliver of life from their bodies. And that was the thing: their Cells had been taken from them, the source of their power, what made them Enhanced.

Once implanted with Cells, there was no way to take them out. Cells were a complicated framework that grew in the body until the human became an Enhanced: stronger build, faster regeneration, better immunity, and longer life spans. They were supposed to be impossible to kill, but it looked like the Cell Destroyer had access to some pretty capable weapons, something the Allseer clearly didn't have. He wouldn't have been throwing a hissy fit otherwise and the Private Guard wouldn't have been desperate enough to ask Sage for help.

"Sad, indeed," murmured the Cell Destroyer after only a glance at his own work. He sipped that beer like he was lounging in his living room, not caring whether or not the Porcupines—the Cut District's very own fastball team—won. It was the last quarter and the score was tied 5-5. "But what on earth makes you think I did it?"

"I don't think you did anything," Sage said. "I'm just here to fetch you because the PG swears you're behind it. You pop up in or around places where Enhanced have died, and you don't do much to hide it, either. I mean, can you be any more conspicuous? Even my teenage nieces would have been able to blend into a crowd with dresses and makeup. Such confidence."

The Cell Destroyer snorted. This really was a game to him. "I'm impressed that the Private Guard sent *you*, though. I wasn't expecting that."

Sage arched a brow. "Oh? You know who I am?"

"Not personally, but you chastise me about being conspicuous in a bar and look at you. You just waltz in here, take a seat next to me, and start wagging your finger at me when you know I've killed Enhanced. You have quite the 'confidence' yourself, miss."

"Is that a confession?"

"Do I really have to hide it? You sound so sure of yourself. Your surety is impressive, but your power even more so."

"This isn't about me," Sage said. "*How* are you killing these Enhanced? What on earth are you using to take their Cells? Not even the Allseer knows how to do that."

"Oh," the Cell Destroyer whispered, not quite looking at her. He still kept his face away, so all Sage talked to was the hook of his nose. "That's what you think, my dear. There are so many things about the Allseer you don't know."

"Well, there is one thing I do know: he's not killing his own Enhanced. So I want to know why you're doing it. Are you competing with the Warlord? He's been acting up as of late, gathering his forces in the Outskirts. But you're not working for him, are you? His attacks are from the outside, and yours are from the inside. The Warlord targets soldiers from the Outskirts where his rebels roam. You, on the other hand, scout out your victims here. Why? More vulnerable?"

"Are you all right here?" asked one of the bartenders when she noticed that Sage was unattended.

Sage was about to wave her off when the Cell Destroyer said, "A cherry soda." He didn't turn his head, but he said to Sage, "I know it's your favorite."

"How do you know that?" Sage said.

"There are certain things I just can't tell you, and that would be one of them. Even so, I feel it's a rather trivial detail compared to your earlier question of why I'm going through the trouble of hunting down Enhanced. Not only is it fun, but let's just say it's time to gather what we so freely gave, to take it back from the sort of people we allowed to come to power. All they can think about are petty wars instead of unity. Just look at the Warlord and Allseer, going at each other's throats like alpha lions."

"Wait," Sage said slowly, " 'take back'? As in 'take back' Cells?"

"Stay out of it. It's none of your business."

"But it *is* my business—"

The Cell Destroyer swung the empty beer bottle at her face—Sage ducked, pulled the dagger from her thigh, and shoved it right through his chest. It happened so quickly that no one saw it, even when the Cell Destroyer slumped in his seat, falling over in what looked like a drunken heap. It happened all the time at Travel the Diamond, to those daredevils who thought Cupid's Arrow was a walk in the park. If only it were that simple for Sage, who got a surprise as she went to retrieve her blade: the Cell Destroyer wasn't dead—he was very much alive, and he proved it by yanking the dagger out all on his own and flinging it right back at her.

Now, people noticed and they started screaming. Chaos erupted, and the Cell Destroyer made a run for it. He wasn't swift about it either: he broke a few glasses, toppled a few tables, and threw around some chairs. Sage had to barrel her way across the bar, and it wasn't easy: she slipped and hit the floor hard. Pain didn't register when she was in fight-or-flight mode, and she kept her eyes on the Cell Destroyer, who just barged through the side door. By the time Sage made it outside, he had already jumped into his car to escape. He would have done it, too, if Sage wasn't afraid to latch onto his bumper and ascend one thousand feet into the air with him.

The wind tore at her body, the pressure about to knock her right off that flimsy lip of the car. Then the car zoomed forward, and Sage held on, fingers clutching metal. Her grip tightened, impenetrable, and allowed her to climb onto the roof without falling to her death. She kept her knees bent, the center of gravity low as she reached over and punched through the driver's side window.

Sage grabbed and yanked the Cell Destroyer right out of the car, and then they sped off course, in line with a cellular service office that was a hundred stories tall. Hotspot was Diamond City's fastest and preferred network, and right now its 3D logo was going to save her life. She saw that happy sun and its rays everywhere, from buses to billboards, and she got the closest look at it yet. With her target secure in one hand, she used the other to latch onto one of the rays as the car crashed into the side of the building just feet away from them.

Sage gritted her teeth. She looked up at her lonely hand wrapped tightly around that steel beam, holding her and the Cell Destroyer in midair. Out of everything she practiced at the gym, dangling with a body close to two hundred pounds beneath her wasn't one of them. Even so, she didn't let go, but then the Cell Destroyer did something unexpected: he slashed her wrist with a blade of his own.

Sage hissed, startled, and dropped the bastard, who fell to his death.

No! She needed him alive! How else was he going to answer all of her questions?

"Damn it!" Sage cursed because all she could do was hang there with a bleeding wound and watch as her target hit the ground a thousand feet below with a sickening splat.

"Damn it!" Sage cried again, squeezing her eyes shut. Teeth clenched, she used both of her hands now to pull herself on top of the ray. Then she broke the closest window with her elbow and tumbled inside, thankful that these offices were empty for the night. Still panting and shaking, she kept her hood up as she trudged across the room to the elevator, heart pounding at what she was going to find on the street. But, to her shock, there was no body.

Only a large crowd. Everyone was gathered around the crash site, the indentation the Cell Destroyer's body had made. But by no means was there a physical body left to gather and study or use as any sort of evidence.

Sirens wailed in the air. Sage's breaths got tight as instinct drove her to step away before she was caught or identified. A few people were already looking at her, muttering to themselves about how she "came out of that building."

"Shit," Sage breathed to herself, taking large strides to get the hell out of there before she recruited any more attention. She had to get back to her restaurant.

Nearby officers came out like roaches, always stationed at every corner and alley of the city. Covered from head to foot in white battle armor and equipped with weapons that shot lasers, they were impossible to miss and that was the point. Despite being human, they were a beacon of power. They were supposed to ward off challengers and troublemakers like the Warlord, but that wasn't working out too well.

On her way to Two for Pizza, Sage saw it on the news, flashing across those large screens on every street: the blurry faces, the gray jumpsuits, and the ruthless way in which those terrorists executed their victims. Sage had to stop because of the red light, so she took a moment to watch what the city wanted her to see.

"*Ise mara topenda*," spoke one of the terrorists in a foreign tongue with a translation of his words at the bottom of the screen: "You don't deserve pity."

The victim, an unfortunate soldier captured along the edge of the Outskirts, shook his covered head, even if he couldn't understand a word. Fear was a universal language among the Enhanced, too. This one had moments to cry out before a single blade ended his life. Stab, crisscross, stab, decapitate.

One blade . . . just like that. Was it, perhaps, the same weapon the Cell Destroyer was using?

And this was in front of everyone, even children. The newscaster stated the obvious—"The Warlord and his rebels are highly dangerous"—and ensured that the people of Diamond City went to bed knowing it. It instigated fear, encouraged more resistance against rebellious forces, and that's exactly why the Allseer played these skits like local channels would Wooly Socks commercials.

Propaganda aside, the Warlord had a reason for putting on a show. Everyone already knew the story of how he and his band of fighters had been exiled from Diamond City for not pledging their allegiance to the Allseer. Everyone had to kiss the Allseer's ring . . . or else.

So the big question was: were those videos for real? Or just a bunch of bullshit?

The footage had been edited to blur out faces and include subtitles. Did the Warlord really know how to speak a different language? Why would he when he could just speak Lucidum, what everyone in Diamond City spoke?

"This isn't about me. How are you killing these Enhanced? What on earth are you using to take their Cells? Not even the Allseer knows how to do that."

"Oh. That's what you think, my dear. There are so many things about the Allseer you don't know."

When Sage was a safe distance away from the Hotspot tower, she updated the PG. She spoke to Penelope, their leader.

"The Cell Destroyer is no regular human," Sage said to her as the rain started to come down. It wasn't unusual to collect a few inches every day, all year round in the city. This place was wet, but district officials made the best of their terrible weather by opening outdoor waterparks, putting on the most impressive light shows Sage had ever seen, and configuring puddle mazes for children to solve. Yes, there was an entire strip of land on the eastern side of the district dedicated to a very inventive game of hopscotch. Sage never got past the first three puddles without landing in them. Her nieces always made it to the very end for the ultimate prize.

"He's an Enhanced. He didn't flinch at my dagger and fell over a hundred stories to what should have been his death," Sage said.

"Come to your restaurant immediately," Penelope said, sounding annoyed. "We need to talk to you face-to-face, Thyme. We've got more than just a Cell Destroyer on our hands now. The Warlord just challenged the Allseer to a duel this weekend."

CHAPTER 2

The Private Guard's New Home

I t was nowhere on the news because that would stir too much chaos. It wasn't every day that the notorious Warlord challenged the Allseer to a duel. It was one thing to see his ruthlessness upon the military, but a complete other to see him fight the Allseer in person. Just the idea of it would create an even greater political wedge among the people, prompt more rebellions among the ones who were thinking about it or entertaining the idea of yet another revolution. In fact, there were many secret Warlord supporters and Allseer haters waiting for the opportunity to take center stage. Only when it was to their advantage, though . . . The Warlord loved to kill the Allseer's people, but the Allseer did the same to anyone who thought about fighting him. Sometimes there were public trials and torture sessions. Those were televised, too. The Allseer had to get creative if he wanted to be the biggest bully in the playground. He was an Enhanced, so, this was his hundredth year in power.

Sage sighed. She wasn't one to involve herself in those conflicts. She had fought plenty during the Unification War and foregone any bickering or power struggles after that. But, how much longer could she keep her neutrality? If the Cell Destroyer wasn't working for the Warlord . . . then he had to be working for the Allseer. The Kilstrongs. Because under the hood, Sage knew now, was someone she did recognize. She had not spent a hundred years of her life researching and memorizing all of Louis Kilstrong's family for nothing.

The curls of brown hair, the hooked nose, the defined jaw—that was definitely Francis Kilstrong, the Allseer's brother. But then why the hell was a *Kilstrong* targeting Enhanced?

"Yo, Oregano." Penelope was hanging out by the door of the restaurant, arms crossed. She was impossible to miss, not just because of her red hair, but the Two for Pizza sign was pretty bright above her. Why didn't Sage see any customers inside? "You're finally here."

"Wait." Sage brushed past her, bursting into an empty restaurant with wiped-down tables, polished seats, and a cleaned-up counter. All the pizzas were gone. Put away. The menu that took up the entire back wall presented customers with types galore, from savory options like the Hippo—all of the toppings, even bananas—to sweet options like the Beat Box, the perfect blend of beets and chocolate on dough.

But . . .

But . . .

Where were her customers?

All Sage saw were the PG members hanging out in the corner like a team of fastball players, fatigued after a long day at practice. They must have had a feast because there were pizza boxes everywhere, and, because they all answered to Bram, the founder of the Private Guard and co-owner of the restaurant, they got *free* pizzas like the overgrown brats they were.

Yes, Bram was their ringleader, like the popular kid hooking up his best goons with freebies at school. And he was also Sage's very spoiled nephew, even if he was human, forty years old, and sported a large beer belly. Sage didn't give a shit, and she let it rip, nephew or not.

"What the fuck's going on here?" Sage sputtered, looking at Bram because *he* was the goddamned owner here and took full responsibility for their business when she was out on missions. Since when did the PG have the right to waltz in here and make themselves at home? They had their own damn headquarters! "Where is everyone?!"

"Chill out, Thyme," Penelope said, holding her hands out. "We cleared everyone out because we have important matters to discuss—"

"Not in my restaurant you don't!" Sage yelled. "Go back to your headquarters and we'll talk there, but not during business hours—"

"That's the thing, Sage," Bram interrupted quietly. The little shit knew never to cross his aunt and put himself above her, no matter how old she was and how much he towered over her. He looked pleading like he wanted another ice cream cone, and he had to do this strategically if he was going to get the sprinkles, too. "The All-seer cut the PG's funding. They haven't been able to pay rent, and so I let them stay here . . . for now."

Sage blinked. It took a long time for those words to register in her brain. That's why she didn't talk, and why Penelope chimed in instead.

"We've been doing a piss-poor job of being useful to the All-seer," Penelope said nonchalantly, as if explaining why she had gotten an F on her assignment. She took a seat at the PG table, re-inforcing the claim that this was her new place of residence. To her right was a guy named Dustin who didn't like to speak much, and to her left was a blonde who had already undone her tie and loosened her jacket. Their personalities varied greatly, but their uniforms were the same, carrying the Diamond City insignia on their armbands.

It was an insignia that Sage held close to her heart. It was on the Diamond City flag, and she had a tattoo of it on her inner arm, right beneath her biceps. It was a diamond with a spear going straight through it, symbolizing the unification of all four districts. Just a hundred years ago, after many battles and tribulations, the city had become whole. She had fought for peace—she had fought for this business—and now she had four lazy asses invading her space.

At Two for Pizza, customers got quality pies and fast service. That's what made the restaurant so successful, attracting people from across the city for a taste of cheesy goodness. Sage wasn't good at a lot of things, but spinning dough and perfecting tomato sauce were in her DNA.

The Private Guard was *not* her problem.

"Piss-poor job, you say?" Sage said quietly. "Really? So in other words, you're not doing your jobs. And because you're not able to provide any meaningful results, you're out of a base?"

"It's temporary," Penelope said quickly. "That's why we sent you out to get the Cell Destroyer. And it seems you've failed to do that, too. Could you imagine the prestige if we had gotten a hold of him—"

Sage flipped over a table. That wasn't enough. She stalked across the restaurant and picked up Penelope, shaking her. The other three PG members stood up, drawing their measly guns, but didn't fire because Bram shouted, "DON'T SHOOT!"

"The PG is *not* my problem!" Sage hissed at Penelope, who remained calm.

"No," Penelope said quietly. "But it's the only way you'll get to meet Louis. It'll get you that much closer to the son who *is* looking to marry, you know. There are rumors that the Allseer will be stepping down soon. Isn't that what you want?"

"Don't bribe me—you have no right to kick out *my* customers and take over my business because you aren't doing your jobs! Just what the hell are you doing all day that the Allseer cut your funds?"

No one was going to answer that. Either they were too ashamed or hiding something. Penelope went with, "You're not the only owner here, Sage. If Bram says we can crash for a bit, use your office to keep us afloat, then what's the problem?"

"THE PROBLEM IS I DIDN'T AGREE TO THIS!" Sage roared at her, then turned to Bram. "When were you going to talk to me about this, Bram?"

"I didn't want to worry you," Bram said with a shit look on his face. "And it's really not a big deal. They can use the office—"

"BUT THEY CAN'T KICK OUT MY CUSTOMERS!"

There was a knock on the door. Sage didn't think twice—she ran and answered it.

"Are you open?" asked the lady standing out in the rain. She had an umbrella, but her hair was wet. She must have run from a taxi just to make it here.

"Yes, yes!" Sage waved her in. "Please. What would you like?"

"Can I have two Hippos, please?" the woman asked, eyeing the PG members suspiciously. She didn't seem to care about the odd company, though. She glanced at the muted TV and the latest Warlord execution video. "I'm not sure what to believe anymore," she huffed. "All this propaganda. Do you believe it?"

"No," Sage said honestly, pressing buttons on the register. "I'm very distrustful of the Allseer and some of their organizations." She glared at Penelope.

"Sometimes we make fun of them, but I think the Clarity District folks are all onto something." The woman lowered her voice as if it was too embarrassing to say out loud. "The Optimum will save us. Just like she did during the Unification War. She brought all four districts together and look how well the districts function now."

Sage looked up at her. "Indeed."

"I think the Optimum is alive somewhere . . . don't you?"

Now this woman truly did sound like a Clarity District resident. Piety was an understatement there. They were very religious with churches and statues in the name of a warrior who had stopped at nothing to unite them in a time when districts had warred with each other. Sage would know . . . because she had been there. She had fought in that horrific war.

As for the woman, she was done speaking her mind. She was here for food, to feed her children, and she wanted to be quick about it because the rain was only going to get worse.

"All right, so we've got two Hippos," Sage said out loud. "Will that be all?"

"Those pizzas are like a meal and dessert in one," the woman commented. "All the toppings *plus* bananas? Genius."

"My idea," Sage said happily, ignoring Bram in her peripheral. She ran to the back, scraped up the pies, and delivered them to the woman, who left, but not before she said, "May the Optimum bless you."

Penelope snickered.

With the restaurant clear again, Sage rounded on her uninvited guests.

"Sage, I'm sorry." Bram beat everyone to the first words. "I didn't mean to upset you, but we closed off the restaurant so we can talk about our very real problems—"

"Our 'very real problems'," Sage hissed, "include not being able to pay rent if this place doesn't make money! These bozos clearly aren't!" She waved at the PG.

"Well, these 'bozos' just got you an invite to Louis Kilstrong's party." Penelope threw the envelope at Sage's chest—Sage caught it. "Here it is, as promised. He'll be turning 114 years old this week-end, and he's throwing an exclusive party at the palace."

114 years old had a strange ring, but all the Enhanced were around that age because most of them had turned during the Unification War. Incredibly, Louis didn't look a day older than Bram. Time slowed drastically for anyone with Cells in their blood, no matter the age they received them. Sage would know because she was turning 118 this year and some bars still asked her for an ID. Longevity, however, didn't cure the trauma of war or a life fully lived. And Sage had been through her fair share of horror. She deserved to go to this birthday party, but something didn't seem quite right.

"Even with the Warlord's challenge?"

"It's the night before."

"And you're still invited?" Sage snorted. "I thought the Allseer 'cut your funding'."

"Of course." Bram frowned. "Actually, we were hoping to present some good news, but now we're up shit creek without a paddle because you didn't get us any worthwhile information, did you—"

"Francis Kilstrong," Sage said tightly. It still felt strange saying the name out loud. Sage had been in a lot of fights before, but this was the first time she had ever gone toe-to-toe with an actual Kilstrong. "Look him up. That's the Cell Destroyer."

Sure enough, everyone sat up. They were confused.

"No way," Dustin said, leaning forward to grab his computer and perform a quick check. Searching up the name procured hundreds of images of the now rogue royal, and Sage was sure that's exactly whom she had chased through the Cut District's skyscrapers tonight.

"Wait." Penelope leaned over the table, peering closely at the screen. "So *that's* the Cell Destroyer? The guy who's been bar-hopping in the Cut District? No way. Our target looks like a run-of-the-mill creepy dude who's been hired to whack Enhanced—not a flawless hunk every woman masturbates to at night."

"Exactly," Sage bit. God, she hated Penelope. "The Cell Destroyer looks like a creepy dude, but he's not."

"Wait a second—but how did *you* know it was Francis Kilstrong?"

"I didn't until I got a good look at him. And you're questioning *me* about what a Kilstrong looks like?"

"Fair enough," Penelope conceded. "But we still have no proof it was him. And let's say you're right—do you know what the implications of it are? If this was Francis, then that means all these attacks in the city were ordained by the Allseer, yes?"

"Not necessarily," Dustin said, looking a bit worried now. "I mean, I don't know . . ."

"Can't we ask Louis at his birthday party?" Penelope said. "See if he knows anything?"

"Absolutely not! We can't just admit we've been tailing a Kilstrong!"

"It was the Kilstrongs who ordered us to stop the Cell Destroyer!"

"Then it can't be Francis." Dustin shrugged, leaning right back into the chair and grabbing another slice of pizza. "Sage is wrong."

"Fuck you!" Sage exclaimed. "Then get off your ass and you chase him—"

"I believe you," Penelope said.

Then they had just uncovered a conspiracy brewing among the royals. If Francis Kilstrong had his own agenda, the question was why? Was this the start of yet another revolution, one that was going to transpire under the radar and in the absence of riots? The Allseer was good about controlling the population, so Francis was taking the solo route on this. The only other question was how did destroying Enhanced help with whatever plans he had against his own brother?

"Before we say anything, let's do some digging at the birthday party," Penelope said. "See what comes up."

Right. The birthday party this weekend. So, at this point, it was out of Sage's hands. She had fulfilled her duty to Penelope and the Private Guard, as she had promised she would in exchange for the invitation, and now it was time for her to go home. Not before laying down the rules, though.

"If they are going to use this place as their new headquarters, they use the offices and never interact with the customers," Sage spat at Bram. "And I swear that if I walk in here again and see that you've closed before hours, I will fucking leave and you'll never see me again. Got it?"

"Sage," Penelope whined, taking a step closer. "Come on. Just take it easy, will you?"

"This is my business!" Sage hissed again. "And you will not interfere!"

"We won't—we promise—and we're sorry."

Sage had had enough for one night, so she turned around to leave without saying goodbye.

"Say you'll help if we need you?" Penelope asked her outside, where it was dark and desolate save for a shimmering street lamp at the end of the block. "Looks like we may. If you couldn't stop the Cell Destroyer, then which one of us can?"

"Wow," Sage said bitterly. "That's quite the pedestal I'm on. Before you know it, I'll be defending the Allseer against his duel with the Warlord, too, right?"

Penelope hesitated. "Actually, I was just about to ask you about that. You know that shit is going to get ugly and that we need positive attention, so if you could jump in—"

"This isn't my concern. Not anymore. And not one word about who I really am."

"Sage, of course not—and this is *all* of our concerns. If the Warlord kills the Allseer, then what will become of Diamond City? You know how those people live in the Outskirts like wild animals, hunting and fist-fighting like savages—that's why they were exiled thirty years ago. We've lived in so much peace and harmony since then—why would you want to jeopardize that?"

"I am not going to take sides," Sage said. "Not anymore. Look, Penelope, it's just one problem after another. I helped you tonight because of Louis, but that's it. I have Bram, the girls, and myself to look after."

"And Louis will need even more help when his father dies."

"Do you really think the Warlord will win in a duel against the Allseer?" Sage said with fake incredulity. "The guy who's been 'hunting and fist-fighting' in the wastelands with nowhere near the amount of resources as the Allseer?"

"Hello!" Penelope waved her hands. "The Warlord has those weapons that can kill Enhanced while we don't! Even if the Cell Destroyer doesn't work for the Warlord, the Warlord still has access to things we don't—those torture videos are for real"

"And how the hell is this my problem, damn it?" Sage spat. "So I'm the sacrificial lamb now—is that it? I'm sorry, but I'm NOT laying down my life for that almighty bastard who, may I remind you, never even told us *why* he was in such a hurry to kick out the rebels to begin with! I know the Warlord's a beast, but did you ever stop to consider that there's a reason for it?"

Penelope's lip trembled. Her hair didn't look so red anymore, not when her resolve was crumbling and Sage's words sank in. The blasphemy leaving Sage's mouth was overwhelming and scary because nobody spoke like that and got away with it. People were put to death for trashing the Allseer's decisions. She was trained to say one thing to Sage's very legit concerns. "That's blasphemy."

"Because the Allseer said so, right?"

"When the Allseer dies, Louis is next in line," Penelope stated calmly. "And he's going to need your help, Sage. We all are. Unless you trust the Warlord to keep Diamond City together. I feel that he is going to completely ruin what we have, because his goal was to distribute power to everyone and not for the purpose you're thinking. He doesn't want to improve everyday life—he wants to watch people kill each other like dogs! This is a man who loves to collect heads and openly punish his own followers if they resist him. It's a sick game of power he plays—even more than the Allseer," she added when Sage was about to argue. "He skins them and eats their organs for dinner."

"I don't believe that," Sage snapped. "Any of it! Do you know why? The Allseer is a manipulative bastard. Don't you remember how he tortured the Warlord in public?"

"Maybe because the Warlord deserved it."

"We don't know what he deserved because we don't have the entire truth. All that bullshit you're spewing? That's what the Allseer told you and wants you to believe so you take his side."

Penelope's mouth hung open a bit. "Are you . . . *siding* with the Warlord?"

Guilt trips and power struggles: the two things Sage avoided like the plague. This wasn't a conversation she wanted to have right now, so she walked away without another word.

She dared Penelope to follow her.

The harpy didn't.

CHAPTER 3
Fight or Flight

The rain never stopped in the Cut District. It didn't matter what time of year it was either. Right now, it was the month of Light, the start of summer, but this was the same drizzle Sage felt in Faith, when parades filled the streets with the celebration of a new year of unity.

Cars sped by in the open air; they looked messy going in all directions. But traffic rules were easy to follow and police ensured they were. Their cars looked like black dots from below, conveniently parked at every intersection. Sage couldn't imagine what it was like to have that job, suffering through ten-hour shifts of just watching for recklessness. While cars had built-in GPSs and automatic controls, teenagers tried their hands at racing whenever they were feeling lucky. They were called Speed Stars because they looked like shooting stars in the sky. More often than not, they wound up dead.

One of Sage's customers, Rick, had been a notorious racer among his underground crew, always boasting about his skills behind the wheel and ability to escape the cops. Bad boy, dangerous, and oh so charming—he had been a huge inspiration to Sage in the pizzeria's early years. Not that Sage condoned crazy behavior, but she admired Rick's drive to pursue what he loved ... even if it had gotten him killed. Cocky Rick had thought he could escape the cops that one time, but his car had spiraled out of control after cutting a corner too close. When Sage heard about it on the news, she had been devastated. In honor of Rick, she had gotten a tiny car tattooed on her left wrist. It was a reminder to do what she loved in life and be smart about it.

Personally, though, Sage didn't need cars because she lived right down the street from the restaurant, and she rather enjoyed her strolls. There were colorful lights everywhere, pink, purple, green, and blue reflecting off of glass and water droplets. Bus stops flashed with the latest events: the Cut Porcupines were playing the Clarity Owls at fastball tomorrow night, and the Art Carnival was coming in the month of Flare, the start of fall. It was a caravan of artists that traveled through all four districts, spending a season in each. Sage bought a painting from there every year, even if there was no more wall space in her room. While she couldn't paint for the life of her, she was good at making bracelets. She felt naked without them.

While Sage should have been looking forward to the Art Carnival, all she could think about was the shitty look on Bram's face and Penelope's annoying red hair. There was a horrible emptiness blossoming in her chest, eating at her body like cancer. It wasn't even the Cell Destroyer chase and the mystery behind the Kilstrongs or the Warlord's tactics—it was the restaurant. Her beloved pizzeria now the PG's headquarters.

Sage sighed. She let her clothes soak up the rain and wiped beads from her face every so often. Ultimately, her thoughts got nowhere because there was no solution to this mess right now—she couldn't open another location because she didn't have the money, and she couldn't get rid of the PG because they were her ticket to seeing Louis. The birthday party was this weekend.

Stupid, said her mind. Her own consciousness called her stupid because she was.

    DIAMOND CITY

Stupid for wanting to see a spoiled prince so badly. Stupid for putting her business in jeopardy—

"It'll warm you right up!" a vendor called from across the street, making Sage look up.

Cinnamon Rings. Soggy as hell, but it was becoming a delicacy here. Cutians made anything work.

Sage wasn't sure she could grow warm right now, though, not with the prospect of another war on the horizon. The moment she pulled her head out of her own ass, she realized there were bigger things at stake than her own measly business. The Warlord was challenging the Allseer, and despite who won, there'd be hell to face. Either the Warlord would take over Diamond City or the Allseer would be free of formidable adversaries. Which one was worse?

More war . . . again . . . It always brought back such dark memories, the days that that was all Sage had known and seen. She had done it for money, but most of all, she had done it because she wanted to be like Star Raider.

Yes, Sage wanted to be like the main character of a kid's TV show. Defenders Unite! was a series that had come out to promote the Enhanced during the Unification War. It was about a bunch of superheroes who fought together to defend their city. Sadly, the series was banned in Diamond City now. The Allseer didn't want any Enhanced propaganda, didn't want to give the public any ideas to attain power themselves. That's why Sage was shocked to find a tent selling Defenders Unite! toys.

Among the piles on the table, guarded by a little girl, was the green head of Star Raider still in her raggedy old box. Sage would recognize her anywhere.

She ran right over, heart picking up speed. She was as giddy as any of the children roaming around the tent, looking for treasure themselves. She picked up the box, then found the eyes of the little girl smiling brightly at her.

"That will be ten Diamonds, please," she squeaked.

"Here." Sage dug into her pocket. "Have fifty."

This reached the mother's ears; she turned around to see who the generous customer was.

The little girl, in turn, seemed ecstatic that she finally had enough money to buy herself a new Virtual Reality helmet—that's what she announced as she hopped back to her mother. She was learning the true value of a Diamond, what it took to make money, and sometimes that meant a bit of sacrifice. Star Raider was still in her box, unused, so the little girl probably didn't care much for her anyway.

The mother looked content to know that it was in good hands now, but thanks were in order for such a purchase in uncertain times. Sure, business boomed in the Cut District, but the city felt like it was sitting on a powder keg and anything could set it off. Something as simple as a challenge, like the one just days away. Every citizen probably had a safe room somewhere.

"You have a generous heart, young lady," the mother said happily, as rickety as the flaps of her tent. Times were tough for her, but she was still holding on. "Are you an Enhanced by any chance?" She suspected this because not many people appreciated Star Raider anymore. There was no way someone who looked like they were thirty years old would get excited over a toy like this.

"I fought with them," Sage said, feeling this woman could keep a secret. "It was an honor, actually. I was a big fan of the show. It's what inspired me to join the Enhanced when I was just eighteen years old." She showed the woman her Star Raider tattoo, an "SR" inside a green circle. The little girl gasped.

"Whoa!"

"You are a brave soul to still be in this city," the mother whispered; some of the customers were standing a bit too close to them. "Why have you not joined the Warlord and his rebels?"

"My fighting days are over," Sage said honestly. "I have a life here now."

"The Allseer will come after you eventually," she whispered, even lower still. "He wants to exterminate all the Enhanced minus the ones in his circle . . . you know that, right? My sister, Gertrude, was a target . . . she had to run."

"But not you? Aren't you an Enhanced, too?" Or else, the mother would not be in possession of a Star Raider toy.

"I have my child." The mother held the little girl tightly to her side. "She goes to school here. The Warlord's camp is no place for children. I have faith this will all come to an end soon. But please . . . if you meet the Warlord . . . he will take you in with open arms." The mother reached into her pocket and pulled out a folded piece of paper. Inside was a hand-drawn map of Diamond City and its outskirts. She pointed to the Circular Forest, the miles of trees that encircled the four districts like a moat, then dragged her finger down to an empty space to the south. There was no indication of a settlement there, in case this ever fell into the wrong hands, but she gazed at Sage earnestly and said, "Here, my friend. Seek refuge if you need it."

"I appreciate it."

"Oh, and one more question," the mother said before Sage stepped away. "Did you ever meet the Optimum? They say she was unstoppable on the battlefield. Clarity residents even say that she wasn't Enhanced or human."

"I . . . met her, yes."

"I believe the Warlord is also searching for her. There is a rumor that she holds the power to all the Enhanced."

Sage cleared her throat. "All the more reason to stay away from her, isn't it?"

Then Sage left before anything went awry. Now she wasn't sure she trusted the woman. She wondered if the woman was a spy for Francis Kilstrong, on the lookout for any wandering Enhanced. However, she had just admitted that the Kilstrongs were looking to eliminate Enhanced that were no longer a part of the military . . . Would a spy reveal that? Sage didn't know. It was a terrible way to think of people, but she was trained to see the worst in everyone.

That's what happened when you lived with Samson for a hundred years. He hated Enhanced *and* humans.

"Greetings, Sage." Samson delivered his usual acknowledgment of her return home after a long day of work. Little did he know, Sage's end of the day hadn't entailed refrigerating dough or wiping down tables. In his own little world, Samson concentrated on his chores, which included cleaning their apartment, cooking their food, and expanding his crafter's business. These were ideal living conditions for someone who looked like a humanoid squid.

Samson had tight raw muscles, razor-sharp teeth, huge amber eyes, sharp-as-hell nails, and if that wasn't intimidating enough, he stood over six feet tall. His Lucidum, Diamond City's language, was terrible, so he spoke in Lolligo, the official name for Squids and their language, which sounded like intelligent garble.

"You look like you've been quite busy tonight," Samson said.

"How can you tell?" Sage took off her coat and hung it on the rack, completely drenched, but at least her new Star Raider action figure was safe. "Because I'm sweaty, dirty, or both? How do you know I didn't get into a fight with pizza dough?"

Samson scowled at her, sharp teeth pinching his puffy lips. "I have known you for more than a hundred years. Are you telling me *I* wouldn't notice these things?"

"You won't ever guess what happened."

"Do enlighten me, then."

To say that she confronted a Kilstrong who killed Enhanced was still strange on her tongue. Foreign, even, as if it would draw the military right to her door. That's because the Allseer loved his Enhanced—kept him and his city safe at night—so entertaining it out loud was like thinking of dogs as being able to walk on hind legs. Samson watched her closely, looking equally unsettled at the amount of attention Sage had drawn from the chase and the sort of consequences it'd have from the Allseer. He didn't like it one bit.

"Well," Samson said slowly, serving her a plate of stripped beef and noodles with a boiled egg on top. This was a portion big enough for two men, but Sage had a huge appetite. "Sounds like you got yourself involved in quite the predicament. That's what happens when you hang around Bram."

　　　　　DIAMOND CITY

Bram.

The restaurant.

"He's the one who started this whole 'Private Guard' to gain favor with the Allseer," Samson snapped without Sage even saying a word about her in-trouble business. "And, conveniently, he drags you into it when he needs you the most. I say get out, change your name, and move elsewhere. Maybe we should look for the Lolligo like we should have been doing since the end of the Unification War and get out of this wretched city. It's always raining!"

"I can't just get out," Sage said quietly. "Bram needs help with the pizzeria . . . and the girls need me, Samson."

"They're just a bunch of humans. Haven't you raised the entire Fraser family, practically? Seriously, how much longer do you need to babysit?"

"They're my *family*, Samson."

"Actually"—Samson pointed at her with a long finger—"they're not. Your mother is dead, and your father is out there somewhere."

"They're my mother's children—of course they're still family."

"How many years removed, Sage? Goddamn it, it's about time you did something for yourself—*And don't even think about it!*"

Sage withdrew her foot. She had been moments away from discarding her boots all over the pristine kitchen floor. It was a bad habit, and Samson always blew a gasket. He was researching ways on how to train Sage's brain to follow simple household rules, and he remembered that yelling was ineffective. Positive reinforcement worked best, so Samson cleared his throat and said, "Good girl."

"I'm not a dog," Sage grumbled. "And to get back to what you were saying before, I am doing something for myself." She mustered all the energy she had to sound as excited as possible to say this, "In exchange for helping the PG, I'm going to meet Louis Kilstrong!" The only plus side in this shitstorm. Sage's cheeks went a bright red. Samson gasped, jaw hanging low. Sage could see all of his sharp teeth.

"Are you kidding me? You would risk our livelihood to meet some despicable *boy*?"

"He's not just a 'boy'," Sage pointed out. "Louis Kilstrong might be the Allseer's heir and living in the palace, but he's a warrior."

"Since when?" Samson sputtered. "Glory to the Forefathers, he's never set foot on a battlefield and knows nothing about politics or wars. Additionally, his mind is not on happy marriages with pizza girls—he wants someone with power. The only way he'll ever want you is if he finds out what you truly are."

"I don't think so. I think he'll like me for me."

"You can't be with this boy."

"Why?" Sage said. "I really have a crush on him. And maybe . . . well . . . maybe I'm tired of the fighting. Maybe I want my fairy-tale ending. Wouldn't life at the palace be amazing?"

"You have watched Defenders Unite! way too much," Samson scolded. "Endings aren't necessarily happy. Or maybe you've been watching The Royal Court too much. You know that's all a show, right? No one's life is that merry."

Admittedly, it was how Sage had grown to love Louis so much. She got to see him and his life at the palace in an annual series that followed his days through school, trainings, meetings, trials, and travels. There was a spin-off series featuring his visit to every Diamond City district, highlighting all the hotspots, monuments, five-star restaurants, and shopping centers. The Color District hosted a festival of lights every month of Faith, and Sage was raring to go one year. Yes, The Royal Court was a soap opera like no other.

"I can dream, can't I?" Sage said.

Samson gave her that look. He sat down at the table, huge quads hanging over the sides of the chair, and very politely picked up his fork and knife, pinkies out. He ate with such grace that it made Sage's manners resemble those of a three-year-old's.

"Either way, it might not be a bad idea to get close to Kilstrong," Sage went on carefully. "The Warlord is coming this weekend."

She explained the challenge. Coincidentally, the day after Louis' birthday party. Now Samson was frozen stiff and it was hard to read his expression, what he thought of the upcoming match and what it meant for their future.

    DIAMOND CITY

"Penelope says the Allseer won't stand a chance," Sage said, trying very hard not to think about the bumbling redhead in her restaurant right now. "Don't know how true that is. If the Warlord can kill Enhanced with weapons and the Cell Destroyer can suck up Cells, wouldn't it be even?"

"I don't know." Samson curled his lip in thought. He looked like a pit bull growling at its prey. "My concern is what the outcome will be. Ever since his exile thirty years ago, the Warlord's been relentless in finding ways to take this city back. He's found a weapon to defeat them, and it makes me wonder if he has any more information on the Lolligo." He peered at her. "We've seen the torture videos. He can *speak* our language."

"He's looking for the Optimum," Sage countered with what she had learned from that woman earlier, "so he can't know much."

"But he lives in the Outskirts, doesn't he?" Samson rubbed his sharp chin, a spark in his eyes. That meant he had an idea, and it wasn't a good one either. "What if he's seen more of our kind?"

Sage hated it when Samson spoke this way. She didn't want to leave Diamond City for anything, especially not to look for their "kind." She was tired of reiterating the same list of reasons they had to stay—family, pizza, and Louis—so she was tempted to yell at Samson and tell him to travel on his own. But the tall-ass, muscular Squid wouldn't dare leave her side, the coward.

"I shouldn't get ahead of myself," Samson said before they started an unnecessary brawl. Like Sage, he was good at strategizing and putting himself in ideal positions. Right now, he had to wait and see what happened between the Allseer and the Warlord this weekend. While he was obviously rooting for the latter, there weren't any guarantees when it came to positive outcomes and beneficial alliances, so he was ready with a weapon of their own.

Samson got out of his seat and stepped toward the back of the living room where he had his computer and desk. Pinned up on the board ever so neatly were the latest commissions from his customers. He had an order for something called the Robo, a small robot that functioned as a living, walking, and talking cell phone, capable of doing anything. This invention was going to catapult Samson to stardom, if society would one day accept a monster like him. For right now, he lay low, charging customers decent prices on whatever they asked him to make, anything from toys to silverware to weapons. But the sword he had on the desk was not for a client—it was for Sage.

Samson had been working on it for months, but Sage never paid it any attention. At last, she laid eyes on the blade that would serve as her companion in upcoming battles, made of impenetrable steel, welded right here in their apartment, possibly on the adjacent table where a ton of test tubes and melted alloys sat in disuse. This blade, unlike the one Sage was used to wielding, was made of Slainium.

"Our weakness," Samson said simply.

Sage's eyes widened. She had never heard of Slainium in her life, but if it was a weakness, then, "Is this what the Warlord uses to kill Enhanced?"

"I don't know, but this is definitely strong. Trust me, I've tested it on my blood. If this blade were to pierce me, it'd take out half of my Cells. My saving grace is regeneration, but I can't say the same for Enhanced who have a fixed number of Cells and can't make any more on their own."

"Is that why you kept asking me for a blood sample?" Not that Sage had given it. She had already told Samson no creepy doctor stuff, but if it affected him, then it sure as hell affected her. She, Samson, and—to some degree—the Enhanced were all Squids.

Sage picked up the blade, long and thin but sturdy. She could slash it and the body wouldn't bend, wouldn't give in to force. According to Samson, it was unbreakable. The bonds were too tight. Sage narrowed her eyes at him. "What are you implying I do with this?"

"I think it's only a matter of time before the Allseer gets you," Samson said honestly. "And when he does, you'll be ready. *We'll* be ready."

"But you trust the Warlord?"

　　　　　　　　　　　　　　　　DIAMOND CITY

Samson hesitated. He watched every news channel every day, so
he knew every player in the game. Like Sage, however, he was skeptical of the propaganda. He just didn't know right now. "Just in case.
But the sword's not done yet," he added quickly. "A few more tweaks."

"Samson . . . I . . . " Sage sighed. She laid the weapon back down
on the desk and rubbed her arms. She looked out the window. The
sight of so many skyscrapers lost in the darkness of those heavy
clouds, lights hardly visible, made her think of the days she'd do
the same in the frontlines of battle. The Unification War was a success . . . but to fight again . . .

"We've learned quite a few things about humans and the Enhanced these past hundred years," Samson said, taking a seat to
look at the side of her face. "Peace doesn't last forever, as today has
proven."

"But you were anticipating this, clearly. Or else you wouldn't
have been hammering away at this sword while I was at work."

"Look at me, Sage—I can't walk out in public without making
a spectacle of myself. If I'm attacked, my chances of survival are
low. Sure, I have muscles and I can tear down a building, but I'm
one person versus how many Enhanced in the military? Ten thousand?" Samson shook his head. "I don't deny that I need you, and so
I try to make myself useful in whatever way I can. I definitely don't
want to drag you into any fights because I know how much this
peace means to you . . . " Samson trailed off. His long fingers curled
on the table and over the back of his chair. He left scratch marks
with his nails. "But it's inevitable, isn't it?"

Sage didn't need him to say any more. She couldn't be mad or
offended because she had already been dragged into a fight, and it
was only going to get worse with this Warlord coming to pay them
a visit. She remained unsure of whose side she was on and who to
defend. Before, when she had been striving to make money and
achieve unity, it was clear. Now . . . her loyalties were a mess. All the
same, she knew she'd have to fight. Only she didn't know for whom:
the Warlord . . . or the Allseer.

"Actually, I was just about to ask you about that. You know that shit is going to get ugly and that we need positive attention, so if you could jump in—"

"Jump in" . . . right.

Sage studied the Star Raider in her hands, already knowing where she was going to put it. Her room, like their small apartment, was lit by dim lamps, the hue pleasant and calming. There were star stickers all over her walls and ceiling, giving off a space effect that went well with the night sky outside her window. Cars raced by silently like little rockets. Sage's imagination went wild.

It transported her to a different time and place. Many years ago, she'd be on the floor playing with her human sister. They'd pretend to be superheroes and defend the world just like all the characters in Defender's Unite! did. Tears burned in Sage's eyes as she placed her new toy next to her other Star Raider collectibles, right in front of a large Defender's Unite! poster on the wall. She took a deep breath, a sad smile on her face as she thought about Aurora.

"You'll go on to fight for me, won't you?" Aurora said on her death bed, holding on to Sage's hand. *"Always do the right thing no matter how hard?"*

"Aunt Sage always does the right thing!" Aurora's children exclaimed. *"Always."*

Sage certainly hoped so, although sometimes she had her doubts. A being like her didn't belong in a city with humans and biologically modified militants. Even so, she wanted to believe she could make a positive difference in the lives of the many. That's what she held on to as she took a shower, went to bed, and texted back and forth with the PG crew until late that night. While it started with their Kilstrong mess and the uncertainty around the Warlord's challenge, Penelope ended it with an announcement:

She was engaged to Dustin.

Jealousy. It burned Sage's esophagus like a severe case of acid reflux. Penelope had finally made it official, that she had someone to spend the rest of her life with. Sage, in the meanwhile, had no one.

Sage gazed out her window, at the droplets trailing down the pane. She pictured herself at Louis' side, holding his arm as he led her up the aisle to the most glorious building in all of Diamond City: the palace. It was for royalty, for those in charge, and that's where Sage wanted to be. Her conquests with the PG put her one step closer to that circle. In fact, if the Allseer lost, she had a feeling Louis would come crawling for the kind of help only the Allseer's secret weapon could deliver.

Sage's heart raced just thinking about it, but for all the wrong reasons. She didn't want to be a secret weapon. Her greatest value was not her physical strength—she certainly didn't want it to be. That's not why she wanted Louis to love her.

She stopped texting at around two in the morning, wishing with all her heart that her dream would come true. After so much training, turning down relationships, and secret missions, she deserved happiness, didn't she? Without any more fighting. Without being called the Optimum. But how was she going to achieve that if she sprang back into fighting . . . again?

She had to keep her secret. She had the invitation to Louis' party, and all she had to do was act like a normal girl. She was an investigator for the PG . . . period.

Sage smiled. Then Samson cursed from his work table. "Damn it, now I have to weld this all over again!"

CHAPTER 4

Happy Birthday, Louis

Samson was still hammering away at that sword the following morning, cursing and grumbling to himself. Although the blade was all Slainium, the nanotechnological part of it had to be perfect or the blade would have faults and break if struck at the right angle. That meant it was up to Sage to make breakfast.

She reported to Two for Pizza as usual, anticipating another shitshow with the Private Guard. Her stomach was all coils by the time she got to the front door, hand shaking just slightly with what she'd find inside, and she *never* got nervous. She held her breath, closed her eyes for a split second, said a small prayer to all the Squids out there, and entered.

No PG. Good. Customers were finding seats, grabbing a drink, or enjoying their slice of pizza. The special of the day was Climb The Mountain featuring a variety of sausages from reindeer to squirrel. Yes, squirrel, although no one knew it unless they read the fine print.

Bram was at the counter like always, shabby-looking due to his worry over last night's mission. Sage had already assured him that she was fine, but he was looking at the bigger picture here, the imminent role she'd be playing in Diamond City's defense *again*. Bram also had a few things to say about the upcoming birthday party.

"It's definitely not such a bad idea to be friendly to Louis," Bram said, taking inventory of all the pizzas they had ready to serve. The cooks were hard at work in the kitchen—the smell would have been uplifting if Sage wasn't weighed down by politics and the fact Penelope and the PG were using the offices in the back.

In regards to the party, Sage's attendance was also a bit of a convenience factor for the PG too, because they needed her to keep things under control. Everyone was nervous about the Warlord's challenge and what would happen if he actually won. Sage didn't think a takeover would be that easy with a military ten thousand strong full of Enhanced. Then again, anything could happen.

But before anxiety set in, Sage was going to take advantage of her chance to meet Louis. She went shopping with her nieces, Candice and Olivia, who were fourteen and twelve. They always made her feel like a teenager again (even though Sage was one at heart) and they were the best mental therapy on the planet. It was just the three of them spending some much-needed time together, since Sage was always at work and the girls were studying hard at school. They were thankful for an afternoon away from Bram, who was strict for all the right reasons, and gave Sage some ideas on what to wear for the party.

"In the last episode of The Royal Court, Louis said he loved coral," Candice said, scanning all of the low-cut dresses on the rack.

"Yeah," Olivia added, "with silver trimmings!"

The girls were quick to find a dress that was suitable for Sage because they already knew what would look good on her. When Sage inspected herself in the mirror, smiling to round out her cheeks and turning her body to see every angle of her new look, she swelled with happiness. She wasn't even in the palace, and already she felt like a princess. Any accessories, as Candice advised, had to be minimal and low-key. Sage didn't need anything else to look beautiful, other than her hair. The humidity in this city birthed a

                                          DIAMOND CITY

frizz that was impossible to tame. Even Candice's hair mask recommendations didn't make much of a dent, but there was always the "wet look."

"You're going to look beautiful!" Candice sang, regardless of what Sage was going to do with her hair. "As long as you show off your muscles and awesome body. And makeup, of course, but you're super good at that."

Sage had done all of Candice's makeup for her middle school graduation last summer. She had done Olivia's, too, making her look like a doll. Not that the two needed makeup—they had perfect caramel skin that they had inherited from their mother. Only the large hazel eyes were from Bram. Thank God they had none of his looks. Sage wished she were more attractive.

"He'll notice you," Candice said as they left the beauty supply store, Sage's hopeful hair creams in hand. "And if he doesn't . . . then he's not the right one."

"You have to feel that spark when you make eye contact," Olivia squeaked, fixing her stylish sunglasses on her head. It was raining, but they made her look classy, sitting atop her tight curls. "Like when I first laid eyes on Adam!"

Candice rolled her eyes. "We've already talked about this, Olive—he's a loser. Sage agrees."

"I say give him a chance," Sage amended, amused. "But if he's still a dick, then no."

"He's not a 'dick'!" Olivia exclaimed. "He helped me with my algebra homework last weekend. Isn't that a start, Sage?"

"It is."

"Aunt Sage, look!" Candice ran over to the corner antique shop, pointing at something behind the glass. "Star Raider!"

An old Star Raider poster. It was easy to miss if you couldn't recognize the insignia, an SR inside a thick green circle, but it was there, perched on the window for all to see, to be reminded of a time long ago. That's what all the antiques were for, and Sage was sure there were treasures galore inside. Samson would strangle her if she brought back any more junk, though . . .

"Poppa says you've been on some dangerous missions," Olivia said to Sage. "Are you going to fight again?"

"I hope not . . ." Sage let her eyes linger over the Star Raider poster, then settled on the tattoo on her right forearm.

"I know you'll defend us when you have to," Candice said comfortably. "That's why I'm not worried. And while Prince Louis seems like a hottie, don't let him take advantage of you, Aunt Sage. Only a very special man deserves someone like you."

Sage's cheeks glowed a bright red. "You flatter me too much."

"You're a kick-ass bitch!" Olivia tooted a bit too loudly, making passersby look their way. "And I don't want anyone to walk all over you."

Sage held her girls close to her sides. They were so wise for their years, far more knowledgeable than she had been at that age. Bram had done a great job raising them since their mother passed away ten years ago, but he attributed a lot of their success to her, too. Sage always practiced what she preached—work hard, get paid—and taught them a thing or two about defending themselves in clutch situations. Unknown to Bram, they always carried a dagger on their bodies, whether in their purses or socks. Candice claimed it had come in handy once when hanging out with her girlfriends and a guy went a bit far when making out with her.

Sage tried not to picture needing one when it came to Louis. The Royal Court was a TV show—actual court was a whole different story. Sage kept that in mind as they entered the arts and crafts shop next for the supplies to make Louis' gift.

Sage was going to make a bracelet. She hadn't done one in a while. And now that Samson had perfected the art of Slainium, Sage was going to start incorporating a bit of that into them, too. Slainium did terribly against itself, rebounding with a powerful clang. Besides, if the Warlord was truly going to invade the city, then any kind of defense was beneficial. Sage still said that the Warlord was using Slainium in his weapons, too, if he was killing Enhanced so damn easily. For Louis, though, Sage kept it simple, incorporating threads of coral and silver like he preferred. By dawn, she was finished and proud of her work, as clumsy as her fingers tended to be. She showed Samson, but he just grunted and waved her off with a massive hand. Of course she didn't tell him that some of those bracelets were for Louis.

The weekend couldn't come fast enough, but when it was here, Sage got ready, giving the most attention to her hair after washing out that mask that did absolutely nothing. She had no idea how Candice achieved such smooth hair.

"Can you make something for hair?" Sage asked from the bathroom as Samson stomped down the hallway. His footsteps were so heavy that complaints were a regular occurrence from neighbors.

"Mm." Samson returned to his desk, back to the sword he was trying to perfect. He didn't compliment Sage's look—never had and never would. He wasn't one for beauty pageants when he didn't quite fit into society, so Sage looked the same no matter how she was dressed. He didn't even bat an eye that one time he had caught her naked in her room (he was delivering laundry and she had forgotten to close the door).

"Hello." Sage waved her hand in his face.

"For the love of all Forefathers," he growled at her, "*what* do you want?"

"Do I look beautiful?"

"You always look beautiful."

"But even more so now."

He eyed her for two more seconds before returning to the sword, the obvious source of all beauty. "Very much."

"Wish me luck?" Sage said.

"Don't have sexual intercourse with him," Samson said. "That's my only advice. You're not ovulating yet, but it always pays to be careful."

Right. Because Samson was very familiar with Sage's menstrual cycle (once a year, always in the month of Loyalty), he knew exactly when she could have sex.

"I'm not selling my body, Samson," Sage grumbled. "I'm not a prostitute."

"You desire this boy. Tell me otherwise."

"I do, but I'm not stupid. This is just a fun night out."

Samson eyeballed her again. This time, he took a bit longer, as if gauging how much sexual desire was coursing through Sage's veins. He couldn't pick up a thing, so all he had to say was, "Be careful. They think you're Enhanced, and they're going to want you to join them. I don't doubt Penelope has already spilled the beans about you."

"What do you mean?" Sage said.

"You know exactly what I mean, Sage—there's a good chance she's already told them everything. Just . . . be careful."

Sage didn't even want to entertain the possibility of Penelope's big mouth informing every royal body in the palace of what she was. Unfortunately, Sage had very little control over the flow of her thoughts when she was this nervous, so her secret was the only thing pounding in her head when she met Penelope and the rest of the PG crew at her restaurant. From there, they headed out to Heart.

Fittingly, it was in the very center of all four Diamond City districts, built after the Unification War as a capital. Outside of its massive walls, there was no mention of the upcoming match between the Allseer and the Warlord. Inside, however, was a different story.

Heart wasn't just comprised of a palace—there were shopping centers, gardens, and an amusement park with a full-fledged Ferris wheel. There were mansions lined up against the east side and training grounds for the military on the west. Not just anyone had access to Heart's facilities, either—only authorized personnel could enter and leave these grounds. Even the four district Overseers needed permission from the Allseer to visit. Hand-chosen media were allowed to make reports and show footage of the Kilstrongs, but they were censored to ensure the districts received filtered information that benefited the Allseer's reign. Sage got most of her news from the PG, and other than the Warlord's challenge and the occasional calls for expansion into the Outskirts, there wasn't a whole lot happening at the moment.

Today, Heart was buzzing with energy at the 114th birthday of

Louis Kilstrong. A long life exemplified power and opportunity, a being who could withstand time, mature, and apply his knowledge for the better of his citizens. Despite his old age, he still looked like a thirty-year-old stud who had just pulled his business off the ground and gotten married. To humans, he was an absolute marvel. The Allseer was thirty years older than Louis, but he had become an Enhanced at a much older age and it showed. While Enhanced were invincible, fresh blood was always a plus. Louis was next in line for the throne, but he didn't seem very . . . excited about it. Media interviews portrayed Louis as accepting of his duty and The Royal Court marketed his future strategies and visions for the future, but all Sage perceived when she met him for the first time in her life was a bit of resentment.

Louis was absolutely fuming and it showed on his face, in the way he treated his guests. He had attendants greeting people at the entrance to the ballroom, all of them dressed in pressed gray suits and forced to smile and be nice. He, on the other hand, was by the juice bar with his arms crossed. His blond curls, brilliant eyes, and fancy clothes with gold bands and buckles didn't hide his poisonous aura.

"Happy birthday, Louis." Sage extended her small gift. She could feel Penelope sniggering behind her.

Louis flashed a smile. "Thanks. Your name is . . . ?"

"Sage." Sage smiled, too, heart pounding like a drum. "Hope you like it."

"I think I will."

To Sage's disappointment, their conversation ended there. More of Louis' guests arrived and they were all here to talk about the Allseer. It made Sage feel a bit uncomfortable, so she stepped back, disappearing into the PG's circle because there was nowhere else to fit into.

There was the Allseer's council, advisors, their families, and some of the military standing around. They worked directly with Heart, the people and families who kept the center of their beloved city functioning. That didn't include the Private Guard, however, which was more like an outside secret service made up of humans. Penelope and Dustin had their own agenda for the night, and they, along with their companions, spread out through the ballroom to network, eat and drink delicacies that were foreign to them (the jelly nuggets were to die for), and observe, leaving Sage by herself.

She got to take a closer look at the structure of the room, the delicate pillars, second-floor balcony, and high dome that captured their chatter quite nicely. There were spheres made of intricate, grooved paper hanging from the ceiling, lit up in an array of colors to celebrate the month of Light. There had only been one Allseer since Diamond City's unification, and so Kilstrong's portrait was impossible to miss, perched right above the Diamond City insignia on the wall behind the mini dais where the council would be honoring Louis. There was a table full of gifts, and Sage spotted hers underneath a few of the larger boxes. One more bag, and it'd be completely out of sight.

This was … boring. Even when the music struck up. The orchestra was in the corner, playing a nice lyrical piece to ease the nerves and get everyone into the celebratory mood, but Sage didn't dance. She retreated to a pillar, watching Louis pair up with every girl he could get his hands on. Unlike some of the more promiscuous and pompous nightclubs in the Cut District, the dancing here was sophisticated and classy. Those were the kinds of steps Sage wouldn't be able to do successfully. Even so, she wanted her chance to be close to Louis. As she watched, hands clenching and unclenching, she wound up thinking, *Look at me. Ask me.*

It was like a mantra over and over again. Obsessive even.

"My lady."

Sage looked up immediately, as soon as she sensed someone had directed their attention to her. Her daydreams never lasted very long, and that was a good thing because they only led to painful realities later. This time, it was a rather pleasant one. Sage had never seen a more chiseled face in her life.

"My name is Dawson Blackburn," said the stranger sweetly, dark eyes twinkling. He certainly was a handsome man, as if he had stepped down from one of the murals in the ballroom himself. He was in a white military uniform, indicating he was here to ensure the party went smoothly. The sight of one of those soldiers never failed to impress Sage, the milkiness of the fabric with black trims around the cuffs and hems. Royals wore gold, but soldiers carried specks of darkness to show enemies that missions often resulted in death. Every soldier had medals for all of his or her participation in battles, terminating skirmishes, or even putting down revolts in the Allseer's name. In addition to the local police, it wasn't unusual to see them in formation on street corners or on patrols at the local discount store. They were around to keep order even if the sight of them was freaky. Rightfully so: they were notorious for their brutality.

Yet Blackburn's hold on Sage's hand was delicate, as if he was holding flower petals, and his steps were as airy as clouds. "May I have this dance?"

"Sorry," Sage said. "But I'm not very good at this."

"Don't worry." He smiled. "Just follow my lead."

Actually, it wasn't too bad. All Sage had to do was reciprocate his movements. The longer she was on her feet, the more confident she felt. She could focus on what was more important.

"Who are you?"

"I've been waiting a long time to see you, Sage," he said pleasantly, cheeks glowing. "You are even more beautiful in person." He stroked her loose hair and eyed her sculpted chest and shoulders. The simple dress was perfect because it didn't take away from her figure at all. "I am the commander of the Diamond City military."

Sage recognized the soldier's uniform, but she hadn't known this was *the* commander. He didn't look it either, not with that smooth face and shiny dark hair that reached his shoulders. She couldn't imagine this man moving any faster than he was dancing now, much less drawing his sword or pointing his pistol. The Allseer's military was hand-chosen among a genetically favored pool of Enhanced, not all of which made rank. Candidates were at liberty to serve if they wished, although the perks of doing so were worthwhile. Any favor with the Allseer of Diamond City ensured fortune, security, and power above all else.

"And you are Sage Arpine?"

"Yes," Sage said carefully. "That's me."

Blackburn bowed his head. "If you would be so kind as to allow me a few minutes of your time. I wish to speak to the great owner of the Cut District's most popular pizzeria. All over Diamond News, my dear."

"And you recognized my face?"

Blackburn chuckled. "Yes. But I also knew you thanks to your coworker, Bram Fraser."

Sage's chest tightened a bit. Bram had never told her that he was passing on her information to the Diamond City military. Her survival instincts flared up, anger brewing at the thought of her asshole nephew selling her out like that, but Blackburn held up a hand to cut off her rage.

"Don't be upset," Blackburn said, never stopping his step to the music. He kept her going, too. "Truthfully, it was only a matter of time before we found out about you. You work closely with the Private Guard, and so, you have been helping us where it matters anyway. We know very little about you, and we certainly don't wish to pressure you, but I wanted to cordially invite you to the Allseer's challenge tomorrow."

The anxiety got worse now. In fact, Sage took a step back, eyes locked on the dark ones above her. This man knew way too much about her, coincidentally inviting her to the challenge that the Allseer had a possibility of losing. Why? So she could keep them all safe? Olivia's advice no longer applied to Louis now—it applied to Blackburn.

"You're a kick-ass bitch! And I don't want anyone to walk all over you."

And Bram was a back-stabbing traitor. Sage fought the urge to run from the ballroom and tell Samson, who'd only retort with a gruff, "I told you so."

But Bram was *family*. He was supposed to be on her side, stuck to her like the rest of the Frasers had since she was a child, kept

                                   DIAMOND CITY

her secret from the Allseer at all costs, allowed her to exercise her power in the PG, and most of all: supported her pizzeria.

"Please, Sage," Blackburn said gently. "Do not fret. Diamond City is in a very tight situation right now, and we need all the help we can get—"

"You're not supposed to know about me."

Blackburn blinked. He really did stop dancing now. Then he composed himself, took a deep breath, and responded, "Maybe not. I am certainly not aware of any of the family drama that has taken place between you and Bram, but I urge you not to see it as a betrayal. Don't you understand what's at stake here? The Warlord has weapons that will most certainly defeat the Allseer, possibly all of us, and you're a fighter from the Unification War."

"I understand the stakes," Sage said, certain that the Allseer *also* had weapons of his own if he shared the responsibility for the Enhanced losing their Cells with Francis. "And I'm sorry if I sound selfish, but this *is* a personal matter and I *do* see it as a betrayal. Now you are forcing me to take sides in what will be an imminent struggle against the Warlord."

"Do you not wish to defend your city?"

"At all costs," Sage said hotly. "But I don't want any part in the politics you and the Allseer played after exiling the Warlord thirty years ago. All that he and his 'rebels' wanted was a voice in your government, and then you turned on them. Not only that: you thought it was necessary to torture them on live television. I still remember those clips, how you cut their arteries, took out their organs, and whipped them until they were all bones and vomit. Then you'd wait for them to regenerate and do it all over again. They were brutal, even more so than the Warlord's videos circulating the web now."

"They were nothing short of barbarians, I guarantee you."

"Whatever they were, it's not my problem. I just know the military wasn't very kind in turn."

"You seem very adamant about this," Blackburn said coolly. "Are you perhaps in cahoots with the Warlord?"

"I don't know him, and I don't know you either."

"Maybe not, but you wish to grow closer to Louis, don't you?" Blackburn chuckled, as if amused by his own cleverness. "What do you think will happen tomorrow, Sage? The Allseer will perish, and then what? Will you allow the love of your life to get hurt?"

"Are you suggesting *you* won't be able to stop the Warlord?" Sage said, inching off the dance floor so she wouldn't be in the way of other couples.

"Even I can't predict everything." Blackburn followed. "If you didn't know, the Warlord has heavy numbers on his side, most of them Enhanced washouts. Add to that those unstoppable weapons he brandishes, and his forces can quickly overwhelm ours if we are careless. But having a fighter like yourself would certainly ensure that we are not."

The song ended. It no longer mattered to Sage and Blackburn, who were standing off to the side, next to a pillar where hardly anyone noticed them. Blackburn continued to hold her, fingertips brushing her cheek. He traced some of her freckles as he leaned in and kissed her forehead. If Sage were any other girl, she'd be blushing, but she was trained to focus on the matter at hand.

"I told Bram that his secret is safe with me," Blackburn whispered to her, eyes glistening again. Sage was starting to understand that was a sign of malice. "The Allseer doesn't know anything about you. We don't have to tell him either, sparing you a lot of drama."

"Do you really know what I am?" Sage whispered back.

"I don't," he said honestly. He raised her hand to his lips and kissed it, dark lashes brushing his cheeks. "May you join me for dinner tonight?"

Dinner? Sage didn't have a chance to answer when he said, "In my private quarters, eight o'clock? That should give you plenty of time with our Prince Louis here."

Then Blackburn walked off, just like that. Sage was reeling. It wasn't long before he was quickly overtaken by other girls, so Sage didn't have the slightest chance of speaking to him without causing a ruckus.

Just what the hell had that been about? Her mind organized all the information for her and drew one conclusion: Bram had sold her out, practically handed her secret over to the military, and now she was expected to take part in tomorrow's affairs or else . . .

Or else what?

Sage backed away, far from Louis, even, who was on the other side of the dance floor. There was no chance of getting to him even if he was a source of comfort—he was busy doing his own share of flirting. She found a corner to phone Samson immediately, and as soon as he answered, she let it all out.

From the beginning to the end of the story, there were no interruptions. Samson didn't speak for a long time after that either, leaving Sage to panic only slightly in that nook next to the bathrooms where there was the occasional *whoosh* of flushing. Nobody found her here, but Sage still felt like she was standing in the middle of the dance floor with breasts and ass out for everyone to see. The windows were awfully high, too, untouchable unless she went out of her way to break the glass and jump out.

Finally, Samson spoke. "Come home immediately."

"Samson, I don't think I can," Sage replied, fighting down terror. "I feel that coming home will only make things worse here." Sage meant it, as uncomfortable as she felt in a one-on-one scenario with Blackburn. There was that pending "or else" that had never come from his lips but lingered heavily in the air, as if someone had sprayed perfume. "If I don't play their games or at least pretend to go along, they'll come after me eventually. They might even target me at the pizzeria."

"Forget the damn pizzeria! We can join the Warlord and set that up anywhere else!"

"I can't just abandon Diamond City," Sage said pleadingly. "Trust me."

Samson had a hard time with that verb: trust. He had known her for years, and that's why he knew how reckless she could be. Sage tended to rely on strength more than strategy, although she was quick to catch on to a lot of details. She noticed, for instance, how Blackburn kept looking at her from whatever corner of the room he happened to land in, a seductive smile on his face, as he whispered to one of his soldiers, *"She's mine."*

In retaliation, Sage returned to Penelope's side. As soon as they were within range of each other, Penelope began hooting at her like a cheerleader, clearly a little drunk from dips in the very-spiked punch bowl.

"You danced with the commander?" She cackled. "Congrats, Sage! Although I thought you were here for Louis!"

Not anymore. As handsome and beautiful as Louis was, strutting around with a bunch of girls around his arms as if he had just gone shopping at the mall, he was long forgotten in lieu of a much more hostile confrontation. Sage already felt it in her bones, and so she asked Penelope about Blackburn.

Maybe these were details she already knew, but her mind was too hazy to remember them. Penelope told her that Blackburn had dedicated his mind and body to fighting, was the Allseer's number one protector. Perhaps that was true, but it certainly wasn't obvious. The Allseer had his own circle of bodyguards that he was willing to discard like cheap toys—Blackburn was a treasured trophy he kept in his closet until it was time to show off. All of that painted a clear picture of just who Sage was dealing with come eight o'clock.

She wasn't nervous anymore because she had been in so many life-or-death situations, but she was cautious, knowing what she had to do to establish herself as a warrior and not a puppet. It could cost her her livelihood, and it could cost her her home with Samson, but she had told Aurora as well as Bram and the girls that she was *not* anyone's dog.

When Sage stepped out of the ballroom, the silence of Heart greeted her immediately. There wasn't a soul in this muggy square. Everyone was either inside the ballroom or at home, retired for the night. No paparazzi, since the birthday party was a private event. This wouldn't be airing as an episode for The Royal Court despite the millions of loyal fans watching the news for any glimpses of it. The season was over anyway. Out here, Sage had the fountain spewing this pinkish water from its head and the palace across the courtyard for entertainment.

Wow. Here was the castle with the tall, twisty spires, a picture taken straight from The Royal Court, and Sage felt no giddiness, no excitement, no emotion. She had been alive for way too long not to sense the dangerous undertones of this date. She sensed it a mile away, especially when Blackburn finally emerged from the cloud of estrogen and found her like a predator its prey.

"My beautiful Sage," Blackburn said royally, wrapping an arm around her shoulders. "Come."

Their steps clicked on the cobblestones. Clouds hovered by the moon lazily. Squirrels were tucked into their coves in the oak trees.

"You fought for this," Blackburn said as they crossed the courtyard. He waved at Heart, the buildings, the little treasure that the elite kept to themselves. Lights blinked in the darkness. "You gave us this."

"I'm going to be honest," Sage said. "It wasn't meant for *you*. Diamond City was for the people to live together in harmony, not for the strongest to create their playground. Although, if you adore it, I suppose I can say, 'you're welcome.'"

Blackburn chuckled. "Such honor and pride. You certainly do carry yourself with a much higher air than any female I've ever met. Of course, I don't blame you. I'm sure you've met the Optimum, take on after her, and hold her morals close to your own. It isn't a wonder the Clarity District pays so much homage to her."

Sage said nothing.

They finally arrived at the double palace doors; Blackburn pushed them back with ease, opening them to reveal a wide, tall foyer that took Sage's breath away. The polished floors, the ruby-red rugs, the plush furniture—royalty at its finest, the kind Sage dreamed about, the sort she wanted to live in—but these weren't luxuries she could bask in right now, nor were they ones she deserved. The waters were turning murky and a storm was coming. Sage felt it in her bones, the nastiness of this date that she was on with Blackburn, who took her down a hallway lined with many quarters for top soldiers. These were full-blown suites that were the equivalent of single-family homes in any district, complete with a living room, dining room, bedrooms, patio, and pool.

"Make yourself at home," Blackburn said, taking off his coat.

Sage would in a moment. First, she had to look around and notice that Blackburn was no family man. There were no photographs, no indications he had a wife, children, or even relatives. The huge portrait of the Allseer didn't count. Everything was just so ... shiny. Plain. Maids made the place feel even more fake and distant. Or perhaps it was Sage who was used to companionship, sharing her space and time with Samson, Bram, and the girls. At home, Samson's tools often found their way to the kitchen counter or table. At the pizzeria, Sage found the occasional fastball cards Bram loved to collect or the cute scrunchies Candice and Olivia left behind. Standing in this room reminded Sage that those happy memories were about to vanish because there was no escaping what Blackburn had in store for her.

He floated toward her, holding a bottle of wine in his hands. It was dated to year one. The Diamond City calendar started the year Heart had been born, the beginning of a complete city with all of its districts in alliance. Nothing else mattered to the residents or Sage, who loved her city more than anything, so while the wine was nostalgic, what was inside it was not wine.

Sage knew it as she watched Blackburn pour it. The wine was crystal clear, glittery, and smooth like the finest blends from the Carat District, but the smell was ... different. Pungent. It took her back to Travel the Diamond where a few brave souls had been popping glasses of Cupid's Arrow.

That's what Blackburn was serving her.

"A toast?" Blackburn offered, holding out his glass. "To the future of Diamond City." Strange ... was he going to drink it, too? Or was he immune to it? It took a lot to build resistance. It was addictive nonetheless, but he sipped it like water. Unless he was counting on *her* to cave in first? If that was the case, just what sort of sick intentions did he have?

　　　　　　　　　　　　　　　　　　DIAMOND CITY

Sage wasn't stupid. But Blackburn must have thought that like any other Enhanced, she'd be under Cupid's Arrow's influence in just five minutes. He directed her to a chair at the table as his servants brought out some appetizers. They were little chicken meatballs seasoned with heavy thyme.

"I noticed you didn't eat at the party," Blackburn said, sitting back and crossing his legs. Without his jacket, he looked loose and comfortable. "Are you not hungry?"

"Not particularly," Sage said quietly, swirling the clear liquid in her glass. "I suppose I was a bit disappointed with Louis. I was excited to meet him and such . . ."

"If only he knew what you were. He probably just saw you as any other girl."

"Exactly. I have to become extraordinary to get attention, right?"

"Don't most men work that way?" Blackburn shrugged his shoulders, as if explaining why birds fly. "We look for women who stand out of the pack."

"Including yourself?"

"Not so much me. As my duty is to the Allseer, I don't particularly care for dating or coupling."

"Is that why your servants have hors d'oeuvres ready at a moment's notice?"

Blackburn laughed. "My servants always have food ready for me."

Liar.

"Truly, Sage. We are everlasting beings with all the time in the world, but my hundred years have gone by so quickly. So much to do and establish in this city with the luxury of getting to see it play out. No . . ." He took another sip from his glass. "Just random coupling doesn't interest me. I am not my brother." He wrinkled his nose as if he was speaking about skunks. "A monster."

"Your brother?" Sage said with interest.

"Yes. He was one of the many fools who fled Diamond City as an exile because he didn't want to remain loyal to the Allseer. He wanted more power, so he set out on his own endeavors, betraying us and everything this city stood for. He uses people, then breaks them, very much the same thing he does to his family."

"So he joined the Warlord?"

"Unfortunately. I'm sure he will show his face here tomorrow." Blackburn downed the rest of his "wine" and served himself and Sage another glass. "I want to capture him. And I need your help to do it." He looked up at Sage, a certain flash in his eyes, one of expectancy. One glass of Cupid's Arrow would have had any Enhanced at a drool, but two?

"Is there something wrong, Commander?" Sage asked.

"Not at all." Blackburn cleared his throat. "But please . . . call me Dawson. There is no need for formalities now that we have grown to know each other, right?"

"I suppose." Sage finished her second serving faster than her first. With the third ready to go, Blackburn looked stunned. "This wine is very good," she complimented. "I'm surprised because I am not much of a wine drinker."

"I'm happy for you. It is a rather strong blend, and not many guests have been able to withstand three glasses."

Not only three, but four. Five. And then Sage finished the bottle.

"I don't think this is wine," Sage said, smacking her lips. "This tastes more like Cupid's Arrow to me. Which, you know, requires waivers for potential side effects."

Blackburn chuckled. He tried to make it sound like he was amused, but he actually looked pretty nervous right now. "This isn't Cupid's Arrow, although it might be just as strong. Typically, guests don't feel compelled to drink the entire bottle like you have, so perhaps you have some experience."

Sage smiled sweetly. "I do. Did you know I've downed hundreds of shots to enhance my immunity? So when people like you try to take advantage of me, I'm well aware of my surroundings." She frowned. "I'm sure not many women are by the second glass. Is this how you get them into bed? They probably don't remember much afterward. The first time I drank Cupid's Arrow, I was out for two days."

"As I said," Blackburn went on quietly, "this is not Cupid's Arrow."

Sage leaned forward. "Do you think I'm an idiot? That I lasted in the Unification War because I didn't know how to read my enemies? Maybe it's not Cupid's Arrow, but it's a fucking strong blend. I don't appreciate you making me look like a fool, Commander. If you're asking for my help in defeating the Warlord, you're going to have to be a bit more genuine than that."

"My sweet Sage." Blackburn got up and walked over to her slowly. In a drunk's hazy vision, he'd be nothing more than a ray of white light—his uniform was blinding. To Sage, he was as clear as day. "I did not mean to offend you in any way. *You* were the one who drank the bottle—I certainly did not force you."

"No, but you would have." Sage touched his face, the smoothness of his jaw. "And I don't know who you think I am ... " Her fingers must have cast a trance on Blackburn, who swayed just a bit as if desire was quickly overriding his composure. It was obvious in his gaze, the way he wanted her. Sage entertained it, made him believe the feeling was mutual, as her other hand snaked down her skirt and glossed up her thigh, tracing the dagger. "But I am not a victim, and I am certainly not yours."

Sage drove the blade up through his jaw, tongue, and nose, skewering him just like those delicacies his servants brought out.

CHAPTER 5

The Challenge

It wasn't raining the day of the challenge. In fact, it was surprisingly sunny. The month of Light was cooperating with them at last, allowing ideal weather as if it, too, was curious about who the victor would be.

The challenge was taking place on a training field right outside the palace. There was a runway for aircraft that came in and out of Heart. It was impressive that the Warlord had his own, that somehow he was able to acquire vehicles of that caliber. His was made of a dark slick steel that wasn't from Diamond City. It was large enough to fit all the men and women he traveled with, all of who assembled in the square like a marching band. Their red and gold uniforms glimmered in the open air, an impressive display of color and wealth as if this was a fashion show instead of a death challenge.

They were nothing like the dark figures depicted in the execution videos, Sage noted. The pack of cruel, dirty, animalistic soldiers who killed their victims without a single blink of an eye. These rebels carried themselves with an air of pride, longing, and—if Sage looked close enough—love. There must have been a hundred of them, all eager to return to the city they called home, but despite how close they were to it, they knew they had work to do. Depending on their abilities, each one carried his or her own kind of weapon, from swords to guns, all possibly laced with Slainium as implied in the videos. Their faces depicted the same rigor, discipline, and respect they held for their leader, who didn't walk to the front—he was *carried*.

Sage's eyes widened. The notorious Warlord was sitting in his very own palanquin, a gilded chair polished until it shined at every which angle, blinding anyone who looked at it for too long. Appropriate, because he was the most beautiful man Sage had ever seen, throwing Blackburn's second place into the abyss.

White, smooth skin like marble; long, black hair like a silk waterfall; and defined, thin frame like the most gorgeous of models. He was a king in his own right, as regal as the chair he sat in, presented as the greatest living creature to grace the earth. It showed on his rebels' faces, even the ones bearing the weight of his godliness: the confidence, the conviction.

The ones who looked ready to crumble were the Diamond City military. Blackburn was as stiff as a rock, and surely it had nothing to do with his sore mouth. The pulsing was a reminder of how much of a scumbag he was, how low he was compared to the rebels who made it a point to show their pride: they saluted their own Diamond City flag flapping from its peak atop the palace. It made Sage's chest swell with appreciation. It was as if they had never lost their love despite their exile.

From her corner, Sage saw a lone man step forward from the sea of Diamond City militants. He walked with his family, flanked by his son and daughter but held back by no one. The Allseer had to do this.

The entire field held its breath, as if it were getting ready to plunge underwater. Only a small number of these people had ever seen the Allseer fight: the ones who had aided him during the Unification War like Sage, and the ones who had witnessed him oust the rebels thirty years ago. A one-on-one fight against another Enhanced, though, was new for the Allseer, who was burdened with too much luxury, lack of training, and servants to pull off a win.

"I will be a prosperous leader, Star," had been the Allseer's words to Sage a long time ago.

Marchello's words.

They sat together in the ruins of the Color District right after driving the enemy out. It had been a two-day-long siege of endless fighting. They bathed in their glorious silence, the victory they had hardly achieved. "I will never lose sight of what's important," Marchello said.

"I want to make sure I don't," Sage said to him, sword in between her knees, braid all messy and speckled with blood. "I can't afford a life of luxury . . . not yet."

"But you deserve it."

"Maybe." Sage gazed at him wearily. "But I still have work to do."

Marchello chuckled. "You always have work to do. Pizza . . . really?"

Sage smiled. It was hard to see it because there were too many shadows on her face. "It's my dream."

"Until you get tired of it, of course. We all get tired of it."

"No . . . I think we all get used to it."

And that's exactly what had happened to the Allseer. He had gotten used to his easy life. Now . . . he was terrified of losing it.

Sage could tell by the way the Allseer clutched his sword. This was a man who didn't think he could win, and he had every right to make that assumption. In the face of the Warlord, whose expression conveyed no sense of doubt, how couldn't he? It was royalty against beast, one that was ready to kill for the glory of stealing the Allseer's daughter for ransom and leverage against the city. Those, Sage had learned from Penelope, were the stakes.

"Just look at him," Dustin breathed, disgusted. "Is he even human?"

Maybe not, but Sage wasn't thinking monster. She couldn't stop staring at the thick swathes of gold on the Warlord's eyes or the glitter on his cheeks, as if he were a sparkling star. Despite the shine, however, Sage detected a hollowness about him, an emptiness that yearned to be filled with revenge against the Allseer. After what

Sage had gone through with Francis, she was able to sympathize with that just a bit.

The Warlord wouldn't have taken the time to mobilize his troops if the Allseer was all righteous, would he? He wouldn't have been here to humiliate the Allseer in front of his own council—in front of the entire city if it were possible—if there wasn't some good reason for it, right? The Warlord made sure everyone who was watching this was aware of it, speaking in fluid Lucidum for all to hear and understand.

"Allseer Kilstrong." The Warlord leaned back on his pillows, the pitch-black eyes lasering in on the enemy. He twirled his foot as if he was bored, but the drawn brows said he was thinking, concentrating. "It has been thirty years since you turned on us, since you had me executed in a public square like a barbarian when all I did was serve you on hand and knee. I followed all of your brutal orders to arrest and execute Enhanced who no longer pledged their allegiances to you. When I discovered your plans to abduct the Optimum to further your own selfish agenda, I stood up to you. Our disagreements turned foul, so you called for my death. It was convenient for you and your experiments on the Enhanced, to see what could truly kill one. As you hung me, you planned to dismember me as you did my comrades. If it wasn't for my loyal followers, my organs would have been in jars, which, I'm sure, you would have taken to feast on when you craved to eat me."

The Allseer raised his hand. "Do not fret, oh one they call the 'Warlord.' The past is irrelevant, for we stand here now."

"The past is everything," the Warlord said stoically. "It's the reason we *are* standing here right now. Your cooperation failed back then, but it better not fail now. My men and women are Enhanced just like your military, and this will be nothing more than a massacre if you don't hand over your daughter when I win."

A challenge and a threat. The entire yard was still holding its breath, all eyes on the Allseer for a rebuttal.

"You must think me foolish if you believe I will be the one to fight." The Allseer stepped back and waved forth one of his close soldiers. This one was not a part of the military—he was one of the Allseer's very own bodyguards, perhaps the best.

At the peak of his power, Kenna used his strength to protect the Allseer at all costs. The man looked a lot younger than any of the Enhanced there, especially the Warlord, who already showed signs of age around his eyes and lips. More than that: he was the most powerful warrior among them, trained from an early age, exceptionally skilled to call himself the Allseer's sworn protector. The battles and trials he must have faced to earn that title were mind-boggling. That's why no one protested when Kenna stepped forward, drawing his weapon and pointing it at the Warlord. Before this battle started, the Warlord wanted to make something very clear.

"He fights in your place." The Warlord nodded. "And Commander fights in mine. Step forward, my love."

From the tight formation of rebels came a man who stood over six feet tall, muscles bulging and breaths even. He passed a hand over the pair of swords at his belt, drawing the first one he touched. The cornrows and tribal tattoos exuded the fierceness of a final boss in a video game.

"These are our substitutes," the Warlord went on, "but the outcome of the battle remains: if your stand-in dies, you die. You are not escaping your fate here today."

Penelope tensed a little bit beside Sage. This was the part, perhaps, where she wanted to usher Sage as the fighter instead. But this wasn't the time to draw attention, and there was no certainty that Kenna wasn't cut out for the challenge. Every square inch of him, from the top of his bald head to the tips of his boots, screamed, *"I was raised to do this!"* In fact, it was his moment of glory.

Then, before anyone could say "go," the first blows rang through the yard, a clashing of metal as sword met sword. Sage followed all of their movements, saw the direction of energy in the air, anticipated Commander's direct blow—a risk on his part for it left him defenseless if he missed—but Kenna was the one who messed up.

One minute? Two minutes? That's how long it lasted. Commander cut through Kenna so viciously that there was no time for regeneration. Enhanced were invincible but not immortal, especially when sliced in half with a weapon laced with Slainium. Commander sawed right through Kenna, blade cutting through torso, neck, and skull. With Kenna in pieces right before their eyes, it was time for Commander to follow through with the promises of this challenge. He did it quickly, too—before anyone could register what the hell had just happened—he flung his sword across the yard and shaved the Allseer's head clean off his shoulders.

The Allseer should have known better than to accept the challenge of someone who was clearly stronger than he was, more prepared, more passionate, and with a lot more to lose. This was all a struggle for supremacy, to show off, and it had cost him dearly.

His head was on the floor.

Commander bent over to pick it up like he would groceries. His strong fingers curled around the thin hair, yanking it up for all to see.

It was quite the sight, forever seared in Sage's memory. The only reason the Diamond City military didn't move was because of fear. An uproar followed, but what could the military do against the Warlord? It wasn't worth the risk to find out. The Allseer had lost, and the Warlord's followers were there to ensure the transaction proceeded as agreed upon. Commander bowed before his ruler, presenting the head of the Allseer, which the Warlord waved away as if it were a bag of trash.

"Please," he scoffed. "I want to keep my lunch down. I rather enjoyed those sandwiches."

Sage stepped back as Louis' howls echoed across the yard. Louis sounded like he had been stabbed in the chest as he watched his sister being whisked away by a monster.

"It's fine, Louis!" Agathe cried, her makeup a mess on her face. "I'll be fine!"

Would she? In the hands of a beast like the Warlord? Agathe would be wed, impregnated, and what would become of the Kilstrong dynasty? By blood, they'd be tied to these barbarians, people who should have been under lock and key like the rest of the Enhanced. That's what the Allseer had wanted . . . wasn't it?

"I followed all of your brutal orders to arrest and execute Enhanced who no longer pledged their allegiances to you. When I discovered your plans to abduct the Optimum to further your own selfish agenda, I stood up to you."

Suddenly, it made sense to Sage: Francis Kilstrong's actions were no coincidence. With his help, the Enhanced would be no more. Anyone considered a threat to the throne would be eradicated.

But it was too late for the Allseer.

"Sage!" Penelope choked, clutching her shoulders. "Do something!"

No. Sage wouldn't involve herself in this, not after a challenge won fair and square. In fact, the Warlord retreated to his ship with Agathe in tow and didn't attack them or try to take over. It was the Diamond City military that got aggressive and reckless, opening a fire that Blackburn tried to put out before they had a disaster on their hands.

Their Allseer was dead, killed so *easily*. The rebels glared them down, more than ready to fight and defend their Warlord. Better to step back and reevaluate their positions no matter how difficult that was to swallow. It showed on Blackburn's face—the strain—and Sage was so happy.

Of course, she didn't let it show. She kept it all bottled up inside as she watched the Warlord leave in his fancy portable throne. His rebels kept order as they evacuated Heart grounds, back to the camp Sage had access to. Her mind was alight with possible courses of action—maybe she'd follow him?—but then she reminded herself that it *wasn't her business*. She'd shown up to the challenge, completed her duties, her tasks, and now she wanted to go home.

So she left. She certainly didn't stick around to discuss politics. She figured that Louis and the remaining council members would figure out their situation, and in the meanwhile, she'd have to consult with Samson about hers.

CHAPTER 6
The Monster's Heart

Poor Samson was worried out of his wits, rushing right to Sage as soon as she stepped through the door. Of course, no one in Diamond City suspected that the Allseer was dead...yet. Although someone at Heart was bound to leak it soon enough—it wasn't something they could hide forever. But for right now, Sage was Samson's only source of information and the outcome of the challenge wasn't surprising to him at all. So now what?

"They're going to use you," Samson said at once. He stomped over to the table and picked up the finally-finished sword. He nearly shoved it into her hands. "They're going to come for you, Sage. We need to get the hell out of here—"

"I can't leave."

Samson blinked at her. "Why not? Because of that damn pizza restaurant? Give me a break—we can open another one anywhere else!"

"I can't leave my city, Samson," Sage replied adamantly. "The Allseer is dead, Heart's in an upheaval, and something bad is going to happen." She needed a seat, so she put the sword aside and pulled up a chair. She still had last night's dress underneath her jacket, but her mind was far from Louis and Blackburn's attempt at rape. "I need to see what happens."

"If they catch me—"

"They won't catch you," Sage assured him. "I won't let anything happen to you."

Samson held his face with a large hand, muscles flexing, even in his knuckles. He gritted his teeth, clicking them against each other before he sagged just a bit. As much as he hated the Allseer, the uncertainty was overwhelming. Sage, on the other hand, grew more and more thankful that the Allseer was dead. She announced her reasons why.

"It would have been worse if he had lived," Sage said, unstrapping those horrid heels from her ankles. "I really do think he was in cahoots with Francis to wipe out the rest of the Enhanced. He was planning something, and one of his plans included capturing me."

"And you don't think they still want to capture you?" Samson said, watching her discard her shoes on the floor. "Isn't it Louis'— your *boyfriend's*—turn to rule? Him and the council? You know they're filing their teeth! *And pick up your damn shoes!*"

"I'm not leaving."

"Think about it, Sage—"

"I SAID I'M NOT LEAVING!" Sage yelled.

Samson looked like Sage had just punched his face. Then he deflated like a punctured balloon and shuffled off, closing himself in his room. Eventually, Sage did the same. She took a shower and reflected on the past twenty-four hours. It all boiled down to this one little detail.

Bram had given away her information as if it were a Cinnamon Ring for sale. He'd had no reason to do that unless money or some sort of personal benefit was at stake, and so Sage confronted him about it the next morning. She arrived at the restaurant before hours, when Penelope and the PG were still ass-kissing at Heart, seized him by the collar, and landed one right in his gut.

"Give me one good reason why I shouldn't kill you," Sage hissed, drilling his already weak body further into the wall. "You told Blackburn about *me?*"

Bram held up his hands, coughing like a diseased hyena. He had never looked older than he did right now, face-to-face with Sage, a woman he had sworn to protect with his life because it was his ancestors' will. He had founded the Private Guard to help the Allseer maintain order in the city, but now he was a withered raisin who'd do anything for a bit of money and fame. Clearly. If the Allseer was recruiting and killing Enhanced, it only made sense to acquire Sage, too. But did they know, specifically, that she was the Optimum?

"I agreed to help you with the PG, but I never gave you consent to speak to Blackburn about me!" Sage exclaimed. "So explain, damn it!"

"I'm sorry, Sage!" Bram croaked. "It's just—it happened so quickly! I mean, Blackburn came by PG headquarters one day to congratulate us for a job well done, and I couldn't help but give you most of the credit! The others did, too—Penelope, Dustin, all of them—because it's obvious they've had help. As skilled as we are, we're just a bunch of measly humans."

"Wait a second," Sage whispered, realization coursing through her veins like ice. "Did you say that Blackburn came by headquarters to *congratulate* you? I thought you said the Allseer cut the PG's funds because you guys were doing a shitty job."

"Well, we've been trying—"

"What have you been doing with the money, Bram? The Allseer never cut the funds—that's a lie—so you've been doing something else with the money. Don't tell me you've been using it for our restaurant because that's a bunch of bullshit—you haven't even paid the electric bill!"

"I get paid, but I don't manage the money we get from the Allseer," Bram said, regaining some of his composure. He was able to furrow his brow now. "That's all Penelope."

"And you haven't been asking yourself what she does with it?

That's a lot of money she's tossing into something if she can't even afford the rent for her own headquarters."

"It doesn't matter—"

"IT DOES MATTER!" Sage exclaimed, shoving him into the wall again. "It does matter, Bram!"

"Please calm down!" he choked. "Please, Sage!"

"I can't calm down! The PG is doing sneaky shit behind my back, and now you are, too, telling Blackburn about me—did you tell him I was the Optimum as well?"

"W-what? N-no—"

"YOU NEVER TOLD ME YOU TOLD HIM!"

"I figured you'd want to get close to the royal family, and that was only going to happen through Blackburn—"

"You *figured*"—Sage seethed—"so that's what you went with. How dare you."

"Goddamn it, isn't it what you want?!" Bram yelled back. He finally had the courage to, maybe because Sage's hands were clenched at her sides and no longer close to his neck. She could snap it in half in the blink of an eye. "To marry Louis and live out your sick fantasy of castles and royals? Aren't you bored with your stupid little life of hiding? YOU SHOULD BE THANKING ME!"

Perhaps Bram was right. Hearing it from him in that manner, in a flurry of high-pitched decibels, made logic and reason sink into Sage's head. Instead of being angry, shouldn't she be thankful? All she did was complain about her miserable life here . . . so now that she had a chance of climbing the ladder, why didn't she?

Something felt wrong. Sage kept telling herself that over and over throughout the day and then weeks. Months. The summer. Despite the passage of time, nothing really returned to normal. There were no leaks in the media about the Allseer's death, as she had anticipated there would be, but the council was in charge now according to a Diamond News update. Gregory Amaryllis, the most powerful man in that circle, was the new Diamond City ruler until Louis and his family gathered their bearings. Whatever the hell that meant.

As for the weather, no matter the season, it never seemed to stop drizzling. With the month of Courage upon them and summer now officially behind them, the nights got longer and the dread of what the future would bring lingered. This terrible time felt like a turning point in Sage's life, not only because Samson was worried about their well-being and Bram was insistent that Sage take the throne at Heart by becoming the council's hero, but because she could make a very drastic choice.

Sage pulled out the map that vendor had given her months ago. She had it in her nightstand drawer and looked at it every so often. If she truly wanted security for Diamond City's citizens as well as the Enhanced who protected it, she could join a force that was willing to spill blood and establish fairness. Or . . . what was it, exactly, that the Warlord wanted? She wished she could speak to that vendor, but to her disappointment, there was no tent sale at the street corner anymore. It was as if the vendor had up and disappeared. Maybe she had joined her sister after what happened to the Allseer. Maybe the tide was turning and it was time to help it along . . . in a positive direction.

And Sage wasn't the only one planning a drastic move. The royal family—or what was left of it rather—Louis—wasn't about to give up either. The knock on the door came one night, and Sage was rather shocked to answer to a depressed-looking Louis on her welcome mat.

As soon as Louis saw her, though, he straightened up. Could he not believe that Sage would be the one to answer the door, the one Blackburn had obviously talked to him about, the one who now held significance because everyone in Heart knew she was a fierce warrior? He looked like a deer caught in headlights. Even for a royal, he struggled to gather his wits, as if Sage was the first woman he had ever seen in his life.

"Hey," Louis said a bit stiffly.

Sage said nothing. Maybe she used to fawn all over him, but she had spent quite a bit of time cleaning out her apartment of anything having to do with him or his image. Since the birthday party, Sage wanted nothing to do with this asshole. Candice had said there'd be a spark if he was her true love, and there wasn't. Even Blackburn had had a longer lasting impact than this coward, as unpleasant as it was.

Having Louis so up close to her right now was just so . . . normal. Sage could reach out to touch his blond curls, long straight nose, perfect lips, and slender neck. She had snapped so many in her life, and this one was no different; if anything, it was thin and frail. Louis was too pretty for the battlefield, and that's why he was here: to recruit the one who'd do the fighting for him.

"May I come in?" he asked when Sage didn't make any moves.

"Sorry." Sage stepped out, closing the door behind her. "My roommate is . . . er . . . indecent. However, I'm shocked by your presence, Louis."

"Are you?" Louis frowned, clearly irritated at being denied entry. "Are you really surprised? I mean, you were there, weren't you? During the challenge?"

When you did nothing to help us, was the unspoken thought that glimmered in his eyes.

"I was," Sage admitted, frowning right back. "But I suppose I'm more surprised that you're actually going to do something about it. Or, rather, that you're here to convince me to do your bidding because even Blackburn is petrified of the Warlord. What really annoys me is that you didn't pay a shred of attention to me at the birthday party and now you're here, ready to ask me for favors. I'm not sure who Blackburn thinks I am, but I don't just do anyone's dirty job."

Especially when your family is responsible for the deaths of so many Enhanced, Sage thought to herself rather than said out loud.

Louis didn't refute her words. Like a wounded puppy, he looked down, head slightly bowed, and whispered, "Come with me to the Art Carnival?"

The Art Carnival.

Sage had completely forgotten about it. Maybe it had sounded interesting before, but not anymore. Sensing her hesitancy, Louis added, "Please?"

If Sage denied him, she'd have to pack up and leave the city. Blackburn would be after her because he and the council already knew too much about her. Wasn't that why they had sent Louis straight to her front door? Goddamn it, just how much had Bram told them about her? She intended to find out, so she accepted his invitation and fought the urge to glance at her door.

Samson was standing right behind it, listening in. His large eyes quivered with fright. She sent him a text that she'd be back later.

Louis held out his arm. He hesitated, as if Sage were someone he shouldn't be escorting but had to for the sake of formalities.

"You don't need to carry me anywhere," Sage snapped. "Now walk."

She surprised herself with her tone of voice. She would've never dreamed to use it against Louis, but the frustration came out of her. This man hadn't looked twice her way before he knew what she was. Now that he was well aware of her potential, he followed her around like a blind man. Sage took the lead, even as she climbed into his own limo. She wasn't impressed and turned down drinks. Blackburn was so right.

"If only he knew what you were. He probably just saw you as any other girl."

Sage snorted.

The carnival attracted all sorts of people from across Diamond City, even if they visited every district throughout the year. It was always interesting to see residents from Color, Clarity, and Carat all in one place. They were so different from each other that they were easy to identify in the large crowds streaming down the street.

Color, unlike Cut, were flamboyant and ostentatious, bouncing around in attire that couldn't hold any more colors, jewels, glitter, and just about anything you could paste on your body and wear. They were head-turners, drawing attention and posing for pictures whenever someone asked them for one. Their fashion shows were extraordinary, attracted crowds by the thousands, and featured wardrobes from stickers (yes, people dressed in only stickers) to fifty-foot-long gowns. Sage had gone with Candice and Olivia just last year, and they had brought back tons of clothes from Color's biggest warehouse. So big, it was like an amusement park in there—five acres worth—with hotels next door because it was impossible to see it all in one day.

Clarity residents were pious people who respected the beginnings of their world and the gods they believe had created it: the Lolligo. Sage wasn't much into religion, but she had spent some time in Clarity studying architecture, paintings, and poring over ancient texts that theorized the origins of Abloudor— the name of their current world—the Lolligo, and the creation of Diamond City.

According to legend, four headstrong Lolligo known as the Forefathers had migrated from some faraway land and established their own territories that would later become the districts. Because of their competitive nature, they had battled each other for dominance quite often. No one knew anything for sure, though—no one had actually ever seen the Lolligo, who had allegedly fled Diamond City after the Unification War. In the Clarity District, preachers claimed the nonstop rain was an omen that the Lolligo were angry with what had become of the city. Sage thought that was the stupidest thing she had ever heard. Aside from listening to crazy logic all day, the hardest part of being a Claritian was wearing those white robes to the bathroom.

Naturally, Claritians couldn't stand anyone from the Color District, so it was kind of entertaining to see them glare each other down on the street. "Praise the Forefathers," the Claritians murmured under their breaths. "They're always watching," they whispered to outsiders when asked why they covered their heads with hoods and wore ridiculous masks on their faces. Apparently, the masks were supposed to grant them immunity to the Lolligo's wrath when the "Lightning Storm" came. There was a prophecy that the Lolligo would be back to "strike them down" and reestablish control of Diamond City. Sage would have to make sure that never happened.

Despite that, Claritians welcomed whoever had the patience to visit their district in hopes of gaining more followers. With districts like Cut and Color, however, not many wanted to spend the rest of their lives in a church.

The one district Sage tended to avoid was Carat. Gangs, black-markets, and drugs ran amuck there, with the district's Overseer completely indifferent to all the lords rising to power. It wasn't unusual for the Allseer to send the military to prevent and quell rebellions. If anyone was communicating with the Warlord and his rebels often, it was them. They got caught sneaking in all kinds of contraband from towns in the Outskirts.

But, in this festival, districts weren't at war with each other because everyone was here for the same reason: to celebrate the arts. Pastels always brought Sage to her childhood when she and Aurora would create canvases of any imaginative thing that had entered their heads. The smell of apples and cinnamon had accompanied those long painting sessions, in times when even phones and computers hadn't been available. The TV and radio were all they'd had for entertainment.

"I want to be a Defender!" Aurora said cheerfully. "Don't you, Sage?"

Absolutely. It was why she had joined the unification cause when she turned eighteen. Always ready to fight . . .

One hundred years later, and this was the fruit of Sage's labor, this beautiful city where everyone walked side by side, visiting vendors, buying Cinnamon Rings, and even playing some karaoke on a makeshift stage. A warm, fuzzy feeling grew in Sage's chest as she ventured farther down the street, passing through groups of people collecting their favorite anime prints or trying the new Cocoa Mocha Locha! at a nearby all-things chocolate stand.

Eventually, Sage lost Louis in the crowd and reached the far end of the festival where very few people lingered. There wasn't much happening here other than some low-key commissions. Nearly all the booths were busy except for one.

This artist was isolated from the rest, wedged in between two supply vans. He blended into the darkness well because all the colors on his palette were black.

"Interested in what you see?" said the man. He was fairly old, with lines on his face, eyes downtrodden with exhaustion. The name on his booth read Melancholy in harsh paint strokes. Was that his pen name or was that just how he felt? Both were possible.

"Umm . . ." Sage took a closer look at his painting. It was of a beast with multiple snouts and rows of sharp teeth.

"The Warlord's true form," Melancholy said. "I have seen it before with my very own eyes. We all know he's not exactly human."

Sage knew that wasn't exactly accurate, but she couldn't help but stare at the painting. It certainly captured the ruthlessness that everyone associated with the Warlord. She wasn't sure that's what she had seen during the duel a few months ago, though. That Warlord had been ruthless, yes—he had to be—and beautiful, pampered like a porcelain doll that everyone was afraid to touch in case it broke. But this beast? Definitely not. Unless there was something Sage wasn't seeing.

"They say he has no heart," Melancholy breathed, as if it was his deepest, darkest secret. "It was ripped out of his chest by his very own brother, before his execution."

"How do you know this?" Sage asked, a bit disturbed.

"*I* betrayed him," he wheezed. "*I* told the Allseer where he ran off to the night we parted . . ." The man shook his head with a great sigh. " 'For the people,' he would say . . . and perhaps he was right . . . "

"Were you a lover of his?"

It was a question the strange man couldn't bring himself to answer. He was off in his own head now, dabbing life into his portrayal of the Warlord. It was obvious that some sort of trauma was wreaking havoc on his mind, and tears quickly welled in his eyes as a result.

"They cut him up," Melancholy went on, drool dangling from his lips. "They dissected every part of him . . . as an experiment . . . to see if he would live . . . Enhanced . . . are invincible . . . they don't die from injuries . . . they wanted to see to what extent . . . and so they took out his heart and gave it to me." Slowly, he picked up a hand and pointed at the table across from Sage. On it, amidst paints and cut-out plastics for stirring, was a jar. It was big enough to fit a heart, but there was no way to see what was inside it because it was wrapped in a thinly-sewed cloth. It was the creepiest thing Sage had ever seen.

"Take it."

Sage froze. The rain came down harder, but people whipped out their umbrellas and the tents held steady. It was the *pitter-patter* that thrummed in Sage's head, drowning out those horrific words. *"Take it."*

"What?"

"Give it back to him," Melancholy said. "I fear what he's become. What will happen to Diamond City once he returns." He turned his pale eyes to Sage. "If he has his heart, perhaps he won't be so monstrous. Without the parts that make them human, it's the Cells that live inside the Enhanced. We all know that's what gives them power as well as what makes them monsters."

Sage couldn't bring herself to move. Now she cursed herself for venturing so far out, leaving Louis to chase after her like a hopeless lover, because she had no idea how she was going to peel herself away from here without taking that horrid jar. Worse was that she couldn't see behind the cloth, so how did she know it wasn't a shrunken head in there instead?

The man said nothing else to her. And Sage had the distinct feeling that she'd never see this man again. The darkness on that canvas was going to consume him, and so this was Sage's only chance to save him. By saving the Warlord . . . perhaps she could save this man. His conscious. What was left of it.

This was crazy—it had to be a hoax. But then she remembered the Warlord's words.

"As you hung me, you planned to dismember me as you did my comrades. If it wasn't for my loyal followers, my organs would have been in jars which, I'm sure, you would have taken to feast on when you craved me."

Sage took the jar.

It was heavy and filled with liquid, some sort of embalming fluid. Sage could smell the salt. Not wanting to be taken for a fool, she peeled back a loose flap of the cloth and screamed at what she saw.

There wasn't anything Sage had never seen in her lifetime. The horrors of war had scarred her mind a hundred years into the future, certain scenes as vivid as if they were happening in real time. But she had never held an actual organ in her hands and she had never accepted such *cruelty*, that the Warlord had been dissected all because he had disagreed with the Allseer's politics.

The scream drew everyone's heads, but Sage quickly contained herself and clutched the jar. Louis found her at last, running her way, looking slightly out of place in a crowd of commoners with his form all wet, white clothes with the gold trimmings ruined. But Sage was his priority, and so he asked if she was all right. Then he noticed the painting Melancholy was still working on.

"Eerie, isn't it?" Louis believed he had found the source of Sage's scream. "Do you see the sort of psychopath we're up against?"

"I'm sure there's a better way to handle him," Sage said irritably, watching the man who was back to muttering to himself, lost in his guilt. "Not all of this fighting nonsense. That seems to be a Kilstrong thing."

"Nothing else gets through to him, trust me."

Not that there was that much effort to try. Louis was already thinking of ways to exact revenge on the Warlord, whereas Sage was looking past all the uglies and formulating a plan.

"But please . . . if you meet the Warlord . . . he will take you in with open arms . . . Seek refuge if you need it."

Sage didn't need refuge, but she had to seek out the Warlord. She had to do so with Louis, to get the Kilstrongs on talking terms with the Warlord so they could get this mess straightened out amicably. No bloodshed. As for Sage, she'd be their mediator. This time, it wouldn't be on palace grounds—she was taking Louis straight to the wolf's mouth.

"We're leaving tonight," she said to him. "The Circular Forest and then the Outskirts."

Everyone knew that's where the Warlord dwelled, but not specifically. Louis was desperate for any kind of information regarding his enemy's location, so his eyes lit up and a grin spread on his face. "Sage, seriously? Oh, that is wonderful! Let me contact my guard—"

Sage drew her dagger, the tip of the blade at Louis' throat.

"No," she said. "You misunderstand. We're leaving ... *alone.*"

CHAPTER 7

The Circular Forest

Louis had no choice but to walk forward. He couldn't say or do anything to Sage because he was a coward. He wouldn't risk fighting her. He did, however, ask plenty of questions.

"Are we seriously going to *walk* there?" was one of hundreds in the short ten blocks they had covered. "How do you even know where to go?"

"Does Blackburn trust me or not?" Sage growled.

"Um, yeah—sure." Louis looked around in hopes that a guard or drunken soldier would notice their new, premature Allseer was out of place. Surely someone had to be following them, but no one had tried to stop them yet. As Sage approached the southernmost point of the Cut District, just miles from the Circular Forest now, she sent text messages to Bram and the girls—*hide*—as well as Samson—*get the moped.* "But he didn't say you were crazy!" Louis exclaimed. "To get to the Outskirts, we have to cross the Circular Forest—"

"I know what we have to do."

"Sage, we need people, reinforcements, power—you can't take the Warlord on on your own!"

"I am not taking anyone 'on'." Sage rolled her eyes and bit back her curses. What had Sage been thinking, falling for someone as clumsy as this fool? Boredom was dangerous, then, if it allowed her to develop crushes on a guy like this. Louis was the biggest liability on the planet. Samson would be laughing at her right now. "We are going to do this like civilized people, trust me."

But the Diamond City military didn't want civilized. They stopped Sage as soon as she reached the Chandelier's Pub, one of the last locales before the entrance to the Circular Forest. Dozens of soldiers skittered out of their hiding places like cockroaches, all in their brilliantly white uniforms with black trims, equipped with guns and swords. At the head of all this was Blackburn, who wouldn't miss a chance to confront Sage one last time.

"Oh, thank the Forefathers!" Louis cried, sinking to his knees. "Commander! So nice to see you here!"

"Indeed." Blackburn looked way too casual: he had a cup of coffee in his hand and an amused expression on his face. He and his lackeys must have been waiting for Sage to come by, so why not enjoy a snack in the meantime? It was a nice, quiet area to discuss terms in, too. "It is nice to see you and Sage had a fantastic date. Sage had been waiting for it a long time, you know."

"Y-yeah. The Art Festival was interesting indeed—"

"Going to see him?" Blackburn said to Sage, eyeing the dagger still in her hand. "With our dear Louis in your clutches?"

"I will find him," Sage assured him. "But I work alone, so I suggest you and your cock-sucking cronies back off."

Blackburn raised his hands like a conductor leading his orchestra. He kept his military under control much like he had when the Warlord had made his retreat. He really did look a little bit too relaxed, though, as if he had been hoping Sage would take the initiative to confront the Warlord all on her own. It certainly saved him the trouble of endangering perfectly good soldiers and doing it himself. He didn't care about Louis either.

"I understand, of course," Blackburn said submissively. "Bram wasn't kidding about you and your … *abilities*. I certainly will not stand in your way here. By all means, use Louis as bait."

Louis' face lost all of its color, whiter than the ghost on the Chandelier's Pub logo. "C-Commander—"

"Let's face it, Louis." Blackburn scowled. "You are 114 years old, but you are nothing more than a pampered child, hardly ready to decide the fate of this beautiful city. This isn't another episode of The Royal Court you're on—this is big-boy business. That's why we have Gregory in charge of affairs until we can secure our people and ensure those heathens don't ever step foot in our city again. Sage … my darling." He floated over to her. For a soldier, he was much more charming and regal than Louis, who continued to whimper on the ground. "How about a little deal for your services?"

Sage glared at him.

"You have Louis, yes? Use him however you see fit—whatever it takes to get to the Warlord. I know you're smart, and you'll bide your time until it's convenient for you to kill him." Blackburn smiled. It was slimy as hell. "Yes, he is an Enhanced, but you can snag his weapons and use them against him. Once you do that, return to Diamond City with his head and we'll give you back your pizzeria."

Sage froze. Her ears rang with that word—*pizzeria*—and it took but a moment for her to register what it meant.

"What did you do?!" Sage pointed the dagger at Blackburn, making his men and women draw their weapons. "What did you do to my restaurant?!"

"Let's just say," Blackburn said smoothly, "that you'll be out of business until you return. The Private Guard, in the meanwhile, will use the space however they wish. After their latest investments, they've been a bit tight monetarily, so I'm sure you understand."

" 'Investments'?" Sage sputtered. "Investments on what?"

"Classified information, of course."

"I'm a part of the PG!"

"Are you?" Blackburn mused, sipping his coffee. The steam

graced his face but did nothing to obscure the malice in his eyes. "I'm not sure you are. You're more like their dog—"

"Fuck off!" Sage exclaimed. "I am no one's dog, asshole!"

God, the willpower it took to plant her feet on the ground and keep her blade clean. The consequences of an attack on Blackburn, however, would be detrimental. Blackburn wouldn't just shut down her business for good—he'd arrest Bram and the girls and use them as bait against her. He knew that, and he was as amused as ever.

"Forgive me, Sage—I hate to sound and behave so despicably, but how else am I going to get you to accomplish this monumental task?"

"You must be mighty confident that I can accomplish it by myself," Sage snarled.

"And so are you." Blackburn waved at her with a gloved hand. Sage wanted to tear the skin right off that pretty face. "Were you not about to march right out of this city on your own? Then again, the *Optimum* should have no problem."

Sage's heart was beating so hard, she started to sweat. Her body wasn't used to all this stress, this pure, unbridled rage that was about to break her collectedness. She had already suspected that Blackburn and the entire council knew she was "special," so why did hearing her nickname take her by surprise? Maybe because Bram had betrayed her yet again. The son of a bitch had told them *everything.*

"I'm not killing the Warlord," Sage spat, hatred in her eyes. "That's not my style. You might think he's a heathen, but I'm currently looking at a band of monsters who aren't too far from that themselves."

Blackburn chuckled, "Trust me, you have no idea what you're getting yourself into, Sage. The Warlord is not your best friend or your trusty counselor—he is ruthless and will stop at nothing to acquire power. Oh, he talks majestically, doesn't he, of how he wanted to stop the Allseer's plans?" He snorted. "Those were *his* plans, my lady. *He* wanted to capture *you,* to use you to create more Enhanced. I won't sit here and defend the Allseer because there is simply no proof of his intentions, but I will say this: be careful around the Warlord." Blackburn glanced at his coffee, as if he could see the Warlord's face in the black depths. "He is very . . . charismatic. He will seduce you until you open your legs for him and fall for his false promises of love. Once he has you wound around his finger, he'll capture you and use you as a source of power."

"And you won't?" Sage spat.

"No," Blackburn said without hesitation. "Simply because it wouldn't benefit us. We don't want to create more Enhanced—we want to control the ones we do have."

Sage doubted that. The Warlord himself had accused these assholes of wanting more power. That aside, eradicating Enhanced wasn't right either. The Cell Destroyer was another problem, though—Sage focused on the here and now—she had to get away from Blackburn and meet the Warlord.

"But please." Blackburn bowed. "Don't let us keep you. Go on and find the Warlord . . . if you can. But do remember what's at stake here."

And that's what had Sage shaking the rest of the way to the Circular Forest. Blackburn and his military retreated rather quickly, knowing there was nothing else they could do or say to persuade Sage to act in their favor. They had to leave it up to her and fate to decide what would happen, but one outcome was clear: Sage's return. She had put too much into that pizzeria. They'd be waiting for her then.

"O-oh my Stars!" Louis cried, shuffling after Sage. "A-are we really going to do this? T-this is suicide! Sage, wait, you're not really going to let the Warlord kill me, are you? This is insane—Blackburn doesn't have this much authority—what does Gregory think he's doing—"

Louis stopped rattling when a giant two-seat moped cut right in front of them. It had a closed cabin with tinted windows, the most ridiculous thing ever invented, but it was cheap and got the job done, transporting Sage from Point A to Point B when she needed it the most. There were always those emergency runs to the discount store when her period flared up or even a snack run when she realized her last bag of vegetable chips was gone. This time, the bulky moped with the huge Samson-customized battery that never ran out of charge was going to get them through the Circular Forest. Strapped to the roof and to the back were sleeping gear, food, and weapons because Samson was raring for adventure and the first opportunity he got to meet a Squid.

"Wait, what?" Louis sputtered, confused as Sage approached the driver's seat. "How . . . ?"

The scream. There had to be one. His Highness' royal eyes had never seen anything like Samson before, a towering Squid with huge muscles and a monstrous face. It was the amber eyes and razor-sharp teeth that scared the living daylights out of him, making him scream some more.

"Damn it!" Samson cried, covering his hole-for-ears. There was only so much screeching he could take, so he threw a wad of slime to cover up Louis' mouth. Sage would have laughed if she wasn't still fuming about Blackburn and her restaurant.

"Really, Samson?" Sage scolded.

"I'm not putting up with that." Samson waved at the crying Louis. He spoke in Lolligo, so Louis had no idea what he was saying. "So either we shut him up or we kill him. Wait—why the hell are we even taking him?"

"He's going to negotiate with the Warlord on Diamond City's behalf."

"Why can't you do that?" Samson growled. "You love and care for this city way more than he does."

Sage glared at him. "He's the new Allseer and I'm not. Now let's go before we waste any more time." She pushed the stunned Louis into the moped, then got in after him.

Louis was screaming through the slime across his lips, turning red from the exertion. Neither Samson nor Sage paid him any mind as they finally entered the Circular Forest, hoping he'd knock himself out.

"Really?" Samson grumbled to her as they rode. "You wanted to have sexual intercourse with *that*?"

"Never mind," Sage grumbled back. She really didn't want to

talk about her stupid crush now, nor did she want to contemplate a future at the palace. She was happiest rolling dough and coming up with exotic topping combinations. Making headline news in food magazines and impressing critics was in her blood—not dealing with this whiny shit or being used as a weapon. She had gotten way too involved with the PG.

Sage knew what the problem was: she had to get laid. That was it. She had divorced her husband thirty years ago and hadn't had sex since. Samson said that Squids were asexual, but Sage was part human and sometimes—she did admit—she was rather lonely. Well, not that lonely since she had never even masturbated—training sessions with Samson always knocked her out at night.

Sage was angry and frustrated. She peered out the window, at the trail Samson followed to venture farther into the woods. It was, for the most part, unused because no one dared to travel this far. No environmental awareness organizations or school field trips ever included a tour through the closest thing Diamond City had to wildlife. The media told ghost stories and spread rumors of nasty monsters to stop people from leaving the city and joining all the exiles in the Outskirts. Even the online forums were convincing, so Sage swore there was more than just fireflies and deer lurking between those trees.

Just last summer, a group of five youngsters had been lynched. Pictures of the scene had floated around all four districts, although many people didn't believe it was real. Still, no one had checked it out for confirmation. Samson, on the other hand, tried to be reasonable: Squids wouldn't hang punks in the woods and leave evidence of it. If anything, Squids kidnapped humans and took them back to their lair—scare tactics weren't their style. That's why Sage said it was the Twig Man.

"Stupid," Samson grumbled. "There's no such thing as a 'Twig Man'."

"Then what else could it be?"

"What if it's a Clarity freak doing rituals?"

"They don't do rituals that involve lynching."

"But they do perform sacrifices in the name of Lolligo." Samson twisted his face. "Disgusting, as if we'd ever bat an eye their way."

Well, whatever was going on, they were going right into the heart of it now.

It was going to be an interesting journey across the Circular Forest, that was for sure, with a disheveled Louis still crying in between them. There was a good hundred miles to cover before they hit the Outskirts, so they'd be spending at least two nights in nature with absolutely no reception; Hotspot towers were far out of range here. Samson had all of his laptops for passing the time, but he didn't do it for work or to catch up on his commissions—he focused on his personal designs and journaling. Louis had his phone, but that had stopped working a mile in. It heightened his anxiety to a fever pitch. At any moment now, those veins on his head were going to burst. To make this camp more bearable, and before Samson strapped him to a spigot over the open fire, Sage dragged Louis aside and ripped the slime from his mouth.

"Stop," she said into his trembling face, speaking in Lucidum at last. "Or he's going to kill you."

"W-what is he?" Louis croaked, sweat pouring down his cheeks.

"His name is Samson. And yes . . . he's a Lolligo."

They were purely rumors in Diamond City and the root of the monster stories in the Circular Forest. Excluding Samson, Sage had never come across a single one in her life despite the fact it was Squids that had controlled each of the four districts before the Unification War. They were elusive creatures, ruling through humans, so not a whole lot of people had actually seen them. The ones who had were already dead, and the Enhanced who had fought in the war had never gotten close enough to one. Where those Squids had fled to, nobody knew. No one dared to venture past the Outskirts, but Samson always had hope they'd meet one at some point.

Louis blinked his two large eyes. At last, he had stopped squirming although he was still panting. He shook his head in disbelief. "What on earth?" he croaked. "A *Lolligo*? So they do exist?"

"Even Claritians know that much." Sage said. "Who do you think their gods are?"

"S-Stars, but they look like giant freaks! L-like humanoid squids or something!"

"Shh—don't let him hear you say that."

Louis blinked cluelessly.

"It's insulting," Sage said. "And he'll cut off your tongue."

Sage had learned that the hard way, although she still called them Squids.

If Louis had ever doubted religion before, maybe he was reconsidering it now. In addition to the crazy stories on online forums, Claritians had their own beliefs regarding Squid behavior. Some thought they mingled with humans and gave birth to invincible hybrids. In actuality, that wasn't too far from the truth.

"B-but I don't understand—where did he come *from?*"

Sage shook her head. "I found him when he was just a baby in the Clarity siege. His guardians must have left him behind when they took off to flee for themselves."

Samson had been a tiny Squid then, the size of a goldfish. Sage had taken him home but never presented him to her mother—only Aurora, who had helped raise and train him. Unlike humans, Samson took forever to grow and age. It wasn't until Sage's mother had died some fifty years later that Samson had officially become an adult at a whopping six feet and five inches with two hundred and fifty pounds of muscle.

"Sage!" Samson called out in their tongue, "Dinner's almost ready." He opened a box of noodles and shook them into the scalding water over the fire.

"What did he say?" Louis croaked as Sage withdrew from their conversation. "H-he can speak another language?"

"Yes, it's called Lolligo. Creative, isn't it? Don't worry—he's just saying that it's almost time to eat."

That was a relief for Louis, whose next question was what kind of diet Squids had. It didn't include Enhanced or humans, so he breathed out, calm for the first time tonight, although he was wary of the food Sage served him. It was noodles and pieces of defrosted pork, but Louis couldn't be certain of that.

"Pussy," Samson murmured under his breath.

Louis snapped his head up. "Oh, um, it's very good!"

"Be nice," Sage snapped to Samson.

"Wait—what did he say?" Louis asked.

"Samson wants to know why you don't fight with other Enhanced," Sage said quickly.

"I can speak for myself," Samson snapped, in Lucidum this time so Louis could understand. "Listen, boy—you're an Enhanced. Do you know what that means? You carry the Cells of a powerful warrior race. You better stop making all those damn TV shows and *do* something."

"Cells," Louis whispered to himself. "I carry the . . . Cells . . . ?"

"Yes!" Samson sputtered, clicking his sharp teeth. "The Cells in your body come from Lolligo, you idiot! Be proud of it!"

"Not everyone is cut out for war, Samson," Sage said lazily.

"Bullshit. If you have Cells in your body, then you can fight. It's just this little shit hasn't learned to do anything but lick girl pussies."

Sage spat out her food. Louis whimpered like an injured rabbit. Samson grumbled more curses to himself.

"Sorry," Sage said to Louis. "He doesn't like other people. Doesn't . . . trust anyone."

"I don't," Samson snapped. "What kind of name is 'Kilstrong' anyway? It's not in any of the Diamond City records."

"Oh." Louis cleared his throat. "My father made it up when he became Allseer. Our family name is actually 'Toussaint'. We're French descendants."

"Was that not a good enough name for the throne?"

"Well, it's pretty common . . . and my father wanted to stand out." Louis took a deep breath, as if it took all the concentration in the world to add, "So Kilstrong it is."

"It's a stupid name," Samson spat. "So you should change it."

Sage glared at him. "Is that really necessary? Who cares?"

"I might change it," Louis said shyly.

Samson was just being an ass, and any little slip-up on Louis' part would set him off. That's why, to avoid any mishaps or accidental deaths, Sage set up her sleeping bag between the two. She didn't need a huge tent like Samson did—she was content lying on the ground and looking up at the sky blocked mostly by branches. The city drizzle didn't bother her either. Being out here meant she'd know if any of her companions were trying to kill each other. Samson never stepped out of his tent again, but Louis was having a hard time falling asleep. The stories of these woods were too engraved in his mind, and now that he knew Squids existed, what was to say there weren't any other monsters lurking around here like the Twig Man? Even so, that's not what Louis asked her about.

"Is it all true?"

Sage looked over at him. "Is what all true?"

Louis hesitated. Even on the ground with some wayward twigs in his hair, he still looked like a pretty boy. Far less powerful and regal than portrayed in The Royal Court, though. "Commander Blackburn said you were the Optimum, the fighter who led Diamond City to victory. There were so many stories written about you."

"I am nothing special," she said truthfully. "A product of my nature just like you are. I can fight because I am a warrior, as Samson said."

"So you were living in secrecy all this time?"

"I was."

Sage knew her life wouldn't be the same again. She'd never be able to run her pizzeria without the council breathing down her neck. It wasn't a wonder Samson had crammed so much of their belongings onto the moped, as if he knew he wouldn't be returning to the city either. Louis' birthday party had ruined everything. But maybe Sage was looking at the glass half empty, as Samson said to her the next morning when Louis went out to find an ideal nook to pee in.

"I feel it now," he said to her enthusiastically. "Our place is with the Warlord. He knows *Lolligo*, Sage. He has Slainium in his weapons. He has to know where the rest of our people are."

Sage didn't say anything. There was no point in arguing without proof, although she couldn't help but think that Samson was right.

This was the beginning of the end of her life in Diamond City. And the beginning of her new one in the Outskirts.

CHAPTER 8

Mousafeld

After another night in the Circular Forest—a successful one because Louis was still in one piece—they finally approached the last line of trees. Dusk was upon them once more, but Sage didn't need lights to assess her surroundings. It was when they reached the Outskirts, still riding their flimsy moped, that Sage got a bad feeling in her gut. It shook her from the inside, like some sort of warning. This kind of terrain was completely new to her, but it was more than that: the rain had stopped, and Sage could smell aggression in the air. Fighting. Violence. She asked Samson to pull over.

"What?" he breathed. "In the middle of nowhere?"

They weren't in the middle of nowhere. They had barren wastelands all around them, but they had followed that vendor's map south to the Warlord's camp, and sure enough, just a few miles away, Sage sighted a broken Ferris wheel.

A long time ago, there had been carnivals here. There were towns peppered across these lands, each of which had been governed independently. After the Unification War, the Allseer had cut all contact with them. He had planted trees around Diamond City, not because he cared about the environment as he had claimed, but because they made an excellent border. As a result, tourism had decreased, famines had struck, and diseases had run rampant in the Outskirts. In the past few years, multiple cases of Red Fever had been reported in Diamond City, which officials attributed to contamination from the outside. Specifically what was doing the contaminating, no one knew, but Sage had a feeling that was yet another council scare tactic. Red Fever was for real—Sage had delivered free pizzas to a customer that had fallen horribly ill once—but it couldn't have been from anything out here. Even Blackburn didn't brave a stroll through these parts often. No one did, for reasons that had nothing to do with diseases.

"Is that it?" Louis said, looking out at the horizon as well. "Where the Warlord is?"

Yes. It was a strategic location, too: a town right outside the Circular Forest for easy access to Diamond City. Sage made the rest of the trek on foot, with Samson and Louis keeping a close distance behind her on the moped, and stopped before the sign that read, *Mousafeld.*

Famous for their rides, attractions, and exertions, it said, like the Thousand Foot Dipper, a roller coaster that sent people into vomit frenzies. Now, there wasn't much of the town left. Not even the Warlord had been able to bring it back up to speed, but maybe it was better that way. The desolation repelled attention and made for the perfect place to hide. Eerie... because above the whistle of the wind and that light smell of smoke in the air, Sage heard something... yells. Shouts. It came from beyond the empty carnival grounds, from an area where Sage could see lights. A marketplace, maybe?

Sage pressed forward despite the rising fear between Samson and Louis. Both of them already knew they were heading straight for danger, and their confidence in Sage's abilities wavered.

Sage, on the other hand, didn't let doubt drag her down. She drew her new and finished sword from its sheath, courtesy of Samson, and prepared to test it out for the first time in actual combat. It felt light in her grip—flexible and impenetrable—just like its prototype, but this blade was thinner and slightly longer, measuring at least four feet. With the Slainium and Samson's meticulous welding, it could cut down a whole building.

"Sage, no!" Louis croaked as Samson kept up with her on the moped, barreling through broken stands and knee-high weeds alike. "This is insane!"

"Ditto what pretty boy says!" Samson called to her. "We don't know what's out there!"

"Hide the moped," Sage said to their white faces. "I'm going to check out what's going on."

They didn't argue with her. It was nerve-wracking, but Sage knew how to concentrate, how to rush past all the disintegrating attractions and dirty teddy bears without thinking, and how to focus on her target.

She was right: there was a marketplace up ahead, in an area that had been rebuilt and refashioned to meet the needs of its residents. There were storefronts on every street, lamps bright, illuminating benches, ponds, and sidewalks. Cars were already at a standstill, making it harder for Sage to get closer without ramming into a hood or bumper. She stopped to compose herself and tune in to the commotion: it was still a good couple of blocks away. She didn't know what the hell was causing such a disturbance in Mousafeld, but it didn't sound like Diamond City soldiers. It couldn't be Squids either... could it? Sage didn't have any idea, so she braced herself for the worst (the Twig Man?) and furrowed her brows when she glimpsed a hooded figure standing at the corner of some pizza restaurant.

Sage's chest swelled with anger at the thought of her own back home, but she didn't allow that to distract her. She kept her focus on the hooded figure, knowing it was male by the size of its torso, and instantly thought of the Cell Destroyer.

But no—it couldn't be. There was something *different* about this guy, a different aura, like a different breed of dog. Sage watched him stand over a pile of bodies on the street with a swagger that said he wasn't going to lose to these weaklings. He was clearly waiting for the stronger Enhanced to find him, to make all of this worthwhile. In the meantime, bullying business owners served as good entertainment.

"CLARA!" screamed a man who was still wearing his pizza apron. He had probably rushed out of the kitchen to find a dear friend of his, or probably his wife, in the clutches of this monster.

But Clara wasn't dead yet. Despite the blade through her throat, her eyes were open, tears streaming from them. Enhanced were invincible, but they still felt pain. If she was still alive, then the attacker's blade couldn't have had Slainium, so these Enhanced stood a chance of living if they weren't cut up into pieces first.

Pizza-man lashed out without thinking twice, but the attacker moved seamlessly, dodging fists and kicks and incapacitating anyone who got in his way. He made the Warlord's fighters look like amateurs, so he couldn't be one of them—he was clearly something more. While Sage was sure that Mousafeld could overpower him eventually, she didn't wait for the massacre to worsen—she leapt right onto the hooded figure's shoulders and flipped him to the ground in one smooth motion.

Her thighs felt muscle—*sheer* muscle. That registered in her brain quickly, so when Sage came back onto her feet, she already had a solid assessment of her opponent: strong as hell. Built like a Squid almost. Samson's body was steel, and this guy's wasn't too far from that.

Sage gripped her sword, the Slainium reflecting all those warm glows from nearby lamps, and flew right at the hooded figure, whose face remained concealed. When she got close enough, driving the blade through his chest, she noticed his features only briefly. She saw amber eyes, gray skin, and sharp cheekbones—definitely not Francis Kilstrong—before strength exploded from the hooded figure's fist—Sage dodged it, but the wave of energy tore a traffic light in two.

The Enhanced were too shocked to move, watching as the hooded figure dislodged himself from Sage's blade. To their awe, he staggered a bit, even with her weapon at his disposal. He never quite hit her with it. In fact, Sage snatched it back, ducked his swing, and

　　　　　　　　　　　　　　　DIAMOND CITY

kicked him hard enough to send him flying into the air. Her sword followed, skewering him to the tower clock.

"What the hell?!" someone cried as Sage jumped right after him, landing on the wall like a spider and grabbing hold of her weapon anew.

The hooded figure gazed right at her, eyes flashing with recognition. Even if his veins were turning black from Slainium poisoning, spreading through his body like cancer, there was something he had to say. His cracked lips curled together, forming the words, *"Sila ilemas fune…"*

A moment felt like an eternity. Even though Sage was looking at a human face, albeit deformed, the broken but slithery language suggested there was way more to this guy than met the eye. This wasn't just an Enhanced terrorizing towns—this was a call to Sage's origins.

Ilemas…

Sister.

That was all the hooded figure had time for. If he couldn't defeat Sage or resist the effects of the Slainium in his body, what chance did he stand against so many Enhanced? Over a hundred of them were assembled at the point of conflict now, and then the Warlord's best fighter arrived.

Commander, the guy who had chopped up Kenna in less than five minutes.

"Duck."

Sage swung away, taking her sword with her, as the bullet struck the hooded figure in the head. He slid down the wall of the tower clock, plopping to the street in a heap. With whatever strength and determination he had left, he fled. Some of the Enhanced followed, but they weren't fast enough to catch him. Maybe Sage should have given chase, too, but she still had that word thrumming in her head.

Ilemas… ilemas…

"Secure the border," Commander commanded to the Enhanced around him. "Although I doubt he'll be back."

"Dough!" one of the Enhanced called, kneeling over the fallen pizza-man. "And Clara! Sailor, Butcher—all of them!"

"Praise the Forefathers!" A crazy one in white robes saw the bloodbath. "Let us pray that they will survive!"

"SHUT UP!" yelled a muscular woman who reached the bodies. "They need help not worthless prayers!"

"Someone call Dr. X!"

"Commander, sir—we've found someone!"

Sage, still on the tower clock, looked over, and her heart sank in horror.

Shoved through the streets like a captured criminal was Louis, whose face was whiter than snow. Samson was nowhere to be found, but he was the culprit, pushing Louis into the spotlight. This must have been Louis' worst nightmare: captured by his sworn enemies, the same barbarians who had killed his father and sent his sheltered life into chaos. He actually peed his pants. If the Allseer had been an expert at dishing out punishment, then these monsters didn't have a shred of mercy in their bodies. Nothing short of hell awaited Louis, and everyone could see it on Commander's face.

Pleasant surprise flickered across his features—the too-good-to-be-true feeling—as if he wasn't seeing quite right at first. Those dark brows furrowed, and his entire body lit with pleasure. From the dark jumpsuit and belt full of weapons, he must have been ready for any sort of attack—just not one from the Allseer's kid. This was his lucky day.

Before that head filled with any ideas, Sage threw her sword right at Commander's feet. All the Enhanced raised their weapons, focused on her. Commander looked up as Sage landed in front of him, the only body standing between him and the whimpering Louis on the ground now.

"Not so fast," Sage said dangerously, pointing her sword at him. "He's mine."

"Oh?" Commander chuckled, eyes alight like a beast's. This man was used to winning every battle because he didn't have a single scar on his body. Like the Warlord, this man had clean, porcelain skin. He was exceptionally tall, just a few inches shorter than Samson, and promised a great deal of damage to whoever confronted him. He was dark enough to prove that he spent countless hours in the sun, but it was obvious that very few people ever got to lay a finger on him. His cornrows were *perfect.* "He's *yours?* Please, enlighten me. How does a young female like yourself own a corrupt prince like him?"

"He came here with me, so we're together. Additionally, he didn't come here to become your slave—he's here to negotiate."

The entire street of Enhanced stiffened, and not in a shocked way—in a this-is-hilarious kind of way. Despite the show Sage had put on in their defense, they weren't about to negotiate with their enemy. So much for righteousness.

"Who are you?" Commander said, scanning Sage from head to foot. "Are you an Enhanced?"

"It would appear that way, wouldn't it?"

"Then you've got quite the courage showing up here and bringing Louis straight to me while thinking that you're going to walk away from this alive."

Sage tightened her grip on the sword. "I'm not a Kilstrong lackey if that's what you're thinking. I am not Kenna."

The Enhanced gasped, swelling with excitement. It wasn't every day a chick showed up out of nowhere and challenged their leader. This was turning out to be one hell of a night.

"Forgive me if I'm not taking you seriously," Commander said slowly, amusement falling a bit, "but I'm having a hard time of it."

"Unless I'm an idiot, I wouldn't be trying to fool you or anyone."

There were ways to test these words, and one of those brutish Enhanced thought that shooting her was the best choice. Louis squealed, but Sage caught every bullet, surprised that these weren't laced with Slainium, and sent them right back. Bullets did very little damage, though, so Sage used her sword to deliver a message and rammed it straight through the brute's chest. All she had to do was slice a major artery for the kill, but she didn't. The rest of the Enhanced were already leaping at her—

"That's right," Commander said loudly, stopping them with his voice alone. "How far do you intend on carrying this quarrel? She is a woman who just saved so many lives from that attacker and has hand-delivered Louis to our feet in exchange for a 'negotiation.' The least we can do is hear her out." He sighed, waving his hand at Sage. "Please, stand down."

Sage did as long as they did. She yanked out her sword from the Enhanced groveling on the ground and sheathed it. "I'd pump out the blood if I were you," she said to his hollering form. Then she turned to Commander, who was frowning now, that cynical glint in his eye gone for good. There was no doubt he had needed that demonstration to understand that Sage wasn't here to play around. Taking things by force was his specialty, but now he had the lives of his men and women to think about. Plus, he couldn't do anything without the Warlord's consent.

"Please," Commander said with a small bow. "Follow me. I'd like to take you to the Warlord to settle this matter."

Even Sage's heart started a quick beating at the thought of meeting the Warlord face-to-face. Poor Louis didn't have any more piss to let out, so he started shaking instead. All the Enhanced smirked: Sage and Louis were sure to meet their deaths now. While the Warlord went around flashing fashion and jewels, Sage knew there was a killer in that thin, lean body. There was a chance she might have to fight for her life after all.

With a whimpering Louis behind her, Sage followed Commander out of the Marketplace. They passed a few buildings until they reached one that was a compound, fenced-in and heavily secured. There were at least a dozen Enhanced lingering around the street and another pair standing guard by the entrance. All eyes were on Sage, a clear outsider in her long trench coat, tight pants, and military boots. These guys, with their drab colors, were all dressed alike. They didn't flaunt the red and gold from the challenge—they were in gray jumpsuits, their everyday wear. Now they looked more like the killers from the Allseer's propaganda videos, but instead of technology to blur their features and hide their identities, they had their names sewed onto their chests. Well, more like nicknames because Blood, Leafblower, Cut-You-Up, and Gambler weren't on the top ten baby names of the century. Fittingly, they all matched the person in some way: Blood had overly large veins, Leafblower had huge arms that could sweep anyone off their feet, Cut-You-Up carried two cutlasses in his hands, and Gambler had slick hair. Perhaps their real names brought too much shame from when they had been exiled.

"Please," Commander said to the two by the gate. "Let us through."

Because this guy was the Warlord's lapdog, there were no questions. They let them pass to the building within.

When Sage stepped through the double doors, it was as if someone had opened the gates to heaven. The walls, columns, and all corners of the room were gilded in gold, gleaming with an unearthly radiance. The polished floors reflected that light, encasing Sage in an ethereal glow and transporting her to a world very different from the one she had just come from. The palace at Heart was striking in its own royal way, but this didn't make Sage think of emperors and kings—this was a place for a god.

Sure enough, the Warlord sat upon his throne. He was in a dark jacket and pants, buttons and chains all polished to match his makeup. He looked more simple today, too: pale white with black around his eyes. There were a few strands of gold laced through his hair, some glittering with what looked like diamonds. He looked like an expensive piece of jewelry that belonged in its own glass case; the people standing around the dais kept their respectful distance.

The conversation between them dropped mid-sentence, long before Sage was halfway across the room. It was hard to hear them when Louis was still crying and sniffling like a baby. Their facial expressions gave away a whole lot more than their words. The the furrowed brows and tight lines of their lips said they knew all about Sage's fight against the intruder already. And, of course, they didn't believe a word of it.

The Warlord stood up. It was the first time Sage had ever seen him on his feet. He wasn't any taller than his subjects, but the air he breathed pressed heavily on everything in the room. Surroundings faded into nothingness when Sage was looking directly into those black eyes that sucked her into an abyss. They ravaged her like a flame, but Sage didn't let them consume her. Her own glistened with resolution, and that's what made the Warlord stare longer than necessary.

"My lord." Commander bowed to him. "We wanted you to meet the warrior who defeated the intruder."

"And incapacitated Fire-And-Ice," spat one of the Enhanced holding Louis. That squat nasty one with the attitude was called Turtle according to his name tag.

"Because he attacked me first," Sage said.

"She is also an *intruder*, my lord. She might have saved a few of us, but the question remains: what is she doing here? With Prince Louis, no less?"

"I already explained why I'm here."

"I don't trust her!" Turtle exclaimed loudly. "She doesn't fight like an Enhanced! I say she's here to kill us all!"

"Hmm." The Warlord tilted his head, as if he were appreciating a fine piece of art. His eyes were eating her alive. "What is your name, darling?"

"Don't call me 'darling'," Sage snapped at him. "My name is Sage. I fought in the Unification War a hundred years ago."

The Warlord gasped. "Tell me it isn't so? I'm afraid I don't remember you at all."

"I'm not sure we've ever met."

"A pity. I would have loved to have seen you in action. Were you one of the ones privileged enough to meet the Optimum herself?"

"Yes," Sage said quietly.

"Marvelous." The Warlord's eyes twinkled. "It is an honor to meet you, Sage. And if you are here on behalf of Kilstrong, then it is safe for me to assume you were on his side during my exile? Most Enhanced play a part in court, and so I imagine you were for his policies—"

"I am not part of the court," Sage spat, and Louis whimpered.

"And I hold special favors with no one. I am not here to turn the tides of any feuds—I only want a truce."

"So you, too, doubt the Allseer's motives?" The Warlord stepped down from the dais so he was at eye level with Sage. He was as tall as she was but lacked the muscularity of every person in the room. It was clear he spent quite a bit of time lounging and giving orders. Still, Sage didn't underestimate the strength underneath his fancy clothes. "But what am I saying? At this point, the Allseer's intentions are obvious. He was too afraid of others wielding extraordinary powers, so he kicked them out of the city like dogs. Me and so many Enhanced helped put him there, yet he treated us like garbage." The Warlord scowled. "Not only that—he wished to capture the Optimum and use her for his own selfish agenda as well. That's all that bastard ever wanted to do—control others—and I couldn't take it anymore. But please. I'm in a rather good mood today, and I'd rather not spoil it with talk of ungrateful savages, so why don't we change the topic?" He picked up a glass of wine from a nearby servant and took a sip. "Besides, there are more important matters to discuss, such as this 'truce' of yours. Does that include joining me, perhaps?"

"Agathe Kilstrong," Sage said. "She wasn't yours to take, even if you did best the Allseer."

"That, I did, so I have every right to take what was at stake. Why not? That fool agreed to the challenge and the consequences if he should lose."

"You still know it's not right," Sage pressed. "No matter what he agreed to. Kidnapping and forcing yourself on a girl is wrong."

"What's not right about it?" the Warlord said. "I want Diamond City back, so what other way is there to obtain it?" He swirled the wine around in his glass. It reminded Sage of Blackburn's wine. "This marriage will force relations between my rebels and the city. I might have killed the Allseer, but I still hold no standing in his politics until I formally marry the girl."

"Then I've come to tell you it's not right—not that way. Return that girl to Heart."

The Warlord laughed. "Seriously? And what the hell makes you think I'm going to do that?"

"If you do, I'll help you with whatever you and your lackeys want to achieve," Sage said steadily. She knew this wasn't a part of Blackburn's plan—and so did Louis because he hiccuped—but this was the only reasonable option right now. There was no way she was fighting the Warlord and his rebels. When it came to Diamond City, Sage hated the Allseer, Blackburn, and all of those tyrants in the council. Allying herself with the Warlord seemed like the best option at the moment, so she ran with it. "Marrying Agathe won't guarantee any position in Diamond City because the council is in charge now. You're going to need numbers and a force that will take out the council. You need to recruit the Enhanced scattered throughout the Outskirts to stand a chance, and I will help you do that. Maybe, with enough people, we can avoid a war."

The Warlord narrowed his eyes. "Who put you up to this?"

"I don't discuss my personal business with others," Sage said tightly.

"I'm sorry," the Warlord hissed, "but you are under *my* mercy now, Sage. And I am still not sure if you are trying to insult me by offering your so-called 'services.' What 'services' might these be, exactly? Keeping me warm at night?" He snorted. "I already have plenty of that, people to fuck and orgies to host. Additionally, you are not very attractive. I'd like to know the man who is ever turned on by the sight of you—"

Sage flung her dagger right at the Warlord's heart, piercing it. That didn't do her any good, though—he didn't have a heart, and even if he did, the dagger was regular steel. The Warlord plucked it right out of his body just as his rebels came to life, initiating the protocol to save their lord. Commander didn't hesitate to draw his sword, but the Warlord waved everyone away.

"But, sir!" sputtered Turtle, now holding a blade to Louis' throat. Poor Louis was as red as a tomato, his breathing coming in tight wheezes. "S-she just attacked you!"

"Indeed," the Warlord mused, touching his chest gingerly. "And

I think she fractured my sternum. No woman has ever done that
before."

"Maybe because you're too busy seducing them," Sage spat.

"I can't help my charm."

"Not charming. At all. You're just an egotist."

"I'm a monster, as my name implies," the Warlord said smoothly.
His entire crew was holding its breath. Even sneezing out of turn
would get them a lashing, much less an insult like that. "Is there
really any point in being nice and caring in a world like ours?"

"If you call yourself a monster, then that's what you are."

The Warlord shrugged. "I don't particularly care what people
think of me. They need to learn their places—period. If they know
what's good for them, they'll submit to me and deal with the scum-
bags in Diamond City. Will you comply?"

Sage arched a brow. "Is that an invitation to join your army or
your bed?"

The Warlord chuckled. "I like the way you think . . . and fight.
But I have no time to waste on you—neither in my bed nor in my
campaigns—if you can't fight." He nodded at Commander. "Kill
her. And when you do, hang her head in the trophy room next to
Kilstrong's."

"S-Sage!" Louis cried.

Sage turned to Commander, who hesitated now. His instinct
was to attack when his Warlord was in danger, but not to follow
through when he was ordered to? Either that, or he had realized
Sage was far more powerful than she let on. *And* her sword was laced
with Slainium. A hit from that, and he'd be Dr. X's next patient.

Even so, Commander couldn't disobey the Warlord's orders. He
meant to make quick work of this, but Sage was faster. She threw
her palm out, smashed his chest, and knocked him off his feet.
Commander recovered in time to use his sword, but Sage jumped
back, drawing her own. Bullets were nothing—she caught them
all—and used her blade as a bullet of her own. When she threw
it, that's what it looked like: a blur until it skewered Commander
through the chest, and pinned him to the floor.

The entire room was frozen. Some rebels were turning purple in the face. Louis had stopped panting so he wouldn't miss a beat of this. The tension swelled to a fever pitch, half of the Enhanced wondering if they should interfere, but nobody moved unless the Warlord willed it. Right now, the Warlord had a dazed look on his face, as if he couldn't believe what he was seeing. Commander was the same Enhanced who had defeated Kenna in just a couple of minutes. Now he lay on the floor, dying, proving to the world that he couldn't defend his own lord.

"Y-you're not . . . " Commander coughed, blood spurting out of his mouth. "Enhanced . . . c-can't . . . be . . . "

Sage grabbed the hilt of her sword. As her fingers curled around the handle, Commander used his gun to shoot her. His hand shook, but at close range, there was no way he could miss. He only did because Sage moved that quickly, then kicked the gun out of his grasp. She broke his wrist while she was at it.

Commander dropped the sword from his left hand at last. Sage pulled her own out of his body. She flicked her eyes at Turtle and said, "If you want him to live, move quickly."

Amazingly, everyone looked at the Warlord.

The Warlord's lips tightened into a thin line. Sage couldn't call him angry or envious, though—drawn brows suggested he was contemplative. Shiny eyes said he was thinking. But first thing was first.

"Get Commander to Dr. X immediately."

A pair of Enhanced stepped forward to do just that.

"Take our . . . *guest* to Building A," the Warlord said, gesturing at the whimpering Louis. "Worry not, my lady," he said to Sage before she protested, "he won't be harmed—only contained. Beyond this compound is a complex where we live. I will ensure that our princeling is . . . comfy."

"Wait!" Louis cried to her, sweating profusely. By now, he looked like he had stepped out of a sauna. "Don't leave me!"

"I'm not leaving you," Sage stated flatly.

"D-didn't you need me to negotiate? To talk?"

It didn't seem like the Warlord wanted anything to do with a Kilstrong. It was clear that his attention as well as that of his Enhanced was on Sage, who was much more level-headed and a breath of fresh air in a pool of corrupt politicians. Still, Sage made the Warlord swear not a hair on Louis' head would be touched.

"You have my word," the Warlord said, bowing his head. "Until we come to an agreement, I will touch nothing." As Turtle led the retreat with a wailing Louis in tow, the Warlord stepped closer to Sage. Despite the tear in the center of his chest from the dagger, he dared to take her hand and lay a kiss on her knuckles.

His lips were as soft as feathers. Like an infection, heat spread through Sage's hand and up her arm. She gazed into the outlined eyes, hypnotized by the fire she saw in them. At this proximity, she smelled teakwood and lavender, as if she were taking a stroll through an enchanted forest where hot, muscular fairy men dwelled. It made her forget all about his call to have her killed. Inside, she knew he'd had Commander fight her as a test to see her skills for himself, so Sage couldn't be too mad about it.

"I am most impressed," the Warlord said huskily, still holding her hand. His fingers were so white, long, and smooth compared to hers. He rubbed hers as if he were massaging her pain away. Each of his rings glistened beneath the lights. The one that stuck out the most was the ruby on his left hand. In the middle of it was the Diamond City insignia, the diamond with a spear running through it. Every soldier who had fought in the Unification War had one. Sage had given hers to Aurora and gotten the tattoo on her biceps instead. "Your fighting skills are incredible," the Warlord went on. "And I am truly honored that you came all the way out here to seek me out. Please … would you join me in my quarters?"

If Sage had truly had any intention of killing the Warlord, it was completely gone now. She couldn't lay a finger on this man, who was so polite, humbling himself before her even if he had every reason to. Sage could have killed Commander … but she hadn't. And if she had, she had a feeling that the Warlord would have attacked her in turn. He was much more powerful than he appeared.

Or else these Enhanced wouldn't have been serving him at his every beck and call. Nor would they have taken him and his ostentatious nature seriously. There was more to this Warlord than met the eye, and Sage wasn't sure she wanted to find out what it was.

CHAPTER 9

Milkshakes and Cigars

The Warlord was still holding Sage's hand like a precious dove as he led her to a set of double doors behind the throne. He seemed to find comfort in her presence because he didn't have Louis decapitated. His features relaxed when he gazed at her, the deep dark eyes that reminded Sage of two tunnels, scary and endless until she saw the light.

But Sage didn't think of Melancholy's painting of a monster. All she saw in the Warlord was a broken man who couldn't trust a soul, who had been betrayed time and time again. His face was angular and smooth, black hair long and silky—healthy—but there were traces of scars and wrinkles underneath his makeup. All the Enhanced were around the same age, but not everyone shared the same experiences. Unlike Louis, the Warlord had spent all his life fighting, running, hiding, and surviving torture. Pity surged through Sage because she knew the Warlord had never had peace, not like she'd had at the pizzeria by Bram's side—by Samson's side. Her respect for him swelled, but not too much—she kept her brows drawn and her body braced. This man was capable of anything. The heads perched on the wall of his common room were proof enough.

"Wow," Sage said, eyeing all those creepy faces with the glassy eyes. The taxidermy on them was so lifelike. Almost as if those heads weren't really stuffed at all … "You sure do like to show off."

"I like to remind myself of my conquests." The Warlord waved at his trophies. "And my most prized one is Kilstrong, the bastard."

Yes, he was up there. Thankfully, his eyes were closed.

"I hope they don't scare you." The Warlord raised her knuckles to his lips again. "I wouldn't want you to feel uncomfortable."

"I'm not here to judge your taste. You do as you see fit."

"As a warrior, I'm sure you've seen your fair share of gore." The Warlord's eyes scanned her face and moved lower to her chest. With so many bulky clothes on her body, there wasn't much to see. The Warlord had a magnificent imagination, though, and it painted a vivid picture of her breasts because his gaze smoldered with heady desire and his nostrils flared with want. Sage kept her breathing under control, but her cheeks flushed when she saw him lick his lips. Then he settled on her hips.

"Your sword," the Warlord said. "May I see it?"

If Samson were here, he'd be raving that the Warlord had noticed his weapon. The son of a bitch must have been lurking in the woods somewhere, looking for an opportunity to infiltrate the camp without being seen. Sage felt his pride all the way from wherever he was.

Sage didn't hesitate to hand over the sword, sheath and all. The Warlord took it as if it were some treasure, gauging its weight, unmasking it, and glorifying it as if he were seducing a woman. His eyes glittered with admiration, taking in every angle of the weapon in his hands before he whipped around and struck down a lamppost with a single swipe.

Sage stopped herself from taking a step back. She had not been expecting that.

"My … " the Warlord whispered, examining the sword again. "Where on earth did you get this?"

"A friend of mine is very good at welding Slainium," Sage said.

The Warlord raised his brows. "Slainium? What is that?"

　　　　　　　　　　　　　　　　　　　DIAMOND CITY

"Slainium destroys the Cells in an Enhanced," Sage explained. "Don't you have something similar?"

"Excuse me?" the Warlord said.

Sage was confused. Didn't the Warlord use Slainium in his weapons? That's what it had looked like in his torture videos . . . how he killed Enhanced . . . so Sage wondered if this was all a trick. But the Warlord didn't look like he was trying to trick her.

"My friend figured out it's particularly effective against Enhanced," Sage went on. "I use it, too." She showed him her bracelets. "A touch of this in your bloodstream, and your Cells are in danger. It acts like a poison until it destroys them all, leaving nothing but the humans we truly are. And if we're all over a hundred years old then . . ." Sage tried not to picture it. "It's not the prettiest way to die. But right now, it's the only known way of truly killing an Enhanced."

"But wait," the Warlord breathed. "Does the Diamond City military know about this?"

"No. I told you I'm not a Kilstrong lackey."

"Who is this 'friend' of yours? I mean, is he a scientist?"

"Sort of." Sage snorted a bit.

"Incredible." The Warlord touched her bracelets gingerly. He must have been afraid they'd zap or poison him, but Slainium was only effective when it touched the blood. "Does it give you immunity, being exposed to it like that?"

"Not really. I keep it around as a form of defense since Slainium doesn't do well against itself."

The Warlord turned back to the sword, fingering its shine. He'd start drooling soon. Somewhere in the trees outside, Samson was wiping his eyes of happiness. "Indestructible, its construction . . . tight." The Warlord sighed with pleasure. "Like the ideal woman."

"I'm glad you can relate my weapon to your vision of an ideal woman," Sage said.

"Absolutely. Choosing a weapon is like choosing a lover. So, because you are her guardian, I must ask you: Do you mind if I hold onto her? I'd love to train with her."

"My sword has a gender now?" Sage said, crossing her arms. "What if it's a male?"

The Warlord chuckled. "This is no male. It's definitely female."

"How on earth would you know that?"

"I've been with both, my dear. I know these things."

"Just a bit dramatic, aren't you?"

The Warlord chuckled again. "What can I say? I'm poetic."

"Sure," Sage said.

The Warlord blinked in surprise. Perhaps he had been anticipating a fight to take the weapon, but Sage didn't need it as much as he wanted it. Not for right now, anyway. Her slew of daggers was enough.

"Come along," the Warlord said, wrapping an arm around Sage's shoulders. "Let us talk business."

The common room was a nicely furnished lounge with a fireplace to hang out by, but the Warlord went straight for his meeting table. He brought her over to it, a protective arm still around her shoulders. Sage couldn't get the teakwood and lavender out of her nose. She was sure they were intoxicating her, brainwashing her somehow, making her want to taste and devour every inch of his body. It was that and his touch, how his hand traveled from her shoulder to her hip, holding her like he would a lover. It wasn't the kind of touch Sage would deem inappropriate, though. In fact . . . it was nice.

Too nice. The Warlord was an excellent manipulator, using his beauty and unspoken promises of explosive pleasure to snag her attention. For a damn moment, it worked because Sage let those fingers caress the outside of her leg. It was a test to see what she would and wouldn't allow. When she made no moves to swat at him, the Warlord grew bolder, just inches away from her thigh now.

"Sage," the Warlord said huskily, bumping his nose against her head. Was he smelling her? God, she probably smelled like sweat and dirt. "Maybe I can use you after all."

"Only if you give Agathe back," Sage said.

"I won't do such a thing until you prove your worth."

"How do I know you can be trusted?"

"You don't have a choice, darling," he whispered against her temple. His hand was practically in her pants' pocket now. If Sage didn't say anything, he'd be all over her crotch the next time she blinked, and—God—she wasn't sure that was such a bad thing—

"I swear that if you keep calling me that, I'll cut cut your tongue," Sage bit out, ignoring the thumping in her chest.

"Aren't you out of daggers—"

Another zipped by the Warlord's head. It pierced Kilstrong's face on the wall.

The Warlord blinked at Sage as if he had never seen anything quite like her. It was obvious that even his most skilled female fighters weren't anywhere near as agile as this. Respect shined in his eyes, but then his tone turned sultry as his thoughts went south.

"Now, I am mighty curious . . . how are you in bed?"

"You'll never find out," Sage snapped. "Because it won't just be your tongue on a silver platter—I'll put your penis there, too. Men can live without both, you know. They'll be much tamer."

The Warlord cleared his throat. It was hard for him to turn away from her, as if she were now his new prized possession, but he did for the sake of alleviating some of the tension in the room. If Sage listened closely, she'd say he was breathing hard. "I give you my word," he finally said.

"That's not enough," Sage said immediately. "Your word means nothing because I don't know you nor do I trust you."

"You don't have much of a choice here, Sage. It's either my word or nothing because I am not giving up the girl. Diamond City means too much to me—you must understand—so I will give you the girl when we have recruited the other Enhanced across these lands."

So Sage consented. She understood the Warlord's goal was to stop the Kilstrongs, and she was confident she'd be able to help. It seemed like the Warlord was, too, because he forewent any doubts about her capabilities and went straight to the details of his mission.

"I wish to seek out the rest of the Enhanced hiding in the Outskirts," he said. "In the past thirty years, I've been fairly successful in recruiting many of the ones in Mousafeld's immediate vicinity and beyond. In fact, a lot of the Enhanced you met today are from other towns."

"But you want more," Sage said.

"Naturally. Right now, I'm about five hundred strong. The bigger my forces, the higher my chances of taking out Diamond City's military. We all know there are more Enhanced out there, biding their time and strength to counter the Kilstrongs." The Warlord waved at the huge map of the Outskirts on the table. There were Xs along the Roaring Mountains up north. He pointed to them. "Their main holdouts are here. I wish to gain their favor through diplomatic means. We are set to meet with Winterfeld tomorrow, and you will join my campaign."

Sage's timing was impeccable. Had she been just a day late, she would have missed the Warlord altogether. But something else caught her attention.

"That's strange," Sage said. "I mean, I certainly wasn't expecting your means of recruiting them to be to 'gain their favor'."

"It is either that or bloodshed. I feel friendly communication is preferable. Resortfeld was a complete bloodbath, and I'd rather not dirty my clothes."

Sage scoffed. "Still. It's not like you. You are the man who beheaded the Allseer."

"I hated him," the Warlord said.

"But not the Enhanced who left you to die?"

"Certainly not all of them left me to die," the Warlord said. "And I am . . . well . . . *confident* we can work something out." He smiled. "I'm curious, you see. What they've been up to all the way out there. What they've invented. Aren't you?"

"Not really," Sage said, thinking of pizza.

"The mysterious being that attacked us today—where do you think he was from?"

"No idea. Friend of yours?"

The Warlord snorted. "Hardly. I would say he's some kind of experiment from Winterfeld, but I don't plan on raising arms unless they show aggression. I think we both agree it's better to avoid fighting, so winning their favor is the next best thing."

"And how do we do that exactly?"

The Warlord laughed. "Other than showing them the Allseer's head? We play nice and ask for their terms."

Sage wasn't buying this. "It's not like you. Why not just take it from them?"

"Then you are just as ruthless as I am, Sage."

"But we have to play smart."

"Precisely. I think you've earned yourself a milkshake."

Sage blinked. "A milkshake?"

"Better than liquor," the Warlord said in earnest. "I've been downing a lot of Cupid's Arrow as of late, so I think it's time to sober up."

"Cupid's Arrow." Sage shook away images of Blackburn. "That's a strong drink to be 'downing' a lot of."

"Yes," the Warlord admitted. He glanced at his feet, as if ashamed. "Pair that with Stars, and you've got a terrible combination. Have you tried it?"

Other than an everyday curse like "damn" or "God," Sage had never heard of that one. It sounded like a drug. The Allseer didn't allow anything like that into the city, at least not openly. The Caratians trafficked a lot of illegal substances, so maybe it was in their stashes. For the Warlord, any kind of escape was welcome. He couldn't do hardcore drugs without becoming an addict, so milkshakes and some high-quality cigars would do for tonight. Especially if he was heading out tomorrow.

"These were imported from Minefeld," the Warlord said, opening a case. "Finest tobacco in all the land, infused with cherry flavoring. Unique, isn't it? Like something Cut would spit out."

"Sounds like it." Sage thought of home.

The Warlord offered her one. "Join me?"

Aurora's husband had taught Sage how to smoke them. *"They take the edge off,"* he used to tell her. They had certainly helped with Sage's post-traumatic stress after the Unification War—the anxiety—and they were sure to fix her now, full of adrenaline and rapid heartbeats. She took a cigar, sat across from the Warlord near the open hearth, and took a drag, thinking of a different time and place.

"Unification War, huh?" the Warlord said inquisitively. He had the sword next to his legs, as if it were his pet. "What do you remember of the Optimum?"

"She was an amazing fighter," Sage said absently. "Managed to push back a great deal of the Squids' soldiers. Humans, most of them, so they didn't stand a chance against Enhanced. But still, she was something to admire. So young … so much to live for … so determined …"

"Did you actually meet her?"

"I did."

"I'm jealous. I'd give anything to talk to her. I'm sure she wouldn't have approved of the Allseer, but I understand why she hasn't gotten involved."

Sage snuck a peek at the Warlord, who was smiling at the fireplace. "You do?"

"She's probably married and has a family by now," the Warlord said, taking a puff of his cigar. "Maybe she isn't even in Diamond City anymore. She held power far greater than any Enhanced did. Her existence in itself was a mystery."

"Why are you so interested in her?"

"She's the whole reason I fought in the Unification War. Gave me purpose when I had none. She made me believe I could do anything."

"Yet you never physically saw her?" Sage asked.

The Warlord didn't answer for a very long time. The silence was a bit too prolonged as if he, too, were stuck in another place and time. At last, he turned to her with a certain sorrow in his eyes and said, "I believe I did … but I'm not sure. It was nearly a hundred years ago, so the details are blurry, but there is one thing I do remember: the Star Raider tattoo on her right wrist."

" … And how did you come to see that?" Sage glanced at hers, hidden beneath the bracelets.

But the Warlord shook his head. "I'm not sure I wish to talk about it right now. The memories of those days are too painful and shameful for me to recall. I wish to remember this moment with you in a positive light."

Sage smiled. "I can respect that."

"So you are nearly a hundred years old like me. Were you eighteen when you became an Enhanced as well?"

"Yes. I joined the resistance as soon as I graduated high school."

"Yet you still look so young," the Warlord said, studying her. Sage blushed a bit. "You must be taking good care of yourself."

"I'm doing the best I can," Sage said truthfully.

"Are you doing anything special for your skin? You have a rather nice complexion."

Full of black heads and scars from teenage pimples? Maybe the Warlord had eye problems.

"Thank you for the compliment, but your skin is tons nicer than mine," Sage said.

The Warlord snorted. "That's because I have makeup on. Without it, I'd look like an old man."

Sage arched a brow at him. No way that was possible. He did look older than she was, but he was still beautiful, like a shiny porcelain doll.

"Physically, how are you holding up?" he asked.

"I think I'm doing fine."

Even Enhanced felt the brunt of their age at some point. Marchello sure as hell hadn't looked like he could wield a sword the same way he could a hundred years ago. Medically, perhaps he had been suffering what humans did in the later part of their lives. High blood pressure, cholesterol, diabetes, osteoporosis, depression, and dementia. Enhanced were still susceptible to all of the above, although much more resilient and easily treatable. Sage, admittedly, wasn't anywhere near as energetic as she had been in her youth but she attributed a lot of that to laziness.

"Dr. X, our physician, makes his own blend of nutrition and vitamins for us to stay strong," the Warlord said. "Slightly better than the shit you get in Diamond City. Perhaps you'd like to see him before we head out? He can evaluate you."

"You are so very kind, but I've lived all my life without seeing doctors." Sage took another drag, the cherry smoke burning her lungs. "I'm not about to start now. Besides, I heard you were the one with no heart."

The Warlord laughed. "Literally or figuratively?"

"Both."

"They're right, and I don't need either one. Now for that milkshake." The Warlord snapped his fingers and a cute old lady stepped into the room. "Cushion, vanilla for the lady. Or would you prefer chocolate?"

"I like strawberry," Sage said.

A night that Sage had thought would end in bloodshed actually ended pretty amicably amidst milkshakes. Not liquor, as she had anticipated. Not counting, of course, the life-or-death battles in between bouts of conversation. The Warlord looked more than impressed at her skill, someone he could battle without worrying about fractures. Or maybe he just liked to play rough with women . . . like he did with men? But, seemingly, outside of throwing knives and shooting bullets at her, he cared about her well-being. He had his personal guards escort her to Louis' room. Their names were Fahrenheit and Celsius.

"Make sure she is fed and rested," the Warlord said to them, sucking up the last of the whipped cream. "I want her in tip-top shape for tomorrow."

The guards were confused by that request because they didn't see how this average-looking girl could play any sort of meaningful role in their campaign tomorrow. They might have seen her fight the night before, but they were still fooled by looks. Yet their loyalty to the Warlord was so great, they didn't question him or her out loud. Actually, they were rather polite as they led her to the third floor of Building A.

"This and the other buildings in this complex is where we stay," Fahrenheit said. "Our home, in other words."

"So you must be special," Celsius said flatly. "Or else the Warlord would not have let you stay here."

"Why?" Sage asked. "Does he have prison cells, too?"

"Indeed," they said. "So you should be grateful."

Sage wasn't. The only reason she wasn't rotting away behind bars was because of her strength. She was quite relieved to be alone in her room, as dainty and ill-kept as it was.

Not that it was too dirty, but the walls, much like the ones in the hall, needed paint. It was a task that Samson wouldn't be able to do on his own, so he had Louis scrubbing off the old coat and stubborn grime first. An odd sight. Sage had never thought she'd see Louis with his sleeves rolled up, bending over to clean like his servants at the palace did. The funny part was Samson with his huge arms crossed, spitting orders and insults. Louis was crying, but he was happy to serve Samson rather than the Warlord.

"Goodness," Samson breathed in annoyance. "Has anyone heard of house cleaning around here?"

"They're warriors," Sage said briskly. "I don't think cleanliness is a priority."

Sage checked all the cabinets and found a lot of canned foods. There was hardly anything perishable in the refrigerator, which meant delivery trucks came by the camp on occasion, cans scavenged from Diamond City or sold by the Carat District's black markets.

"So," Samson said as Sage investigated the bathroom and bedroom, both tidy but in need of renovation. That's what Louis was for, and he was smart enough not to stop his cleaning to listen in. God only knew what Samson had threatened to do to him. "What did the Warlord say?"

"He wants me to fight for him in exchange for Agathe."

It didn't sound so bad, but Samson's face fell a bit because he knew Sage was doing the very thing she didn't want to do. She was back in the lines of battle, the sort of life she had left behind a long time ago. Sage sat on the edge of the bed, but she looked up at him with determination.

"If I have to do it to get back into the city . . . to get my"—Sage clenched her fits—"my *pizzeria* back, then so be it."

Ironic. Hadn't she wanted a life at the palace? All she had to do was kill the Warlord and bring back his head. A not-so-easy task now that he had her sword in his possession.

"What about the Lolligo?" Samson spoke up, hope in his voice.

"I don't know, Sam. The Warlord can't speak Lolligo like we thought, and his weapons . . . they don't have Slainium either. He's fascinated with your sword. In fact, he took it from me."

"Wait," he sputtered, "but in the torture videos—"

"They're fake," Sage whispered. "Propaganda . . . most likely by the Allseer . . . to get people to think the Warlord is a monster. Well, he is, but not to that extent."

Louis really had stopped scrubbing now. Sage could see his shadow in the hallway.

"Impossible!" Samson sputtered again. "They actually spoke *Lolligo*, Sage!"

"It's not the Warlord. It must be that weird hooded guy I fought earlier. He spoke Lolligo to me. Broken, but he knew the words."

"Who was that guy?"

"Don't know. But it seems he's been traveling around the Outskirts. And there's something weird about him, too—he's not a normal Enhanced."

Sage wasn't sure how to describe him. Because she had so few answers, there was no point in Samson asking her any more questions. He agreed with her—they had to stay here for now—and he stomped away, ignoring Louis, who peered into the room and squeaked, "Sage?"

"What?" Sage said.

"Y-you're going to fight? You're not even going to call for backup?"

"The Warlord isn't our enemy," Sage said, taking off her boots. "And I'm not going to betray him. So I'm going to do my part by helping him recruit the other Enhanced your father kicked out of Diamond City and get your sister back. Isn't that what you wanted?"

Louis hesitated. He shrank a bit from her, as if he wasn't used to being scolded, before Samson whisked him away, shouting, "Get your ass back to work!"

Sage quickly tuned out Samson's shouts. She went for the shower. There were comfortable clothes in the closet, and the bed's mattress was firm enough to provide a rejuvenating sleep. Despite the open window with a nice view of the midnight sky, it didn't take Sage very long to fall asleep. Not that it was deep . . . for she kept an ear out for peepers . . . but there was no one out to kill her.

Not that night, at the very least.

CHAPTER 10

Winterfeld

When Sage woke up the next morning, she smelled toast. It reminded her of home. That made her think of Candice and Olivia, and so she wondered, as her phone came into view on the nightstand, how they were doing. She hadn't communicated with them since leaving Diamond City, and she wasn't able to now because there was no reception. Unfortunately, Hotspot didn't service the Outskirts. While Bram had revealed her identity to Blackburn, at least the Frasers were safe . . . for now. Sage feared what would happen when the Warlord did take over the city, if there'd be some kind of revolution.

Another war.

Sage examined the toothpaste in the bathroom. Gleaming White was the same brand she used at home. Were companies like this in cahoots with the Warlord, supporting him and his rebels from a distance? What would the Allseer had done if he had found out? It seemed the torture videos didn't convince everyone, after all.

"Sage!" Samson called. "Breakfast."

"Yeah." Sage grimaced as she brushed her very bushy hair. She couldn't blame the rain anymore, so it had to be that shampoo from last night. How did the Warlord have such silky hair with products like that? "Damn it," she cursed after wrestling her hair into a braid. "I keep telling you to invent something that will fix this frizz."

"Does it matter what you look like?" Samson said from the sink as Sage sat down. Louis was still scrubbing walls—they looked much brighter now. "You're not trying to impress anyone, are you?"

Sage glared at Louis' back. "Not anymore."

Louis turned his head slightly. He had nothing to say about the rocky start to their relationship or their current position. He only had one question as Sage prepared to leave for the day.

"Are you sure you can handle this?"

Sage didn't know what would happen if the Warlord's plans failed. She supposed she had to fight for him just like everyone else here did. Fahrenheit and Celsius were already waiting for her outside her door, holding a dark gray jumpsuit that would serve as her uniform. It even had her name on it. No nickname for her, though.

"The Warlord says he rather likes your name," Celsius said dryly; Fahrenheit didn't look very amused either. The two were similar enough in looks and behavior to be twins. Fraternal, perhaps.

Sage took her suit, slipped it on, and followed them down the hall. As she adjusted all the gold zippers and latches, she realized she was missing something very important.

"The Warlord regrets that he cannot return your sword," Fahrenheit said in Sage's ear. "But he offers another weapon in her place." He gave her the one he had in his hand—the Warlord's very own sword. It was heavy and a bit too bulky for Sage, but she could wield it all the same. While she should have been honored, she was annoyed now. The Warlord taking and using her weapon was manipulation at its finest.

Outside, Sage found a lot more people on the streets than there had been last night. They were all preparing for the voyage to Winterfeld, lining up and heading toward the hangar on the east side of the camp. Because they were all dressed in the same dreary jumpsuits, it was hard to tell them apart. Except, maybe, for the preacher guy who was sporting a ridiculous mask of arbitrary shapes and saying a

                    DIAMOND CITY

prayer in their name, asking the Squids to keep them safe. Sage wasn't amused for long because it wasn't the preacher people were rolling their eyes at—it was her. It hadn't taken them very long to realize there was a newbie on board; so the rumors from last night were true.

"That's her?" they whispered to each other. "I thought she'd look . . . stronger."

"Seriously? She's huge—look at her! Her biceps are bigger than my legs!"

"Is she an Enhanced?"

"Yeah, I think so."

"But is the Warlord seriously bringing her along? I mean, how can we trust her?"

Sage kept her eyes down. She certainly wasn't here to fit in, and that's not what the Warlord was intending either, not right away at least. The bastard came out of nowhere and swept her out of the group, drawing her to his side. Both tension and jealousy spiked in the air like a heat wave.

"I want and need to keep an eye on you," the Warlord said to her.

Sage was about to retort and ask why he wasn't on his beloved palanquin, but she was taken aback by how . . . beautiful he was. Unlike yesterday, he wasn't wearing black on white—he had royal gold eye shadow, gold glitter on his skin, and gold accents on his jumpsuit, turning lackluster into . . . wow. He looked like a god leading his people, and maybe it was him that sleazy preacher should have been worshipping instead of some ugly Squids.

"I didn't know we could customize our clothes." Sage looked down at her plain gray. "Were we supposed to?"

The Warlord chuckled. "No. I let my Enhanced dress how they want—within reason, of course—unless it's a serious challenge. Like the one with the Allseer, in which we were a little bit more . . . coordinated."

"And vivacious." Sage would never forget that wave of red and gold across the field, like a marching band cheering on their home fastball team. All they had been missing was the color guard. "You are definitely from the Color District."

"Actually, I was born in the Clarity District." The Warlord eyed the preacher, who went on with, "And the Forefathers never relented!"

"It was always my dream to get away from the seriousness of piety and indulge in life's flares," the Warlord went on pleasantly. "But war got in the way of that. Then you know I had no life when I worked for the Allseer. And now ... well ... I'm here. How about you? By your quick wit and keen observations, I'd say Cut. You certainly do look like a fantastic businesswoman."

Sage smiled. She was proud of it.

"And you can tell that I'm trying to impress you, right?"

Sage arched a brow. "I think you've impressed me quite a bit."

"No." The Warlord drew her closer, lips to her ear. "*Really* impress."

Sage stiffened at that implication, but there was no way in hell she was going to let it show. She said smoothly, "I thought you were wondering what kind of man would be turned on by the sight of me?"

"I can be an asshole at times," he admitted. "And say things I don't mean."

"That's dangerous. I would have impaled you for that comment, but you sort of redeemed yourself when you revealed you wanted to negotiate with the Outskirts peacefully. Either way, I don't appreciate men who can't control their mouths."

"Will you forgive me?" The Warlord pressed a kiss to her temple. Now they were really drawing a ton of attention. "My mouth can, of course, make it up to you."

"How?" Sage's head was spinning.

"However you wish," the Warlord whispered. "A kiss, perhaps?"

Sage's mind exploded with so many inappropriate and explicit images that it threw off her concentration entirely. These weren't innocent make-out sessions she was envisioning either—she wondered what it'd be like to have those lips *everywhere*. On her neck, chest, and even in between her legs as his tongue slithered inside her and those pearly fingers traveled up her legs, his rings cool on her skin—

"I have to think about it." Sage's lungs were on fire. Her heart was thudding, too, as if she had been intoxicated. She felt like she was in some sort of trance, whisked away by the Warlord who kept his arm around her shoulder as he bulldozed his way through the crowd and led her right into the aircraft with conviction.

Up close, it was huge, like an apartment complex, capable of fitting the hundred comrades going on this mission comfortably. It had the resistance of a bull, making for a smooth ride thanks to the exterior panels infused with the latest anti-force technology. They were much more durable than the ones the Diamond City military used, so Sage wondered who in the Outskirts was helping the Warlord obtain them. There were dozens of rooms inside, but the Warlord made for one in the back, already occupied by what looked to be his closest warriors.

First, there was Commander, his right-hand man. For someone who had been stabbed with Slainium just the night before, he stood by with his shoulders round, chest out, and back straight, eyes piercing and perceptive. Showing any kind of weakness was a strict no, especially if he was the Warlord's personal assassin. It didn't matter that the woman who had bested him had just walked into the room—he kept his features smooth. They were still flawless, and so were his braids, despite his recent loss. Sage was impressed by how composed he was: serious and appropriate, polite, and never questioning the actions of their leader. While this was loyalty at its finest, Sage wasn't sure how to characterize the others in the room. They, too, had been present during the fight at the Warlord's compound. Sage remembered them. Their facial expressions hadn't changed too much.

It was obvious that no one was thrilled to have her on board. The woman who was muscular and bulky—the one who had yelled at the preacher after the attack yesterday at the Marketplace—introduced herself as Mega Woman, but generated waves of hatred with her scowl. Gertrude, less in size and intimidation, smiled briefly. The men looked even more annoyed: Turtle was a midget with attitude and Little Man was ready to pummel something with fists that were like boulders. With knuckles like that, he probably won every fastball match he played.

A long time ago, Sage had challenged a guy of Little Man's caliber to a game of fastball and gotten clobbered on the court. She had meant to teach her girls a lesson about being brave in the face of people who were bigger and stronger than them, but it hadn't turned out too well. That guy had been *really* good, and Sage was sure Little Man was, too. She eyed those massive forearms with respect.

"She may not look it," the Warlord said, devouring Sage with his eyes, "but I wouldn't cross her. She threatened to cut off my tongue and penis, and I believe her."

Little Man laughed wolfishly. "Really?"

Sage was ready to demonstrate, but the Warlord stopped her. "That's not why she's here, of course. Well, that's not all accurate—she *can* fight—but what's most important is that she knows people. She fought in the war, so she knows all the Enhanced who live in these lands. Most of them, anyway."

Sage backed down when the circle of rebels used their brains and not their brawn to validate her usefulness. She let the Warlord do all the talking on her behalf, waiting for specific instructions of her own. She knew Winterfeld was extremely cold and isolated, the farthest town from Diamond City. There was a good four hundred miles to cover before they made it to the base of the Roaring Mountains. It was sad to think there were Enhanced stranded all the way out there. Hopefully, the rebels could convince them to come back.

"We will all be meeting with Craddock," the Warlord said, sitting down in an armchair and crossing his legs. "He is throwing us a feast, as we are welcomed guests. I will be speaking with him directly, and you will wait for further instructions. You'll be able to tell if we've been ambushed, although I don't predict they have the balls for such a move."

"You never know," Little Man said. "These Enhanced can be feisty motherfuckers, most of them old and retired. They couldn't care less about Diamond City so long as they're comfortable."

"That's why we have to be convincing," Commander said. "We can't take no for an answer."

So what did that imply? That the rebels were going to do this by force, even if Gavin and the people of Winterfeld didn't want to fight? Sage didn't think that violence was necessary, and she wasn't sure the Warlord would advocate for it either. There wasn't any point in friendships if they were going to turn into liabilities. Sage grew curious and fearful of the outcome of this visit. There were too many what-ifs, so it was useless to plan any further. Their success depended on Gavin's level of cooperation.

As the Warlord's circle broke off into separate conversations, he called Sage over.

"Louis," the Warlord said a bit out of the blue, bouncing his foot in agitation. "I dislike him greatly. Just like his father."

"I'm sure he dislikes you, too," Sage said blandly. "Captured and held hostage by you."

"He asked for it, didn't he?"

"He did." Sage thought for a moment. "Actually, I kind of dragged him along. He would have much rather stayed at the palace, even if his sister is in your custody. He's a coward."

The Warlord shook his head. He looked exceptionally jumpy, and Sage wondered if it was his nerves or withdrawals. He must have been itching for a hard drink or cigarettes. "What a fool. He doesn't understand anything, does he? I am doing this for the sake of Diamond City, and meddling will only get him into further trouble." The Warlord frowned. "He tried outwitting one of my guards this morning, and it didn't go very well for him. I believe he's been sent to the infirmary as a result."

Wow. Had Louis actually tried to run away? Or was that Samson teaching him another lesson?

"You must not kill him," said Sage.

"I know that."

"He could be out of your hair if you just did what I said. Let him and his sister return to Diamond City. We really don't need them."

"Not a chance," the Warlord said curtly. "Not yet. He will have to learn his place first."

"Just like the Enhanced do."

"Just like everyone in the world does."

"Your strength is admirable and frightening at the same time."

The Warlord laughed. His eyes twinkled with amusement. "I rather like your hair, Sage."

"I'm not sure what there's to like. It's in a braid, and your shampoo is terrible." Sage touched her flyaways.

"Did you not use conditioner?"

"It did absolutely nothing. I bet your personal hair products are ten times better than everyone else's. Not like they care." Sage glanced at the unruly members of the room. "If it wasn't for you, I'm sure they'd all be fighting in rags."

The Warlord huffed. "Alas, 'looking good' is the least of everyone's concerns. I, of course, always strive to look beautiful." He passed a hand through his silky locks, throwing back his head with elegance. He smiled seductively at her. "Would you like to touch my hair?"

"No."

"I'd like to touch yours," the Warlord said, sitting forward. "Will you let me?"

Sage didn't need to be here, so she wasn't. She made a beeline for the door, passing by all the rebels, who kept a close eye on her. Mega Woman, especially, who took this chance to engage with the Warlord, thwarting his attempt to stop Sage from leaving.

Sage found a lonely seat by the control panel Justice manned, who was checking the ship's coordinates. They'd be arriving at their destination in an hour. Right now, they were in the middle of nowhere, tundras for miles. So much of this area remained unexplored for fear of running into Squids. Sage wished she could have Samson's company now . . .

She had nothing to do, so she meditated. In this mission, she was following the Warlord's lead, a simple enough task. Then, after a few more towns, she had to help him take Diamond City.

And then what? she thought.

Who was going to govern the city if not Louis and Agathe? Just what was the Warlord planning?

"Penny for your thoughts?" Commander found his way to her, and Sage was surprised. He hadn't expressed much interest in her presence earlier, not after their fight last night. The gleam in his eyes said differently, though: there was nothing in the world more intriguing than her right now.

"I haven't been on a mission in a very long time," Sage said slowly. "I guess I'm just nervous."

Commander arched a brow. For a woman who beat up everyone she fought, Enhanced or no, it sounded kind of silly that she'd be worried. But Sage didn't want anyone to get hurt, including Commander.

"Shouldn't you be resting?" she asked. "I stabbed you with Slainium."

"Trust me," Commander grumbled, rubbing his shoulders. "I know. I feel like shit."

"So then why the hell are you here?"

"How can I not be? I serve the Warlord whether I'm alive or dead."

Sage didn't respond. Commander had to elaborate further.

"It . . . um . . . " He rubbed the back of his head. "Took me a long time to gain his favor. To become his favorite fighter. I stand by him no matter what."

"Are you in love with him or something?"

"Oh—n-no!" Commander's cheeks turned an ugly red. "I don't think it's love or anything like that—"

"It's love, doofus."

"No," Commander said more seriously. "Maybe it is love, but out of brotherhood. Not romance."

"You're interested," Sage said.

Commander sighed. "Perhaps there was a time I was—and still am—but I've accepted my place. I am content enough being his sword."

"All because you can't get into his bed?"

Commander looked like he had been stabbed again. Sage shook her head, overwhelmed with disgust toward the Warlord now. This was all one big game of chess to him—he, who didn't care about anything but power and control. He had Commander wrapped around his little finger, and now that Sage had bested Commander, it was all eyes on her. Sick. Disgusting.

"Anyway." Commander shook his head. "What counts here is the now, and I'm sure we'll be fine—"

"Commander."

He jumped at the sound of that voice. He whipped around as if he had been caught robbing jewelry, facing his superior with an apologetic air. Talking to the new recruit must have been off-limits because the Warlord was frowning.

"You're needed in the back. The crew's getting restless."

No terms of endearment said the Warlord was annoyed with the two talking in private. It made Commander stammer, "Y-yes, sir," and Sage scowl. There was nothing wrong with chatting before a mission, but this wasn't a matter of protocol—this was a competition.

The Warlord had the balls to take a seat right next to her, pretending to speak to Justice about their coordinates. Sage couldn't wait to get off this damn ship, and, thankfully, she didn't have to wait much longer. The Warlord did get one final remark, though.

"I didn't upset you . . . did I?"

The question was unnecessary and irrelevant. It had nothing to do with their mission, Sage said to him very tightly.

"Then will you at least have dinner with me when we return to camp?"

"No!" Sage hissed. "You're getting *married*, asshole!"

"That is a political alliance, not a romantic one."

If Sage wanted to keep all her daggers, then she had to step away quickly. Her ears were still ringing with that bastard's invitation to dinner. He had thrown off her concentration again, made her incapable of hearing their next set of orders as they stepped off the ship and kept her from surveying her surroundings like she usually did. She was doing all in her power to stay away from the Warlord as they crossed a very large snowy field and arrived at the gates of Winterfeld. Soon, she had to focus on staying warm because this cold was unlike any she had ever felt before.

Diamond City's first snowfall was always in the month of Energy, the second to last month of the year. That day was special because everyone came out to see the lithe flakes and make a wish. Snow was a nice change from rain, and people took it seriously, deeming whatever day it happened a holiday. Businesses closed and school was out. Candice and Olivia always came over to Sage's apartment to watch movies and make a wish. Luck for the new year, they said.

This cold, though—shit. Sage dug her hands into the pockets of her jumpsuit. She remembered Samson's training, one of the few times they had practiced endurance in severe weather. Once in a while, Diamond City fell prey to devastating thunderstorms. Even rarer than that were the snowstorms that blew in from these very mountains, but they did happen. It took a while for Sage to adjust her body temperature, but she was fine once she did.

A line of guards equipped with rifles was already waiting for them. Sage had never seen them before, and none of them were Enhanced, so maybe they were townsfolk who had deep roots in this place. Diamond City had never bothered to reach out this far; money and resources were always scarce, and the ones in charge were too comfortable to make any waves without guarantees of success. That meant these people were living very isolated lives.

Even so, the town didn't feel primitive. The guards sported thick uniforms laced with silver, equipped with earpieces and high-tech watches. Living so far out in the Outskirts, they probably had a lot of technology that helped fend off attacks by rogues or bandits. Perhaps, like Samson, they had discovered something similar to Slainium. It certainly was possible . . . It wasn't a wonder the Warlord was so obsessed with Sage's weapon. Sage only hoped he wouldn't have to use it here.

Gavin already knew his guests had arrived, so he emerged to meet them outside the gates. This was an Enhanced that Sage had never met, but she read a lot from his face, the weariness of all the years he'd lived. Even as an Enhanced, he looked like a human well in his sixties. His eyes were droopy, his skin was off-color, and his entire aura suggested easy prey. He was wrapped in furs, shivering too much for his own good, but he played it off smoothly, bowing just like his guards did.

"My lord." Gavin took the Warlord's hand and kissed it in the most outright display of respect ever given.

"Of course." The Warlord smirked. "I come with a gift for you."

The Allseer's head, preserved in a display case. That brought a lot of joy to the war-torn Gavin, who started salivating at the sight of his rival's head on a platter.

For that reason, Gavin was worse than a woman when it came to the Warlord. He took his arm and dragged him and his crew past the gates for a grand celebration in town. The welcome party was much bigger than Sage had anticipated, and she wondered if this was a trap. Just how ecstatic was Gavin to learn that the Allseer was dead? Sure, it was a relief, but was he going to put his tired old body through another war all to become a puppet to the Warlord?

Sage joined her fellow rebels in Capital Square, the heart of the town. There weren't towering skyscrapers, but the buildings were sturdy, squarish, and lined with lights, forming a nice semicircle around the plaza they entered. There were storefronts and offices, but the main attraction was the ballroom with an entrance in the shape of an arch. Two large fir trees blanketed with snow stood on either side of those exotic doors, lights blinking lazily. There were signs written in Lucidum that said *Benediximus* or "well wishes", a Clarity phrase that honored the Squids and their power.

Inside the ballroom was a sweeping space with shiny tables, silverware, and bouquets of flowers for the Warlord. The windows were stained glass, casting soft shades of colors in every corner of the room. The procession went smoothly as waiters and waitresses in thick overcoats came out to serve them, assisting the Warlord and rebels into their chairs.

As Sage took a seat along the far wall, a napkin draped across her lap and her glass filled with wine, she understood why it was important to make alliances here, but something didn't feel quite . . . right. She watched all the bright exchanges between parties very closely, munching on bread and then the salad absently. When she finally looked down and saw the jumbles of arugula, she thought of the sides at Two for Pizza.

Sage sighed. She was so far from Diamond City now . . . from her world of dough and sauce . . . but then anger took centerstage, poisoning her concentration with images of Blackburn and Louis, who had taken it away from her, blackmailed her—

Sage jumped when someone touched her shoulder. She looked around to see Gertrude standing behind her.

"Hey," Gertrude said, hands up. "Sorry, didn't mean to startle you. Guess you must have really been into that salad."

Sage shook her head. "Not really. Just . . . concentrated."

"Yeah, definitely see that. Can't say I blame you—it pays to be careful. Anyway, can you . . . um . . . join me outside for a moment?"

Sage arched a brow. She searched for anything amiss, but the energy was positive and the environment was carefree. Then she caught the Warlord's eye from across the room despite the fact he was talking to Gavin.

"All right, let's go." Sage stood up, leading the way outside. She walked quickly, feeling every bit of the Warlord's gaze searing into her back. She just had to ask Gertrude as soon as they were in the silence of the garden, "What is his problem?"

Gertrude blinked her large eyes. "Excuse me?"

"The Warlord—does he have to dominate everyone he meets?"

Gertrude continued to blink. It was really starting to annoy Sage. Then a fervent blush crept into Gertrude's cheeks, betraying her not-so-innocent thoughts of the Warlord.

"Um, no." Gertrude cleared her throat, rocking on her feet now. "I mean, he is really handsome and I did see him naked in the showers once, but that's about it. He's never disrespected any woman, at least not me. Oh, God, why are we talking about him again?"

"*He's a nutcase!*" Sage hissed. "Maybe he knows his crew, but he has a strange fetish for dominating everything with genitals! He won't stop looking at me, and I want him to stop!"

Gertrude couldn't seem to figure out what the problem was. She was at a loss for words, mouth moving, but no sounds coming out. It was hard for her to believe that anyone would turn down the Warlord's advances, but she acknowledged Sage's preferences and shook her head.

"Just ignore him, Sage. If he's not your type, I mean."

"I didn't join you to get laid—I joined you to help in your mission and that's it."

"Got it." Gertrude raised her hands. "But we are still human and have feelings. Perhaps the Warlord sees in you someone he can rely on or something the Allseer's daughter can't give him. He did have a wife and daughter ... and he's probably still mourning them."

A wife and daughter? Sage was rather taken aback by that, not seeing the Warlord as the family type at all. But Gertrude's seriousness said it was true, and everyone who followed him had witnessed the tragic fall of the two people he cared for the most. For some reason, Sage suspected it had nothing to do with dying of old age, one of the many problems that an Enhanced faced when they outlived their human family members.

"I'm sorry for whatever happened, but we all have our skeletons, and that doesn't excuse inappropriate conduct," Sage said. "I feel like he's about to pounce on me at any moment."

Gertrude blushed a stupid red again. She must have been picturing the Warlord leaping on her in the middle of the night. She tugged on her jumpsuit's neckline and hummed, "Umm ... "

"I think I'm done talking about the Warlord right now," Sage snapped before this got out of hand. It was obvious that Gertrude had a *huge* crush on that man, reduced to nothing more than a giggling, uncertain schoolgirl with the rosy hair, cute freckles, and folded hands. This was not a woman about to fight for her life right now.

　　　　　　　　　　　DIAMOND CITY

"Right." Gertrude composed herself. She reached for her phone and pulled up a profile, which she showed to Sage. "Nova Church. We need to find her."

There was an address, but Sage didn't know the reason for this untimely visit. Gertrude said that their target held an important antidote, one that was going to save all their lives. The Warlord and his rebels had just been poisoned.

"Poisoned?" Sage breathed, thinking of Slainium.

"*Thickener*," Gertrude said. "That's what it's called. It thickens the blood until it suffocates you."

"Are you serious?"

"Never underestimate the Outskirts—these Enhanced don't have the Allseer breathing down their necks. They have liberties that the scientists in Heart don't, and we also suspect they have connections to the Lolligo."

"So if you knew that, why put yourself at risk?"

"We sort of already anticipated this," Gertrude said hurriedly, jumping over the wall to land on the street outside of Capital Square. From here, it was all about being discreet and avoiding guards. "This was all a trap."

"Wait a second—Gavin was all over the Warlord, practically kissing on him—that was all a show?"

"You know that these Enhanced can't be trusted, Sage. A lot of them hate the Warlord because he was the one who got them into trouble with his revolutionary ideas—the reason they were kicked out—some of their closest companions executed. Or tortured." Gertrude shook her head. "They're looking for any way to backstab us."

"What about Nova?" Sage said, head spinning with all of this. Why hadn't the Warlord given her a bit more insight? "*She* can be trusted?"

Apparently, that, too, was a gamble. How the Warlord had made these sorts of friends, Sage didn't know, but those were some dangerous risks he was taking. There was no guarantee that Nova was really on their side, so the antidote was one big gamble, too. What if it just finished the job faster? Sage's mind was still buzzing over the fact that they had all been poisoned; then she learned it was all in the wine, which she had not tasted. Neither had Gertrude, who was designated to make contact with Nova.

Nova lived in a house a few miles from the capital. These homes were right along a large forest, ideal for hunting and firewood, but it wasn't like there was much necessity for the outdoors when there were electric fireplaces to keep warm and door-to-door food service. Now Sage was starting to see why treachery was on Gavin's mind: disrupting the lives of his people just wasn't worth the reward of getting back into Diamond City. Sage felt bad for them, but she didn't understand why they had to be sneaky with their approach to saying no. Was the Warlord that ruthless? Or maybe the Warlord knew how to pressure them, so the only way out was to get rid of him completely. But, even if that was the case, there were other ways to help in battle if it came down to forced tribute. These poisons that the people of Winterfeld were so adept at making could also be used to wipe out the Diamond City military. The Warlord wouldn't say no to something like that, so maybe Gavin was just a traitorous bastard by nature.

That's why Sage didn't trust Nova. It didn't matter how innocent she appeared or how relieved she was to see some of the Warlord's troops. This woman, who looked way too young to know so much, was a scientist for this town and worked hand in hand with Gavin. She was blond, blue-eyed, what Sage would call a snowflake, and too terrified to keep allegiances . . . surely.

"Come on." Gertrude waved her over. Then she looked at Sage and said, "We're taking her with us," and that's when there was gunfire.

Sage jumped, whipping around to face the town in the distance. Instinctively, she raced right back to the heart of it, adrenaline soaring through her. Patrol was on high alert, making it impossible to dodge them without a fight. On top of that, Sage learned that those so-called guards weren't humans—they were androids.

All it took was one hit, and Sage knew she wasn't punching muscle and bone. While Samson's body was practically steel, this hurt the hell out of her knuckles. The worst part was looking into a face that appeared human and taking a hit to the gut because she was so damned mesmerized by the hunks of pure technology in front of her. Samson's annoying Robos paled in comparison to this.

Get it together.

She had to stop thinking of Samson right now and what he would say if he saw these clusters of full-fledged androids. She braced herself for combat, ignored the throbbing in her hand and stomach, then struck. She ducked bullets, broke arms, cracked noses, and pierced hearts, tossing the androids aside like toys. Her motions were fluid but powerful, and it wasn't long before the street was littered with broken bodies.

"S-Sage . . . ?"

The softness in the voice cut through Sage's roaring mind, distracting her from an incoming android who screamed with rage. He sprayed her with a myriad of bullets, and they weren't made of just any metal either—these were pure Slainium, catastrophic as soon as one of them made contact with Sage's back, rattling her entire skeleton. It made Gertrude and Nova scream as if they were the ones who had gotten hit. Sage didn't waver, refocusing on her attacker and taking care of him like she had everyone else. In less than two minutes, his body joined the pile, sirens now roaring in the distance.

"SAGE!" Gertrude ran to her, huffing and puffing. "Oh my God— Oh my God! Y-you're hurt—shot!" She clutched her head. "W-we weren't supposed to—"

"We have to get back to the ballroom," Sage said, starting to run again, but Gertrude caught her arm.

"Don't move! Y-you're injured!"

"I'm fine, Gertrude."

"YOU WERE JUST SHOT IN THE BACK!" Gertrude roared. "WITH SLAINIUM!"

Enhanced couldn't survive a blast with Slainium—no way. Gertrude was thinking of Fire-And-Ice—the one who had gotten all his blood pumped out at the clinic because of Slainium poisoning—and

Commander—who could hardly hold a bottle of water when he drank. But when Sage touched a wound in the back of her shoulder, there was only a bruise left. The bullet plopped to the ground.

Gertrude tripped over her feet, scooting back to Nova, who was too shocked to move. Sage didn't have time for this, so she grabbed them both, threw them into an alley for cover, and finished racing toward the ballroom herself.

The struggle still wasn't over in there. Sage pictured the Warlord commanding his rebels to fire, engaging in a bloody battle that was costing the lives of many more Winterfeld androids than rebels, thankfully. Of course, a lot of that was thanks to Sage, who unleashed hell on any and all aggressors by jumping around like a spider, twisting necks, flinging daggers, dodging bullets, and turning momentum in her favor.

As the battle died down and only a handful of Winterfeld's androids remained, Sage spotted the Warlord finishing off a few foes with equal ease. She was a bit mesmerized by how he moved, so swift and agile with his new sword. It had already killed Gavin, whose body lay slumped on the floor, and was proving equally effective against machinery. Samson's weapon was being put to the test, and it was passing with flying colors because the androids weren't able to put a dent in it, even if its wielder was slowly dying from Thickener. It showed on the Warlord's face, but it hadn't taken enough effect to slow him down yet. Despite all his rides in the palanquin, he clearly was the strongest among all his fighters, and with Sage joining him, he was unstoppable.

Sage took care of the last android in his path with a swift decapitation. The Warlord turned around to see it, eyes on her as he registered how she had just taken care of half of their foes by herself. Then came Gertrude and Nova, who was clutching the antidote, both stopping at the sight of all this carnage. And not just at the bodies—but at their own fallen comrade.

Commander was dead. Sage saw him, too, sprawled in the corner among the heap of Gavin's androids, thrown away like trash.

Sage had told him. She had told him it was too dangerous, but he hadn't listened to her. Instead, he had gone on this suicide mission to please his lord. While he had assured Sage that all would be well, it wasn't. He and the Warlord had suspected this would turn into a massacre, and yet, Commander had come anyway. But worst of all: the Warlord hadn't dissuaded him from it either.

Had the Warlord set him up on purpose? Gotten him out of the way because Sage was the new best thing?

No, the Warlord wasn't that heartless . . .

"My lord," Justice panted, reaching the Warlord's side. "We did it."

"Indeed," the Warlord said, eyes still on Sage, and that's when Sage realized he had sent her away on purpose. He must not have been sure of her abilities or her actions in the face of danger despite the fight at the Marketplace yesterday. Now his eyes shined with a new light, his breath hitched just a bit, thoughts of what Sage's performance meant interrupted by Gertrude, who pulled Nova further into the room to deliver the antidote.

"This better work, girl," the Warlord growled as Nova opened a cache of syringes with a clear liquid, the substance that was going to save them all from suffering a terrible death. A few of the rebels were already starting to cough up blood. "Or you'll have your head on a platter." He motioned at Sage, who stood there with her hand on her—*his*—sword, ready for another fight.

Nova had seen enough. Her loyalty was clearly genuine, so she handed over what she had promised without resistance. Her life, however, was still in danger here. She was too valuable, and anyone from Winterfeld could capture her and use her as leverage. Even though the Warlord was assigning temporary leadership posts for the rest of Winterfeld's citizens, Nova would be returning to Mousafeld with them.

As everyone filed out of the ballroom, Gertrude spoke to the Warlord in a low, worried tone. Her frightened, quivering eyes kept looking at Sage. Whatever she was saying made the Warlord stop in his tracks, as if he had hit a brick wall. He whipped around, found Sage, and stalked right up to her, yanking her up against him to get a better look at her.

Sage grabbed his arm, about to flip him around and slam him face first into the bloody floor, but he pulled first, capturing Sage in his arms. She rolled away, drawing her sword and pointing it at him; that sparked a chain reaction among the rebels, making them all draw their weapons, too.

"Get your hands off me, asshole!" Sage exclaimed. "Don't you *fucking* touch me!"

The Warlord raised his hands to show he meant no offense. "I wanted to ensure no harm has come to you."

"When I need help, I'll ask for it. But don't you ever assume that I'm like one of your prostitutes, at the ready to suck your dick."

The entire room grew quiet. The rebels still had their arms raised. The Warlord's face remained smooth, unaltered by that insult. It was embarrassing, maybe, but no one knew him better than his followers.

"I'm sorry you think that way of me," the Warlord said quietly. "But that is not the sort of life I lead, nor is it one I instill in my Enhanced."

"You're forcing Agathe to marry you," Sage spat, "and you're trying to seduce me, you sick son of a bitch. Commander's not good enough for you anymore, is he? Well, he's dead now!"

If the room had been quiet before, it was dead silent now. Once in a while, a small wind whistled through the broken stained glass, ruffling the snow atop the overturned tables, spilled food, and dirty floors. But no one heard it. No one moved. No one dared to look Commander's way. Maybe Sage was talking shit, but she was starting to see the situation very clearly now—just who the Warlord was—and Blackburn was right.

The Warlord wanted to dominate everyone.

The Warlord kept his hands up. "I told him not to come, but the son of a bitch insisted. I even thought about ordering Dr. X to sedate him, but I didn't want to take away his choice or his honor. That is not something I will ever do to anyone, not to a lover or a soldier. And if you really must know, I have never bedded anyone to take advantage of them. Forgive me if I came across that way."

"Don't give me that bullshit—you're a master manipulator! I can see it!"

"Believe whatever you must," the Warlord said. "But my words are the truth. Either way, I didn't mean to offend you. Please." The Warlord waved down his team. "Lower your weapons. She is no threat to us."

Sage wasn't here to fight them and she made that clear when she put away her sword. She stalked out of the ballroom, ready to get the fuck out of this town, to relay everything she had seen and experienced to Samson, and to talk about what the fuck was going on with the Slainium in her body.

That was just it: nothing.

She boarded the aircraft without another word to anyone, tucking herself into a corner and falling into a meditative state as the Warlord finished his business here. In fact, they took off without him.

"He'll be staying for a bit," Sage overheard Justice say to Gertrude and Nova, the latter who was also seated in a solitary corner.

All Sage could think of was, *Thank the Squids.*

And God was always her deity of choice.

CHAPTER 11

Overdose

When they arrived at the camp, Sage headed straight for Samson in Building A. She walked with purpose and conviction, stopping for no one. She didn't have anything to say and she was on a short fuse. She ignored the annoying preacher going on about how "The Forefathers have graced them yet again!" and braced herself for the battle of a lifetime with Samson.

"We're leaving," she said curtly, without taking a thing. "Let's go."

"Leaving?" Samson breathed. He was in the middle of mixing paint, ready to beautify their walls. "Why? Did everything go well?"

If Sage was in one piece and the Enhanced were trickling back into camp, then yes. That meant a successful mission regardless of Gavin's death, and Commander's. But Sage didn't want to stick around these people one moment longer, knowing she was going to get sucked into another war and a whirlwind of turmoil. She knew what it was like to lose comrades, had never really gotten over the deaths of people she had once known, and right now all she wanted was her life in Diamond City. If she could snag Louis (who had gotten thrown in prison for trying to run away) and Agathe (whom Sage had yet to even see in Mousafeld) now that the Warlord was busy at Winterfeld, she could leave here and never look back. She ignored the voice in her head that said she'd be recruited and forced to fight for the Diamond City military instead, and didn't wait for Samson to respond—she turned and stormed out.

"Sage!" Samson caught up with her, not caring that he was a massive monster thundering through the halls. "W-wait! Why can't we talk about this?"

"Because there is nothing to talk about."

Sage stalked to the prison block across the street. She had her hand on her—the *Warlord*'s—sword, ready to attack anyone who got in her way. This was going to get nasty, but she didn't care. Sometimes, ruthlessness was the only way to survive. Her first victim was Mega Woman, who came out of nowhere, exclaiming, "You bitch!" and threw a punch right at Sage's face. A grand mistake because Sage dodged it, punched Mega Woman in the gut hard enough to break a rib, then flipped her to the ground.

Mega Woman scurried back. She clutched her abdomen, half gawking, fear giving way to awe. All the other Enhanced on the street were frozen, too, not knowing how to approach a fighter who was clearly a cut above them all.

"Just what are you?" Mega Woman croaked.

"It really doesn't matter," Sage said curtly. "I'll be out of your hair in just a little bit."

"Wait—you're leaving?"

Why did Mega Woman sound concerned about that? She had looked ready to pummel Sage just seconds ago. Maybe it wasn't in the camp's best interest to allow someone like Sage to run away despite how much everyone hated her. Now that it was happening, tension rose like a wave. There was only one thing that kept Sage right where she was.

"He wants to see you in his quarters," Mega Woman said. "Now."

Damn it, so the Warlord was here? Already? Sage had thought she'd get out unscathed. She was confident in the face of all these Enhanced, but against him? She might not be able to win, especially if he still had her sword.

Releasing all her tightly-held air, Sage said nothing as she headed for his compound down the street. Fahrenheit and Celsius were waiting for her by the gate. They no longer had those disinterested expressions on their faces; in fact, they grew rather nervous when they saw her. They bowed their heads and stepped aside.

Sage was back in the Warlord's throne room. She shoved down memories of her fight with Commander. She shouldn't have pierced him with Slainium. Disarming him would have been enough.

In the common room with the display of heads, she found a new addition. Gavin was now perched next to the Allseer, right above the fireplace. It was barbaric and unnecessary. But more pressing than that were the Cupid's Arrow bottles everywhere on the floor. Those hadn't been there last night, and neither had the empty glasses.

"I've been highly addicted to Cupid's Arrow as of late, so I've been trying to sober up."

Oh.

Sage knew it before she saw it—her brain had conjured it up in her head before her eyes could confirm it—the Warlord had been drinking. Past one of the ajar doors, hunched over the table, was his body.

He had his head down, still in his uniform from the campaign. But something was *wrong* and it had nothing to do with all the liquor hanging around him. It was Samson—who had found his way into the compound like he did any other place—that found the syringe on the floor.

Sage ran to the Warlord. She tripped over a bottle and smashed another into pieces with her foot. She ignored the hand-written letter on the table and lowered the Warlord to the ground. She focused on his still face, felt his cheeks—how cold they were—and checked for a pulse—there was none—and remembered he had no heart.

That couldn't be for real, though, could it?

Sage tore open his jumpsuit, breaking buckles and buttons, and exposed his chest. From top to bottom was a long scar like the kind that open-heart surgery patients had. She laid her head on it, listening for any signs of breathing. At the very least he had lungs . . . but all was quiet.

Did that mean the Cells were quiet, too? If so . . . just what had the Warlord overdosed on?

"Samson," Sage croaked, turning to the very still Squid who was watching all of this in horror. The Warlord's death meant so many things aside from the fact they'd be found as culprits—everything he was trying to achieve in Diamond City would go down the tubes. "Please give me the vial!"

The vial that contained what the Warlord had injected into himself was sitting on the table, half full, its contents red like lava. It didn't look like something he had bought from a pharmacy. There must have been a stash of it in this room, but Sage wasn't about to look for it right now—not when CPR was futile and she was about to lose the Warlord for good. She had to see something first, and Samson already knew what she was thinking.

"Sage!"

"Now!" Sage yelled.

Samson grabbed the vial and gave it to her—Sage yanked the cap off and poured its contents down her throat. She coughed immediately—the sharp tang of Slainium struck her insides like a hot poker. It was the only known substance that tore up Cells, making them swell and explode. Sage's head spun and her vitals shot up, but she already knew what she had to do.

She grabbed the used syringe on the floor and yanked up her sleeve. Her veins always showed, so finding one was easy even if the room was spinning. Samson was crying because he was nervous, and so was Sage—she just kept it together better than he did as she stuck the needle into her arm and withdrew an entire 100 milliliters of her blood. For the love of Squids, she had no freaking clue what she was doing and if her Cells were going to save the Warlord's life, but it was the best she could do given what she had.

Her breathing hitched as she grabbed the Warlord's arm and found the prick from earlier. It was still red and bleeding, the idiot, but Sage couldn't blame his addiction on idiocy.

He was trying to sober up, said a voice in her head. *And you sent him over the edge by insulting him.*

Bullshit. Sage had done no such thing. This wasn't her fault—it couldn't be—but it was going to be if she didn't revive him. She had never done this in her life, but there was no reason why it shouldn't work. Wasn't it the Cells of Squids that gave Enhanced their power? She injected every last drop of her blood into his vein and then watched for any signs of life.

"Please wake up," Sage croaked, shaking his body. "Damn it, wake up!"

"Sage, someone's coming!" Samson cried, head to the door. "I think it's the two guards!"

Sage didn't care—she transferred more blood because there was nothing else to do.

Then Fahrenheit and Celsius came bursting inside. These weren't ordinary sounds coming from the Warlord's study, and they were right in sensing distress.

"Help!" Sage cried. "A-a medic—we need a medic!"

"What the hell happened here?!"

"What the fuck's going on?!"

Sage stumbled back as the two crowded around their comatose leader. Then Dr. X came fumbling inside with a shot that would revive the Cells in the Warlord's body somehow, if there were any to revive at this point. Sage prayed to God that her Cells would be enough to carry him back to consciousness. Of course, there were no guarantees. At this point, Sage had no idea if he was capable of resuscitation, would even live—how long had he been out like that? How could this have happened when he had literally just sent for her minutes ago? And where the hell was Cushion, or had he dismissed her? The fireplace in the common room was dark, small embers nearly out in the mantel, so no one had fixed this place in a while.

"There's a reaction," the doctor stated nervously, shining a light into each of the Warlord's eyes. Pupil dilation said there was brain activity and short tremors said that his body was starting up again. "Let's take him to the clinic—hurry."

"Oh, GOD!" Mega Woman cried from the hallway; Fahrenheit and Celsius carried him out. "W-what happened to him?! Was it that bitch?! Did she do this to him?"

Before her accusations got out of control, one of the Enhanced showed her the vial of Stars. Mega Woman's lip trembled. Then she whipped around and followed the Warlord to the clinic.

Sage, in the meanwhile, just stood there, hyperventilating. Everyone left her, as if she didn't exist. For a few moments, she embraced the solitude. Her head was still pounding and tears were burning her eyes. First, it had been Gavin, then Commander, and then the Warlord. All the stress was pressing down on Sage's soul, making her lose focus. Samson was moving around the room, but Sage had no idea what he was doing.

"Sage," Samson called, head in a filing cabinet. "Here."

There it was: a crate full of those little vials filled with red. Only there was no name, no indication of the seller, because whoever was making a business of this was doing it for two purposes: money and claims to the lives of Enhanced like the Warlord, who probably shared it with others, too.

Sage grabbed all the vials and dumped them in the sink. She flushed it all down, watching the crimson dilute until it was gone. She grabbed the edges of the countertop, panted, then looked up at the mirror. Her body was still trembling, but it was because of anxiety, not so much the drug's effects.

A drug that killed Enhanced? Where on earth had the Warlord gotten that from? Who was selling it to him? And was there more of it?

Instinct told her to open the mirror, too.

Sage gasped. So did Samson, who croaked, "Oh, my . . . "

A collection of pills—from sleeping aids to insulin to erectile dysfunction medication—graced their view. Why the Warlord would need all this, Sage could only guess. But she knew these things couldn't kill him, only alter his mood. Perhaps that's what had driven him to take Stars, the only drug that had a real effect. Either way, these weren't necessary, so she dumped them, too.

"Sage," Samson croaked. "Maybe that's not such a good idea."

Maybe not. But it was Sage who had nearly died of a heart attack from seeing the Warlord unconscious on the floor, and she wasn't about to go through that again. Maybe she was overstepping her boundaries, but this was her business now that she had gotten involved. That's why she took great pleasure in flushing the toilet and watching all those capsules disappear into the sewers where they belonged.

Sage was too anxious to return to her room, so she went to the clinic. She stayed in the waiting area for any word on how the Warlord was doing. Out here, at the very least, neither Mega Woman nor the other Enhanced would bother or chastise her. She drew her knees into her chest, looking at the dull walls, the nutrition posters, and the lone TV screen in the corner. There was nothing playing right now.

"Sage?" Gertrude entered the clinic; she must have just heard about what had happened. Thankfully, Sage didn't need to explain anything because Dr. X came out to tell them the Warlord was stable.

"Indeed," he said seriously, looking from Gertrude to Sage through those thick glasses. Add the crazy hair, lab coat, and stethoscope, and he looked like a mad scientist. There was something off-putting about him, and Sage realized it was his huge eyes. "If Sage hadn't found him in time . . . we wouldn't have been able to bring him back. He would have suffered a great deal of brain damage, which, without the right amount of Cells, we would have been unable to fix."

"But how did this happen?"

Apparently, the Warlord's addiction to Stars was news to everyone. This was a secret the Warlord must have kept to himself out of shame.

"I want to see him," Gertrude said. "Coming, Sage?"

"No, thanks," Sage said quietly. "I need some time for myself. I'll be at the Marketplace."

The entire camp was alight with conversations about their precious leader, from the street vendors to the shop owners. Commander's death was second to that, the concern over who the new "chosen" would be. Without him, who would defend their camp if they were ever invaded? Talk out here was far more stressful than in the clinic, but Sage tuned it all out.

She entertained her mind with the scenery, the fresh air, and the twinkling night sky above her. These were sights she had never appreciated much in Diamond City. Most of the Marketplace was closed off because of that intruder yesterday, but at least there was a decent chunk of it that was up and running. There were some pretty unique trinkets for sale, and one in particular caught her eye. A tiny projector in the shape of a ball, completely portable. With that, she could watch whatever she wanted anywhere.

Drawn to it, Sage entered the store. The owner was on the phone with Fahrenheit and Celsius, getting an update on the Warlord's condition. He had no idea it was Sage who had saved his life, so he didn't speak to her as she studied the Portable Projector in her hand.

"Excuse me, sir," Sage said. "But how much are these?"

"Two hundred Diamonds," answered the owner dismissively, getting back to his conversation.

Sage had no money on her. All she had was enough for necessities—or more like the scraps from Diamond City—so she purchased a new set of clothes, a jacket and pants. Then she went for pizza; Dough glared at her from behind the register.

"How's Clara doing?" Sage asked.

"Why the fuck do you care?" Dough spat. "You're an outsider and you shouldn't even be here. I bet it was you who led that monster here!"

"That makes so much sense: I purposefully let a monster attack a random bunch of Enhanced. Brilliant."

"I don't trust you, girl! Get the hell out of my restaurant!"

With no pizza to enjoy, Sage bought a granola bar from someone who didn't spit in her face. She munched on it at the fastball stadium near the edge of town, looking out at the court below longingly. Twenty-four meters long with a net across the middle, the one players had to avoid touching at all costs. Even in the Outskirts, fastball was extremely popular, if those championship flags were any indication. Behind those was a wall with the banners of

　　　　　　　　　　　　　　　　　　　DIAMOND CITY

different teams, a lot of which Sage had never heard of before. They were from Sunfeld, Steelfeld, and Forestfeld—Outskirts towns—and there was also the Porcupines from Diamond City in the far corner.

Sage swelled with pride. She was no expert at anything fastball, but she thought of Candice and Olivia. Once in a while, they played a few games with the ball Bram had gotten them as a present. Fastballs were not for the faint of heart because the rubber was thick and hard to punch. That's what made the game exciting: to see players break their knuckles or shatter their palms. The impressive ones were stars in their own right. Sage was slowly getting there.

"Phoebe played a lot, you know."

Sage whipped around and found Nova. She took a few steps back, startled that she hadn't sensed anyone approach her. This girl looked just as gloomy as she had at Winterfeld. Despite her loyalty to the Warlord, she had seen people die today and that was no easy thing for a human so young. She was in a fresh coat with mittens, so at the very least someone had clothed her.

"Phoebe was a friend of mine," Nova went on softly. "She was the Warlord's daughter."

"'Was'?"

"Phoebe ran away from here . . . from her father . . . a few years ago. I suppose after her mother betrayed him to the enemy, she couldn't handle siding with him anymore."

Sage shook her head because something didn't make sense to her. The mother had betrayed the Warlord? So the daughter had sided with the *mother*? What?

"At the time, there was a group of Enhanced traveling through the Outskirts, asking for money in exchange for protection. Phoebe's mother, Ileana, reached out to them and brought them right into the Warlord's lair to have him executed as he slept. Somehow, he managed to survive but killed his wife in the process. As for the assassins—well—they're the heads you see in the common room today."

"My God," Sage breathed. "In the middle of the night?"

"His wife thought it'd be the only way to defeat him."

"Why would she do that?"

"She thought he was a monster," Nova whispered. "And from then on out, so did Phoebe. She couldn't take the violence he brought upon himself and everyone around him, so she sought guidance in our town . . . but she was executed, too. By Gavin. The Warlord and I gave her a proper burial and put her to rest in peace."

Sage was stiff. She knew the Warlord had a deceased wife and daughter, but she hadn't imagined their deaths to have been so . . . brutal. Some exiled Enhanced hated the Warlord, but Nova must have felt sorry for him. Or maybe she'd had no one else to turn to for revenge. Gavin had promised the Warlord his daughter back, in exchange for the Allseer's head, but had already killed her and poisoned the rebels.

"Wait a second," Sage said, "so Phoebe's death was recent?"

"Very," Nova answered quietly.

"I'm sorry to hear that. Perhaps Phoebe was a good friend to you, but I'm still wary about the way these Enhanced out here treat us. I didn't imagine they'd be so traitorous. Gertrude told me not to trust them either."

"Yeah . . ." Nova lowered her head. "It's always been a struggle. The Enhanced are devastated because they had to leave Diamond City. On top of that, they have new threats to deal with. There are a lot of wandering thugs and thieves out there, both Enhanced and human, who are looking for places to raid. Gavin didn't have a lot of alliances, so he trusted me to build the town's defense systems. The androids became an ideal way to keep an eye on what was happening in Winterfeld."

"And what was happening exactly?"

"Women were going missing," Nova said.

Sage furrowed her brows. " 'Missing'? Or ran away?"

"No—missing. As in never to be seen or heard from again. Two of my closest friends are gone. They just up and vanished one day. For that reason, Winterfeld tightened its borders and heightened security. Since we did that, kidnappings have died down a lot."

                    DIAMOND CITY

"All women ..." Sage murmured thoughtfully. "Any idea who or what might have done it?"

Nova nodded. "I know Enhanced love to worship them, but I say it was the Lolligo. They're up to something, and they're sneaky about it."

"Have you gotten any traces of them?"

"Not a one," Nova said. "I'm hoping the Warlord will help with this. I fear the Lolligo are building a powerful army of sorts to take revenge on us after the Unification War. We have every right to fear them."

"So you're in cahoots with the Warlord's plans to gather all the towns?"

"I think we stand a better chance of survival if all of us are working together. I am confident he will gain the Outskirts' favor. Already he's built quite the force in Mousafeld, and I think it's only going to get bigger from here. When it does, he'll be able to take back Diamond City. The only problem is a lot of these Enhanced don't trust him after the rebellion. So many of their comrades were tortured and imprisoned. To be honest, our leader, Gavin, didn't believe that was really the Allseer's head. I knew there'd be retaliation, so that's why I created the antidote to Thickener. I hear, however, that the Warlord's first-in-command is dead, and the Warlord himself is in failing health."

"Yeah," Sage said. It was hard for her to get the picture of the comatose Warlord out of her head. She was still in shock, even if she didn't show it. "He overdosed on Stars. I wanted to ask—did the traveling Enhanced you mentioned earlier have a name? Were they some sort of group or something? Surely they came from somewhere."

Nova narrowed her eyes, not because she didn't know the answer, but because she grew suspicious of where Sage was going with this. "Those Enhanced called—or rather, *call*, because they're still around—themselves 'Jackals', although they are more like glorified hyenas. They attack weaklings and take away other people's conquests. Worst of all, they're proud of it."

"Interesting. So in addition to bribing people, do they also sell drugs like Stars to Enhanced?"

"It's . . . possible." Nova gasped. "Is that how the Warlord got a hold of such a drug?"

Probably. Sage only wondered how she was going to deal with it, fearing that if those Jackals made enough rounds through the Outskirts, they'd eliminate a lot of the Enhanced. Sage had to cut them out of the picture as quickly as possible because she already anticipated they were working hand in hand with the Diamond City council.

"Either way, we must be vigilant." Nova bowed respectfully. "And thankful that the Warlord will recover. I will go visit. Please stay safe."

Perhaps Nova could foresee that Sage was going to take a walk toward the Ferris wheel. The farther out she ventured from the Marketplace, the more desolate it got. Where there should have been lights, people, and explosive energy around concession stands, games, and rides was an eerie silence.

"What are you thinking?" Samson asked, bursting out from in between a pair of trees like an overgrown dummy. "To pay the Jackals a visit? Do you even know where they're located?"

Sage did. And she didn't need the map the vendor had given her to figure out where. It didn't take long for a voice to call her, making her look up and Samson startle. The poor Squid jumped right back into the woods, shocked to see who had found them all the way out here.

"Sage, it's us! It's us!" cried the same voice right before Sage made good use of her blade.

Penelope, Dustin, and a handful of the Private Guard showed themselves. It was a bit unexpected to see them out of the office and in the thick of shrubbery, but it had been a good number of days since Sage had left Diamond City. Most of all, she had custody of Louis.

"God," Penelope breathed, eyeing Sage in that gray jumpsuit. She had never dreamed to see her trump card in the ranks of their enemy, but that's why Sage explained the situation.

She had to help the Warlord's campaign in order to get Agathe back. As soon as that happened, they'd be marching right back to Diamond City for negotiations. Perhaps it sounded too good to be true, but it relieved a lot of the anxiety the PG had brought with them. They had their own ideas on how to eliminate the Warlord, too.

"Why can't we attack him *now*?" Dustin hissed, making Sage want to punch his face. "He's not expecting us! And with Sage—"

"The Warlord's too powerful for you," Sage said curtly. That was true, except he was in a hospital bed right now. "It'd be best if you let me handle this. Tell Bram I'm . . . fine."

Sage had just thrown away her perfect opportunity to attack the Warlord and end his life. But it had never been her intention to do that, and despite her wariness of his goals, she stuck with her decision. Maybe it was stupid to put all her trust in him, but everyone else in Mousafeld seemed to. Even Nova, a friend of Phoebe's, sided with him. Besides, the council and military were hiding quite the secrets themselves, and the PG was no exception.

Stars.

Goddamned *Stars*.

So *that's* where all their money had gone.

Sage knew it as did they: the bastards sent those drugs across the Outskirts in hopes they'd wipe out as many Enhanced as possible. While it was as clear as day now, and Sage was incensed at the fact no one had bothered to tell her the PG was this shitty, it wasn't something to fight about at the moment. The last thing she wanted was for the PG to suspect that she was against them, not for them. The Diamond City military would be out here for sure.

"Are you sure, Sage?" Penelope asked worriedly.

"Yes, trust me," Sage said. "I don't want to put Agathe and Louis in danger either."

"Where is the Warlord now?" Dustin asked desperately.

"He just got back from taking Winterfeld," Sage said. "A lot of Winterfeld is here now."

"Goddamn it—we can't let him get any more power! Sage, what are you doing?"

"Do you want to save Agathe and Louis or not?"

"FORGET THEM!" Dustin yelled. "The Warlord is gathering more numbers!"

This was the first time Sage had ever heard Dustin yell. For good reason, though—Sage had been sent out here to kill the Warlord—not help him.

"These were *not* Blackburn's orders!" Dustin spat. "And you know it. You're helping him, you filthy traitor—"

Sage whipped out her sword, the tip at Dustin's throat. She braced herself, eyebrows drawn in the face of her former allies, who drew their weapons as well.

"Stand down," Sage said to him. "Right now. You forget I'm not your toy—I make alliances with whoever the hell I please. I told Blackburn I wasn't here to kill the Warlord. We're not going to war and taking lives over petty squabbles. I know what I'm doing, dick-face, so back the fuck up."

No one moved.

"*Now,* damn it!"

Were the PG going to attack her? The pussies wouldn't dare. They knew exactly who she was thanks to Bram's scheming ass, so they backed down. A lot of them fled right back to their nest, possibly to tell Blackburn that they had lost Sage.

Good. They had taken away her damn pizza. They had involved her, the bastards.

"I thought we were friends," Penelope whispered, one of the last to leave.

"I don't have friends," Sage whispered back. "Clearly."

The PG crew had never been her friends. Those manipulative bastards had only used her when it was convenient, and Bram was no better. Sage wasn't about to become the reason for war, so she trusted the Warlord to accomplish his task without fighting. That's why she was going to stick with him.

As obnoxious as he was.

CHAPTER 12

Gifts

Sage thought about the Warlord all the way back to her room. She got a message from Gertrude that read, *He's awake!* but she was too tired to see him now. It was five in the morning and she had gotten no rest since her first campaign.

That meant sleep came easily. It was so deep that she didn't have any nightmares, just the blissful dark until she woke up to someone knocking on the front door.

"A guest has arrived," called Samson, who shuffled into the room. He burrowed into the closet for cover and left her to deal with whoever was out there.

"Damn it," Sage mumbled, rubbing her weary eyes. She could do with a few more hours, but Gertrude was way too happy and hyper to let her stay lazing around all day.

"Sage!" Gertrude jumped up and down like an excited schoolgirl. "Wow, were you still asleep? You must have been tired! Look at what I got for you!"

It was a gift wrapped in gold, sparkly paper. There was even a bit of confetti for decoration. It excited Sage, but then she remembered her stoicism and kept it plastered on her face. She grew suspicious of what it was and was surprised to find a pot of . . . hair conditioner?

Gertrude giggled. She must have found it cute because her cheeks were flushed and her freckles were glowing. "It's from the Warlord. He sent me to buy it for you as a token of appreciation. He said you were asking about hair, so he wanted you to try what he uses." Clearing her throat, she eyed Sage's not-so-tamed strands of frizz. Falling asleep with her hair wet was the worst thing she could have done. The tips were twisted and crunchy. "I didn't know you cared so much about it. I mean, it's hard to find someone who actually pays attention to that sort of thing around here."

"My hair is untamable," Sage mumbled, reading the name of the conditioner. Suave-Suave.

"Just leave that in your hair and you'll see improvement." Gertrude beamed. "The Warlord says he's throwing a party as soon as he's out of the clinic. You know, to celebrate his recovery. Will you let me do your hair?"

Sage frowned. Parties made her think of spoiled princes and manipulative commanders. She made it clear that her interests were elsewhere. "I'm not going to any party. Commander is dead."

Gertrude sighed. "I know. We held a special sermon for him last night. Preacher led the prayers. It was very beautiful."

Sage was astounded. Gertrude sounded like she was describing a boring movie.

"He's not our first casualty," Gertrude said quietly. "And we're all devastated by his loss. But in this kind of life, we can't afford to mourn for long."

"He was your best fighter."

"Definitely so."

"You just lost your best fighter and now you're thinking of parties?"

"And what do you expect, exactly?" Gertrude said defensively. "We're all hurting here, Sage, but we're trying to make the best of it. Now you're suggesting we can't relax for an evening because we have to be holed up in our homes and praying to a pantheon of fucking Squids?"

Against a response like that, Sage had no words. Gertrude changed her tone.

"Oh, come on, Sage! You have to go—at least with me." Gertrude cleared her throat. "There's this guy I want to impress. Turtle."

"Who?"

"The guy who's always staring at you?"

Sage snorted. "That dwindles it down by a lot."

"Please, Sage?"

Sage didn't know. Her silence was a maybe, and Gertrude didn't want to push her any further than necessary.

"Anyway, I think you should get ready and have some break-fast." Gertrude cocked her head to the side. "Are you visiting the Warlord today?"

Actually, no. While Sage wanted to see him, she didn't know how to look at him or interact with him. On top of that, she had prowlers like Mega Woman, who were raring to beat her up, thinking that Sage had been the cause of the Warlord's overdose. Appar-ently, the Warlord had already clarified those little details.

"You actually *saved* him," Gertrude croaked, still astounded her-self. Tears welled in her eyes.

"I didn't have a choice," Sage said. "I mean, he was nearly dead."

Gertrude shook her head. "You're mighty brave, Sage. I think I would have panicked."

"I've been trained to remain calm in the face of danger," Sage said softly. "Although I will admit . . . " She floated toward the counter where Samson had prepared some eggs and frozen tater-tots. The bacon was still frying, so she gave that a stir. "I was a bit scared, too."

"Doc says he's going to be fine but wants to keep him in obser-vation for a while longer. That Stars drug is no joke, and he wants to wait a full forty-eight hours to ensure all is stable. Anyway, the Warlord wanted me to show you around camp. I know you've seen most of it, but usually we're up training during the day and everyone's wondering where you are. Training begins at five in the morning, and you … well … slept right through it." Gertrude cleared her throat. "Not that I blame you."

"Training?" Sage had seen the grounds yesterday, right next to the runways. She wasn't very thrilled to go back to see it or the people using it.

"Yes. You don't have to participate today, but I would like to show you around."

Sage figured it'd be best not to make too many waves, so she dressed up in training attire (tank, spandex, and boots) and followed Gertrude out of her room. They took the elevators down with a happy Gertrude looping an arm through hers.

"*He's* there, you know," she chirped.

"Who?"

Gertrude's jaw dropped. "*Turtle*, Sage! I told you! Huge crush!"

"I thought you liked the Warlord?"

"OH MY GOD!" Gertrude's face was redder than a tomato. "Y-yes, I like him, too, but I know he's off-limits, not for me—"

"Why not?"

"Sage!" Gertrude whined. "I'm not good enough for him!"

Sage blinked. "Why?"

"I'm average compared to some of these other women. Some of them brag about how they make out with him in his compound whenever he calls them to talk about important stuff. Mega Woman gloats all the time, says she's had the pleasure of giving him a blowjob—"

"Yeah, yeah!" Sage grimaced, shoving those images away. "I get it."

Gertrude's face couldn't turn any brighter. She radiated warmth with her skin alone, beating the sun at its highest point in the sky outside. Sage truly had overslept—she felt like the late student who barged into the middle of a class when everyone was already taking notes.

Down the street, past the Warlord's compound, were the training grounds. The Enhanced were sparring in pairs of two, some three. A few of them stood around, watching, some betting on their friends to raise the stakes. They were all in the same gear as Sage, not so appropriate for chilly weather, but no one noticed when the training was this intense. Sage recognized some of the faces such as Justice, their pilot; Little Man, the not-so-little dude who had clubs for fists; Turtle, Gertrude's crush; and Mega Woman, who had the sassiest attitude of all.

The one Sage hated.

"Hey, guys." Gertrude waved at a group of Enhanced standing close by. "You've all met Sage, right?"

No. Maybe they had seen her beat up Commander in the Warlord's throne room or dancing around the ballroom in Winterfeld, slaughtering androids, but no one knew what her voice sounded like or how she carried conversation. Sage didn't care to demonstrate because she sensed these couple of guys—Eye Candy and Rockstar—were looking at her . . . and it wasn't good. In fact, Sage got a shiver through her body in response to the negative vibes they released, both of them with those ugly sneers. It reminded her of Blackburn, so she couldn't help herself.

"What are you looking at?" Sage spat.

"Sage!" Gertrude said, grabbing her wrist and reeling her away from that toxic circle. "Watch it! You don't want to antagonize anyone."

"Did you see how they looked at me?" Sage breathed incredulously. "What do I look like to them—a piece of meat?"

"They're just a little rough around the edges, but you'll get used to them. Please remember that most of these Enhanced are war-torn, fighting to survive."

"*They're* war-torn? Damn it, what about me? I don't use that as an excuse to glare people down like I'm some sort of predator!"

"Take it easy," Gertrude said quickly. "They're also in competition to become the Warlord's next fighter. You know—like our camp's own version of the Optimum."

"That, and they blame me for Commander's death and the Warlord's condition, don't they?"

"Of course not! We already know what happened to the Warlord, and everyone knows that Commander *chose* to come with us yesterday despite his injuries—"

"Ones I gave him," Sage said.

"You were defending yourself," Gertrude said flatly. "The Warlord wanted him to kill you. What were you supposed to do otherwise?"

Maybe that was logical in the mind of a normal person, but these Enhanced out here were brutes. That's why training with them was a bad idea. Gertrude isolated Sage before any punches flew, instructions she had probably received from the Warlord if interactions out here turned sour. He was perfectly aware of Sage's personality as well as that of his Enhanced, all of who were a bunch of assholes, including the women. Even as Sage watched one pair in particular practice their sword movements, they eyed her with disgust and curled their lips, flashing their teeth. What on earth did one have to do to gain any favor around here? There was another pair at the far end of the grounds that were much more welcoming, a blonde with pigtails and a guy with a mohawk. They had their swords out, too, but they were courteous and tried to include Sage.

"I appreciate it." Sage bowed her head. "But I think I'll just watch for right now, thank you. Although . . ." She looked at Blondie. "You can try keeping your elbow out when you're parrying." Sage showed her, pushing her arm up. "That way, if he comes at you, you're at liberty to swing wherever you need to. Down here, you won't have much leverage."

The two went at it again, and Blondie's performance improved greatly. Sage felt good about herself, and Gertrude finally relaxed.

"Thanks for trying," Gertrude said on their way back to Building A. "I'm sure that will make the Warlord happy. Maybe you can try sparring tomorrow?"

Sage didn't know. She didn't like fighting in front of others because she wasn't used to it. She also knew it wasn't a very wise military tactic because even though these were her "allies," a lot of them were looking for opportunities to kill her. They'd learn her movements and style, putting her at a grand disadvantage.

As soon as Gertrude left, Sage headed straight for the Ferris wheel. There, she could practice without being seen by anyone else. Samson was always the ideal sparring partner because he was twice her size and so much stronger than her. He could shape-shift and grow tangles of tentacles that forced her to cover every angle or else she'd break a bone.

She'd broken every one at least once in her lifetime. Femurs were the absolute worst, and Samson had shattered them both during a training session once to teach her a lesson. Sage hadn't let her guard down since.

"Wow," Samson panted, stopping her blade with a mere hand. "You sure are motivated."

"I have to be," Sage panted, ducking a tentacle. "These people want to kill me."

"You'll get used to them."

"Maybe."

They went at it for an hour or so. By the end of it, Sage dropped the sword (she was still using the Warlord's) and used nothing but her hands to fight. She didn't have to shape-shift because her power and speed were enough to faze Samson, who coached her movements, showed her where she left open spots, and corrected her when she fell.

"Get back on your feet and slide!" he shouted, coming at her again. "You know the left side is your weakness—cover it at all times!"

Yes, and she had cuts and bruises by the end of their session to show for it. Not only had Samson destroyed her, but he reminded her that they had been training for five hours, it was midnight, and it was time to return home.

"Nutrition is very important," Samson said to a sitting Sage. "You have burned enough calories for a feast. Let's go—"

"Stop." Sage held out her hand, senses acute. She looked right at the wild shrubs, the footsteps and voices getting closer. They were coming from the Marketplace, and she already knew who they were before they showed their faces.

"Well, well…" sang Eye Candy, who looked just as surprised to see Sage as the other two flanking him. Rockstar and Turtle were equally smug. They had packets of powder and bongs, so this was going to be a great time, but with Sage in attendance? This was going to be a blast.

"Aww, look at the little *girl.*" Rockstar sniggered. "What are you doing out here? Writing in your journal about how scary everyone looks?"

Stand up and walk away, was Samson's advice from his hiding spot. Sage got up to do just that. She had the Warlord's sword at her hip, and the three of them noticed. It was Turtle who laughed loudly this time.

"How did you get that, little girl?" Turtle cackled. "Did you do him any *favors?*"

"Why don't you show us a little something-something?"

Sage grabbed a dagger and flung it at Rockstar, catching him in the eye. Rockstar seized his head, yelping loudly as the other two drew their weapons.

"You wanted me to show you something?" Sage said dryly. "There. Now leave me alone and do whatever it is you're going to do. I'm done here anyway."

"Hell no!" Eye Candy exclaimed. "Do you think *I* am going to let you walk away after that?"

"You antagonized me first."

"Bitch!" Eye Candy lunged at her, as fast as a bullet, but Sage was faster, ducking his blade, elbowing his chin, then swinging back with her sword to cut off his hand.

Eye Candy screamed, as loud as all the colors in his hair and on his clothes.

With two of his comrades down, Turtle stepped back. He was shaking in his boots because this had gone totally wrong. They were supposed to be the bullies here. Maybe he'd thought her conquests were a fluke, or maybe it was entertaining to see how far he and the other two could tease her.

"If you mess with me again, I'll make sure your heads join the Warlord's collection," Sage said to him. "And just so you know, I won't ask him for permission. He'll get a nice surprise in the morning."

"IS THAT A THREAT, BITCH?!" Eye Candy shrieked, clutching his bleeding stump. "Do you think you can just walk in here and start talking like *that*?!"

"Yes," Sage said honestly. "Now good night."

Having had enough, and with a hyperventilating Samson in the trees, Sage left before this escalated. She was sure that if she showed up at the Warlord's compound with three heads, he'd kill her. There was no way he'd see her side and take the loss of his hard-earned comrades lightly.

Hostility certainly brewed among the Enhanced the next day after they learned what had happened to the three idiots the night before. Even though Sage stuck to Gertrude, Blondie, and Mohawk, the latter two looked at her ... differently. They were more reserved around her now, as if they didn't trust her, and they even had the gall to ask, "Are you really an Enhanced?"

"What else would she be?" Gertrude snapped. Sage's love for her swelled. "She just has much more experience than all of us."

Gertrude was a godsend. Truly. She was genuine and kind with a purpose: her dream was to return to Diamond City to be with her sister. And something about her was awfully familiar, too, even if the face wasn't. Sage had a hard time figuring it out, so she was at a loss for an uncomfortable moment. She just stared at Gertrude, who was preparing the hot iron to do their hair for the Warlord's welcome-back party tonight. The lines on Sage's face were drawn and intimidating, making Gertrude hesitate.

"Everything all right, Sage?"

"Fine."

"That's a nice name, you know. An herb. It's supposed to be

very rich in nutrients. Sage also means wise and good judgment. My name is as plain as it gets."

"So Gertrude is your real name?"

She nodded. "Well, it used to be Gerard before I became a woman. I kept my female name close to the male one, but it still sounds horrific. Maybe I should have gone with something new . . . but my name was the one thing I didn't want to lose. Even though I've joined the Warlord, I never want to lose my ties to the people I love in Diamond City. But you're right—maybe I should have chosen Thyme or something."

Thyme reminded Sage of Penelope. Those weren't people she wanted to think about right now, so she shoved the PG out of her mind and focused on herself as Gertrude did her hair.

"Just watch, Sage," Gertrude said happily, portioning it into sections. "You're going to look beautiful." When she beamed, her cheeks rounded, freckles popping out. She was well-built with round shoulders and thick legs, a woman who could hold her own in hand-to-hand combat. Like everyone else here, she was in this to fight. But when it was time to relax, she knew how to show off. Her dress was long and beautiful, hugging her curves in a very modest way, mostly accenting her shoulders and upper chest muscles. Sage's dress was plain, looked more like a box, and that was fine. This was the cheapest, quickest thing when funds were low and Gertrude's closet was scarce. There weren't a lot of dresses in their import crates, although the Warlord did make it a point to acquire any fine materials he could grab. Those were mostly for him, though.

"For him?" Sage said. "What does he do with all those fabrics?"

"Well, you know he loves fashion. He doesn't talk about it often, nor does he dress up like he's been doing lately, but he's always designing outfits and such. I think his dream is to put us all on a runway."

That didn't come as a surprise to Sage. She only wished she had the dress from Louis' birthday party, but this would have to do.

And speaking of Louis, she had not gone to see him at all. From what she knew, he was still in prison, visited twice a day by that crazy preacher who blessed him with "good thoughts" and urged him to "please the Forefathers." Sage laughed. Maybe that was a good change for Louis, considering he had spent his entire life in a palace. Samson was going crazy because he "desperately needed" his helper back. Who else was going to clean and renovate their space? Maybe Sage would ask for Louis back soon.

"So, Sage, anyone on your radar?" Gertrude asked innocently, moving on to makeup. "You know … any special someone in your life?"

"No, actually," Sage said softly, eyes closed as Gertrude applied some shadow. "Not currently. I mean, I was married for a few years, but then I divorced. I haven't really looked for anyone since. I've been busy with the pizzeria and such."

Gertrude gasped. "Pizza?"

"My sister and I started our own pizzeria a long time ago. It was our dream since we were little. We really loved pizza. Our mother would buy it for us almost every night, and we'd watch movies and play board games."

Gertrude giggled. "That's so cute."

"It was the only food my mother could afford," Sage said. "She was a prostitute for a long time, but then she got sick. She died at forty years old. My sister took it hard, but she had me to hang on to. She had children—my nieces and nephews—who kept the family line … " Sage stopped for a moment. She didn't realize how hard it was talking about her ancestry, about people she had loved, because aging, disease, and weakness were part of being human … and that was difficult to deal with sometimes. A divorce was just as bad. The heartache had torn her apart, especially when her ex had taken the Allseer's side during the Warlord's Rebellion and gotten involved in politics, leaving her and the restaurant behind just to serve royalty.

That, however, was nothing compared to what the Warlord had gone through. Divorce was one thing, but being betrayed by your own wife and daughter?

"How about you?" Sage asked, changing the topic. "Other than Turtle, who's a nasty bully, anything else going on with you?"

"Nope," Gertrude said, ignoring that comment. "I never fought in the Unification War, but I did join the Warlord's cause and participate in the rebellion. I've been here ever since, training and getting stronger. I do have a niece, though. Her name is Sally." As soon as Gertrude showed Sage a picture, Sage knew immediately where she had heard Gertrude's name before.

Sally had been the little girl with the Star Raider toy, and the mother, Emma, was the one who had sold it to Sage and given her the map. Heart pounding, Sage told Gertrude all about that exchange. Gertrude couldn't be any happier.

"So they're doing well!" Gertrude clapped. "It's almost impossible to communicate with them all the way out here, so we send letters back and forth. But you've actually *seen* her, and that's a relief."

Sage hoped they'd be reunited soon. The longer she stayed here, the more confident she felt that the Warlord would be able to bring together all the Enhanced and create a strong enough front to force the Diamond City council into a draw. They'd be able to work *something* out . . .

"All right, done." Gertrude beamed into the mirror, marveling at Sage's makeover.

Her face was smooth with blush and shadow in the right places, and her hair was straight with no frizz thanks to the Warlord's conditioner. Suave-Suave really did work. Sage touched her strands, a much lighter color now that they were ironed and clean. Gertrude wrapped half of them into a fancy bun because she said it accented Sage's face a lot better.

Sage truly looked beautiful now. But this was only because of the party tonight. Tomorrow, it'd be right back to a sweaty forehead and dangling tank top. That's why Sage wanted to enjoy herself tonight and she also wanted to see Gertrude win Turtle over. There'd be nothing else to do because Louis and Agathe weren't allowed to attend—this was for fighters only.

It took place in a large building quite the walk away from their quarters in Building A. Back in the day, when Mousafeld had been occupied by non-militants, it was a museum. Sage recognized the parking lot, now overrun by massive tree roots and weeds, as well as the kiddie playground in the back, all rusted and breaking apart. The entrance to the museum was well kept, and now there were lights to welcome all the guests to the party.

Inside, the space was massive: there was an open floor for guests to mingle, and tables lined all around what used to be the lobby. There was a buffet of food against the back wall with a podium for announcements in the corner. The rest of the museum was used for storage, a bunch of doors closed except for the ones that led to the playground. Couples came and went.

"Let's grab this seat," Gertrude said, dragging Sage to one in the corner. "We'll put down our stuff, then we can make our rounds!" She was the only one with a purse, so she placed it on her chair, then dragged Sage right back into the crowd. She was quick to find Blondie and Mohawk, who both greeted Sage but showed signs of that uneasiness from before.

That left Sage to stand aside awkwardly. She looked out at the ceiling, the old chandeliers that barely lit up. The bulbs were dim and unchanged, because it was the newer lights that provided the most power. There was an orchestra for music, but no one was dancing yet. Classical music was always a nice way to relax, which was the idea—there was a lot of energy, crying, and emotions around Commander's death. Then there was the Warlord himself, their beloved leader who had almost died. The love his rebels showed him was impressive, but Sage could tell he was trying to escape the attention. He kept looking around, as if in search of someone, and then their eyes met.

They made contact for the first time since the battle at Winterfeld. The Warlord's face, always so hard and lined with fierceness, softened ever so slightly. It was easy to see because half of his hair was tied, but it was in no way plain—he had light blue streaks in those beautiful long strands with matching eyeshadow and lipstick. That went beautifully with his navy coat, white trousers, and black boots, reminding Sage of a dreamy sailor on a boat flying across a moonlit sky. His attention to detail was always outstanding. Sage couldn't stop staring. The Warlord stared at her in turn, inching toward her; he wanted to reach her, to say something to her, but he had so many people in his way.

Then Sage noticed Gertrude bouncing into Turtle's circle. Her conversation starter was a complete and utter failure, winning her snickers and insults from the savages.

"Wow," Turtle sneered at her. "As if you care so much about museums."

"I do, actually," Gertrude said in earnest. "This one was dedicated to the history of carnivals and how they started in Mousafeld before all the surrounding towns—and Diamond City itself—got into them. Did you know it was a ten-year-old's idea to invite people into his own backyard and charge them to ride in his playground?"

"I don't care."

Gertrude didn't stand a chance. Turtle didn't even look twice her way, actually, edging back at the smallest opportunity he had to escape her. It was sad to see. Gertrude's shoulders deflated, depression settling in, but not for long: Blondie and Mohawk reeled her back into their space to cheer her up. It didn't work very well—Gertrude was wiping her eyes.

Sage started toward Turtle. She didn't hesitate to get in his face, interrupting the pitiful manly exchanges with his dimwit friends. To her satisfaction, Rockstar was still missing an eye and Eye Candy had his arm in a sling. Bastards. "She really likes you, if you couldn't tell," Sage spat at Turtle. "The least you can do is give her the time of day."

Turtle snorted, eyeing Sage cruelly. "And who the hell are you to tell me who to give attention to? That bitch used to be a man, and there's no way I'm laying a finger on her—*it*—whatever the fuck *it* is—"

"I'm a friend of Gertrude's, and I care about her," Sage said. "And I just wanted to point out that you're an asshole. You fucking target me in the woods when no one is looking, and then you pretend you're high and mighty around all these dicks. It's called being humble—you should try it sometime."

"Bitch!" Turtle exclaimed. "Get the hell out of my face—"

Sage punched him in the nose. She broke it, making blood gush out of his nostrils. Everyone who saw that gasped, making way, as brave souls like Blondie and Mohawk jumped in again, lassoing Sage with their arms and pulling her away before this celebration turned into a bloody fight. Thankfully, there were enough bodies between them to stem hostility, although the Enhanced continued to glare and whisper about Sage's violent tendencies.

"Really?!" Gertrude squeaked at her. "Did you have to do that, Sage?"

"Yes," Sage said hotly, taking the glass of water from Blondie. "I did. He could have at least looked at you."

"You're fierce," Blondie admitted with more admiration than fear now. "Do you know that? Or are you blind to your own badassery?"

Sage wasn't sure if her actions were "badass"—she just didn't like assholes. Gertrude, on the other hand, thought it was super heroic. The three of them were impressed, sparking conversation about abusive relationships, but Sage didn't engage with them further.

She looked up to see the Warlord bulldozing his way to her. It was obvious she was his only goal at this point because he ignored anyone else who tried speaking to him.

"Sage," the Warlord said huskily, reaching her at last. "I've been looking for you."

"Well, you found me."

The Warlord extended his hand. His lips spread into a seductive smile.

Sage knew better than to fall for that. Even so, she took his hand. It was nice to feel its warmth after feeling how cold it had been just days ago. The Warlord raised hers and gently kissed it, lips lingering over her knuckles. Then he caressed it with his smooth cheek, eyes closed as if he were rubbing up against a pillow.

"I thank you from the bottom of my heart. You saved my life and care greatly about my men and women." His words were genuine. He chuckled, glancing at Turtle, who was still white in the face. "Sometimes they need a little discipline."

"I couldn't let you die," Sage said softly. "And Turtle is an asshole."

"I certainly see that. What he and the others did to you last night was unacceptable. Their comments of Gertrude were equally abhorrent. I will personally execute punishments for all three of them. One I will enjoy stabbing to near death while the other watches, and as for Turtle—well—he'll be cleaning up around here for a very long time. Then, perhaps, I will teach them a thing or two on how to be respectful to a lady. Allow me to demonstrate." The Warlord ran a hand through Sage's hair. His eyes blazed with passion, like two coals on fire. "Your hair looks beautiful. No frizz."

"I guess your conditioner really works."

"I know it does." The Warlord touched his own hair, the silky strands pinned behind his head. It was like a waterfall.

"I'm so damn jealous," Sage muttered.

"Give it a few months." The Warlord kissed her hand again. "And you'll see you'll be nearly as beautiful as me."

Sage smiled. It made her eyes and cheeks glow. This was such a rare sight, that the Warlord took his time marveling at it. Eventually, he spoke.

"Can you please follow me outside? I . . . want to show you something."

There were a lot of eyes watching them in here. Mega Woman had her gaze fixed on them, the conversation with her friends forgotten. There was always something jaw-dropping about the Warlord in all of his creative outfits, but he wasn't the one she was looking at.

Sage looked away and focused on the Warlord. She let him take her out of the room and wondered why. What had changed within her? The sight of his comatose body? Learning that he'd had a wife and daughter who were both dead, a pair of traitors? Or that damn conditioner he had sent her, a sign that he was clearly thinking about her?

Sage learned that the conditioner was the least of his gifts. When he took her outside, into the darkness of the night where there were only small lamps for light, he pulled another trinket out of his pocket. Sage wasn't sure what it was at first, but she quickly realized it was the Portable Projector she had marveled at at that store in the Marketplace.

"W-what?" Sage breathed incredulously, taking it.

"When I was investigating the attack on you at the carnival grounds, Trader told me you had happened by his shop and looked particularly interested in these," the Warlord said. "I know it's the latest piece of technology. You can store whatever you like in it. I know that you enjoyed Defenders Unite! when you were a child, so I had Trader download the entire series on here. Nighttime can be boring at times—"

"You *what?*" Sage couldn't believe her ears. She had to see it to believe it, so the Warlord turned on that little ball with a press of his finger. It lit up, threw its light across the bare field, and projected a menu with all of Defenders Unite!'s episodes.

"Do you not enjoy this series?" the Warlord said. "I saw the tattoo of Star Raider's crest on your wrist."

"Wait, but how do you know about the series?"

"I, too, used to watch it when I was a child." He started the first episode. There was a lazy smile on his face, but the triumphant gleam in his eye was more potent. The bastard felt accomplished.

Sage wasn't sure how to react. She studied the Portable Projector in her hands, knowing she'd be pulling an all-nighter with this in her possession. Her chest swelled with happiness, as if she had just purchased another action figure, but this was a different happiness. She pursed her lips to keep her emotions in check, eyes gleaming even more brightly than his. The nostalgia hit her hard, but she didn't let the Warlord see the weakness—only the appreciation.

"Can I at least get a kiss?" the Warlord asked hopefully.

"Do you have to seduce everyone you meet?" Sage said.

"Not everyone, no. Only the ones who are loyal . . . and save my life."

"Doesn't that include everyone in the room?"

"Absolutely not. Those men and women who fawn over me are not necessarily in love with me. They just want a good ride."

"But I'm different?"

"You know you are."

"I'm only here because of Louis and Agathe," Sage admitted. "Nothing else. I am loyal to them before you."

That was such a lie. Her mind was quick to remind her that she had turned Penelope away in a moment that could have ended the Warlord and his dreams. But then, having gone on a campaign with him and talked to Nova at the fastball stadium a few nights ago, she acknowledged that she *did* side with the Warlord. He sensed that.

"Maybe so," the Warlord muttered. "But if you truly hated me, you wouldn't have rescued me, would you?"

"You scared the shit out of me." Sage crossed her arms. "That Stars is a potent drug. I thought you were trying to sober up."

"I was," he said softly. "But it's not easy. I am already experiencing severe withdrawals, stemmed only with medication Dr. X provides. Speaking of, I imagine it was you who wiped out my stash in the bathroom?"

"Erectile dysfunction?" Sage arched a brow as the Warlord laughed. "Really?"

"It's hard to get in the mood sometimes."

"Maybe I can see that, but what about the rest of the shit? And Stars, no less? You've got people to lead, so please don't touch that stuff again. Well, I flushed it all down, so you can't unless you go out of your way to buy more."

"I should kill you," the Warlord said simply. "For throwing away ten thousand Diamonds' worth of drugs."

"Screw you," Sage spat. "You're going to kill me over those worthless drugs? Then you really are crazy."

"I am. Stars is highly addictive."

"Then you shouldn't have ever started it."

"I know ... but I needed something to take the edge off."

"Find something else to take the edge off."

"I think I have." The Warlord laid his hands on Sage's shoulders. It was a test of her reaction to his touch, of whether she'd pull away or not. Maybe Sage did flinch at first, ready to throw him and pummel him, but she stopped herself. Instead, she wrapped her arms around his trim waist, embracing him. She gave in to the moment she had wanted to cherish ever since finding him on his desk. She rested her head on his chest, and she took a moment to search for his heartbeat . . . and there was none.

What the hell? Was what that old, creepy man had said true? Was that really the Warlord's heart sitting in a jar in her room?

"It was taken from me a long time ago," the Warlord whispered against her hair.

How? How could the Allseer have done something like that?

"We truly are invincible, Sage. Immortal, even, if we don't count Slainium."

Sage tightened the embrace because she was trying to keep her sympathy in check. She screwed up her face, thinking about the Warlord's torture and his family's betrayal. No heart . . . his own wife attacked him in the middle of the night . . . lost his daughter . . .

Sage released her breath. She could smell the teakwood and lavender on his skin and clothes, intoxicating her. The Warlord did the same with her, nose against her throat and lips against her skin. He kissed her gently, so softly that it wasn't enough to warrant a punch.

"Your name is Damianos," Sage said.

The Warlord stopped from planting a second kiss. Hearing that from her lips took him by great surprise.

"I read the letter from your brother," Sage admitted. "The one on the table, where I found you. How he . . . hated what you've become. A traitor."

"May you call me Damian?"

"Of course. There's no need to be ashamed of it."

"I haven't heard that name since I left Diamond City," Damian said. "I was branded a traitor and taken to be executed, but I escaped thanks to Mega Woman. She and I led the mass exodus of Enhanced from the city we helped construct."

"That doesn't mean you forget your name," Sage said.

Damian resumed his kisses. He sucked on her skin in a very tantalizing fashion, as if he genuinely enjoyed the taste of her sweat.

"You said I was unattractive," Sage reminded him as his hands traveled from her shoulders to her waist. "And you wanted to know the man I could 'turn on.' Are you one of them?"

"I am. I've been wanting to kiss you ever since you threw that dagger at my chest."

"I'm not kissing you," she said. "I'm not sure what your intentions are. You're being kind and generous because you want to have sex with me, but is it because you want to dominate me or you truly love me?"

Damian chuckled. "Who says I'm the one who's dominating you? I think"—he touched her hand, fingers kneading hers—"it's the other way around."

Sage looked up at him. She raised a careful hand and caressed his face. Her fingers brushed smooth skin, freshly shaved. She liked the feel, tracing it all the way down his neck to his chest. She kissed his collarbone, right above where his heart should be. She wondered if she should give him the jar . . .

"Just one kiss," he whispered against her hair. "That's all I want."

"That's not all you want."

"Maybe not. But if you don't want it either, then tell me to stop." The sadism in his eyes was gone, replaced with a sultriness that Sage didn't want to sink into. She wasn't going to let herself, even if it became harder to resist him. She let him trail his hands to her back, fingers finding the zipper to her dress. Maybe she was giving in too much because Damian's moves were becoming bolder by the second.

"I want to take off your dress," Damian said.

"Then go ahead," Sage said.

He lowered the zipper slowly and steadily. He loosened the top, letting the straps slide off her shoulders. Then he gripped the hem of her dress and pulled it up and over her head.

Damian stiffened immediately. His eyes locked on her breasts. It was as if he couldn't believe they were real, small but round enough to make his breaths tight. He hadn't expected it to be this easy, so he was completely floored when Sage pulled down her underwear, too. Now she was butt-naked minus her flats, but those weren't what Damian was staring at.

"Heavens," he breathed. "You're so … very beautiful …"

"I'm glad you think so."

"I've never seen such muscularity in a woman." His eyes raked her shoulders, her chest, and then her abdomen.

"I've been fighting for a long time," Sage said.

"I want to touch you …" His eyes settled in between her legs. "Every part of you … and then I want to taste you."

"Do you?"

Damian tugged on his collar. Sage was teasing now, but he followed her like a puppy. "I do. Everything on your body is a beautiful piece of art that deserves attention and respect."

"Everything?"

Damian continued to stare at her. He sounded like he was in a trance. "Everything. I think of my fingers, squeezed to death as you writhe at my touch. I think of my tongue and all the wonderful tastes there are to find, especially as I make you climax with my mouth alone."

"Wow," Sage said. "That's quite explicit."

"I rarely hide what I'm thinking," Damian said. "And that is only the foreplay."

"Are you sure you have erectile dysfunction?"

Damian chuckled, but he looked like he was in pain. "Maybe not at this very moment."

"Obviously," Sage said.

"Please, Sage," Damian said huskily, visibly trembling. "Allow me to fulfill my fantasy."

"Go on," Sage said. "Get it out of your system."

What the hell did that mean exactly? Yes? Had she just said *yes*? Damian's pulsing, sex-hazed brain registered nothing else. He didn't waste any time reaching for one of her breasts, a preliminary to what awaited him between her legs, but he didn't get the chance to touch anything because his phone went off.

Damian jumped. That ring was louder than a bullet in the sky, killing the mood instantly. The look on his face was death.

"Wow," Sage teased, "what timing." She laughed as he answered the phone with a loud, "WHAT?!"

"Your lordship, we are about to perform the toast," said poor Justice, who was sure to get his ass kicked for this horrendous timing. "We are in need of your presence."

Damian threw the phone across the grounds. He raked his hand through his hair in pure, unbridled frustration.

"Better stop while you're ahead," Sage said coolly. She had no problem putting her dress back on, but Damian needed a moment... and a private corner. She laughed at the way he walked, more irritated than uncomfortable. She didn't want to be seen entering the ballroom with him, so she went on ahead.

"There you are!" Gertrude grabbed Sage's wrists. "Enjoying the view?" She looked outside.

"Very much," Sage said happily, hoping Damian was doing well out there.

Apparently, it had been the most distasteful masturbation of his life. When Damian returned to the party, he was outraged and it showed not only on his face but in the way he treated guests, hissing and spitting at everyone like a rattlesnake. Poor Damian had been breaths away from getting what he wanted all to be interrupted with a toast he no longer cared for. He was too angry to lead it, so he had Justice do the honors. Damian's eyes were wide and wild, locking onto Sage's in the crowd.

"Holy damn," Gertrude breathed in Sage's ear. "Think he has a stomachache?"

Sage laughed. "I don't think it's his stomach that's aching."

This was the best revenge she could have asked for. Thank goodness she had paid attention to Justice's earlier call of "Ten minutes until it's time to toast!" She had known that was exactly how much time she'd had to tempt him. Unfortunately for Damian, he wouldn't get another opportunity to seduce her tonight—there were way too many people trapping him.

After everyone toasted to Damian's health, it was time for dinner. Sage stuck to Gertrude in the back corner, where they spent the rest of the evening talking about the week's training schedule. This was the part of the conversation where Sage checked out. She didn't care about training with these Enhanced. She was more concerned over where Damian was going to take his crew next, how he was going to recruit the other Enhanced now that Winterfeld was theirs, and how they were going to move back into Diamond City. This whole process was going to take a while . . . and maybe it'd be a good idea for Sage to keep Louis and Agathe in the loop.

She planned to see them soon.

CHAPTER 13

Sold

After the party, Sage and Gertrude returned to Building A. It was a nice walk because the night was cool, allowing Sage to think more openly about her future. Penelope and Dustin invaded her thoughts often, what they were doing now ... Were they looking for more ways to infiltrate Damian's camp? Were they employing the military to do so?

"So ... " Gertrude cleared her throat. "Anything new with the Warlord? The two of you were out there alone."

"Not really," Sage said. "He just thanked me for saving him. Told me he was grateful."

"Did he kiss you?"

"I didn't let him."

Gertrude's jaw dropped. "What? Are you crazy?"

"Why am I supposed to kiss him?"

"He's so *hot*."

Everyone could agree that the Warlord was handsome, but that wasn't the only quality Sage looked for in a man. An image of Louis in royal garbs popped up in her mind, and her stomach churned. Louis ... did she truly like him? Not any more than she liked her ex, she supposed. Both men had priorities higher than her. Damian, however, didn't when his drive to win a kiss was even greater than the one to take back Diamond City.

That night, Sage turned on the Portable Projector. Tears welled in her eyes when she heard the theme song of Defenders Unite!. She watched three episodes before falling asleep, swimming in the past, in a memory of her cherished sister when they used to binge episodes all day long.

The following morning, Damian held a meeting with his team about their next course of action. He promised to fill in Sage afterward because he wanted her to spend some time with Agathe, who was holed up in a cottage that the rebels referred to as their very own "retreat." This was where Damian's late wife and daughter used to stay. It was a house, lake, and garden, with maids and servers galore. Agathe looked worried, but she was well taken care of for sure.

She was plump. Not fat, but full. She had round cheeks, a stubby chin, and a square body. This wasn't any different from the usual Agathe in Diamond City, but now Sage was looking at her up close and realizing something very important: Agathe was far from having been whipped, raped, chained, and starved. If anything, Agathe's life was much more quiet and calm without royalty lessons shoved down her throat.

"Sage!" Formalities thrown aside, Agathe jumped on her. The girl was so relieved to see a familiar face that she started crying. Happy tears ran down her cheeks. "Please, come in!"

The inside of the cottage was just as beautiful as the outside, with plush furniture, clean rugs, and shiny decorations. There weren't any paintings, portraits, or pictures of Damian's family here. The simplicity would welcome anyone.

"It truly is nice to see you." Agathe beamed as a few of her personal maids tended to Sage's jacket and offered her something to drink.

"Yeah," Sage said slowly. "Me, too. I was worried about you."

"I know it's hard to believe, and despite the circumstances, I am . . . fine." Maybe Agathe had a hard time believing it herself. After witnessing her father's decapitation, she must have forecasted nights of sheer agony with Damian forcing himself on her. But, according to Agathe, there was nothing forceful about this. After a couple of dates to the Ferris wheel and a few shopping sprees at the Marketplace, she had simply fallen for him.

Sage arched a brow.

"We kissed," Agathe admitted in a way that Candice or even Olivia would when talking about their school crushes. "And I know this sounds weird, but I *liked* it, Sage. I mean, who wouldn't? He truly doesn't compare to any man in Heart. He's not overly built, and sometimes I feel like he's more . . . I don't know . . . feminine than most? Like he understands me, what I feel, and how I want to be held." She giggled. "It excites me in a way nothing else has before."

"This is the guy who killed your father—you know that, right?"

Agathe shrugged as if Sage had just told her the grass was dying. "Maybe so, but what many people don't know is that I was a prisoner in that place. I *hated* that place. Shortly before the challenge, I was planning on running away."

"Well, that's good to know. Does Louis know?"

Agathe shrugged again. "No. He loves it there, but I don't. I like it here. The Warlord is so sweet and handsome. I wanted my first time to be with him, but just as we were undressing, he . . . stopped. I think he was the one who was uncomfortable." Agathe sighed with longing. "He has a hard time opening up to people, but at least he's trying. He did give me this."

Agathe picked up a box from a nearby table. She showed it to Sage. Inside was a necklace that had once belonged to Damian's wife, encrusted with diamonds. It was the flashiest, most expensive piece of jewelry Sage had ever seen, making her wonder if he had stolen it from Diamond City.

Agathe shook her head. "It belonged to his grandmother, I think. It was the only heirloom he ever received, but he didn't tell me any more. So weird. I mean, I'm lucky he's so nice to me, but

I feel terrible, Sage. He wants to empower the Enhanced—maybe even create more of them—and I fear they are only going to cause turmoil and violence in our city. We've already created a dutiful army, so why do we incentivize people to obtain more power? I mean, he's a living, breathing example of why we shouldn't have superior beings wandering around! All they want to do is fight for control."

"The exiles do want to return to Diamond City," Sage said, putting the necklace down. "There are no doubts about that. But it's for a reason. Not only is Diamond City their home, but there's talk that the Squids are up to something." She told Agathe what she had learned from Nova after her first campaign.

"Oh, Sage . . . " Agathe whispered, eyes welling with tears again. "I-I'm so sorry you got sucked into all of this. What's going to happen now?"

"The Warlord wants to acquire as many exiles as possible before returning to the city, and he's taking advantage of my help to do it. I suppose he wants to make sure there are no more enemies before taking the throne for himself."

"H-he's using you?"

"Yes," Sage replied. "In exchange for Louis' and your safety. More like Louis' from the looks of it."

"Oh, God!" Agathe cried. "He wants to kill Louie?"

"That was his plan after Louis got caught, yes."

"A-and Louie—at least he's well?"

"From what I know."

"I imagine Louie sent you here after I was taken from Heart?"

"His idea, yes." *More like bribery*, Sage thought bitterly, wondering how her pizzeria was doing.

"Sage, I . . . Well . . . " Agathe took a deep breath. More worry etched across her face like badly-drawn lines. There was some sort of guilt eating her up alive, something she needed to say or else she was going to explode. There wasn't any guarantee they'd have another moment together in the future, so she spoke, "This isn't right. And I'm sorry."

"I'm not sure it's your fault," Sage said, thanking the servant who brought her a cherry soda. "All of this happened so quickly. The Warlord has his own agenda."

"I'm sorry for *you*," Agathe said. "You don't deserve this."

"Do any of us?"

But that's not what Agathe was getting at. She was implying that Sage, in particular, was suffering the brunt of some unfortunate circumstance. Sage didn't quite understand why, because she was stuck here like all of them were, but then she would have never imagined what Agathe was about to say next.

"Sage," Agathe whispered, "Bram sold you to us. If he had never given you over . . . well . . . you wouldn't be here right now."

Sage blinked. Agathe was hysterical with guilt now—she clapped two hands over her mouth, as if she had just given away a deadly family secret.

"Bram told us that you were the strongest being in all of Diamond City," Agathe went on with a sob. "That you were the Optimum, and that your blood could be used to empower the Enhanced even more. Not only that—your children would be invincible, and so we purchased you with the hope that you'd mate with Louis."

"What the fuck?" Sage croaked. Horror crept into her veins like a disease. "What the *fuck* do you mean by that—'*sold*' me?"

"You're a weapon, Sage. You know that." Agathe gathered herself enough to take Sage's hands, holding her in place. It was a futile move because Sage could tear those fingers apart like paper, but Agathe had to make sure she was listening for this next bit. "I needed to tell you because you need to know. Bram wanted a better life for you, more than your dabbling with the Private Guard. He wanted you to move on in life, get married—"

"You mean become Louis's concubine? Is that how I was supposed to 'better' myself?"

Agathe shook her head. "I don't think that's what Bram intended. He just wanted you to be happy, to be with someone you loved. He knew you had a massive crush on Louis—"

Sage punched the wall, leaving a hole. She didn't mean to be destructive, nor did she wish to inflict any damage on a property that wasn't hers, but she needed an outlet. The next target would have been Agathe's face, even if the poor girl wasn't at fault for this crazy transaction.

Sage was shaking. Her entire body was up in flames. "How dare he," she whispered. "So his solution was to sell me? Without my consent? That's supposed to make me happy?"

Agathe broke out into more tears. The sobs were irritating as hell.

"That was the only way Louis was going to look me in the face, right?" Sage spat. "When there's money involved? Promises of stronger children?"

"I'm sorry, Sage! R-really! I promise that if I'm the next Allseer, I won't ever let that happen—you have to believe me! But I wanted you to know the truth. I can't bear to see you treated like some sort of toy, but know this: Louis outright refused to play along. That's why he ignored you at the birthday party—he didn't want anyone to know that he was interested. Either way, it was futile because Blackburn was going to take you regardless of whether you and Louis hit it off." Agathe breathed out raggedly. "Of course, Blackburn never had the chance. Not after the Allseer's death."

Sage should have known. Damn it, hadn't she known? Blackburn had known she was the Optimum all this time, so why were Agathe's words taking her by surprise?

Damian wasn't the monster.

Blackburn was.

When Sage stormed out of the cottage, she wasn't thinking straight. In all her years of living, she had been trained to remain calm and collected, the only way to win battles. But this was a different kind of battle, one that required blood and a satisfying snap of bones. Unfortunately, Blackburn wasn't here. She couldn't pummel his face, so she needed another way to relieve herself. Maybe not with destruction, though—she had to acknowledge that, at the very least, Louis agreed that selling people without their consent was abusive.

The prison block was on the other side of camp, close to the training grounds. It wasn't easily distinguishable from everything else around it because there were no fences, just a lot of guards. Its structure was sturdy with very small windows, so no one had any hope of crawling out of there. It had an open yard in the back where prisoners were lined up, questioned, and beaten. Most of them were bandits, but there must have been people from Winterfeld there as well. Sage didn't particularly care what sort of protocol Mousafeld's prison followed, and she ignored the coppery smell in the dank air as well as the soft waft of mold coming from the walls because there weren't signs of needless torture.

Sage had broken into a lot of prisons during the Unification War. The sights she had seen then were nothing compared to the clothed and sleeping bodies she saw now. The horrors of those days took root in her mind, throwing her back to a time when the fighting and blood had never stopped. Sage entered a bit of a frenzy, ignoring the calls of guards who moved to apprehend her and the cries of prisoners who sought escape. Instinct took her right to Louis at the end of the hall; he had been huddled up on his cot until he saw her.

"Sage?" Louis got up, grabbed the bars of his cell, and peered at her. Relief washed over his face. "Oh, thank the Forefathers you're here!"

"Release him," Sage said to the guard. "He's coming with me."

This wasn't up for debate. That's why she came at the guard with her fist, landing one right across his face. There was a *crunch* from shattered cartilage. It shocked the rest of the guards, who had no idea what was going on and why they were being attacked by a woman. They could call a breach all they wanted, but Sage favored people who were honest and moral, and that's the sort of lesson she was trying to teach Louis right now.

"Sage?" Louis croaked, stumbling after her. He was dirty and a bit too thin, but at least he had all his body parts. There weren't any obvious lashes, but there was a bruise on his cheek. "What's going on?"

"Nothing," Sage said. "I'm getting you out of prison. Samson's been dying for your help, so can you get back to the room and finish up whatever he wants you to do?"

"Oh, thank the Forefathers!" Louis cried. "Anything is better than that horrid prison! They fed me this disgusting porridge for dinner and I've had the runnies ever since! Thank you, Sage!"

If that was the worst of it, then Sage had misjudged the Warlord big time. This wasn't the torture camp she had believed it was. These exiles weren't perfect, but they had to survive, and that meant fighting and taking prisoners. Sage knew she'd never be able to sustain a camp like this on her own, with so many people depending on her and her leadership. All she knew how to do was wield her sword . . .

"Later, Sage!" Louis ran toward Building A with impetus. Quite impressive. That's how Sage knew he wouldn't be trying any tactics to escape ever again. Samson would probably get the surprise of his life when Louis burst through the door.

Sage didn't follow, though. She fell to her knees and held her face. Her eyes burned with unshed tears. Any desire she'd had to break something in half died along with her spirit. She had come here to rescue Agathe and Louis, but now she realized they were better off as prisoners. All those assholes in Heart were corrupt. She appreciated the Allseer's head on Damian's wall that much more.

Sage supposed she had every right to feel frustrated. The only person who had shown any semblance of interest in her was an evil, greedy bastard who wanted to dominate the world. Sure, Damian was civilized and proper, but that didn't mean he was pure. Sage suspected ulterior motives, a side he wasn't showing to any of them in order to win their favor. She didn't believe he was anywhere near as good-natured as he pretended to be. But if she killed him, then that meant Blackburn and the council would win.

And she didn't want that . . . right?

Sage shook her head, curling tighter into herself. She planned to stay like that for a moment while she composed herself. She had to be quick about it because this was a busy street—there were Enhanced walking up and down, and there was one who had been raring to get to her ever since she arrived.

"My lady!"

Sage whipped around.

Oh, no.

The preacher . . . who was nicknamed Preacher.

Oh, God.

Always in those long robes and that weird mask, Preacher fumbled over to her like an owner who had found his dog. He was protective, glaring at the other Enhanced, who backed away before they were sucked into another sermon. Everyone avoided the little chapel next to the prison like the plague. It was the only building in Mousafeld that Sage had yet to enter. Looked like today was her lucky day.

"Please," he urged her. "Come in."

"I really don't want to," Sage said. "I'm busy."

"You look quite upset, my lady, and I have just the thing that will cheer you up."

"Please . . . just call me Sage." Sage stopped herself from rolling her eyes. She couldn't feel too annoyed, though—Louis wasn't anywhere near the scumbag she'd thought he was. And while she was upset over Blackburn, she was furious over Bram. So much so that it blinded her. Her body went into autopilot, picking itself up and following the bumbling Preacher into the chapel. At least he took off the mask when he was inside.

There were hundreds of these in the Clarity District. Sage had visited a great deal of them during her travels there, and they were all more or less the same: stained glass, altar, pew, and books. The lighting was dim and the air was musky with incense, all in honor of the four Squids whose images were hung at the far end of the room.

The Forefathers. They were blurry and obscure because no one knew what they truly looked like, even all the way out here. Sage had seen those portraits a hundred times, but she felt especially drawn to them now.

" . . . pray much?"

Sage had only caught a part of Preacher's question. It was enough for her to snort out an answer. "To Squids?" *I live with one.* "Ah, no."

"Shh!" Preacher shushed her. "You must not call them that!"

"Squids?"

"Shh! Or they will rip out your tongue!"

"Sorry, but that's what they look like. And it's not like they can hear me."

"They can always hear, my lady! That's why we must be respectful."

Amusing, yes, especially when Sage pictured herself kneeling at Samson's large feet, but it was no laughing matter. A lot of people dismissed Squids, but Sage knew they were real. And one of the four up there—the second one to the right—was awfully familiar to her. The Claritians had given them names, but the only one who mattered to Sage was *Pugnator*. It was Lucidum for fighter. For Sage . . . that Squid up there was father.

Stay away, were the words that Sage remembered so clearly. She hadn't known much Lolligo at that young age, but she had derived their meaning from the glow in the amber eyes above her. They had looked right at her.

Sage blinked. She looked at Preacher, who was watching her with held breath, intrigued at her apparent reverence. After so much eye-rolling from other Enhanced, Sage's respect was a shock to him.

"Do you worship often?" the Preacher pressed again.

"Worship?" Sage said, trying to hide her disdain. "Are you asking if I worship the Squids that I fought against in the Unification War? No."

"Respect! And you *fought* the Lolligo?"

"Not directly, but who do you think was in control of the districts? There were four of them." Sage waved at the portraits. "Hence why there are four of them up there."

"There must be some mistake. The districts were all separate bodies controlled by vicious Overseers. What proof was there that Lolligo were behind this? If anything, it was the Lolligo who gave us power. Where do you think Enhanced came from?"

"Enhanced came from laboratories," Sage said quietly. "Not Squids."

"Respect, my lady!" Preacher scolded. "And did you know that the being who gave life to Enhanced was a hybrid? A mix of Lolligo and human?"

"I know . . . trust me. But I think that hybrid was captured by scientists, not given as a gift by Squids. In fact, the Squids wanted to keep their all-powerful DNA to themselves."

Preacher breathed in and out as if he was exercising patience. He didn't chastise her this time. "You claim that the Lolligo were in the districts, controlling them behind the scenes. What proof do you have of this?"

Samson. That was all the proof Sage had, the only living Squid who had been left behind in the Clarity District. If Squids hadn't been in control there, then where the hell had Samson come from?

Sage suspected the Squids had dabbled with humans as an experiment, to see how much they could control and manipulate. They wanted to observe humans and their behaviors in order to initiate a full takeover. According to Nova, that's what seemed to be happening now. If women were going missing in Winterfeld . . . then it had to be Squids. What they were planning, Sage didn't know, but there was a reason all these towns were terrified of them.

"You cannot deny that the Lolligo are powerful," Preacher said. "And it is because of them that we have Enhanced. In just three months, we celebrate the 100th anniversary of the first Enhanced. The month of Birth will be one of silence and piety."

Here? At camp? Sage doubted that these Enhanced cared enough about their origins to bow their heads and worship monsters. The month of Birth was also the first month of the year, and everyone would be too busy lighting fireworks and throwing parties. Only Claritians turned off all their lights in reverence.

Sage said nothing as she made her way to the front of the chapel. She noticed a large case of books in the corner, which she assumed were the usual prayers, preachings, and hymns from the Clarity District. While there were some she recognized, there were others that were written in . . . Lolligo?

Sage furrowed her brows. She recognized the wavy, slithery text because her mother used to read books like this to her. In fact, back at home, she had all kinds of fairy tales written in Lolligo, given to her by her father at a very young age. It was simple text, but it was enough to learn the language. It was how she had taught Samson to read, who then had gone on to write the entire alphabet, decipher grammar rules, and write his own journals. Yes, their fluent Lolligo was based on fairy-tale writing.

But these books were not fairy tales. These were history books as Sage read in the titles—*Yësselé*—and her heart started a vicious pounding.

"Where did you get these?" Sage asked Preacher.

"Those we've acquired in our travels through the Outskirts," Preacher replied. "The only problem is we know not the ancient text of the Lolligo. I've kept them anyway since they bring good luck. Look at how successful the Warlord has been."

His success came from his own battle strategies, but Sage wasn't going to start an argument. She eagerly asked if she could borrow them, and Preacher was ecstatic that someone was so interested in what these books represented. Suddenly, Sage was overwhelmed with excitement, wondering if there was a way to haul all these texts to Samson, but she wanted first dibs so she grabbed four of them and sat down at the front pew to read.

Wow, Sage was a bit rusty with her reading. It was frustrating that she couldn't fly through the words, but she did make out most of them. This text was from before the Unification War, a journal of sorts, as if a Squid had written down his or her experiences in the Outskirts. It was hard to concentrate with Preacher looming in front of her and asking her questions.

"Do you feel empowered?" he asked excitedly.

"I do," Sage replied honestly.

"It is a shame we can't read what it says!"

Yes, it was. Sage was completely engrossed in what this was saying. This Squid was taking note of human persistence and intelligence in places Sage assumed were faraway towns, how they interacted in stores, at hospitals, and at border skirmishes. Like Samson, these Squids were elusive, invisible to humans and Enhanced alike, who fought for survival against each other. Not only that—they watched all their puppeteering come to fruition. Why destroy humans when they destroyed themselves?

This was fascinating and all, but Sage wondered if there was a book here on Diamond City, if some humongous Squid who could squash a building with his fists had documented the rise of her city. Sure, there were all kinds of historical texts about Diamond City, but none ever mentioned the how and why those four Squids up there had strayed from the mainland to establish their own districts. So what if there was one such book here—

"Wait," Preacher rasped, "are you *reading* it, my lady?"

"Wish I could," Sage murmured.

"No, tell me the truth! I see your eyes, the revelation—"

"I'm just so moved," Sage choked, trying not to laugh. "A Squid wrote this!"

"Wow," said a voice from the doors. "I certainly had no idea you were so religious. Or are you here to confess your sins after breaking my guard's nose and freeing Louis without my permission?"

"My lord!" Preacher ran down the aisle as if he were in a race. He grabbed Damian's hands and kissed them. "You're here—"

"May you give us some privacy?" Damian said. "I might have to execute proper punishment for unruly behavior. Would you remind me what that is again? My clerical days are starting to blur."

"Oh, yes!" Preacher cleared his throat. "For aggression and defying orders? Thirty days of imprisonment with ten lashings each morning and night. Don't forget just the basic food rations as well."

"Now I remember."

"My lord, I had no idea she holds so many transgressions!"

Damian snorted. "I thought you knew everything. Or were you more interested in *her*? She is beautiful, isn't she?"

"Well, I was—am—interested, of course! She is our most experienced fighter, part of the reason for our success in Winterfeld! Physically, however, I must control my sexual urges and abstain from any inappropriate behavior that would offend the Lolligo! I wouldn't want them to see us giving in to our temptations."

"No, you wouldn't," Sage muttered to herself, still reading the journal on her lap. "They'll cut off your balls."

"Understandable," Damian said. "Go to the prison block. I believe they need you to bless a few transgressors who are acting out."

"Yes, sir!" Preacher ran out, mask back over his face in case he met any Squids on the way.

Finally rid of distractions, Damian made his way down the aisle. Sage kept her eyes on the book, but she could see the smugness on his face. He was in all black today, so he stuck out like a sore thumb in her peripheral. Or maybe this was his way of protesting the church, which despised dark colors, making him all the more rebellious. Sage could be rebellious, too.

"If you touch me, I'll kill you," Sage said simply.

"Are you going to answer my question?"

"Please leave me alone."

"I'd like to know what happened," Damian said. "What triggered your behavior? Why did you release Louis? And here I was hoping to hang him. Please give me the order. His daddy misses him so. I think he spoke to me the other day."

"I think we should give Louis a chance," Sage said, ignoring that comment. "I think some discipline and work is all he needs to become a decent human being."

"I'll leave you to that, but I want to know what he did to redeem himself. Certainly, he wasn't writing you love letters behind my back, was he?"

Sage glared at Damian.

"Why do you look at me so?" Damian asked innocently.

Sage threw a dagger at his chest. She got the hit, but Damian just laughed.

"Goodness." Damian yanked it out. "You really are mad. But I think it's quite unfair of you to take it out on me. Let me guess: Agathe let you in on some little secret that shed some positive light on Louis so you felt inclined to set him free." He gave her back the dagger. "I want to know *what* he did that was so great. I'm a little bit jealous."

"He's a much better person than his father," Sage whispered.

Damian snorted. "Anyone is."

"I guess I know that now."

"That's why I want to take back what he stole from me. I'm curious, though: what did Agathe say?"

"That you tried to bed her but couldn't get it up."

Damian sighed. "Regarding you, Sage."

"It's none of your business."

"I suppose it doesn't matter." Damian took a seat next to her. He put his feet up on the altar. "A betrayal is a betrayal. How long have you been here, going through books you can't read?"

"For a while now." Sage closed the journal, knowing she wasn't going to get any more reading done. Now she had to figure out a way to borrow these books without anyone knowing she could read Lolligo. "I've never seen books like these before."

"We come across numerous items in our travels. It chills me to know that Squids really do exist. Not sure I would worship them, though."

"Yet you're from Clarity."

Damian scowled. "I hated it there. People become way too obsessed with worshipping beings they've never even seen. Everything has to be proper and pious. I think it's all an excuse to control people." He picked up one of the books from the pile. When he did, Sage saw his hand, the long pale fingers, the multiple rings, and the blue spider-like veins in his wrist. That's when she noticed a faint sort of scar, a sight that took her by great surprise. She seized his hand to take a closer look, and her heart sank.

"It was a long time ago," Damian said softly. "When I was still human. I fell in love with my best friend, and because he was a boy, my father kicked me out of the house and claimed I was possessed. One of the churches took me in, and I am very grateful for the preacher and his wife, who gave me food and shelter despite my sexuality. They are examples of kind, giving people. I lived at the church for three years, watching all these families worship beings I didn't think existed. When I wasn't in service, I spent my days studying and watching Defender's Unite!. I applied to an art school in Color, but they weren't accepting anyone from Clarity. As you know, the districts were at war with each other back then, and intermingling was forbidden."

"So what did you do?" Sage asked. "Did you stay at the church?"

Damian snorted. "No. I'd rather die, and that's exactly what I tried to do. I cut my wrists behind a dumpster because that's what I felt like—trash. No pious Claritian freak would ever think to look there, but there was one person who did."

Sage's heart was beating so hard, it was a miracle Damian couldn't hear it. She didn't even realize she was holding her breath until she whispered, "And who was that?"

Damian closed his eyes. He shook his head. "I don't know her damn name. But I remember her face when she found me, her strong-as-fuck hands as she grabbed my wrists, stemmed the blood flow with some pieces of her shirt, and carried me all the way to the hospital. She *carried* me, Sage, and she couldn't have been any older than I was. Some time later, I woke up and found her holding my hand. She didn't want to leave until she made sure I opened my eyes. That's when I noticed the Star Raider tattoo on her wrist.

" 'You're fine now,' she said to me. 'Things are going to get better. The Enhanced are forming a coalition, and we're going to unite Diamond City.'"

Damian smiled. "Would you believe those words lit a fire in my chest that hasn't yet gone out? It was because of that girl that I got my ass out of that hospital and decided to fight. I was the ideal candidate—eighteen, young, determined, and ambitious—and the coalition took me in. They were some sort of secret society recruiting people to become Enhanced so they could topple the Overseers, and I think she had some sort of ties to them. Whatever her role, I'm sure of one thing: she was the Optimum."

"How do you know that?" Sage asked. "I mean, I have a Star Raider tattoo."

"Because I could feel that she was different. I met a ton of Enhanced afterward, and no one was like her. Yes, I was practically unconscious when I saw her, but I *felt* it, Sage. Sadly, I never saw her again. But whoever she was, she saved my life."

Sage ran her thumb along the jagged scar of his skin, feeling the raised bump. She had seen plenty of scars on his body, but this one was the saddest.

"Does it disgust you?" Damian asked quietly.

"No," Sage whispered. "It's what makes you human."

"And that's not good. I've been trying to find a way to snuff out my humanity. I feel it is a rather weak trait to carry."

"Humanity doesn't necessarily equal weakness, Damian."

"I feel it does. Very much so."

"I feel it's what opens my eyes to certain things," Sage said. "The reason I left Diamond City and haven't killed you, for example."

Damian smirked. "You have a grand opportunity right now. Why don't you do it?"

"First of all, a blade alone wouldn't kill you. Secondly, I . . . " Sage exhaled. "I also believe that we need to take back Diamond City. Come to some sort of agreement so one party doesn't have all the control."

"I believe there is another reason, too."

"There isn't."

"You want to taste my lips, don't you?" Damian leaned in and puckered up. "If I were dead, they'd be cold and stiff. But when I'm alive, they're full, soft, and oh so warm—"

Sage used the dagger, but Damian jumped off the bench, laughing his head off.

"Careful, Sage, we're in a place of worship."

"I think the Squids would be pleased with your blood sacrifice," Sage grumbled with a glare. But then she softened her brows and smiled lightly. She stood up. "Do you know what would please me?"

Damian stopped laughing instantly. "What?"

"Would you let me take these books to my room? I really want to study them."

Damian blinked. He didn't understand why Sage would be so interested in unreadable books, but he didn't care enough to ask. He was way too distracted by Sage's lips. He kept staring at them as she drew closer. "Then can I come with you?" he asked.

Sage cupped his face with her hands. His cheeks were angular and smooth, the pads of her thumbs resting easily on his skin. The rest of her fingers were in his silky hair, rounding the back of his head. For someone so fierce, Damian was thin and . . . elegant. He was just as Agathe described. Warmth spread through Sage's body. She gazed into his eyes as she leaned in, lips nearly brushing his as she said, "Shouldn't you be with Agathe? Aren't you marrying her?"

"Why are you teasing me?" he growled angrily. "You already know the answer to that. It is a political alliance and nothing more. You already know I can't get hard with her."

"Maybe you didn't take your pill that day."

Damian shook his head. "It's not that, I swear."

"Being with her doesn't mean you have to have sex with her."

"What if I want to be with you instead?" Damian touched her hips. "I've been in meetings all morning, which I do need to fill you in on, but I don't want to ruin this moment with war tactics right now. There are so many other things to do together."

"Do you think I'm a weapon?" Sage asked him.

Damian furrowed his brows. "What?"

"Am I a weapon to you?"

"What on earth is the reason behind that question?"

"Commander was your greatest fighter, and now that he's gone, you've set your sights on me."

"You can fight, Sage," Damian replied softly. "It doesn't make you a weapon. I thought you were fighting for me because we had an agreement, not because you're some kind of tool."

And that's why Sage kissed him.

Innocent and ginger, not because that was all Damian deserved but because Sage wasn't sure how he'd react. Before she got too far back, though, Damian touched her cheek. He held her face and gazed into her eyes with a tenderness that felt out of character in a warlord. The black orbs burned with a certain longing for love and attention. When he leaned in to kiss her, it wasn't violent or dominant.

At least not at first. His lips captured hers, upper and then lower for a full taste. Then, when Sage reciprocated his movements, he pulled back to gaze at her again.

This time, the kiss was far more intense. Damian pushed his tongue into her mouth, as if it was something he had been dreaming of for decades. Sage matched every lick, swipe, and thrust with her own, unsure if it was out of spite toward Blackburn or sympathy toward Damian—it felt good all the same. That warmth in her body quickly turned to heat because his tongue was relentless and so was hers, as if they were battling at his compound all over again. There were so many ways and angles to taste each other, and neither one was inclined to stop exploring, not when they finally had the privacy they needed. It turned into a competition of who was crown dominator, and Sage wasn't about to lose that title.

Sage kept his head pinned against hers and Damian had a hand at the base of her neck. Eventually, they were going to need support, but this was a chapel and there was no way Sage was going to do more in the presence of four ugly Squids, even if they were just a painting. Plus, Preacher was racing right back to them.

"Damian," Sage breathed as Damian bit her and sucked on her neck. "He's coming. Preacher's coming back. I can hear his footsteps."

"I don't care." He forced his tongue into her mouth again. That gagged her for a bit, but Sage found another opportunity to speak.

"Do you want him to catch us?"

"Do you know how long I've waited for this moment?" Damian croaked to her, eyes huge. He was so dramatic. "How hard it was for me to get just one kiss—*this* kiss—"

"My lord!" Preacher burst through the doors, exclaiming, "I did it! I blessed the prisoners!"

"DAMN IT!" Face red, Damian stomped down the aisle and grabbed Preacher by the robes. He shook him. "Make yourself useful!" he spat at him, "and move all those Squid texts to Sage's room—*now!*"

"Yes, my lord!" Preacher croaked without asking questions or noticing Damian's swollen lips. "R-right away!"

Wow. If Preacher wasn't protesting the loss of his beloved texts, then he was absolutely terrified of Damian. Sage couldn't say she blamed him—Damian was ferocious and extremely seductive. Her heart was still hammering from that kiss, which Damian had every intention of finishing that night. He shot her this intense look, sparks in his eyes. After Preacher carried all those Squid books out of the chapel, he held out his hand.

"He is very . . . charismatic. He will seduce you until you open your legs for him and fall for his false promises of love. Once he has you wound around his finger, he'll capture you and use you as a source of power."

Even so, Sage wanted Damian. He cared about her despite what Blackburn said. Thanks to him, she and Samson had full access to all those books. Who knew what was written in them.

Squids aside, Sage had to think about Diamond City, too. The only way to restore peace was to help Damian, and that's what she intended to do. Her life. Her choice. There was no secret transaction here.

Sage took his hand. Damian leaned down and licked her lips. She smacked his ass.

"Behave," she warned.

"Or else what?" he challenged.

Sage smiled. "No cigars or milkshakes tonight."

"Whew." Damian wiped his forehead. "I thought you were going to say sex."

Sage pulled out her dagger; Damian raised his hands.

"Cigars and milkshake it is." He nodded.

CHAPTER 14

Brother Versus Brother

I t was cigars and milkshakes every night for the next three months. Oh, and kissing.

A lot of kissing.

They did it in the common room, but most of the time it was in Damian's study because Sage got creeped out with all the heads on the wall. It turned out, those hadn't been stuffed after all—they were alive. Enhanced didn't die without Slainium, so they could actually watch everything going on around them. Damian loved to show off to his enemies, but Sage preferred the space with his designs and fabrics instead.

Gertrude was right: Damian was an artist. He had twenty-plus sketchbooks full of drawings, some of which he had actually brought to life with his own hands. Sage couldn't believe she had missed his rack of coats and shirts when she was in here the first time, but his overdose had taken center stage. Now that Damian wasn't dying, she got to see his talents and his clear passion for fashion. Damian had designs for every occasion, from promiscuous clown costumes for birthday parties to revealing swimwear for the beach.

"Wow," Sage said, impressed, as she flipped through the pages. She had definitely never seen a mermaid outfit quite like this one, with breasts in the air and frills in the crotch. "I can definitely see why you left Clarity."

"Phoebe used to give me her feedback all the time," Damian said with a sad smile. "She'd approve. I always trusted her judgment when it came to fashion."

Instead of training, Damian went to Winterfeld every day to visit her grave. Sage always offered to go with him, but Damian insisted he go alone. Besides, he wanted her to train with the others.

The key to surviving without breaking faces or getting into unnecessary brawls was sticking to people she considered friends, like Gertrude, Blondie, and Mohawk. They were under the tutelage of Trainer, an old-time Enhanced like Damian, who had served in both the Unification War and the Warlord's Rebellion. Not all these Enhanced had those credentials, so bonding was a bit difficult, but Sage was happy with her circle of friends. They were people she could talk to and confide in, especially when it came to Damian's Stars withdrawals.

She spoke about it with Gertrude one afternoon after hours of training, when they were in the cafeteria drinking nutritional blends made especially for Enhanced. Sage gagged because it tasted like cardboard. Nutriblend was the worst drink she had ever had.

"The withdrawals would be natural, wouldn't they?" Blondie said. "After overdosing on Stars?"

"I know a few Enhanced who've died from it," Mohawk said, arms crossed. "It's no joke. At the very least, we took care of those Jackals."

Little did they know, the Private Guard was very much alive. Only the PG wasn't dumb enough to attack the rebels because they'd lose. Thanks to Nova, Mousafeld held all of Winterfeld's resources, particularly their weapons with all the laced Slainium. Those were undergoing distribution now, making the camp's confidence swell. At last, they were on even fighting ground with Sage and stood a chance against Diamond City, who was sure to make a move soon. In the meantime, Sage focused on Damian, who could very well lose his life to Stars poisoning.

Sage saw it every time she was with him, how he flew to the bathroom at random moments to throw up. It happened again now.

Sage was there to hold his hair, wipe his mouth, and ensure he didn't hit the floor if he passed out. It concerned her because he didn't seem to be showing any improvement. Sometimes it looked like he was getting worse.

"Damn," Damian grunted as Sage helped him into a chair in front of the fireplace. His chest heaved with every breath, as if he couldn't inhale enough oxygen into his lungs.

"Here." Sage offered him a water bottle.

"Withdrawals," Damian said dismally, eyes closed. "They're no joke. I crave Stars so badly that sometimes I think I'm losing my mind."

"You'll get better once your body adapts to not having it. You grew dependent on it, but you can also grow independent of it as well. It just takes time."

"I know." Damian rubbed his temple. "But in the meanwhile . . . I'm so fatigued. Everything I eat, I throw up. When I try to sleep, I'm so fucking paranoid that I can't close my eyes for two damn seconds without thinking someone's going to kill me. I sleep at the clinic every night, but even then . . . " He sighed. "I don't feel safe."

Sage already knew why. Damian had never gotten over Ileana's betrayal and he wouldn't anytime soon. She didn't blame him for that, but she did wish he could rest. When he wasn't worrying about assailants in the middle of the night, he was thinking of their upcoming campaign tomorrow.

They were traveling to Wolfeld. It entailed more than just persuading exiled Enhanced to join them—they were warding off an attack by the Diamond City military and had their eye on an Enhanced named August Vaughan. Damian's goal was to save August from capture, unless there was resistance.

"Sage," Damian said after some silence, the fire cackling loudly. "I'm worried."

"That's obvious." Sage pressed some ice to his forehead. She sat on the armrest next to him. "Why wouldn't you be worried?"

"No. I'm worried about you."

"Don't," she assured him. "I'm the last one you need to be worried about."

"Such confidence. Who taught you how to fight?"

"A close friend of mine. His name's Samson, and he's been a part of my family for a while."

"I see. Was he in the Unification War as well?"

"He doesn't like to fight in wars. He just knows how."

"Is this Samson still around?" Damian asked, drinking some more water. "I'd like to meet him."

"He's ..." Sage hesitated. "Shy."

He was also a killer handyman. With Louis as his helper, he had renovated their entire living space to make it look like a luxury apartment. He couldn't go shopping in public, so he sent Sage and Louis out to the Marketplace to buy the nicest everything in Mousafeld, from couches to glass tables to lamps to silverware. Of course, all of that came with a price, but Sage earned enough money for her services to afford it. Samson managed every Diamond.

"There is nothing to be shy about," Damian said. "Neither me nor my people will hurt him. We would love a few pointers. You are an amazing warrior. I'll never forget what you did at Winterfeld—you decimated those androids."

"Wasn't that my mission?"

"Indeed." Damian touched her cheek. His thumb glided over her skin. "I wanted to tell you something ... about this campaign." He hesitated now. "It's my brother. He'll be there ... leading the attack on Diamond City's behalf. He's the commander, has been for many decades."

Sage froze. "Wait a second ... Diamond City's commander is your *brother*?"

Blackburn? What the hell? But now that Sage thought about it, and now that she was looking right at Damian's face, she saw the resemblance instantly. It was so quick that it was like a spark, jolting her from the inside, throwing her back to that horrible night she had gone to dinner with him.

That's right . . .

Blackburn had said it.

"Your brother?"

"Yes. He was one of the many fools who fled Diamond City as an exile because he didn't want to remain loyal to the Allseer. He wanted more power, so he set out on his own endeavors, betraying us and everything this city stood for. He uses people, then breaks them, very much the same thing he does to his family."

"Wait—so you're Damian Blackburn?"

Damian snorted. "I don't go by my treacherous family name. I adopted 'Damaris' when I married Ileana. I definitely didn't want any of my children burdened with a rotten legacy."

And for good reason. Sage told Damian about the date, and he guffawed.

"What?"

"He's a perverted son of a bitch." Sage scowled. "So I stabbed him."

"Oh, shit!" Damian turned red from laughing. "That bastard had it coming to him! If only I had been there to see it. My brother is the most entitled person on the planet—he thinks he can manipulate everyone and everything."

"But didn't he criticize you for doing the same?"

"He did. But he is and always has been the Allseer's puppet, handing over his will as if it were a bargaining chip, all to keep his power." Damian snorted again. "Pathetic."

"Do you feel uncomfortable confronting him?"

"I'm trying to keep my head straight. If I see his face, it might move me to anger. But if I can't finish the job, I need you to step in."

"So you want me to kill him?"

Damian rested his head on her shoulder. "Capture him," he said finally. "Chances are he'll be waiting for me once we land. I've assembled two units: I will be in the first, entering Wolfeld as planned. I'm anticipating that my brother's forces will be waiting to strike me down. I may or may not be successful in holding him off, and that's when you come in. I don't think it matters if he's expecting you or not."

Sage drew his hair from his face. The tie was messy, so she undid the ponytail and combed through his strands. "Will you let me braid your hair?" she asked.

"Absolutely."

Just one braid. She did it in the inside so it wasn't easily noticeable. She thought it was a nice touch.

"Does it make me look less manly?" Damian asked.

"No way." Sage rubbed her cheek against his head.

"My one and true fear." Damian chuckled. "How else am I supposed to impress you?"

Damian was impressive regardless, but Sage wasn't going to admit that out loud. She smiled to herself instead.

Damian touched her cheek. "Stay with me tonight?"

"Shouldn't you rest? You look like hell."

"I'm sure a night with you will make me feel a lot better."

Sage climbed on top of him, straddling his hips.

Damian held her waist. "I want to make love to you." His voice turned thick. "I want to touch every inch of your body, and then I want to thrust deep into you. I want to know what it feels like inside you."

"What did I say about being explicit?"

"I'm being honest," Damian said hoarsely, longingly. "That's what I spend a lot of time thinking about."

"What my vagina feels like?"

"Among other things, of course."

Sage glared at him. "There's more to a relationship than just sex, Damian."

"I know." Damian slipped his hands into her shirt. He kneaded her ribs with his thumbs, then felt the plane of her abdomen with his palms. His skin was so warm despite how cold his rings were. He traced the ridges of her muscles. "You know I'm just trying to turn you on."

"You're going to have to try harder than that."

"Then tell me what to do," Damian said innocently. He dragged her hips up against his crotch. "I already got rid of the heads like you wanted me to."

That was true. Damian had moved each one to the museum, so the common room looked much more presentable. There were paintings in their stead, of happy things. Sage was proud of him, and she supposed she could reward him, but then she remembered something.

"I'm watching a movie with Gertrude tonight," she said.

"Ah, right. Because she's more important than I am?"

"Are you jealous?" Sage teased.

"Very," Damian admitted. "I want you to spend some time with me."

"I'm in here every day."

"Hump me."

Sage laughed. She slumped forward onto his chest in her fit of giggles. "No, Damian. No humping."

"I know you want me," Damian said, chuckling, too. "Would you like me to prove it?"

Sage smiled against his chest. "Nice try, but no. You'll have to find another way."

"Unfortunately, my camp only has access to so much Defenders Unite! merchandise."

"I don't need toys to turn me on."

"Then tell me what holds you back." Damian stroked her hair. It was always in a braid, and it didn't look anywhere near as nice as Damian's.

Sage sighed. She clutched his shirt. "I just think there's too much going on right now. I'm anxious and so very uncertain about my future. To this day, I don't know if what you feel toward me is lust or love. You barely know me, Damian."

"Give me a chance."

"I am." Sage listened for his heartbeat again. There was none.

Damian tilted her chin, finding her eyes. "Kiss me."

Sage did. Without any hesitation. Her feelings for him strengthened with every day that passed, and it was dangerous. The closer she grew to him, the more possessive and loyal she became. But maybe that's what Damian wanted and needed. Despite all the

Enhanced surrounding him, he didn't have that one person he could trust...

Or the one he could use as weapon, said a voice in her head.

No way. Damian wasn't manipulating her. This affection couldn't be fake, not with the way he kissed her, with a fervor Sage's ex could never match. He even asked her if she was sure she wanted to go with him tomorrow.

"Of course, Damian," Sage said gently. "I'm with you on this." She petted his head, then played with his hair. They kissed one more time before parting ways. The pained look on his face made Sage swell with sympathy. She hated to let him go, but he wouldn't be able to rest if she stayed. Separation was for the best.

"Please...do right by the Warlord," Cushion said to Sage, offering her her coat on the way out of the compound. Damian withdrew to his study, at the table now for another designing session.

"I'm trying," Sage said.

"That boy has been through so much in his lifetime, so much heartache. Life is cruel, but it has been especially cruel to him." Cushion shook her head. "Treacherous family members, traitorous love interests...I don't know how he's still sane. Even without a heart, he keeps himself together." She wiped her eyes. Was she crying? "All I want...is to see him happy. What more can a mother ask for?"

Sage's eyes widened. She couldn't believe that this cute little old lady she saw and greeted every day was the Warlord's *mother.* Why the hell hadn't Damian told her anything?

"I'm here for him," Cushion said earnestly. "And I want you to be, too. He loves you so very much."

"How do you know that?"

"His fashion. He has passion for it again. When he asks me to model, I know I'm catching glimpses of my son." Cushion's eyes welled with more tears. "My beautiful little boy. And when he plans to dress up his entire camp? Well...you know he's happy. Don't tell him I told you that, though—it's a surprise."

"I'm sorry to disappoint," Sage said quietly. "But he was already doing that before I got here. He dressed up his whole army for the Allseer's challenge. That was way before he met me. What I'm trying to say is: he doesn't need me to be happy."

Cushion smiled wryly. "A mother knows. He is different. I don't know what it is about you, but you seem like an honest, strong girl. Please . . . take care of him tomorrow. He can't fight, much less against Blackburn. I only ask that you don't kill him."

Her firstborn. Right.

Sage nodded. Then, with her mind reeling, she left the compound.

Talk about a dysfunctional family.

"SAGE!"

Gertrude jumped out of nowhere and clambered onto Sage's back. She was awfully giddy and she smelled like alcohol. She must have been out drinking with Blondie and Mohawk, gossiping about the fates of Turtle, Eye Candy, and Rockstar. The last two hadn't been seen in months, and the first, well, he was nicer to people for some reason. Now it was time to dig up truths from Sage, and Gertrude already knew a few.

"Where have you been?"

"What?" Sage said.

"You know 'what'—everyone's been talking about it! So you *are* with the Warlord!"

Sage allowed herself a small smile. "Maybe I have fallen for his charm a bit, but swear not to tell."

"Promise!" she said a little bit too happily.

That promise didn't mean anything when people were already noticing there was a new couple on campus. Mega Woman, for example, didn't approve of Sage's one-on-one time with the Warlord at all. Either she had forgotten that Sage had defeated an army of androids by herself, or she didn't give a damn because she stalked right up to her before boarding for their mission the next morning and swung a fist at her face. Sage was always in the back of the line, isolated, so no one noticed the attack. There really wasn't anything to watch because it happened so quickly: Sage dodged, swept Mega

Woman right off her feet, and pressed the tip of her blade to her throat.

"You *bitch*!" Mega Woman huffed from the ground. "You were the one who tried to kill him! I don't believe for one instant that you have his best interests at heart!"

When the Enhanced started to whisper and point, Damian noticed and rushed over to them. He got Sage to back down, then helped a furious Mega Woman to her feet.

"What is the meaning of this?!" Damian exclaimed.

"I don't trust her," Mega Woman spat, eyes spewing fire. "I want her gone!"

"Gone? She is in charge of the second unit, which is responsible for following up on the first. With her on your side, you stand the best chance of a successful counterattack."

"What the hell do you see in her? She is nothing but a brain-washed warrior who can't be trusted."

"*I* trust her," Damian said strictly, grabbing Mega Woman's arm. He glared her down like he would a prey, daring her to challenge him on his judgment. So far, he had never let them down, so there wasn't a negative track record to use against him. That left Mega Woman hyperventilating in his face with the occasional evil eye to Sage. "Now will you stand down and work together?"

"Fine," Mega Woman breathed. "But I give the orders and if she breaks them, her life is at stake."

"Sage knows what to do."

"*I* am in charge, Damian!"

The rebels froze. The runway had never been this quiet before, not with so many people in one cluster. Speaking Damian's name was like uttering the foulest word in the dictionary, and only Mega Woman had the balls to do it.

"*I* tell her what to do!" Mega Woman repeated firmly. "Or I end her. We can't afford puppets or traitors."

Why didn't Damian say anything against that? He kept quiet, turned around, and stalked off to join the first group ready to take off to Wolfeld. Either he was too tired to argue or he just didn't see the point. He had to focus his energy on their upcoming mission.

Sage stood back as Damian's ship took off and left them far behind. They had to wait exactly an hour before they could follow. Sage was glad that she could hide in the farthest recesses of the cabin, far from Mega Woman. She stuck to Gertrude, who didn't speak until they were strapped in and ready to go.

"Don't listen to her," Gertrude whispered. "She's very jealous . . . as you can see. The entire force knows she's been after the Warlord for years, helped him escape from Diamond City. She feels that he owes her something."

"I thought they were a couple," Blondie said, voice low. "I mean, Mega Woman is always bragging about those blowjobs."

Gertrude had mentioned that once, too, and Sage would rather not be reminded. Unfortunately, her silence and discomfort didn't discourage them from discussing these rumors further. Sage ignored them because Damian hadn't had another lover since Ileana's betrayal, and if he had been married to her for a number of years, then the blowjobs were from ages ago. Or this could be Mega Woman spreading gossip for the sake of looking good, which Sage had no intention of entertaining.

"Who cares what sort of wet dreams Mega Woman has," Gertrude said a bit too loudly; some rebels turned their heads. "The truth is Sage and the Warlord are together."

Blondie gasped as Sage kicked Gertrude in the ankle. "For real?"

"No," Sage said at once. "I just help him out with his withdrawal symptoms. It doesn't mean anything."

Yeah, right. The entire crew already knew that was bullshit, and judging by the looks on their faces, they were outraged. Turtle and Little Man, both of who were sitting across from her, glared at her as if she were a murderer. Turtle never forgot their scuffle at the carnival grounds and Little Man wanted to prove that he was stronger than the new woman in town. Above all, they hated the idea of said woman manipulating their leader.

"Whatever," Gertrude said. "Bitches will be bitches. Anyway, am I the only one who's a tad bit nervous around here?"

No. The closer they got to Wolfeld, the more jittery Sage grew, too. They arrived within ten miles of the town just as they had planned. They set up camp in the woods, with portable, full-fledged housing units courtesy of Winterfeld. They came in crates that opened up into mini hotel rooms, equipped with their own furnishings and private bathroom. It was kind of incredible because the only outdoor adventure Sage had been on was in the Circular Forest with her sleeping bag, but she didn't stick around to admire convenience. From this area, Sage noticed as she wandered around the perimeter, they could detect any oncoming forces. Damian and his crew were just up ahead, probably already infiltrating the town. At least, that's what Sage hoped for. They had the Diamond City military to factor in, and the thought of Blackburn made her anxious.

So anxious that Sage took a seat on the snow. It helped with the shaking in her limbs because she didn't have to use that much energy to calm herself down. She wished she could be with Damian, but it was strategy over protection. They had to make Blackburn believe that Sage wasn't with them, that he had the upper hand, so the counterattack would work.

Daddy says the entire city is worried about you, had been Candice's letter to Sage some days ago. *They're growing bolder.*

That was true. The Diamond City military was panicking now that Sage wasn't holding their hand. Sage only knew this because of Candice—she flat out refused to speak with Bram. She was confident in the face of the military, especially with their new set of Slainium-laced weapons. What she grew the most troubled about were the Squids.

Three months later, and Samson was still reading through all of Preacher's texts. In those scriptures were tales of the Squids' very own metropolis somewhere far out in unreachable territory. Their mission when it came to humans was just as Sage had feared: toys, experiments, *opportunity.* Slainium was powerful against the Enhanced, and numbers were a huge advantage against the Squids, so what was the next best thing? Something in between—something that could blend in with the human population easily . . .

"Enhanced of their own, then?" Louis said. "Maybe they came up with a different breed."

"There are only so many ways to shape a human," Samson said with half a snort. He glanced at Sage. "Besides, Enhanced are like toys, so easily contained. They need something . . . stronger."

Sage clutched her knees. Those missing girls from Winterfeld weren't a coincidence. The Squids knew exactly what to do with them.

"It'd be best not to get involved, right?" Louis said. "I mean, keep away from them. What business do we have with the Lolligo anyway?"

"The Enhanced, idiot!" Samson exclaimed. "Where do you think they came from? We have everything to do with them, and this is not counting my interest in actually meeting them! You don't honestly think they'll stay away forever, do you?"

"Well, we have even more Enhanced now. As strong as the Lolligo are, do they actually have the means of toppling us? Where were they during the Unification War if they're so high and mighty?"

Samson didn't have the answer to that. Neither did Sage.

Sage gazed at the bracelets around her wrist. She felt the heaviness of the metal but never the stinging, not on her skin or beneath it. True, she had Cells just like an Enhanced did . . . but she wasn't an Enhanced. She was a hybrid, trained—a warrior—with her share of advantageous immunities. That's what made her so valuable. Squids were huge and conspicuous, but Sage? She was just right. She had defeated humans and led a bunch of Enhanced during the Unification War. She was the perfect weapon . . . What wouldn't the Squids give to have someone like her . . .

"We can't get into contact with him," Turtle was saying to Mega Woman out of earshot of everyone else. Sage could hear them, though, and she lifted her head. "Is there something going on over there?"

Bad reception was too good to be true. Mega Woman tried to play it off, but it was possible that Damian had already been

attacked. With no confirmation of his safety since their first inter-
action with him just an hour ago, they had to move into phase two.

"All right," Mega Woman called them around. "Let's get ready—"

"SAGE!" Gertrude cried, taking off after Sage just as an explosion shook the area.

Sage flew through the woods and right into the clearing, entering what looked like the last skirmishes of a brutal struggle. From
miles away, Sage spotted the rebels across the field, all overwhelmed
by the multitude of troops and vast airships that Diamond City had
deployed. Sage recognized the crest across those steel frames, exactly like the one on her biceps, so there were no doubts about who
was leading this attack. That spear through the diamond was supposed to symbolize unity, but these barbarians weren't thinking of
peace. Wiping out Wolfeld was so worth it if they were killing the
Warlord as an added bonus: they had him chained up like an animal, shirt off, with decorative bruises all over his body. Blood trickled down his face, one of his eyes swollen shut. All his glamor and
shine were gone, leaving a beaten, broken man on the ground. The
troops restraining him kicked and spat at him, laughing, "Come on,
you faggot! Get up and stab us now!"

The sight tore Sage up from the inside. It threw her into a
frenzy in which her entire being grew numb to emotion and pain,
thoughts filled with blood and violence. Her conscious and re-
morse faded away to nothingness as survival instincts took over
and adrenaline pounded through her veins.

She pulled a dagger from her belt—that was all she needed.
With that small blade alone, she was able to deflect bullets, parry
swords, and stab enemies. Past allies were now her enemies, ones
she knew how to maneuver like the back of her hand. All soldiers
were trained to fire, dodge, then use close combat as a last resort
while nearby numbers moved in. Against Sage, they weren't fast
enough to do any of that.

"S-Sage!" Damian choked on his blood as Sage shot down each
of his captors with her gun. He stumbled forward, exposing his
wrists, which Sage freed with another bullet.

                                    DIAMOND CITY

Stopping to make sure he was safe was Sage's grand mistake. As soon as she had Damian on his feet, she had a gun to the back of her head.

"Don't move."

Her surroundings slowed down a little, adrenaline giving way to reason. She already knew that a bullet to the head would incapacitate her and endanger Damian, so she could either duck quickly or do as she was told. The latter was out of the question because she wasn't going to become someone else's hostage.

Her movements were so quick that they caught her captor off guard. She got a bullet in the back, but she preferred that over one to her head. When she whipped around to disarm her enemy, she hesitated because the person aiming the gun at her looked just like Damian.

Maybe at first, but a closer look told Sage there were significant differences. Blackburn was taller and much more menacing despite the lack of scars on his face. His perfect features didn't fool Sage anymore. For someone who criticized his younger brother for violence, he reminded Sage of a crow.

"Sage?" Blackburn whispered, eyes widening in shock. He knew damn well what Sage was, and in his eyes, she was no longer a shy girl looking for a way into the prince's bed—she was a weapon that had gotten away from them.

"I'm not sure it's nice to see you again," Sage said. "The first time, you wanted to rape me. This time, are you going to admit I was an item to be purchased? How much money did the Allseer pay Bram?"

Blackburn shook his head. Even so, he never dropped his guard and his eyes never so much as flickered from hers—not for a moment. Explosions continued across the battlefield, but Sage wasn't aware of who was in the line of fire. She trusted the rebels knew what they were doing. Her priority was taking out this son of a bitch. "It isn't anything like that," he had the gall to say. "We weren't purchasing *you* for money, only your services."

Sage flashed forward with her dagger and slashed Blackburn's face. Blackburn retaliated, but Sage deflected his strike; with momentum in her favor, she was going to win that scuffle, so Blackburn took a step back before they clashed again. He used that break to regain his composure, stalling with words as his troops quickly gathered around them.

"Quite outstanding," Blackburn muttered, wiping blood from his face. That was Slainium traveling through his veins now. He was a skilled warrior, but it was nowhere near enough to dent Sage. The only other leverage in sight was Damian, who was struggling to stay on his feet; he sank back to his knees again, coughing up blood. "It looks like the rumors are true … You *are* powerful. We could have definitely used you in our ranks, and you still have that chance. My worthless brother's ideas of domination will only end in more heartache. Bringing those exiled Enhanced back to Diamond City is a mistake—it's like letting delinquents back into a palace."

"Depends on your definition of delinquent," Sage spat. "Do you know what's a mistake? You. Your entire regime that treats people like puppets."

"And what do you think my dear brother does with you?" Blackburn sneered. "I'm sure he must have jumped at the idea of having you join the rebels, with all your sweet potential and all. What I don't understand is why you've allowed him to exploit you. We were so sure that Louis and Agathe were in your best interests, but I think I see what's going on here." He smiled cruelly. "He's making you believe that he loves you, right? My brother is so very charming. It's how he's managed to win over all his partners in life. It started with that worthless boy who spawned ideas of resistance in his head. Soon after the Unification War, he left him to seduce David, another 'love interest' who gained him favor with the Allseer. Then there was Ileana, another 'love interest' who served to bear him a daughter. But since when does Damian care about being a father? I think he just got tired of penises."

Sage struck again, landing another slash on Blackburn's face.

"What is it with you and my face, girl?!" he yelled angrily, touching the blood. His veins around the wound were already turning black, but it didn't give Sage anywhere near the satisfaction she craved.

"You're such a fucking hypocrite," Sage spat. "You accuse your brother of manipulation, but look at what you do. I'm sure you rejoiced when Damian became the outcast of the family because that meant you took the pedestal. Then you conspired with David to betray him and promote yourself to commander of the military."

"I sound so terrible, don't I? What you don't see is that my brother is just as bad as me, and maybe even worse because he went against the Allseer's wishes. The Allseer is what kept our city together, one that my foolish brother was trying to dismantle with his ideas of power." Blackburn attacked, but he didn't have a whole lot of energy left. He tied with Sage, then took a step back. "What do you think he wanted for himself? The Optimum—the warrior who led us all to victory in the Unification War! That was the sort of information he was gathering from David while they were sucking each other's dicks at night!"

"Sage," Damian choked. He finally found his footing and grasped Sage's arm. He made her look at him. "Please get out of here."

Sage touched Damian's cheek briefly, indicating that she needed to take care of this. There was no other way to ensure his safety, so he could escape and find a place to recover. His wounds weren't healing at all, and that worried her, but at least he was conscious.

"He criticizes the Allseer, but he's a traitor himself," Blackburn spat. "Betraying Enhanced, even ones who joined his cause long ago. Let's not forget he still takes pleasure in killing them, too. Is that truly the man you're going to stick out your neck for?"

Sage turned to Blackburn. "I love how men think that women are so naive. As if I'd follow him around like a lost puppy because I want to feel loved and kept warm at night. I know exactly who I'm dealing with, and Agathe made it very clear to me."

"I am sorry that you feel so betrayed, but why don't you come with me, Sage, so I can clarify this?"

"Fuck you."

Every soldier standing around her opened fire. Sage dodged the blasts, then knocked them unconscious or dead until it was only Blackburn who engaged her again, struggling to keep his sword up. He must have been hoping she'd fatigue by now, but something even better happened: more troops stormed into the clearing, overpowering Damian, who was so banged up, he couldn't defend himself. The Cells in his body weren't doing anything for him. Sage stopped to keep her eye on him as Blackburn continued his taunts.

"Don't you want to see Bram, your fifth generation nephew?" he panted, three ugly slashes across his chest. Those were strikes he had barely dodged, and the slip-up was costing him quite a bit. The Slainium was all over now, weaving through his body like a sewing needle. "To tell him how you really feel?"

"You don't even know the least of it." Sage pointed her dagger at his face. "Now let Damian go, and I might think about sparing your life."

Indeed, Blackburn was at a stalemate here. Fahrenheit and Celsius soon made it to the scene, followed by the rest of the rebels, who had been fighting out in the distance, and formed their own circle around the Warlord and Blackburn's last line of troops. This was going to get messy, but Blackburn was no fool. He was just as adept at making the right choice to spare as many of his troops' lives as possible as he was with his sword. He called them back, wary of Sage and the rebels, and escaped with his life. It was better to live today and fight tomorrow.

"DAMIAN!" Mega Woman cried, rushing to his side. "Oh, God, what the hell happened to you?!"

Damian was beat up pretty badly. There were some abrasions on his torso that indicated fractures and internal bleeding. Mega Woman wanted to take a closer look, but Damian turned from her. He had no such success with the rest of his rebels, who moved in to evaluate him,. They overpowered him, laid him on the ground, and mended his most worrisome gashes.

"Sage!" Gertrude made it to her at last. She was panting, blood smeared all over her body. The rebels had been through their share of hell today—the Diamond City soldiers were no joke. But their situation was about to get a lot worse because another force entered the fray.

This one didn't harness weapons or brute strength. It was an explosive power that flew at them from across the field, invisible to the naked eye. Maybe a few rebels noticed it, but there was nothing they could do to stop it. Sage was the one who caught it with her bare hands.

The rebels were stupefied. They didn't understand what was going on because they had never seen a power like that before—it showed on their faces. Like zombies, they watched Sage throw the unseeable energy right back at its deliverer as if she had caught a ball. Everyone looked across the field and found the lone figure standing in the distance.

Chubby and a bit out of shape didn't accurately describe this Enhanced. Looks were so deceiving. After a display of skill like that, no one judged him by how round his gut was. Sage, unfortunately, was at the end of her rope: her form drooped a bit and her breaths got tight. She was trained not to falter before the enemy, so she kept it together, but that didn't mean it was easy. She kept her place between that overweight Enhanced and her comrades.

"Star!" clapped the Enhanced from so far away. "Thank the heavens! It's you, girl!"

The rebels froze in place. Sage kept a frown on her face.

"Come!" called the Enhanced, waving her forward. "Come! Enough fighting! You already took out an army! Was that Slainium in those weapons?"

"Sage?" Gertrude croaked, getting closer to her, still confused by all of this. Sage was sheathing her dagger as if she were done fighting.

Sage looked at Gertrude. Then she turned to Damian, who was back on his feet.

"No," Damian stated. Despite his ugly injuries, adrenaline kept him focused on her. "No, Sage, you're not going anywhere with him."

"Wait a second," Celsius breathed. "Is that August?"

"It is," Sage said softly. "I must go."

Damian grabbed her—roughly—and yanked her back. His brows were drawn, veins popping out of his forehead. "No," he said again. "Absolutely not. We are too weak to continue with this mission."

Sage touched his hand, wrapping her fingers around it. She gazed into his eyes earnestly and said, "There's a lot I haven't told you. There's no time for it right now. I have to go . . . but I'll be back."

"Sage—"

"Do you trust me?"

"*Trust?*" Mega Woman spat, coming to life at last. She was as furious as all the rebels who were starting to feel betrayed, but it's not like Sage owed them any explanations—all she owed them was her fighting and loyalty as promised.

"I know what I have to do," Sage said steadily, ignoring Mega Woman. "I know how to get August to come to our side. Please trust me on this, Damian."

Damian waved at Gertrude. "Go with her. I don't want her alone."

Gertrude gulped, but she didn't hesitate. She was ready to follow orders with a determined look on her face. Sage didn't protest Gertrude's involvement because maybe it would be a good idea to have a witness. But Damian wasn't doing this for tactics—he was doing this for insurance of Sage's safety and return.

"Come back to me," Damian whispered to Sage.

"I will," Sage said. She kissed his hand before letting it go.

With one final look at Damian, she turned and faced August. She had a field and a litter of bodies to cross, but nothing stopped her from carrying on.

"I'll be waiting for you, Sage," Damian said.

It wasn't a hope . . . it was a command. Or else Damian would come for her.

CHAPTER 15

Cell Extraction

"S-Sage." Gertrude was brave enough to interrupt the silence to ask a simple question. "What's going on?"

"I have to speak with August," Sage replied softly, trudging across the field.

"B-but wait—you know him?"

Almost all the Enhanced knew each other in some way ... but some of Sage's relationships were personal. This was one of them. It was a very long story, and Sage wasn't up to talking about it right now. As adrenaline died away, her body grew sluggish. But she couldn't afford to drop her defenses because she anticipated a struggle. August was eccentric and a bit unpredictable, angry like the rest of the Enhanced who had lost the rebellion, and Sage didn't know how he was going to act when she got closer. She told Gertrude to stay back and drew her dagger again, pointing it at August's face.

August raised his hands, laughing heartily. "Really, girl? Is that how you treat me after all these years?"

"The number of years since I've seen you last doesn't change the hell you put me through in Diamond City."

August shook his head with a *tsk, tsk.* He turned to the wary

Gertrude and said, "We threw parties in her name. She was our Optimum, our very own Star Raider."

"I am not an Optimum," Sage said to Gertrude quickly. "They're just fascinated by my fighting skills. I didn't have a choice—I had to fight to survive."

Gertrude already knew this, but it didn't stop her awe from settling in. Maybe it was different hearing it from an Enhanced who had known Sage from the very start of her fighting career. Nearly all of the Enhanced who had fought in the rebellion had heard of the Optimum's greatness, but so few had actually *seen* her. It was mind-boggling.

"You have to admit it is something to revere," August said to Sage. "You practically dismantled each of the four districts' military force single-handedly." He took a glance at all the bodies strewn across the field. "Then again, Star isn't an Enhanced. She's a hybrid between a Squid and a human."

"It's cold out here," Sage said.

August chuckled. He waved her forward. "Come on then."

"How do I know you won't try to kill me?"

"Didn't Gavin already try that? And look what happened to the poor fool."

"So you just want to talk all of a sudden?"

"Isn't that the reason you're here? I'm willing to listen." August turned around and continued toward Wolfeld, where a line of troops led by a couple of Enhanced stood waiting for commands.

Before making the trek, Sage took one last look at Damian. He was standing in the front lines of his own fighters, watching Sage like a hawk. His eyes flashed with intensity and fear, as if he were never going to see her again. He didn't care about taking over Wolfeld—he just wanted her in his protective bubble. Sage appreciated that, making her love for him swell. She showed him with her eyes. She wanted to say it out loud, but she didn't.

Then Sage had to break away and follow August into Wolfeld. She and Gertrude were welcomed among these people's ranks without conflict. Sage took a look around at the faces, some of them drawn in suspicion of who she might be. She didn't recognize any-one, not even the Enhanced sprinkled throughout the crowd.

"Please," August said, waving away his guards. "Let us pass. I think we're secure for right now, although I would make sure the rebels out there don't get any closer."

Damian wasn't going to fight, Sage reassured herself. He was no idiot, retreating when it was necessary. Sage could rest easy. Her focus shifted to surviving her confrontation with August, who en-tered town as if he were in a parade. He strutted right down the street, past businesses where a lot of people were holed up due to the fighting so close to home.

Like Winterfeld, most of the citizens here were humans who felt comfortable being ruled by an all-powerful Enhanced. They must have liked the protection and security that came with some-one who was that capable. Their weaponry consisted of guns that could detect and latch onto moving targets. For everyday life, they enjoyed hover cars and clean-up bots, but the most striking piece of technology was the force field that controlled the elements. Sage noticed it as soon as she looked up at the sky: just minutes ago, it had been gray and cold with snow floating down. Now, it was bright and sunny as if they were in the middle of spring. The Roar-ing Mountains didn't allow a lot of reprieve from the cold, so this technology made farming and outdoor sports possible. There was an upcoming fastball game this weekend at the Off-Center Arena. It was the Wolves versus the Suns, a team from a town called Sunfeld. Sage wondered if she could build a team in Mousafeld . . .

In the middle of all this was a one-hundred-story tower. Sage had to crane her head to see the very top, overwhelmed by how im-posing it was. At the same time, it was fitting for someone like Au-gust. He probably didn't come down from there often. Sage wasn't the only one recruiting him to start another rebellion against Dia-mond City.

"Let's talk more in my office," August said.

Inside the tower, they took the elevator to the hundredth floor. Because the walls were all glass, Sage got to see a lot of the building's interior on the way, the many offices, swathes of people, and life-sized robots that served as maids. Aesthetics were impressive, but Sage paid particular attention to the work ethic, the drive people had as they zipped through hallways.

"It's all about innovation," August stated, picking at his teeth. "Even all the way out here, so far from home, I never lose sight of that."

Gertrude shot Sage a concerned look. Her priority wasn't how innovative the Enhanced were and how their technology surpassed even that of Diamond City's—she was thinking survival. They were headed to the top with a one-hundred-story drop for an emergency exit. Sage was confident they wouldn't have to resort to such extreme measures now—she sensed that August wasn't here to hurt them. Not anymore.

In fact, the more he walked, the wearier he appeared. It looked like he was a bit drunk, semi-limping down the hallway. He held open the door to his office, head inclined, and trudged in after them.

Sage and Gertrude didn't make any moves to sit down just yet. They took a glance at every corner of the room and confirmed there weren't any immediate threats nearby. The office was accommodating enough with a full set of furniture, pillows, and tables. There was a bowl of some sort of candy on one—Icy Mints—and a few books about physiology on another. More of those kinds were stacked on the shelves that lined the walls, as if August had been doing nothing but reading about different ways to use his skills as an Enhanced. Sage glimpsed some of the titles—*Immortals: is That What We Are?* and *The Limitations of an Enhanced*—but now wasn't the time to ask August about his interests.

"Please," he said politely, waving at his couch. "Why don't you have a seat?"

Sage got a good look at his face. His eyes were squinting because his cheeks were round and huge, but it wasn't because he was fat. August was puffy, as if he were undergoing an allergic reaction to something. Beads of sweat trailed down his temple.

Even Gertrude couldn't help herself. "Are you . . . all right?"

"Oh." He waved her off. "Yes." He opened a drawer and pulled out a syringe. The reddish liquid screamed Stars, making Sage tense with the unpleasant memories of a comatose Damian over his table. August didn't look too keen about shooting himself up in front of them, but this wasn't by choice—this was a necessity, or else he'd die, suffer those horrible withdrawals like Damian, who was skating on thin ice. He gave a harsh little wheeze, frustration evident as he shot the substance right into his vein.

"After a while," he whispered, head down, "it just doesn't do much . . . does it?" He caught Sage's eyes. "What a horrible thing. And here we thought we were truly immortal . . . but it seems we have a weakness."

"Did you purchase it from the Jackals?" Sage asked.

August nodded. "I did. Although I got a bit more than I bargained for. Are you ashamed of me, Star?"

"No," Sage admitted. "The Warlord went through much of the same, but he quit. Maybe you can, too."

August chuckled, shaking his head. The poor man seemed to be getting bigger and bigger by the minute, as if his cells were swelling and about ready to burst right out of him. Wasn't that exactly what was happening?

"Always the optimistic one," he mused. "I remember those days . . . You were just a girl with no experience on the battlefield. Yet, you always won. We came to depend on you because we had no one else if we wanted to oust all those tyrants in our city." August looked at Gertrude, who was like a child in his eyes because she was so young and inexperienced. "They probably don't teach this much in the districts anymore, but the Overseers were no saints. In the Cut District, for example, they exploited people like you wouldn't believe, all to control them like cattle. Everything from their diets to their vaccines, just to *see what happened*, to see what the Overseer could get away with. The saddest part? The people didn't even know it." August sighed. "I know . . . as well as Star . . . because that's where we were born and raised.

"My mother had myocarditis. It was especially bad when she

hit her fifties, and to this day I don't know if it was because of those fucking doctors or the actual medication itself. Perhaps a bit of both. The antiarrhythmic drugs weren't doing shit for her—they were killing her. It was all one big experiment for Overseer Callus, who was funding all kinds of research on his own people. He viewed us like his very own lab rats, never letting us leave our district in fear we'd become 'contaminated.' We were all pawns in his schemes . . . except for Star, of course."

August beamed with pride. His cheeks were as radiant as the sun.

"Overseer Callus had no damn clue there was a Squid hybrid in our ranks. It was all thanks to the *Pugnator*, her father, who had had a kid in private. He loved her mother so much—"

"August," Sage said quietly. "Please stop."

August held up a hand. "Forgive me. But if it wasn't for him, we would have been stuck in that hellhole. We wouldn't have had *you*, Star, to help us fight. Yes, your father disappeared afterward and you went through hardships, but he was a *Squid*. If the other Squids had found out about you, they would have taken you away. You know that."

Tears formed in Gertrude's eyes. Both fists were clenched at her sides, shaking with the strain of keeping her emotions in check. This had been such a long damn day that she couldn't take any more surprises. Hearing about Sage's father, a Squid, overwhelmed her like a wave, but she held it together impressively well. That's what she was trained to do. It didn't matter that the Squid had had a child who had become her best friend the past three months. She had to sit there and listen.

"Star and I fought to make a difference," August went on. "We became lovers in school, swore to always protect each other. We plotted the Overseer's demise, and so we joined the resistance. Or, rather, I did because I was human. Star, on the other hand, didn't need to become an Enhanced. I fed her all of the resistance's battle tactics, where we'd be striking and when, and Star was always there to guide us." He took a deep breath in and out. His eyes swam with the glorious victories of those days. Ones he would never see again.

"We fought to make a difference, and while we did, I was foolish enough to try to overpower the Allseer when he wanted to implement that same control over the entire city. Star refused to fight in any more battles at that point. She tried to convince me to let it go, but I couldn't. I went on to live in Heart, conspired with Damaris— the one you call the 'Warlord'—to overthrow the Allseer, but it didn't turn out too well, did it? I got kicked out and look where I am."

"The Warlord defeated the Allseer and wants to take Diamond City back now," Sage said. "So why don't you join us?"

August laughed a bit too abruptly. "Oh, my Star! If only it were that simple . . . You're not the first one to utter that phrase—'So why don't you join us?'—to me. Your sister was here, you know. And she wants the same thing."

Sage remained stoic. Gertrude stiffened at the mention of yet another revelation. Aurora was dead . . . so that meant this sister was *another* sister?

"That's impossible," Sage whispered. "My sister left the Clarity District with the Kilstrongs and never looked back. She's a part of their circle . . . has been for a long time."

"Joined, she did," August said pointedly. "But she's here, my Star. She wants cooperation, and her idea of it is not as noble as yours. I will gladly lay down my life to take Diamond City back, but your sister . . . well . . . she wants my Cells. And I . . . " His hands tightened around the armrests. "I'm not giving them to her."

" 'Cooperation'?" Sage said, breaths tight. "Exactly what does that mean? Cooperation for what?"

"She wants me to oblige with her requests, Star. I have no idea what her agenda is, but if she wants my Cells, then I wager everything I own that she's been traveling the Outskirts and taking back what she's given. As of right now, she's camping out at the Junkyard a few miles north of here, waiting for me."

Sage's heart started a fast beating. As soon as the words had left August's lips, she thought of the PG cases in which Enhanced had been found without Cells, slumped over, dead, in their own pool of drool and blood. But that couldn't have been her sister, could it? That had been the Cell Destroyer.

"I don't know what she intends," August said quietly, hands fidgeting on his lap, "but I am terrified. Not just of losing my Cells to her, but of what she's going to do with that power. If it's true that she was with the Kilstrongs, then I wonder if she is working on their behalf."

"My sister doesn't work on their behalf," Sage said confidently. "My sister is working independently."

"How do you know that for sure? You've never even spoken to her, have you? Well, either way, before she gets me, I have a few loose ends to tie up."

Then August did something unexpected. He called in the guards so they could be witnesses to his actions, so there'd be no doubts that Sage was innocent in this upcoming freak show. August drew what looked like some sort of asthma inhaler from his pocket, but it was nothing that simple. Uncapped, there was a large needle sticking out of it, meant for someone's vein. With a push of the button, this contraption extracted the Cells within an Enhanced's body.

Sage stared at it. Diamond City would *salivate* to acquire something like that. The PG cases suggested that someone was capable of it, with the way Enhanced were killed and left Cell-less, but then Sage concluded they had nothing to do with the Allseer... or the council. The council didn't know how to kill an Enhanced, but someone among them *did*. They didn't know who, so they were turning to August. Now Sage understood why Blackburn and the military had been here. August explained it further.

"I offered them this Extractor," he said, "which my scientists created. It was my ticket to Diamond City. Now that you've scared them away, I have nothing."

"That's not true," Sage said at once, a bit of panic blooming in her stomach. "I want to return to Diamond City, too."

"I understand, my Star. And I am honored that you would invite me, but my rejection has nothing to do with you. It's just..."

August exhaled loudly. Sweat rolled down his face in huge globs, as if he had just finished running a mile. Sage hated to see him like that, but she didn't get a chance to offer to take him to Dr. X—August's mind was already made up.

"I can't take it." August stabbed himself with the Extractor, making Gertrude scream. He pressed the button, and like a vacuum, it sucked all the Cells right out of his body. He then deflated like a balloon, shriveling up like a raisin right before Sage's eyes. The guards were too shocked to move, unable to do anything unless they were ordered. All they could do was watch as the last few Cells left August's body, leaving behind what was essentially a one-hundred-year-old human who shouldn't have been alive. With death around the corner, August had minutes to relay what was on his mind.

"Sage, I leave this burden to you," he drawled, slumping in his seat as the life quickly oozed out of him. "I leave Wolfeld in your command. Defend these people well. Your sister . . . is a monster."

And he died.

Gertrude couldn't stop screaming. The guards were in raw panic. The tension reached a fever pitch, the temperature skyrocketed, and Sage's surroundings spun uncontrollably. Gertrude couldn't take it anymore: she threw up on the floor. All Sage could see was August, his wasted body imprinted in her mind, the weight of his Cells in the Extractor growing heavier by the minute.

August was dead. And, in some way, Sage was, too.

CHAPTER 16

Close

Sage didn't move for a long time. Despite Gertrude's heaving noises and the guards' full-blown panic at their dead leader, she sat there like a zombie, body starting a massive tremble. At some point, she had to pull it together. She had to address a crying Gertrude and a wave of new guards that found the commotion. She did get to her feet, knees buckling, to face her company, who were now her allies.

"Please," Sage croaked, motioning at August. "Take him . . ."

The guards did just that. They tended to poor Gertrude, too. Sage took a few steps through August's office before collapsing on the desk, head in her hands.

She had met August at a fastball game in the Cut District. They had bonded over their lack of skill to make it onto the school team but swore to always have each other's back, especially in chemistry. Three years after that, there had been an outbreak of test subjects from one of the district research centers, a flurry of people who had joined the resistance against the Overseer. Sage had used to see them on the streets as a little girl, freedom fighters her mother would quickly walk away from.

"They'll notice us," she'd say hurriedly. *"They'll come after us."*

Little did anyone know, the little girl she had dragged along was a hybrid. The Squids in charge, if they had suspected it, would've come after her. Maybe, at some point, they had. Sage had been eighteen when she graduated high school and come home to soldiers raiding her mother's home. That fight had quickly led to another, an all-out war that she and August had led. Together, they had toppled the Squids. Or rather, the humans who had worked for the Squids. They had created their own militia and sought to help the other districts to freedom.

After an entire night of sorting through August's immediate files, Sage decided to contact Damian. She hoped he was healed and rested after suffering a brutal defeat at the hands of his brother. She tried not to correlate August's demise with Damian's eventual fate at the hands of Stars; any of those thoughts went away as soon as she heard his voice.

"Sage?" Damian sounded relieved, as if he had been holding his breath all through the night.

"It's me," she said. "Gertrude and I are safe. We have a new situation on our hands, though . . . "

Sage didn't think it was very appropriate to talk about August's developments over the phone. She yearned to see him and was shocked when she learned he wasn't that far away.

"I camped out a few miles north," Damian said. "Report back as soon as you can."

Camped out a few miles north? Was he crazy? He was supposed to have returned to Mousafeld!

"No one is going to attack us out here," Damian assured her. "And I wasn't about to leave you by yourself, damn it."

"You're injured and you're not well!" Sage exclaimed. "What if your brother had come back and found you?" Or worse: what if her sister had found him?

"I'm a liability now, aren't I?"

"For now you are until you get over those damn withdrawals! If you had never started those damn drugs in the first place, then maybe you wouldn't be such a damn weakling!"

Sage couldn't let go of August and it made her cry. She hung up on Damian before he could retort, slammed her head down on the desk, and sobbed.

"Sage?" Gertrude entered the office with a tray of coffee and biscuits. She hadn't expected to become in charge so soon, but Sage had to deal with the Warlord. Gertrude understood. She was equally worried about his proximity but not surprised. "Sage," she said one final time before she was all alone in this town. "I'm worried. Not just about him, but about everything. About *this*. The Extractor, Diamond City, and now your *sister*? I-I didn't know you had another sister."

"Actually," Sage said softly, "she's my twin. My mother had twins but gave up my sister to pay for expenses. Remember how I told you that she was poor and desperate?"

Gertrude blinked rapidly. Sage took the tray before it hit the floor.

"The Cut District was huge into research," Sage went on dismally. "And so they paid my mother a lot of money for her."

"That's horrible," Gertrude croaked. She shook her head, as if she couldn't imagine losing her own sister to the greedy clutches of scientists.

"Yeah. I've never officially met her, but I know she's out there."

"Is she a threat?"

With the way August had phrased it, the answer was yes. But Sage didn't know what her sister's intentions were, nor what her sister had to do with the Enhanced in Diamond City.

"I'll take care of it." Sage pocketed a few biscuits and downed the coffee despite burning her tongue. "But I have to see Damian first."

She kept her head down as she left Wolfeld, doing her best to ignore guards and the whispers from staring passersby. They didn't associate her face with that of her sister's, of trouble, but they did know she was their new leader. Shock toward what had happened to August was still prevalent among them, and those images drowned Sage's sanity.

August was dead.

Sage trudged across the battlefield. Wolfeld troops paced back and forth, counting the bodies, both human and Enhanced. The extent of the battle's damages was grand thanks to Slainium and the ability to kill so quickly. She recognized a few faces, but one made her stop completely.

Blondie.

Sage stared at the glassy blue eyes. She noticed the wound on Blondie's chest, a direct hit to the heart. One of Blackburn's men must have used her own weapon against her. Or maybe it wasn't hers—it was Mohawk's, dead before he had gotten to see his lover jump in to defend him.

Sage held her mouth. Tears burned her eyes, but the nausea was worse. She scrambled to the nearest tree and threw up. Then her heart started palpitations, sending her into shock. It was a horrible, vulnerable state because she was neither here nor in the throttle of bloody memories from the Unification War. She was stuck in limbo, enduring this massive explosion of pain that she was pretty sure was grief.

"My lady?" said one of the Wolfeld troops, rushing over to her.

"I'm sorry!" Sage wheezed at the confused face. "This wasn't supposed to happen! So many people weren't supposed to die!"

Again. Just like before. More blood and death just like a hundred years ago. Just when Sage thought she had put it all behind her, it was staring right at her face again.

"My lady, it's fine," the Wolfeld troop reassured her. "Just stay clear of the area for now." He helped her to the next tree outside of the bloody field. There, Sage stopped and threw up again. He asked if she needed any further assistance making it back to town, but Sage had to see the Warlord.

Right now, though, she couldn't walk. She just sat there, knees up and head down. She entered a meditative state to cleanse her anxiety and shaking. Thoughts of Candice and Olivia always brought a smile to her face. Samson and Louis made her laugh. Damian did, too.

An hour or so later, he called her. Sage lifted her head. Slightly more composed now, she answered him.

"Sorry," she said briskly, climbing back to her feet. "I'm coming."

"Do you want Fahrenheit and Celsius to escort you?"

"I'm fine."

Damian's camp wasn't too far away. It was well hidden, tucked in between thick trees and shrubbery, but Damian was waiting for her by the lake out in the open. His wounds were tended to, some of them healed and others bandaged, but he was a lot weaker than he let on. No makeup showed the dark circles under his eyes and the age on his skin. Even Fahrenheit and Celsius, who were stuck to him like glue, wouldn't be enough to defend him if someone of worth attacked.

Of course, Damian was stubborn. His safety didn't matter when he was waiting for Sage. Their ugly conversation about his drug addiction and battle liability flew out the window when he saw her. Like a schoolboy, Damian took off to reach her that much quicker. He swept her into his arms, held her face, fought the urge to kiss her in front of people, and sighed with relief.

"You idiot!" Sage pushed against his chest. "What the hell are you still doing here? You're too close to Wolfeld if something were to happen!"

"Like what?" he challenged.

"Everything is under control for now, but how do you know that, you bastard?"

"All the more reason for me to be around." Damian scowled. "I'm not going to leave you alone. How many times do I have to say that before it settles in your thick skull?"

"I can take care of myself!" Sage yelled. "You can't seriously be this obsessed with me, enough to put you and your troops in danger!"

"Is that what you call it, Sage? 'Obsession'? The last time I checked, I was in charge of these Enhanced and my word is rule. You are certainly not going to change that nor go against my judgment."

"You're falling to pieces, Damian—tell me how camping out so close to the enemy is strategy?"

"We are a team," Damian said quietly. "And I leave no one behind."

It sounded noble and praiseworthy, but Sage knew Damian all too well now. She didn't approve of his reckless decisions just because he wanted to "ensure" her safety and, therefore, ensure his ultimate weapon. This had everything to do with his obsession over her—the fact that his health was on the decline and that Sage was the only one capable of bringing down forces like his brother—than out of sheer love. It was painfully clear.

Sage clenched her fists, outraged by her own thoughts. The burning started up in her eyes again. She turned her head so Damian wouldn't see the tears. As she battled with herself, she wanted to give Damian more credit than that. His love for her couldn't solely be for his war gains . . .

"Come." Damian wrapped an arm around her. "We have much to talk about."

He took her the rest of the way to camp, ignoring Fahrenheit and Celsius. His arm was heavy and warm, bringing a sense of comfort to Sage as they walked together, mostly in silence. She thought of what she was going to say, what information to withhold. If she told them everything, she might endanger them. There were too many hotheads raring to prove themselves in battle.

Like Mega Woman's camp, there were makeshift houses scattered around the grounds. Damian took her to one that served as a meeting room. Most of Damian's rebels had returned to Mousafeld, but the ones present would brief them later. Sage stood by the table as she recounted August's suicide with the Extractor, his surrender of Wolfeld to her, and his wish to take back Diamond City. She didn't mention the Optimum or her sister, but everyone was too busy marveling at the Extractor to inquire about August's enemies.

"What the hell?" Little Man breathed in awe as Sage showed them Wolfeld's most prized possession. "How the hell was he able to create something like that?"

It was scary. But it was also a relief that Wolfeld was now in their control. They had beaten Diamond City to it, and that was a blessing in itself. What they didn't understand was the *reason* behind the suicide. Sage muttered a low, "I don't know," and kept her eyes downcast.

And that's what tormented her all throughout the day and well into the evening. The rebels stayed here with plans to enter Wolfeld in the morning. Sage stuck to Damian because his warmth made her feel better. After dinner and tearing through some roasted deer meat, she quietly decided she wasn't going to return to Wolfeld with the rebels... She was going to intercept her sister at the Junkyard. Her imminent encounter with a *monster*, as August had described it, terrified her more than she let on. As dusk grew near, her fear began to skyrocket, bringing on that fever again.

"You seem awfully distracted." Damian offered her some tea, which he had just brewed. It had sage, too...

"Your feud with your brother," Sage started softly, eyes on the ground. The snow was mushy. "It doesn't bother you?"

"I've come to accept it. I had to when I learned my brother was on Kilstrong's side after the rebellion. He always used me as leverage to gain favor with others. First, it was my parents, and then it was the royal family. When I was arrested, it was he who tortured me. It was he who cut out every organ from my body."

Sage looked up. "What?"

"Indeed." Damian sipped his tea, as if those were details he had already come to peace with. "He would have had me executed, too, in public before putting my body parts into boxes... if it wasn't for Mega Woman."

Sage had already had a good idea of Damian's traumatic past, but now she filled in his torturer's face with that of Blackburn's. The tea wasn't so soothing anymore.

"There are situations in life we have no control over," Damian went on. "And we have to be grateful for the opportunities we are given to start anew. I owe my life to Mega Woman."

"But you don't love her."

"I thought I did. When we escaped from Diamond City, I was lonely. I had been betrayed by my partner and brother, so I turned to her for comfort. I came to realize that it wasn't love . . . just lust. Despite my promiscuity"—he laughed as Sage rolled her eyes—"I don't just sleep with anyone. I never betrayed Ileana after I married her."

"Yet she betrayed you."

"She did." Damian sipped some more tea. "But surely it is not my past love interests that worry you. I know that no one can plant seeds of doubt in your mind when it comes to my love for you. So tell me: what truly bothers you?"

Sage couldn't bring herself to say it. She kept quiet, hand rattling around her cup.

"Sage," Damian said softly, grasping her chin. "What's wrong, darling?"

"I told you not to call me that."

"I feel that things are different between us now, are they not?"

Sage's lip trembled. The answer was yes. She touched the Portable Projector hanging around her neck, still unscathed.

"Talk to me," he pressed softly. "What bothers you?"

"I . . . " Sage hesitated. "I have a sister."

"Aurora?"

"No. I have a biological sister."

"Is that so?"

"Yes. Apparently, she's been traveling the Outskirts. I"—Sage cleared her throat—"I have to see her tomorrow."

"You are estranged?"

"A bit, yes."

That was such an understatement. But Sage said all the right words to convince Damian that she was in no danger, that this would be any regular visit to a sibling. Little did he know, her sister was the reason Sage hid in her pizzeria.

"You will be fine," Damian said. "In the meantime, get some rest. I will retire now."

He retreated, but he didn't let go of her hand. He wasn't the only one who held on tightly either. Sage's fingers squeezed hard.

"Don't go," she whispered.

"Come with me."

Sage followed him into his room. There was a bed and furnish-ings to make for a comfortable space. In fact, it was even more luxu-rious than the rooms in Building A, although it didn't best Samson's renovations. It was warm, too.

"You have fought long and hard," Damian said, taking off his jacket and shirt, then pulling down his pants. He had gotten fresh clothes after medics had tended to his wounds. "Aren't you tired?"

Very. But Sage was looking at all the visible bruises on Damian's skin—red and purple. Then there were the old scars from lashings many years ago. The most prominent one of all was that scar in the middle of his chest.

Sage's eyes burned with tears again. Damn it, why was she so emotional today? And worst of all, she was in front of Damian, so he could see her trembling, in clear distress.

"Sage?" Damian said gently. "My penis isn't that small, is it?"

Sage laughed. She had the handkerchief the Wolfeld troop had given her to wipe her eyes and blow her nose. While she felt horri-bly sorry for him and his past, it wasn't those injuries that worried her. Sage couldn't stop thinking of August, his swelling body, the craze in his eyes as he dealt with the effects of Stars. How close had Damian been to that sort of addiction? What would Sage do if he ever relapsed?

"Join me," Damian said.

It wasn't in a sexual way. And even if it was, Sage was compelled to slip into bed next to him because she wanted to hold him. She didn't take off all her clothes like he did, but she was in her tank top and underwear, which made him stare. Still, he didn't make any advances when she curled up against his side. Damian wrapped an arm around her, holding her close.

Sage closed her eyes, breathing in his scent. Teakwood and lav-ender. He was clean because he had taken a bath and scrubbed off all the old, caked-on blood and dirt. She knew how to take a moment like this and hold onto it, grateful for the opportunity she had to be with him, thankful that he was still alive and healthy.

"Sage," Damian said softly, combing her hair. It was surprisingly tame after all the fighting. "Why are you so tense? What worries you—"

"You can call me darling."

"I was going to call you that even without your suggesting it."

"I just wanted to make sure. I didn't mean to scare you earlier."

Damian chuckled. "You didn't."

Sage settled against his chest. Once in a while, she pressed kisses to it. She wanted to show him that she loved him, that she valued his person and body. She didn't want him to ruin it with drugs... but most of all... she wanted him to stay away from her sister. She wanted him to go back to Mousafeld.

Damian could sense all those thoughts in her head. He whispered to her, "Talk to me, darling."

"The Cells," Sage whispered back, eyes gazing out into the darkness. There was a window in the corner with some moonlight peeking through the cracks of the blinds. "I think... they turn us into monsters. I know I've been one for a very long time. I feel like I don't have a soul, as if my emotions don't exist. I'm a killer and that's all I'm good for. It's what I was going to be *sold* for."

"You have lived an entire life in Diamond City, been fed so many lies," Damian said. "Sage, you weren't the only one who was being treated like a commodity. It's the very reason I left."

"This goes beyond politics. I understand how Diamond City works now, but perhaps there is a valid reason for their violence against us. I don't feel human anymore."

Damian's face contorted. "There is *no* valid reason for any violence, especially against people like us, who sacrificed themselves for the good of others."

"I'm a weapon," Sage croaked, eyes quivering. "No conscious... no emotions... "

"That is not true."

"I feel like a robot."

"I don't understand why you are talking this way."

"Blondie and Mohawk are dead. I-I saw their bodies—I couldn't defend them—and I'm just supposed to pick up again? Keep on fighting while they stay dead?"

"That is a life we all must live," Damian said, holding her cheek. "Until this war is over."

"There will always be wars." Tears slipped from her eyes. "And I will always be dragged into them."

"You don't have to fight," he reminded her. "You know that."

"We had an agreement. I have to help you fight."

"Forget the agreement. You decide what you want to do."

"What do you see in me, Damian?"

"Determination and loyalty," Damian said firmly. "With a soft spot for Defenders Unite!. I don't know why or how you got this into your head, but you are not a machine. You can feel and rationalize like the rest of us. I'm not sure you would have been able to free Louis from prison otherwise, and you certainly wouldn't be feeling a thing for your fallen comrades.

"Sage, you have lived many years. It is human nature to develop thick skin, especially someone who has seen and experienced so much. I wanted to snuff out my humanity, but wasn't it you who told me to hang onto it?"

"I've killed so many people . . . " Sage croaked.

"We live in very violent times. How many of us haven't killed someone?"

Sage sobbed. She clutched her head as the ugly poured out of her. They were words that were foreign to her because she had never voiced them to anyone—not even Samson—and sounded so strange to her ears: "I deserve to die," she cried. "I-I deserve to die for what I've done!"

"Darling." Damian held her wrists before she could start yanking out her hair. He laid her on her back and leaned over her, using his body as a blanket. He touched her nose with his, waiting until she calmed down some, then kissed her lips. His were so soft and warm. They absorbed some of the cries and lessened her sobs to loud pants. "You deserve nothing but peace after everything you've done," he said to her. "After everything you've sacrificed to help those who were and are oppressed." It was safe to let go of her hands now, so he did. He wiped her tears with his thumbs. He combed back the small frizz on her forehead. He kissed her there, too. "Look at me, Sage." He nudged her nose again. "You are good. And after all the trials you've been through, you deserve nothing but happiness. I vow to ensure that happens."

Sage wrapped her arms around his torso. She brought him further onto her so she could feel the weight of his body. It grounded her because he was the only thing she could focus on then. At this point, there was nothing more for Sage to say. Any more words about her sister and future battles would only convince him to go with her tomorrow, to ensure her safety, so she kept quiet. Sage wanted to forget her troubles the only way she knew how. Slowly, she wrapped her legs around his hips. He hardened instantly.

"Why are you doing this to me?" Damian whispered against her face.

"I think I love you," Sage whispered back. "And I want you close to me."

Maybe this wasn't Sage-like behavior, but Damian wasn't about to question her. With permission to take their affection further, he pressed his lips to her neck and trailed kisses to her chest. This time he slid his hands up her shirt without hesitation, finally coming into contact with the mounds of flesh he so desired. He squeezed them slowly, as if he was working a stress ball, then kneaded them like dough, up and down against her ribcage. Sage took off her tank top as Damian dipped his head to suck on her right nipple. The pressure of his lips made colors erupt in her vision. Tingles shot through her body and a steady pulsing started in her lower belly.

"You have no idea how long I've waited to do this," Damian said heatedly, dragging his tongue across her chest to her other breast. "Your breasts are so beautiful. Every time you trained, I'd see them through your shirt and I'd want to touch them, but I was afraid you'd cut me."

"I would have," Sage admitted, hands in his hair. "You have to learn to control yourself. Besides, don't they all look the same?"

"Definitely not. Breasts come in all shapes and sizes, and not all call to me like these do." He rubbed them again, up and down with his rough palms. "These are firm and fit perfectly in my hands."

Damian was such a horny bastard. Right now, everything about Sage's body fascinated him and fueled his arousal. Maybe it always had. What was most impressive was how thorough he was as he moved farther down—his hot mouth scorched every inch of skin it touched, leaving a trail of saliva and sweat all across her ribs, abdomen, and belly button.

Sage squeezed her eyes closed, anticipation swelling as he headed for that spot between her legs. She was already seeing stars and the pounding was driving her crazy. She gripped the bedsheets as he hooked her underwear with his thumbs and pulled them down over her hips. He was quick to discard them on the floor, eyes devouring what he had been dreaming of for months.

"I don't understand why I am so attracted to you," Damian said, spreading her legs wide. "Physically, I've always desired men. Maybe the occasional woman caught my eye if her breasts were just right or if her legs were thick. But you? Everything about you is so damn enticing. I felt it when you threw that dagger at my chest the first time we met."

"No," Sage panted, "you just like dominance."

"Yes ... that is true. I've always desired to hear you groan with the pleasure *I* elicit from you. A strong woman in my mercy." Damian lowered his head. Sage held her breath. Then she felt his tongue ride up her slit, and Sage wheezed.

"Stars!" Damian panted. His breath was scorching, making the pounding down there worse. "You are so slick right now." He licked her again, so goddamned slow that Sage felt the entire plane of his tongue. "It must be so hot in there, so tight. I need to see what my penis is in for." This time his tongue slipped inside.

Everything after that was a blur. Sage wasn't capable of thinking in the throes of passion, in the waves of heat Damian's tongue sent through her body. Those slow strokes and swirls made the pulsing inside her faster and hotter until Sage had to bite her tongue if she wanted to keep quiet. Her face turned red from the strain and sweat trailed down her body. Damian, of course, wasn't going to let the silence linger.

"Come for me, darling." Damian pressed her legs even farther apart. "You are so tense, I feel that you are close." Then he closed his lips around her clit.

That was it: Sage groaned as the heat burst and she climaxed against Damian's mouth. Pleasure burst through her body as Damian lapped up every bit of her with his tongue, like a thirsty puppy. She seized his head to keep him there.

"My sweet Sage," he spoke huskily against her very swollen folds. That tongue made another pass along the seam. "You taste so delightful . . . I want more."

So did Sage. For that reason, she sat up, body still throbbing, and climbed onto his lap. She was ready for him. She'd never thought she'd share this moment with him, but it was here. The desire for that explosive pleasure he gave her drove her nuts; its remnants were still in her veins, keeping her alive. She straddled his hips, braced herself, then sat on him completely.

Sage hissed. For a second, the moonlit room went pitch-dark. As colors filled her vision, all she could hear were their ragged pants and the pounding of her heart. His penis was pounding, too, so thick and hard inside her. She clutched his back for support, nails digging into his skin, as her body adjusted to his size. It didn't take long.

The pulsing urged her to rock her hips, and so Sage did. Slowly at first, because the pleasure was searing. Eventually, when that wasn't enough and she needed more, she went faster. Damian was egging her on, too, chanting in her ear, "There, there . . . just like that . . . so good . . ."

Sage squeezed him with her thighs, and that was the end of poor Damian. He had been hanging on by the skin of his teeth, and now he was a hot mess. "Stars!" he cried as he exploded. His seed was hot like syrup, thick and dripping down her thighs in silvery trails. Sage wanted all of it, so she kept on squeezing, annihilating Damian, who was still amidst the throes of his orgasm.

"Fuck, Sage!" he exclaimed. He tipped his head back as he reveled in every second of this moment. He touched her hip. "Keep rocking . . . just like that . . . up and down . . ."

Sage only stopped when the pleasure subsided. Then it was just their breathing again. Sage kept her head on his shoulder, hands traveling up and down his back, tracing his spine. Damian did the same to her until they parted enough to look at each other.

"It will be hard for me to stop here," Damian whispered thickly to her, eyes glowing in the darkness.

Sage brushed back the hair from his face. She found the braid from a couple of days ago, still neat and tight. Then she kissed his forehead, nose, lips, and chin. She ran her hands down his chest before lying back and spreading her legs for him again. Damian was already hard, but that sight put him in a frenzy.

"You're driving me crazy," he croaked, using his fingers to tease her, in and out. "You truly are, my love."

"I'm not doing anything," Sage admitted, although it was hard to speak.

Damian grabbed her hips, picking them up to meet his. He filled her up again, crying out as if someone had belted his ass cheeks. The theatrics made Sage laugh. "So tight . . . so hot . . . " He wrapped her legs around his waist. "Just like I dreamed."

"You dreamed about me?" Sage asked weakly.

"When I actually slept, yes. One time I woke up in the clinic with a huge erection. I was lucky that Dr. X wasn't around to see it. I slipped into the bathroom undetected. I was in so much pain—I had a fever and everything. Masturbation is absolutely dreadful when the star of your dreams is so close by and completely off-limits to you. But I am a man of honor and I have never taken anyone by force. If this is now my reward, then it was so worth it."

"Damian, please stop talking."

"Does it feel good?" he asked huskily, holding her hips before they started moving. "Me inside you?"

"I swear," Sage hissed at him, "if you're going to be an asshole, I will ban you from my room."

"Please don't do that to me, darling. I just want to know how you feel."

"You know how I feel, damn it! Can't you see it on my face?"

"I want to hear it."

"It feels so good," Sage said, about ready to flip the bastard onto his back and take him herself. "You feel so good."

"Do I stretch you a lot?" Damian asked.

"For the love of Squids, Damian!"

"Please answer my question."

"Y-yes!" Sage choked. "You do!"

"Is this better than any other penis you've had inside you before?"

"Are you seriously going to make me think about my exes now?"

"Am I better?" Damian asked innocently.

Sage threw her hips up, but Damian kept her still. She yelled in frustration. "Yes! So much better! You're thick, hot, and pulsing, and I'm about to explode just by having you inside me, something I've never done before! Sometimes, I wouldn't even climax after sex!"

"How sad," Damian lamented. "Who was the poor sap who couldn't get you to climax?"

"My ex-husband."

"He must not have been doing it right."

"How hard can it be?" Sage panted. "This isn't rocket science."

"Sex is an art, darling. You have to hit the right angle or else you're wasting your time. Let me show you."

He leaned over her and started thrusting, fast and hard. He did most of the work that time, and it was a good thing he did because Sage was completely numb in this position. She contributed hardly anything because Damian kept a tight hold on her hips and legs, an angle that made them climax within minutes. Damian didn't lower her body for a long time after that, riding out every wave of pleasure, sometimes with a small rock of his hips.

"You are beautiful," he said to her, a hand on each of her knees like a king on his throne. "And so strong."

After releasing his last grunt, Damian lowered her back onto the bed and rested on top of her. At that point, it was mostly kissing and touching. Eventually, they worked it up to another round, but then it was lights out for them both. Limbs tangled, they settled in, but before they went to sleep, Sage had one final request.

"Promise me you won't ever take Stars again," she whispered. Her fingers lightly traced some of the bruises on his brow.

"I promise," Damian whispered back, dark eyes boring into hers. Then they fluttered and closed.

CHAPTER 17

A New Enemy

Sage needed to leave before anyone saw her in Damian's room. She didn't want dirty looks from the rebels as they realized she had stayed the night with him. Her subconscious did a good job of pestering her until she opened her eyes and realized that she had, indeed, had sex with the Warlord.

Sage herself had a hard time believing she had finally caved in. After so many months of resisting his advances, here she was in his embrace. But she didn't have any regrets. There was warmth in his arms that seeped into her body, a love and security that Sage had been craving for such a long time. When she craned her head to look at him, she saw his face: smooth and expressionless.

He was at peace. His breathing was even. Sage ran a hand through his hair, over his shoulder, and down his hip. She got to see more scars, some from battle and others from lashes. She touched them with light fingertips, knowing his mind was as war-torn as hers. Yet, last night, he had been her rock. He had kept her together when she had been so close to snapping.

Damian's phone went off. Sage heard it, but he didn't. He kept on snoring. She got up, not to answer it, but to make her escape.

That was impossible to do unnoticed, though—it was like taking a sleeping kid's teddy bear. Damian searched for her body and sprang up as soon as he realized it was missing.

"I'm here," Sage said to calm him down.

"Where are you going?"

"To get away before anyone sees me. And to bathe."

Damian frowned. "Why do you care if anyone sees you? We don't have to hide it, do we?"

Sage hesitated. She thought carefully about how to say this without hurting his feelings, but she didn't know any other way. "I just joined your camp three months ago and already we're sleeping together. That's going to make me look like a tramp."

Damian chuckled. "Or maybe it makes me one hell of a stud, able to snare even you—"

Sage threw a dagger at his face. To her irritation, she missed. Damian was all out laughing. "I'm glad you're amused," she growled, grabbing her clothes. "But I'm going."

"Please don't. Or rather"—Damian got to his feet—"I'll join you."

No chance. His phone went off again, so duty called. Damian, cursing, couldn't ignore it. Sage laughed at his look of death and finally slipped out of the room.

Without the sun, it was cold and dreary out here. The wind cut in on occasion, filling the silence with its howling. Anything could be watching from the shadows, even if there were rebels on guard. Thankfully, Sage didn't run into any on her way to the lake.

It was way too cold for a bath, but Sage could regulate her body temperature. As soon as she dove into those icy depths, she warmed up from the inside out. She came up for air five minutes later, gazing at the sky, at the sun as it finally rose, thankful she had gotten to see another day.

She couldn't say the same for August. The thought of him was like a knife to the heart. She'd never forget that fastball game, when they had sat next to each other on the bleachers and bonded over Wooly Socks. August had had a whole collection of them and he'd always worn them everywhere. Even in battle.

Blondie and Mohawk. Sage's insides twisted. It was hard to breathe. All the anxiety from last night came back with a vengeance, especially when she remembered her mission today.

Her sister.

She had to meet her sister, but she couldn't risk Damian staying in Wolfeld. They had to evacuate immediately—

Sage threw a dagger at the intruder. It wasn't Damian who emerged from the trees, blade in between his fingertips—it was Mega Woman. She must have been on patrol.

"Do you carry these everywhere?" she asked tightly, eyes as intense as ever. Her lips were pursed, showing her usual annoyance, but her face was gaunt and her stance wasn't as steady as usual. Perhaps she was just as tired of fighting as everyone else.

"I do," Sage said, returning to shore to pick up her sword. Stark naked, she pointed it at Mega Woman, whose intentions were anything but good. Sage smelled it like a bad odor.

"Put it down," Mega Woman said.

"You don't tell me what the fuck to do."

Mega Woman raised her hands. "I'm not here to fight or start anything. Sorry I interrupted your bath." She dropped the dagger. "I did, however, want to give you a warning."

Sage didn't lower her sword. The tips of Mega Woman's lips curled ever so slightly.

"He does that to everyone who's beneficial to him, you know that? He did it to me after I saved his ass from Diamond City, and he did it to Ileana before she bore him a daughter. Neither turned out well for him, so he's moved on to his next project." She narrowed her eyes, her scowl turning ugly. "*You.* He needs you now that he's falling to pieces thanks to Stars. Who else is going to come to his rescue?"

"I appreciate the advice, but I can take care of myself, thanks."

"You don't know him like I do, Sage."

"Do I look like an idiot to you?" Sage hissed. "I know enough."

Sage pulled on her clothes. Mega Woman continued to watch her, as if she had never seen another woman before. She must have been burning up with anger, unsure of how to act in the face of competition. Attack Sage, and there'd be consequences to pay, ones that weren't worth the strife right now.

"Out of the way," Sage spat. "Unless you want to settle something? Maybe get that pent-up jealousy out of your system."

Mega Woman didn't dare. Fuming, Sage brushed past her, free of her glare at last. That had been the most unpleasant bath she'd ever had. She was glad Damian hadn't been with her, or they would have had an audience.

Back at camp, Damian was standing next to the meeting house. He was dressed in a brand-new jumpsuit with a heavy coat over his shoulders, engaged with his guards about their day's activities. He had makeup on his face, so he looked like his usual self, minus all the bandages. He had a thick mug of coffee in his hand, the only drink he was able to gulp down before heading out to Wolfeld. Little did he know, Sage had other plans for them.

"Damian," Sage said, approaching him. Her heart fluttered when she saw his face lighten at the sight of her.

Damian smiled. His lips were all glossy, as sparkly as his eyes, which ravaged every bit of her body anew. Not much to see with her thick layer of clothes, but he was thinking of last night. Sage's cheeks flushed a bit. He stepped closer and wrapped an arm around her despite how many people were watching.

"Darling," Damian sang. "How was your bath?"

"Terrible," Sage admitted. "Your lovestruck bitch couldn't keep her eyes off me. Maybe she finds me alluring, but I can't say the same about her. She's one of the most unpleasant people I've ever met."

Someone roared with laughter in the distance. Leave it to Turtle to find this humorous. It wasn't every day that someone had the balls to rat on Mega Woman's obsessive behavior.

Damian frowned. "I'm sorry about that. I will talk to her."

"I don't think it'll make a difference," Sage said honestly.

"It will, trust me."

"Oh, it will!" Turtle called out with a grin. "He'll bitchslap her so hard, she'll see stars! If only that worked with every woman . . . "

"Ignore him," Damian grunted. "I will take care of it. I promise."

　　　　　　　　　　　　　　　　　　　　DIAMOND CITY

Sage was annoyed by it, but she had other problems to deal with. Those wormed their way to the surface again, taking shape in the form of weariness on her face. Damian picked up on it right away.

"You'll be leaving now?" he said. "To speak to your sister?"

"Yes," Sage said softly. "But I was going to ask you for a favor." She clenched her fists and pursed her lips. It was a command she didn't want to give, but she had to for the sake of survival. Who the hell was she kidding? Her *sister*? No human would last two minutes in a fight against her, so that's why she had to say it. "Damian, please take everyone in Wolfeld back to Mousafeld. *Everyone.*"

"To Mousafeld? Why?"

"We won't all fit there," Fahrenheit said at once.

Sage wasn't here to negotiate with anyone other than Damian, so she grabbed him by the wrist and pulled him aside. With their small moment of privacy in between a few trees, Sage delivered more of her earnestness. "Please," she whispered. "Please do as I say."

"Absolutely not," Damian said. "Not without an explanation. A worthy one, Sage. I know you so well—last night, you were tense as hell and now you look ready to break down again. What is going on?"

"My sister is going to attack Wolfeld, and I might not be able to stop her."

Perhaps Damian had already been anticipating that her sister wasn't the lovey-dovey sibling waiting for her at home. A blood sister of Sage's meant being just as old as she was, advanced in the ways of Enhanced. He still didn't know that Sage was the Optimum, though, and that a twin had the potential to do some serious damage.

"Your sister is going to attack us," Damian repeated slowly. "Or Wolfeld, rather."

"Yes. For this." Sage grabbed the Extractor from deep within her pocket. She tucked it into Damian's palm. "She's collecting them. *All* of them. And if she runs into you and the others, she's going to hit the jackpot."

"So she has an Extractor, too?"

"Um." Sage flexed her fingers. "Sort of."

"Explain, damn it!" Damian exclaimed. "I want to know what's going on—why is she doing this? For what purpose?"

"My sister is a maniacal bitch. Maybe it's not too different from me, but at the very least I don't want to take over the world. That, I suspect, is what she's doing with all those Cells—taking them back from the people they were given to in order to fulfill some unknown purpose. I don't know what she wants because I haven't spoken to her in a very long time."

"If she's stealing people's Cells, does that mean she is working directly with Diamond City?"

Sage didn't know. She wasn't sure it mattered.

"This changes everything." Damian shook his head. "Sage, how on earth can you think I am going to let you confront your sister alone? We need to do this strategically. We don't have much of a force right now, but we can always regroup."

Sensing she was about to argue, Damian held her cheek to stop her. "You care for me . . . but I care for you as well. Instead of meeting your sister, help me move everyone from Wolfeld to Mousafeld, and then we can figure it out."

Sage would have agreed to it, too, if Fahrenheit and Celsius didn't barge into their conversation.

"M-my lord!" Fahrenheit was the first to croak amidst their panting. Right now, he cared little for formalities and more for getting his message across. "Our drones have picked up movement five miles north of here—someone is making their way right to us—to Wolfeld—"

"Gather everyone and tell them to evacuate Wolfeld immediately," Damian said without a stutter. "Send word to Mousafeld as well, to deploy as many airships as possible to get the people to safety."

"We're evacuating everyone to Mousafeld? But, sir, there is no space—"

"We'll make space," Damian growled. "Now go."

One attempt at a rebuttal was enough, so Fahrenheit and Celsius didn't stick around for another. Damian was about to follow, but Sage went the other way. Confused, he grabbed her by the arm, hauling her back.

"Where are you going?"

"I have to go," Sage said quietly. "I have to buy you time—she's too close."

"Don't be ridiculous!" Damian hissed. "Come with me to Mousafeld this instant and stop acting like a damn martyr!"

"I am not going to fight her, Damian! I am simply going to stall. If she catches us in the middle of an evacuation—catches *you*—we're done. I refuse to let her anywhere near you or the others. I have to do this."

"Then you can defend me where I can keep an eye on you."

"And allow her to use you as a liability?" Sage said.

"Goddamn it, why do you keep saying that?! I am not a liability—I am not a child who needs to be defended, Sage—"

Sage knocked him in the chest with the palm of her hand, winding him. That moment was all she needed to grab his wrist, twist him around, and hold a blade to his throat.

That hit a nerve. Damian didn't even struggle against her hold because an enemy would have slit his throat already. The only reason he started shaking was because he was fighting the truth and a very harsh reality.

"Do you see?" Sage said softly, letting him go. "You need to get to safety."

Tears welled in Damian's eyes. His weakness meant he couldn't defend Sage the way he wanted to. For that reason, there was a good chance he'd lose her. After a night of so much passion, he was going to lose Sage . . . like this?

His turmoil contradicted everything Mega Woman had mentioned at the lake, his so-called manipulation, because the love in his eyes was true. It was impossible to hide, even if he swiped at them viciously, disgusted with himself and his feelings.

"Damian, look at me." Sage gripped his face with her hands.

She peered into his watery eyes. "I'll be back," she said steadily. She kissed his lips. "I promise. I'll see you at Mousafeld."

Damian shook his head. "I can't lose you, too. Not you, too."

"You're not going to lose me, Damian." Sage kissed him again. "I promise. I promise."

"No, Sage," Damian croaked, holding her face now, thumbs on her cheeks. "I *can't* lose you. I cannot lose you because if I do, it will destroy me. It will shatter what is left of my black soul, the only thing my brother hasn't been able to take away. I have lost Kevin, David, Ileana, and Phoebe, and I am not going to add you to that list. Do you understand, Sage, that I love you? I love who you are and what you stand for. I love how you do the right thing no matter the cost, and that . . . " He choked. "I-I have no words for."

Sage's lip trembled although she kept her composure. She noticed that he didn't say, *I love you because you are invincible.*

"If I had my heart," Damian whispered to her, "I would cut it out and give it to you."

"You don't have to do that, Damian," Sage said softly. "Because you already have given it to me." She wiped the tears from his eyes. She kissed his lips again. There was hardly any gloss left on them. "And if that is the case, then that must also mean you trust me. If you love me, you trust me. So trust me when I say I am not going to die. Not today." She smiled at him. "Not today, darling."

Sage embraced him just to take in his scent one more time. He did the same to her, nose in her hair, until she decided it was time to step back.

Damian let out a breath, strained. He didn't let go of her hand until she tugged it out of his grasp. He kept his eyes on her as she turned away, leaving him in the cold, determined to confront her sister after so many years.

"Say it, Sage!" he called after her. "You will return to me! Or else I will come find you."

"I will," Sage affirmed before disappearing into the woods.

CHAPTER 18

Junkyard

age had never met her sister—only seen her. She didn't consider eye contact a formal introduction to anyone, and that's what had happened right before the final battle of the Unification War in the Cut District. Sage had been in the frontlines, ready to lead the Enhanced into Overseer Callus' sanctuary, when she had briefly glimpsed her sister loading an aircraft.

Long, beautiful, light brown hair, milky arms tied behind her back, straitjacket tight around her body. Sage wasn't supposed to have seen her, but she had. It was instinct when a twin sibling was so close, to look that way, and her sister had done the same, lifting her chin ever so slightly, dark eyes glistening like a pair of black jewels.

Ilemas.

The voice, even though Sage had heard it so long ago, was as clear as a crystal in her mind. As she trudged past the last of Wolfeld's forestry, she thought her sister was speaking directly into her head.

Sister.

Out in the distance was a massive junkyard, piles upon piles of metal. It could have been Wolfeld's trash heap, but it also could have been scraps of leftover debris from some kind of war. The explosions were in Sage's head, only until they were cut off by an obnoxious shriek.

"Do it again, Taz! Do it again!"

Taz. That must have been what was making those guttural sounds followed by crashing noises, as if a monster was throwing around everything it came into contact with. It must have been funny to see a behemoth create chaos because there was high-pitched laughter. The closer Sage got to the hills of steel, the more of this "Taz" she saw, a massive body with long, shifting limbs.

People had vivid imaginations, as Sage saw in the Art Festival every year, but no craft had ever taken the shape of that. David, Damian's former lover, hadn't come close to capturing a monster like this. Even Sage, who had been in countless battles, so many they blurred one into the other, didn't know what that was.

It had sharp senses, too: it detected her from a mile away, stopping just to turn its unshapely head to her. Its eyes were like dark tunnels, endless and without a scrap of humanity in their depths. They reminded her of Damian when she had first met him, of someone who had lost everything. Whatever it was, it was male. If Sage looked closely enough, she could see stubble along the jawline and a very small sac of genitals between its legs. This thing had lost its ability to reproduce a while ago.

Sage stiffened in the face of an enemy she had never confronted before. She had no strategy to conquer it, and that unsettled her. It wasn't like her to wobble or to take so long to evaluate her chances of surviving.

Then, ever so slowly, Sage turned her head to find her twin. Perhaps in looks with the pale skin, tight body, and hair color, but not in demeanor. Not in aura.

That Sage was grinning, eyes an amber color, evidence of her Squid roots. Her sharp teeth were bared, showing every bit the monster she was. She sat perched on one of the junk heaps, long, slender legs crossed in front of her. She flapped her arms like a bird, wild and mirthless, enjoying herself over something as trivial as

                    DIAMOND CITY

dumpster diving. Either she was finding her weight in gold or she thoroughly enjoyed unearthing bones.

But then her grin fell. Her entire demeanor changed when the slitted pupils focused on who was standing in the distance. Taz, sensing discomfort from his master, went a bit limp as well.

Sage drew her sword, pointing it at her sister. It took all the energy she had to say the name out loud.

"Wren."

"What?" Wren came to a full stand, letting the hem of her long white gown fall to her ankles. Her mouth was shaped in an O, clear confusion on her face. That look-alike knew her name, but was she supposed to know hers? The answer was yes. Their bond didn't exist, but their knowledge of each other did. Still, surprise didn't fade. Wren's lips simply curled into a sneer.

"Sage. Dear sister. Do my eyes deceive me?" Wren rubbed them innocently. Along her skin, like a ripple, tiny mouths opened and closed, all teeth. "Is it really you?"

"It is." Sage didn't move from her spot. She wouldn't be getting a step closer, that was for sure. Half a mile was more than enough distance to dodge whatever might come hurtling her way.

"What on earth brings you here? And here I thought you were that fat Enhanced." Wren giggled. "You may not be as big as he is, but your hair is ugly. Have you heard of conditioner?" She had no shame flaunting hers. Sage didn't stir. "Well? Aren't you going to speak?"

"I have nothing to say."

Wren shrieked with laughter. "*Nothing?* Oh, sister, we haven't seen each other in a hundred years! In fact, we haven't even formally met. I've heard of your feats on the battlefield, and it gives me great pleasure to see that you have sought me out at last! Where have you been all this time? Hiding?"

"I had to. I couldn't afford another battle. It would have destroyed me."

"Oh, please." Wren snorted. "Don't pretend to have a heart, oh Queen of Diamonds. You are the reason there *is* a Diamond City.

But you are also the reason all these Enhanced were exiled. Didn't dream to defend them?"

"Not my problem." Sage tightened her hold around the hilt of her sword. She wasn't going to let her guard down for a moment. "Not anymore. Not until now, when I learned you've been going around stealing their Cells."

"You mean *my* Cells." Wren frowned, as if she had swallowed something bitter. "*My* Cells, sister. Don't you know it by now? I am the creator of all the Enhanced. Those nasty scientists took *my* blood—*my* DNA—and injected it into humans. I am simply taking back what is mine."

"What for? Why don't you just let it go?"

"That would be too boring." Wren smiled graciously at Taz, who was staring at Sage. "Just look at him—isn't he beautiful?"

"And what is he, exactly?" Sage already had a guess: her sister wasn't collecting Cells for nothing. She was using them for her own experiments, to see what would happen to a person when they had too many. By the looks of Taz, a hundred doses too many. It was already wreaking havoc on coherent thought and human processes. This thing probably didn't even remember his own name. The only reason he was bound to Wren was because of strength; he knew damn well she was his master. Now he was curiously studying Sage, wondering how a look-alike played into all of this.

"This is Taz." Wren introduced him, kicking her feet back and forth. She looked like she was tap dancing. "He is my savior."

Savior?

Wren nodded. "Yes, he gave me freedom in exchange for power. He took me out of that miserable lab. There were already so many Enhanced, so why did we need more?" She smiled cruelly. "He was so kind to me, too. He took me in, taught me to read and write, gave me pleasure . . . oh, so much pleasure . . . " She laughed. "And I gave him Cells. A lot of them. More than anyone else."

" 'A lot of them'," Sage whispered, eyes widening. There was only one person she knew who was going around taking Cells. "So . . . he's a Kilstrong?"

Francis Kilstrong. The one who was supposed to be dead, who Sage had driven into a car crash in Diamond City . . . and the one she had fought in Mousafeld. Had to be, because nothing else made sense—the Cell Destroyer and the Marketplace intruder were one and the same. The more Cells, the more monstrous the form, which was why Sage hadn't recognized him before. At last, Sage got to see his true face, which had changed drastically from his human one. Standing amidst the trash heaps was a new creature, eyes shiny and focused like a pair of lasers.

"Wow, sister," Wren drawled. "You sure are smart. But I guess it wasn't much of a secret that the Kilstrongs wanted to contain the Enhanced. While the Allseer found ways to manipulate them into his army, Francis wanted to do away with them completely."

"So those torture videos," Sage said slowly. "That was you. It wasn't your weapons that killed the Enhanced like everyone thought—it was *you.*"

Wren clapped. "Bravo. We've certainly been hard at work. So far we've recovered about a thousand of my beautiful babies." Wren ran her hands over her body, up her arms, over her breasts, and in between her legs. She blushed a bright red, laughing shrilly. "That's a lot, isn't it? Out of ten thousand, give or take? The military was too difficult to topple at first, so after targeting all the stragglers, we came to the Outskirts. What have you been up to, big sister? Any crazy battles lately?"

"I gave up that life," Sage said curtly.

"Ah, that's right. You refused to fight in that rebellion some years ago. I don't blame that on you, of course—I also don't like fighting." Wren cocked her head to the side. "But . . . if that's so . . . then what's with the sword?"

"It doesn't mean I wander around unprotected. I happened to be paying Wolfeld a visit when I learned that you were on your way here."

"Ah, yes! August promised me his Cells—*my* Cells—so I'm coming to take them."

"It's too late. He's dead. Committed suicide."

Wren's face fell. Taz's stoic features reflected her surprise at this revelation. "You lie."

"Why is that a shock?" Sage said. "After your crazy threats, I'd probably do the same."

"Did you interfere?"

"Not really. He extracted his Cells before I knew what was going on. It's all over the local news, so you can confirm if you'd like."

Wren didn't like that at all. No sense of understanding crossed her face whatsoever; if anything, her fists tightened even more. Like a little child, she was angry that she hadn't gotten what she wanted, as petty as it was. What were a few Cells from a single Enhanced? But it was like missing a puzzle piece, and Wren grew furious. She gritted her sharp teeth.

"*You* have it."

"Actually, I don't," Sage said truthfully. "Not anymore. I got rid of it."

"It wasn't yours to dispose of."

"I didn't know you were so interested, sister."

Wren screamed like a banshee. It was a screech that shook the ground, destroying eardrums. Then came the tantrum, but not by her hands—she ordered Taz to do the dirty work for her with a point of her finger, teeth bared like a wolf's.

Sage braced herself for Taz's strike and it happened fast—in the blink of an eye—she threw her sword up in time to block his punch. The impact nearly sent her flying, but she held to the ground, snagging momentum in her favor. She stole it from Taz, surprising him with her own swiftness and punch, breaking his sternum and a few other bones as he stumbled back. Sage didn't stop there—she flew forward with her sword ready to pierce his skull. All she had to do was land the hit now that Damian's sword had been laced with Slainium, too.

But this wasn't just another Enhanced, as Sage quickly learned. Having more than the recommended number of Cells made a difference because Taz no longer thought as a human—he didn't even behave like one. His instincts were sharp, locked onto her every move so she couldn't attack without him already knowing what she was going to do. It made dealing any blows difficult, nearly impossible, especially when she started to slow down.

"Give it up, sister!" Wren called. "You don't stand a chance!"

This was only supposed to be a distraction, Sage told herself as she dodged all of Taz's swipes, flipping back onto the ground. *I should run while I still have the chance.*

But that was just it—could she outrun Taz? If she took off, giving him her back, would she be able to make it to safety?

Sage knew she wasn't going to win this battle. After another clash that shook the ground, she rebounded as far away from Taz as possible. Her opportunity to run shattered when Taz crossed that distance in less than a second, head-butting her to the ground with that robotic look in his gaze.

Sage wobbled but kept her sword up. Blood trickled down her lip. Neither the taste nor the smell of it distracted her, even when Taz turned wild and pummeled her to a pulp: he smashed her face, cut a tendon behind her heel, and locked her in a death grip.

Sage battled his hold, fighting to loosen it from her body. In the distance, she saw her sister bouncing up and down like a cheerleader. This was the greatest show she had ever seen, the only person to put up a fight against Taz. Ever so slowly, all of that turned blurry in Sage's vision. Taz must have been cutting off her airflow. With a final burst of strength, Sage managed to overturn Taz. She couldn't, however, run.

Sage collapsed, face down. She heard her sister come closer. She stirred, turning to watch her.

"Let's see . . . " Wren stroked her chin. She had a huge smile on her face. "How do we kill a hybrid?" She picked up Sage's sword. "This has that special metal in it, right? Slainium?" She thrust the blade through Sage's throat, pinning her to the ground. "I know it won't kill you right away. Slainium in our blood takes *forever* to have any effect. We have too many Cells, dear sister, and our bodies regenerate them naturally. How do you think those scientists at Cut were able to extract so much from me? *But* there are ways to kill us." Wren walked around her body. "With enough Slainium, and enough damage, there is a way to silence us forever. Let's see if it works with you—we'll start by cutting off your head—"

Wren jumped because something flew at her own head. If she hadn't moved in time, she would have been skewered by Damian's sword.

Sage barely saw it in her hazy vision. She hardly heard him rush to her side. She didn't feel him tear the blade out of her throat. She could tell that he was screaming because his eyes were huge and his mouth was open. His hair was messy, whipping in the wind, in tune with his open jacket. He was as frazzled as Sage had ever seen him.

"Oh?" Wren breathed in surprise. "Who is that?"

"D-Damian . . ." Sage rasped, shuddering as blood continued to spurt out of her neck. "B-behind . . ."

"Don't speak!" Damian was panicking. He had never seen this much blood on her. Not the cool, collected Sage, who danced around her enemies like a fly. Because of that, he lost his composure and any sense of conduct amidst battle—he was an open target—and Sage had to reach for the bloody sword sitting next to her body and fling it at the incoming Taz, who would have ripped Damian to pieces.

Damian whipped around. Wren shrieked with laughter.

"Big sister! Who is this? My goodness . . ." Wren licked her lips. "He looks delicious."

Sage grabbed Damian's coat, lifting herself to a sitting position. Her wounds were healing despite the dose of Slainium in her bloodstream, but her energy was low. Still, she was in survival mode and that meant pushing her body to its absolute limit. Damian kept her behind him and finally turned his attention to Taz, who yanked the sword from his chest. Damian grabbed his, confident all of a sudden in the face of a monster he'd never seen before because he trusted the weapon in his hands. He hadn't let go of it since he had confiscated it from Sage. It definitely suited him more than it did her. Wren and Taz both appeared unfazed.

"Stand down, Damian." Sage reached for one of her daggers. "You'll only be a liability."

"I am no liability," Damian said, eyes on Wren now. "Or else I wouldn't be here."

The resemblance was uncanny. But the personality ... was so different. It must have really unnerved him because he grew stiff, not just with fear, but with wonder. Wren helped fill in some of those gaps.

"Are you really here to kill me?" Wren asked innocently. "You don't even know me, you sweet hunk of a man."

"I am not here to kill anyone," Damian said calmly. "I am here for Sage and no one else."

"My sister?" Wren frowned distastefully again. "Really? And what does she have that's so great?"

"She's not going to let us walk," Sage whispered urgently to Damian. "Don't even think about turning your back."

"Forget August! I want *him* now, Taz!"

"Fuck off," Sage spat.

"Ooo!" Wren giggled. "Are you two lovers? I am so jealous—"

Sage lunged at her, but she wasn't quick enough to make contact. Wren jumped back, laughing away. Taz struck Damian, whose movements were surprisingly quick for someone who was sick. In fact, he held his own impressively well, indicating he had consumed more than just a mug of coffee at camp.

August's Cells.

No.

Sage turned around, watching as Damian and Taz duked it out; the latter was already fatigued from a full hour's fight against Sage, but that did nothing to land him on the losing side of the scuffle. Taz had too many Cells, completely overpowering Damian, who quickly lost his momentum and got run through with his own sword.

Damian grunted. Sage flew to him, but Wren smashed into her.

"Out of the way!" Wren cackled. "He's mine!"

"DAMIAN!" Sage yelled as Taz jumped back, letting Wren hop on Damian.

"My *Cells*!" She cackled, seizing his face. "Give them back!"

Wren didn't need an Extractor to take what was hers—all she

needed was blood. There was plenty spurting out of Damian's wound, a big enough incision for Wren to grab and call the Cells back into her body. Not that there were many to begin with—Damian had destroyed all of his Cells with Stars, and what was left used to belong to August. So how was he still alive now?

"What?" Wren breathed as Damian struck her, throwing her off him. He yanked the sword out of his body, staggering to his feet in a pitiful show of defense. "How are you still alive?!"

Damian shouldn't have been. He shouldn't have had any Cells left, and now there was a steady dose of Slainium traveling through his veins. It was perfectly visible, stemming from the wound in the center of his chest like a spider's web. While he'd have to get his blood pumped, there was one advantage to having no heart: the Slainium didn't move through his veins as quickly. Wren was confused, but she quickly figured it out.

"You!" Wren exclaimed at Sage. "You gave him your Cells?!"

Damian fired his gun, shooting Wren's face—Taz lunged at him, but Sage got to Taz first. Taz wasn't going to win another battle against her, and he couldn't afford to waste time when Wren had a bullet in her brain, so he made the smart move and put whatever energy he had into escaping. He jumped back to hide behind his mother, cowering like a scared little boy. Wren didn't look very amused because she had to call a truce here.

"Sister," she said softly, with blood trailing down her face. "Must we fight?"

Sage staggered a bit on her feet; Damian held her tightly, an arm around her waist. "Must we?" she said, breaths shallow. "You attacked me."

Wren shrugged. "I was mad about the Cells. Such a petty thing when there are much grander goals to accomplish, though." Her eyes glistened at Damian. "A pity he is the least of my worries. As hybrids, we are valuable, Sage. We are wanted."

"Hybrids?" Damian whispered.

Wren scowled. "Do you not know who I am? Who *Sage* is? We are the perfect being, the perfect blend of Squid and human. While

Slainium is still our weakness, we can overcome that easily because our bodies are like machines. As for Enhanced?" She snorted. "We are much stronger than they are. So bow to me, you insolent man!"

Sage held out an arm. "He bows to no one."

"Sister, you've got to put him in his place . . . or else he'll walk all over you." Wren touched her lips. "Not that I'd mind that, of course."

Damian drew Sage even closer to his body. He didn't turn around and leave until he was sure Wren retreated first. It was crazy how the tension lifted like a veil once she was out of the perimeter. The adrenaline fled just as quickly, making Sage sag against Damian's chest.

"I've got you," Damian said, his voice ringing in her ears.

Sage hoped so because she fell unconscious after that.

CHAPTER 19

A Proposal

Sage had woken up by the time Damian made it back to the airship. The rebels had already packed up and left, so the camp was gone. He seated her inside, then got to work on the controls. He looked composed, but Sage knew the Slainium had to be tearing his body apart. On top of that, his thoughts were probably traveling at a hundred miles per hour. With the coordinates locked in, he sat down next to her to enjoy the ride. He communicated their safety to his crew, then turned his full attention to her.

Damian touched her cheek, fingers feeling her skin. There were no longer any open gashes. Sage was going to be fine.

"You're a hybrid?" Damian whispered.

"Yes," she said. Her head was against the headrest, arms on her lap. Her sword was on the floor by her feet. "My father is a Squid . . . and my mother was human."

"Is that so?" Damian's face remained expressionless, so it was hard to tell if she disgusted him. If she did, he was hiding it very well. "And you know this for sure?"

"Of course. My mother told me, and just look at my sister—how she created Enhanced—and look at *me*, Damian. Do you think all the training in the world can elevate an Enhanced to my level? Even if I was riddled with Cells, I wouldn't look this human. Francis doesn't."

"So if it's true that these Cells came from your sister, then why were you not in a lab, too? Why only her Cells?"

"My mother sold her for money," Sage said softly. "And kept me a secret."

At last, Damian gasped. It was as if the idea of a mother selling her child for money was far more scandalous than being a Squid. Sage appreciated his reaction, but right now she was wrapped up in memories she'd rather forget. Watching her mother die had been no easy task, but learning the truth at a time when she couldn't ask any questions had been even worse. Even her half-sister, Aurora, hadn't had any idea that there was a long-lost twin in a lab somewhere.

"So you, too, can create Enhanced?" Damian held his breath. "But you didn't, not like her. Wren was used as a lab rat whereas you're the—"

"Optimum," Sage finished for him.

She gazed into the dark eyes above her. The tunnels sucked her into nothingness. There weren't any flashes of emotion or judgment in them or his expression. Damian just took a lot of time to process all of this and kept whatever thoughts he had to himself. One of his rebels' missions was to find the Optimum, and now that he had . . .

Ever so slowly, Damian's eyes grew shiny. They welled with tears as they dropped to his wrists, to the scars from so long ago.

"Damian," Sage whispered gently.

He was going to need a lot more than the sound of his name from her lips to compose himself. In the meanwhile, past the emotional breakdown that made Sage nervous, she noticed the sallowness of his skin. She was going to need to give him more of her blood soon, but Damian's focus wasn't on his health.

"It was you," he said quietly.

"It was," Sage said.

"You saved my life."

"Maybe I did, but you saved yourself afterward. You found a purpose, and that is far more impressive than what I did."

"I FOUND A PURPOSE BECAUSE OF *YOU!*" Damian yelled. His face turned red, and huge veins popped out of his forehead. "And because of it, I've lived a life of death, blood, torture, and betrayal! It would have been so much easier to die!"

"It is much easier to die, isn't it?" Sage said. "And that's what makes you so powerful, Damian. You have lived. And as much as you're pity-partying now like the drama queen you are, you know it's been worth it."

Perhaps, but Damian had more crying to do before he could acknowledge it. This whole mission had done a number on him, and it was definitely time to rest. When he grew weaker, slouching a bit in his chair, Sage got up to look for a med kit.

Those were easy to find in the clinic. They had syringes, which was all she needed. When she returned to Damian's side, he had stopped his sobbing. He didn't have the strength to at this point, but he did watch her. He didn't stop her from withdrawing her blood then pushing up his sleeve to transfuse it into his vein. This would hold him over until Dr. X could tend to him.

"I love you," Damian said.

Sage smiled at him. She injected him. "I love you, too."

Damian touched her cheek. Sage held his hand. Then they leaned toward each other and kissed. Five minutes later, they arrived at Mousafeld.

There was a crowd waiting for them there. Damian lowered the ramp, and then he was walking with his head up and shoulders back, every bit the warlord his name indicated.

Impressively, nearly all the Enhanced were on the runway, clapping, hooting, and cheering. They screamed for their leader, prostrated themselves, kissed his rings, patted his back, and congratulated him on his success. Not just his, but they had good news to deliver, too: they had rescued all of Wolfeld's residents, who were now being accommodated in the fields outside of Mousafeld. Sage saw them in the distance, aircrafts racing to provide supplies for

the people living in tents. It was temporary, as Damian told his Enhanced on the way to the clinic where Dr. X was waiting for him.
There were updates galore for him, so he was going to have a busy
night. Even busier days were ahead because the rebels had a lot of
preparations to make. It wasn't just Diamond City anymore—it
was Wren and Taz now, also.

"Come with me, Sage?" Damian asked her.

Sage looked up, interrupted from her thoughts. They were at
the clinic already, and Damian wanted to know if Sage was going
to be holding his hand while Dr. X pumped out all of his contaminated blood. It'd be the right thing to do, but Sage wanted to talk to
Samson. It'd be her only opportunity to do so because she was sure
Damian wouldn't be letting her out of his sight now. Of course, she
couldn't talk about her Squid companion out in the open, so she
used Louis instead.

Perhaps it had been the wrong thing to say because Damian's
face hardened. It was slight, but Sage knew all his looks by heart
now. *Him over me?* he seemed to say with the blackness of his eyes.

"Don't be a baby," Sage said. "You'll be fine."

Nobody talked to the Warlord like that and got away with it.
Their audience was very vested in how Damian was going to react, and he did something they didn't expect in a million years: he
stepped up to Sage, held her jaw, and kissed her lips tenderly. It
wasn't rough because he didn't want to come across as possessive,
but that's exactly what it was.

Sage glared at him.

"I'll see you later, darling," Damian said to her. Coldly.

Sage didn't appreciate that. But she said nothing as he entered
the clinic, flanked by his closest Enhanced. The remaining ones
whose ranks weren't high enough to warrant their presences glared
at Sage with something akin to hatred. Sage sensed it. They hated
her, didn't know her, and didn't trust her. They already knew she
wasn't like them, and that made them very uneasy. Additionally,
the Warlord had just kissed her and confirmed the rumors: they
were a couple now.

Thank God Mega Woman wasn't around to exasperate her. She was with the Warlord in the clinic, happy as a bird by his side. Sage was glad because she couldn't handle any more drama.

Sage went straight to her room. There, she had Samson and Louis to greet. Both of them were at the counter, cooking in . . . harmony? Samson was speaking Lucidum, and not in a snappy or spiteful way. He was telling Louis about spices and how the right blends brought out the right flavors. They had two pots of tomato broth going, an accompaniment to the beef ribs baking in the oven.

It wasn't just the food that made Sage freeze—there was a stack of presents on the table. There was a banner that read *Welcome Back, Sage!* hanging on the wall. Sage was speechless.

"Oh, thank the Forefathers" Louis exclaimed. "You're in one piece! We were worried about you—"

"*He* was worried about you," Samson corrected. "I knew you'd be back. Missions can get complicated sometimes, but you always pull through."

Louis flushed, pronouncing his boyish cheeks. "I went to the Marketplace every day looking for Defenders Unite! merchandise, and I heard things about the mission. Diamond City hit hard, didn't it?"

Sage rubbed her temple. This was a bit too overwhelming for her, so she took a seat at the table, in front of her mountain of gifts. She gazed at them in wonder, then glanced at Louis, who actually looked pretty good in an apron. Who would have thought a spoiled prince could be so useful around the house? The room was immaculate, fresh, and up-to-date because of him (and Samson). It was all to show that great things were earned, not given.

"And . . . you're not upset about that?" Sage asked quietly. "That we fought off your people?"

"I think they're *our* people," Louis corrected her. "And I'm not mad you were able to drive them off—those assholes dumped me! As if I'm just some cargo they can use!"

"Impressive, Louis."

"Right?" Samson said. "I think Mousafeld has been good for him. Sometimes one needs to be a hostage in order to appreciate life."

Louis sure had grown in the three months he'd been here. But that didn't mean Sage could divulge secrets about the missions, did it? At this point, perhaps, it didn't matter. Diamond City already knew so much about her, so she said it anyway.

"Wren is alive and well."

Samson stopped. He blinked his large eyes, which only continued to grow the more Sage described the encounter: Taz was the unknown intruder, a body just filled with Cells; and Wren was among them, free from Diamond City, traveling the Outskirts with some unknown purpose in mind. Other than retrieving her own Cells, of course.

"But *why?*" Samson said.

"She didn't say," Sage replied, folding her hands on the table. "She's just collecting Cells . . . and sicking her pet on everyone because it's easy."

"But since when did Francis become a 'pet'?" Louis asked quietly. "How did this duo happen?"

"You don't know anything about it?" Samson asked incredulously.

It was more than obvious Louis had been kept in the dark about a lot of things. The Allseer and his brother had kept quite a number of secrets from each other and everyone around them, too. Even Blackburn didn't know Francis and Wren were working together. He only knew about the Optimum—Sage—and that was because of Bram . . . Did he even know about Wren?

"So that means it was Taz killing all those Enhanced the Private Guard was investigating," Samson said. "Meaning it's not likely that even the Allseer was aware of it."

"Wouldn't he have known about Wren, though?"

"Maybe he didn't. Maybe Francis kept all his actions a secret."

The memory was so vivid in Sage's mind, that day that Wren, in her straitjacket, had loaded the airship. Sage had focused so much on her that she hadn't noticed who else was with her. Francis had broken her out of that laboratory in the Cut District, but for what purpose? As a sex toy, or something else?

"They're obviously experimenting with Cells," Louis said, playing with the frills on his apron. "But for what purpose?"

To find the Squids was Sage's immediate answer. It was probably Samson's, too, but they kept that to themselves because they weren't sure and there were other concerns between them at the moment. Wren and Taz would return to Mousafeld eventually, and so the Warlord had to be making preparations for that inevitable confrontation. Sage had to stay tuned for what those next moves would be, but first, she had all of Louis' gifts to open. They were a great distraction, lighting joy in Sage's chest. She marveled at an old clock with Star Raider's face, bracelets, a T-shirt, and socks.

"There was a thrift sale," Louis said happily. "And I thought of you, of course. It's to say sorry for being an asshole that day during my birthday party. It's just—"

"I know," Sage said quickly. "They were forcing you to make a move and you didn't want to appear interested."

"Yeah," he replied grimly. "My sister told you?"

"She did. It's why I didn't let you rot in jail."

Louis' cheeks went a bright pink again. "I'm glad you heard something positive about me. I've heard nothing but positive things about you from Samson. Except for how you leave your shoes in the kitchen. He hates that."

Sure enough, Sage had already taken off her boots. There they were on the floor. Samson grumbled as he picked them up and tossed them into her room.

"Why don't you take the room tonight?" Louis said. "You need to rest."

"I appreciate that." Sage got to her feet. Louis' fidgeting got worse.

"Oh, and, Sage?"

Sage looked at him.

"How about we get some pizza at the Marketplace?" Louis asked nervously. "When you're up for it, of course. Dough makes these incredible pies that I'm sure will remind you of home."

Sage blinked. She looked at Samson, who refused to look at her, the asshole. But he must have approved if he kept quiet about the date. Little did he know … *they* know … that Damian wasn't going to let her go that easily.

"Sure," Sage said, smile falling a bit.

Troubled by thoughts of Damian, Sage went for the shower. She took off her jacket, her jumpsuit, and her socks. She inspected her body, the bruises in the most random places, and then her tattoo of Star Raider's crest, right on her wrist, over her pulsing vein.

"Sage … you are a hero," Aurora said to her on her deathbed. "A defender of the people."

After a hot shower, Sage applied conditioner to her hair. She combed out the strands, waiting to see the silkiness in her locks. Better than usual, but nothing like Wren's. Not that she wanted that sort of comparison.

Instead of going to bed, Sage curled up on her armchair and used the Portable Projector to watch a few episodes of Defenders Unite!. She laughed when someone made a joke, grew worried when characters got into trouble, and sighed when Star Raider found out her beloved was the villain after all. Sage thought of Damian. Speak of the devil, there was a tap on the window.

Sage drew her gun and shot at the intruder. Glass exploded, curses rang through the building, and Damian shouted to the angry residents, "It's all right! Just a mistake!"

"Damn it," Sage grumbled, hoping that Samson and Louis weren't too startled. "It's you."

"Must you try to kill me every time you see me?" he spat. He came inside and shook glass off his coat. "You almost blew my head off."

"That was the intention. I knew you were coming to see me, but I didn't think it'd be through my goddamned window."

"I'd rather not deal with Louis," Damian growled. "Because if I see him, I'm afraid I'll hurt him. I only wish to see you—I need to keep you updated."

"Am I your secret weapon now?"

Damian scowled, shadows darkening the lines on his face. He

looked more irritated than menacing. "Didn't I already tell you that you're not a weapon? We had an agreement, Sage: you fight for me, and I give Louis and Agathe back to you."

"Can you tell your people that?" Sage spat. "Because every time they look at me, it looks like they want to tear my throat out."

"I know." Damian sighed. "Despite our successes at Wolfeld, they need time, Sage. Please understand."

"I understand they're frustrated because they're weaklings who get their asses kicked."

Damian chuckled. "Precisely. Either way, they have to follow my commands. They will accept you in due time."

Sage finally lowered the gun. "Did you tell them what I am?"

"I did. There was no other way to explain what they saw when you defeated my brother. If possible, they are even more terrified of you now . . . but they also realize they can utilize you." Damian paused. He finally finished straightening out his coat, then fixed his hair. He ran a few fingers through it, eyes downcast, thinking of ways to tell her what Sage already knew.

"You have fought for so many years," he said. "Because of you, Diamond City is the beauty that it is today, with its united districts and driven people. I understand your need for retirement from fighting, but you also understand that you are here by contract. You work for me, and I spare the lives of Louis and Agathe. However . . . we can change that."

In the throes of love-making, Damian had suggested the same thing. Then again, sex-crazed Damian was very different from battle-strategy Damian, who was standing before her now.

Sage watched him closely. "What do you mean?"

"I'm feeling generous and I'm willing to compromise those terms. Also, our situation has changed drastically. As you have probably already figured out, we will not be able to stay here much longer. We fear that Wren will find our camp, so it'll be best to move back to Diamond City as soon as possible."

"But, wait—Diamond City? They're going to let you back in?"

"Not me," Damian said. "You. My brother wouldn't dare attack you head-on. He'd much rather listen to reason and spare as many lives as possible. We also have Louis and Agathe, whose safety we will barter as well."

It sounded like such a long shot. Damian was banking on his brother's cooperation in order to stay safe from Wren. Sage thought it was way too soon to make a move against Diamond City—Wolfeld's forces weren't nearly enough to give them a fighting chance, even if all their weapons were laced with Slainium. Not only were they at a disadvantage against Diamond City when it came to numbers, but what would happen if Wren decided to make her move at the same time? They'd be overwhelmed on both fronts.

"I think we should stay here," Sage said. "Build our defenses, gather more towns. It won't take long to persuade them—everyone is terrified of Wren."

"I fear for my people's safety, Sage. That I will not sacrifice."

"Our chances are better here, Damian. Trust me—I'd much rather fight my sister with an army of Enhanced than your brother's army, which triples ours."

"I have sent word to my brother," Damian said softly. "For a truce. We will see how he reacts. But either way, regardless of what we decide to do, my concern is you."

"Why?"

"I know that we had an agreement, but as I said, I'm feeling generous." He cleared his throat. "Do you want to do this, Sage? Do you want to fight for me?"

"I told you from the beginning," Sage said quietly. She didn't want to, but she had to. She couldn't stay idle while people put their lives on the line. She had come here to complete a mission, and she had to see it through to the end. "I am with you until the ordeal is over."

"You are a traitor in the eyes of Diamond City."

Sage snorted. "A traitor? Do you think I care about that? Those idiots were the ones who bribed me into this predicament, so if anything, it's their fault."

"What do you care about?" Damian asked.

"Unity."

"I was hoping you'd say me."

Sage narrowed her eyes at him. But Damian wasn't looking at her—he was looking at the stack of gifts in the corner of the room. He understood exactly what was going on here, the dynamics between her and Louis, which were more worrisome to him than Wren's next move.

"The moment I let Agathe and Louis go from my custody . . . will you kill me?" Damian seemed to be bogged down by the thought of it. How couldn't he be? He had been betrayed by so many people in the past, including his own family. He took a seat in the armchair with Defenders Unite! continuing to play in front of him.

"Is that what you're worried about?" Sage said.

"Very much so," Damian replied quietly. "This can turn around so quickly. I can strike a deal with my brother, return Agathe and Louis to Diamond City, but then be backstabbed by you. I wish to know where your loyalties lie."

Damian sure was being frank with her. There was no way he'd had this much time to think at the clinic with all his Enhanced asking questions, so these must have been concerns from way back. It was a bit unnerving, actually, hearing him talk this way to her, as if they were enemies on a battlefield and not lovers occupying the same room. Sage wasn't used to the Damian who bullied his way around his opponents . . . She wanted the kind, attentive, and loving Damian. It was childish of her, but she knew why Damian had to be this way.

"I can't betray you," Sage said honestly. "It would mean betraying Gertrude and the handful of people I actually like. Besides." Sage sat down on the footrest, looking into his eyes. "I meant it when I said I love you."

"Did you?"

"I'm not giving you a blowjob to prove it."

Damian laughed. "A kiss would do."

Sage crawled up next to him, squeezing her body in between his left hip and the armrest. She ran a hand through his silky hair, pushing it back from his face, and gave him a kiss he deserved.

Positive reinforcement. That's how one trained animals. That's how Sage intended to train Damian's monstrosity, by showing him that this act of kindness and consideration on his part was appreciated. She gave him everything he asked for in that moment, nipping his lips, stroking his tongue, and just relishing in the feel of his mouth. He didn't ask for anything more, anything that would make her feel uncomfortable or like he was taking advantage of her. If anything, it was Sage who touched his throat, fingers beneath his shirt to feel his chest.

"I have cut off my engagement to Agathe," he murmured against her lips.

Sage stopped. This took her by surprise. "What? For real? Damian, marrying her guarantees you a place in Diamond City once we return."

"It doesn't," he said. "Not at all. My brother doesn't honor such unions. You were right from the beginning."

"So you have her as a hostage instead. Then why did you propose marriage?"

"I was bored," Damian said truthfully. He stroked her hair, tucking a strand behind her ear. "And horribly lonely. Agathe is such a sweet girl . . . I'm not sure how you'll take this, but I pictured her taking care of me, holding me. I want someone to love me the way my family used to, even if their shows of love were all fake. I suppose they gave me a taste of it, so I want something genuine now. Is it wrong for a man to want these things? Even if that man is a monster like I am?"

"Not at all," Sage said softly. "But maybe forcing yourself on someone isn't the way to do it."

"You're right. Which is why I've called it off. I swear I never touched her."

Sage already knew that because Agathe had been honest about it. What impressed her the most, though, was Damian's admittance of it, as if it was something he was proud of. Out of all the horrible deeds he had committed in the past, at least he had some good ones to hold onto.

"So now you've set your sights on me," Sage said. "Is it because I'm convenient? The Optimum you were looking for?"

"Absolutely not." Damian let his fingers trail to her collarbone. "I am trying to tell you that I love you."

"I think you just want to dominate me. It's a sick game power-hungry people like to play. You'll move on to the next person as soon as you're done with me. Whatever will help you get to the throne quickest."

Damian's hand fell. Her accusation offended him.

"You are the man who kidnapped Agathe because you were bored," Sage reminded him. "She was convenient for you then. How am I supposed to believe that I don't fall in the same category? Kisses and sex don't prove anything."

"Then give me a chance," Damian said. "Stay with me . . . and allow me to show you that I have nothing but your best interests at heart." He took her hands hopefully. "Forego your loyalties to Diamond City and join me instead. Wholly and heartedly." Before Sage could answer, Damian asked another question.

"Will you marry me?"

Sage froze. It was one of those moments when everything just stopped, as if someone had pressed the pause button. She blinked rapidly, mouth falling open. Worst of all? No words came out. She hated being put on the spot like this. Damian kissed each of her hands.

"How am I supposed to let you go?" Damian croaked, as if the answer was too difficult to ponder. "In the short time we've worked together, you have proven to be my most faithful ally. I trust no one with my life but you."

"You seemed to be doing just fine without me."

Damian chuckled wryly. He shook his head. "On the contrary. I didn't have the manpower, skill, or persuasion that you have to keep this camp together. To gather so many allies. I don't believe for one second that you're a weapon, but surely you see that you have value."

Sage said nothing.

"If you wish to leave after our agreement is over, then you'll have to fight me because I am not going to let you, Sage. I have spent a lifetime being rejected, betrayed, and backstabbed by everyone I know, so what on earth makes you think I am going to let you walk away from me? Are you really so damn selfish? I believe the answer is no, you won't leave." Damian held her cheek, forcing her gaze on his. "You'll stay with me."

Sage touched a strand of his hair, playing with it. She already knew what the answer was and so did he. What they didn't know . . . was what awaited them *after* they captured Diamond City. What sort of rule would there be? Dare she mention Louis and Agathe? Did it really matter what Damian promised with words—wasn't he going to do what he wanted anyway?

"I'll help you," Sage said softly. "If you swear to put Louis and Agathe in charge. I won't do this if it means you'll be a tyrant."

"Is that why you think I'm doing this?" Damian whispered, her words hurting him anew.

"I don't know, Damian. How can I know? I hardly know you. I want you to swear to me that this isn't for you. This is for Diamond City."

"I swear. If I prove it, will you marry me?"

Sage lowered her eyes. "I may have to leave anyway. After all of this is over."

"Leave *where*, Sage?"

"I'm not all human, Damian."

"And neither is anyone in this camp. Neither am I—"

"You don't understand," Sage insisted. "I told you that I was a hybrid. I am human *and* Squid just like my sister. That makes me very valuable, not just to you and Diamond City—but to the Squids. I am nearly immune to Slainium, but more than that: I'm far more powerful than an Enhanced. I'm the perfect blend, and they know it. I read about it in Preacher's books because I can read Lolligo. They're going around kidnapping women to reproduce—Nova told me so many in her town have gone missing—because they want *more* hybrids. They're out there, and there's a chance that I . . . " She hesitated. "That I might have to get involved."

"Why?" Damian said.

"Because I can't ignore it. Those are my people and I have to make sure they don't hurt Diamond City. My fight in the Unification War will not be for nothing. I will *not* stand down and let them take over again."

"Sage, you don't have to do anything alone. We'll do it together, understand? Just like we've been doing all this time."

Sage breathed out. At long last, she had expelled all that bad air from inside her lungs, the insecurity she'd kept bottled up for so long. Hearing Damian's declarations of loyalty certainly made her feel better about her mission. He'd never given her a reason to distrust anything he'd ever said, even if Blackburn's warning kept ringing in her head. But Sage was long past listening to Blackburn—she knew Damian now. Somewhat. It was only fair she gave him a chance . . .

"Please," Damian whispered.

Sage rested her head on his shoulder as she admitted, "I suppose if you say it like that, I'll have to give in. That 'please' will get me to do anything."

"*Anything*?" Damian traced the outline of her breast.

"I'm not sucking your dick," Sage said flatly.

"I understand that, and I am willing to compromise. I want you to touch me instead. Squeeze me, then pump me until I explode."

"You do know that Louis is listening in, right?" Sage glanced at the door. She didn't doubt Samson was there as well. She raised the volume on the Portable Projector; there was a boom as Star Raider entered a fight against Metalman.

"I'll keep it down," Damian said huskily. "I promise. Please?"

"No."

"Then come to my room where we will have more privacy."

"I'm not moving from here."

"Please, darling. Have I not been good to you?"

"You sound like such a sap."

Damian kissed her cheek, letting his lips linger. "You've already aroused me. So either I will do it . . . or you will."

Sage glanced at his crotch. "How the hell is that possible? We only kissed."

"That's all it takes," he whispered.

Sage was so thankful she wasn't a man. To some degree, she supposed she did pity him. "One sound and you're doomed, got it?"

There was no way Sage was going to put herself in that very embarrassing conversation with Samson and Louis tomorrow morning. If they even suspected Sage was engaging in sexual encounters with the Warlord, she'd be a laughingstock. Not a peep from Damian, or she'd stop immediately.

Damian sat back, arms on the armrests. He closed his eyes as Sage unbuttoned his pants and lowered his zipper. He hissed as the cool air hit his penis. He bit his lip when Sage's fingers skimmed over his abdomen, past his belly button, and to the tuft of hair beneath it.

"Relax, Damian."

He was extremely tense. Maybe it was the teasing and the anticipation that drove his temperature to burning, making him sweat. Sage couldn't help a laugh as her hand finally traced his length, finger gliding over the tip—Damian bucked his hips, but she kept his body down and under control. He groaned when her strokes became more defined, squeezing and pulling in perfect rhythm. Sage laid her head on his chest, right under his chin, fondling him like she would a pet.

"Stars!" Damian croaked, hands clutching the chair. "This is so much better than doing it myself."

"You're being obnoxious again."

"I'm hoping it turns you on."

"Maybe a little."

"Have you ever masturbated?"

Sage smiled sweetly. "No."

"You wait for the real pleasure." Damian groaned. He rocked his hips in tune with her hand. "Like my tongue inside you, touching and tasting every crevice in that tight snatch." Sage pumped harder, and he groaned louder. "Harder, darling." He gritted his teeth, trying to keep the sounds inside. "Don't be afraid."

Sage wasn't. That's why Damian climaxed in seconds, with Sage's mouth on his, swallowing the cries. This was going to keep him quiet as pleasure crashed through his body. He ejaculated all over Sage's hand, and it was a while before he stilled his hips, riding out every wave of pleasure until there were no more.

"Mmm..." Damian hummed against her kisses. "That felt so good..."

Sage was sure it had, and it had been a mistake to oblige him because now he wanted more. He indicated so with his tongue inside her mouth and the fist that crept up her shirt.

"Damian, no," Sage said, stopping him. "Not with eavesdroppers."

"Why?" he rasped desperately. "Will it make Louis jealous? Good. You're *my* lover—not his."

"We don't have to prove anything." Sage shooed his hand away from her breast. "And we're not going to tonight. Now can you settle down and go to sleep?"

Impossible. At least at first. All Damian did was lick her lips like a dog and try to snake his hand up her shirt or into her pants.

"Damian, cut it out!" Sage hissed.

"Why?" He tried to outright cup her crotch, but Sage blocked him with a fist. "I know you want it."

"Yes, but not right now."

"You are probably so wet right now."

There wasn't a doubt that with all of Damian's groaning, climaxing, and attempts to touch her that she was aroused as hell. But Sage was going to have to exercise some control if she was going to keep her honor. Samson was a pervert who'd hear everything and Louis would never look at her the same. Sage was supposed to be a serious woman on a mission, not a lusty wench sleeping with the Warlord every chance she got. No Defenders Unite! episode would be loud enough to drown out their wild sex, so the answer was no for tonight.

After more kissing and attempts at touching, Damian got the hint. Or maybe he was so exhausted that the last of his energy vanished and his body slumped on the couch, head on Sage's. It was nice to hear his snores.

Sage stayed awake through another few episodes of Defenders Unite!. Eventually, she succumbed to fatigue, too. The day's aches drifted away and the fog around her brain cleared up. When she woke up some hours later in the darkness, she was surprised to find Damian was still sleeping. Unlike her, he had a hard time getting a full night's rest.

Slowly, Sage raised her head. Defenders Unite! was on episode fifteen now, running without viewers. A tap of the Portable Projector stopped it and any sound that filled the room. Now there was only soft rain and wind that snuck in through the broken window. Any rain they got always came from Diamond City.

"Why did you have to break it?"

Sage was on her feet, attempting to free herself from Damian's embrace without disturbing him. Fat chance.

"Unless there are any more starlit boyfriends coming to see me tonight," she said, unlatching the buckles on his boots, "I shouldn't need to break any more." She slid them off his feet. "You'll be safe. Damian, get some sleep."

The man needed it. The circles under his eyes were as dark as ever and his skin was looking a bit too sallow. This was that pivotal moment of sleep or drugs, and Sage already knew how many times he had picked the latter.

She pulled him forward and hooked her arms under his. She lifted him off the couch and hoisted him onto her body. His one hundred and fifty pounds felt light, almost fragile. Or maybe Sage was that powerful, something Damian made no comment about as she sat him on the bed and took off his coat, shirt, and pants. There was no way he could rest with all that heavy clothing.

His electronics were next. Sage reached into his pockets and pulled out all his phones, communication devices, and spyware. To her surprise, Damian didn't snatch them or demand them back. He said, without opening his eyes, "Don't leave."

At first, Sage thought Damian meant don't leave the camp. Then she realized he meant the room.

"I won't," she assured him. "If you let me braid your hair."

Damian smiled because he was too weak to chuckle. Sage combed his strands until they were silky locks over the pillow. Then she worked on another braid, this one in the back, and laced it with a colorful thread. Damian fell asleep as soon as she made the first knot.

It was mission accomplished. Perhaps this was Damian's first true rest since his last overnight stay at the hospital a few days ago. Dr. X would be so thrilled to hear it, maybe more so at all the messages Damian wasn't answering at five in the morning. Sage didn't read them either, only made sure they were silent . . . although she did wonder what sort of information she was missing out on.

Was it related to a mission? Gossip? Or people asking to share his bed?

Caring for him was a mistake. Sage was already wrapped around his finger, confined by the very emotion she feared: love. She *loved* this man. What had sealed it?

The damn Portable Projector. Dangling around her neck like jewelry. Better than any engagement ring he could have gotten her.

CHAPTER 20

Gathering Forces

Sage stayed with Damian for the rest of the night. After his braid, she slipped into bed behind him. At some point, she had come to lie on his back. Despite the heavy weight draped over his body, Damian snored on.

When morning came, Sage got up. She did so carefully, replacing her warmth with that of the comforter. Damian stirred, but Sage whispered that she was getting breakfast. He went back to sleep.

Samson was in the hallway. Louis was nowhere to be seen, so he must have taken off to visit his sister or stroll the Marketplace. Had he heard them? Samson surely had.

"What the hell, Sage?" Samson said in Lolligo. "He's sleeping in *your* bed?"

Sage rolled her eyes. "Relax. We didn't do anything."

"Do you think I'm dumb, naive, or both? I *heard* you—"

"Yes, and if you had been paying closer attention, you would have known it was a hand job with no intercourse."

"What is this?" Samson stomped after her, ready to explode with the barrage of questions he had for her. Damian was fast asleep, so this was his chance, but he still had to keep the volume under control.

"Why do you insult my intelligence? You must think I'm really stupid, Sage, for me to believe that you haven't had intercourse. A couple of nights out of my sight, and you're already spreading your legs for him?"

"I love him."

"Stars, you say that about a lot of men!"

Sage glared at him. "About August? It wasn't really love, just camaraderie. Gregory? I did love him because he was my husband. Louis? I don't think it was meant to be. And Damian . . . well, he's different." She made it to the refrigerator. "Don't look at me like that, Samson—you of all people love it here even if no one knows you exist. So wouldn't you be happy that I'm with Damian?"

"Yes," Samson said a bit stiffly. "It's just I already know how this is going to end. As soon as we're back in Diamond City, he's going to take over and he's going to break your heart. Goddamn it, Sage—you're doing the very thing you swore you wouldn't do! Working for him is one thing, but *sleeping* with him? And right when you are about to ovulate?"

Sage ignored the dip in her stomach. She masked the concern she felt because she had already prepared herself to deal with it. She had been perfectly aware of her actions and what the consequences would be. Unprotected sex always equaled a chance at pregnancy, but she was still many days away from the start of her new cycle, which came once every year at the beginning of spring, around the month of Shine. She had dodged pregnancy with August and Gregory, and she could do the same with Damian. Besides, yesterday night's romp was just a hand job.

"I know what I'm doing," Sage said. "And I needed to do this. It was the only way to wrap him around my finger."

Samson burst out laughing. "Look at you—the manipulative one. So you think he's going to listen to you just because you pumped him hard last night?"

"You really are a sick, fucking pervert."

"I *heard* you and I wasn't even standing by the door. Thank the Forefathers Louis hadn't been here or that boy would have been heartbroken."

"Oh, so you care about him now?" Sage crossed her arms. "He's no longer the spoiled little brat, is he?"

Samson waved at the room. "*Is* he?"

"You can't control me, Samson. I value what you have to say, but at the end of the day, I know what I feel."

"And what is that?" Samson sneered. "Horny?"

"What the hell's up your ass, Squid?"

"Goddamn it, Sage—don't you see the bigger picture here?! Forget warlords and Diamond City—if your sister is here, you know there's a reason for it. She is not a power-hungry female who has nothing else better to do. Maybe she's gathering strength because there's no other way to win."

"To win against what?"

"The Lolligo, Sage!" Samson exclaimed. "If you had tried talking to her instead of swinging your sword, maybe we would have figured it out!"

"She attacked me first," Sage said thinly.

"Are you sure about that?"

"Are you questioning *me*, Samson? If you want to find out so badly, why don't you start hanging around her instead?" Sage pulled out the eggs and milk in a non-too-gentle way. "I already know what you're suggesting: Let's go see the Lolligo, right? Well, why don't *you* go, Samson?"

"I can't," he said quietly. "You know that. They'll execute me."

"So then what the hell's your problem?"

"I'm curious, Sage!" Samson yelled a bit too loudly. "Aren't you? About your origins?"

"Then ask my fucking sister!"

The conversation didn't end well at all. They had to stop here or else Damian was going to wake up, so Samson shrank a bit and shuffled away. To where, Sage didn't know and didn't care because she was fuming and in the middle of breakfast now. Her hand shook violently as she grabbed a pan, the cutting board, and a pair of knives. There was emergency preserved food in the refrigerator because Samson was a paranoid prick who was always ready for the apocalypse, a Squid invasion. Thoughts of him turned fierce, his face pounding in her eyes, the only thing she could see as she started cutting onions and sliced her damn finger wide-open.

"Damn it!" Sage cursed, holding it under the running water. Her breathing escalated until Damian's hands settled on her shoulders, calming her.

"Darling," he whispered, concerned. "Are you all right?"

"Yeah."

Damian took her hand and inspected her finger. The wound was nearly gone by now. Either way, he slipped it into his mouth, tongue cushioning the cut and easing the pain. He caressed her cheek and peered into her eyes. His own were so naked without makeup and his hair was still wet from the shower, combed back from his face. All bare like that, Sage could see the light wrinkles, a few scars, and a tiny blemish on his temple. In her eyes, he was still the most beautiful man she had ever seen.

"What's wrong?" Damian asked her gently.

Sage kissed him. Doing so made her forget about Samson because the feel of his lips and then his tongue intoxicated her. She wrapped her arms around him, hands sliding up his back, and clutched his shoulders. He didn't have a shirt on and his skin was so smooth—it was hard to get enough.

This was the deepest she had ever kissed anyone. Their teeth clashed, tongues so far down each other's throats that they nearly gagged. Sage sucked all the moisture from Damian's swollen lips. Then they gazed into each other's eyes.

At that moment, Damian had her wrapped around his finger. He could ask her to do anything and she'd do it. When he whispered not to worry, Sage had to let Samson go. She couldn't muster up the will to leave this man, to abandon the love she felt for him.

She couldn't stop thinking about the sex, either. Their hips were touching, and all Sage had to do was thrust. One move, and Damian would be pudding. They'd both be on the counter or on the floor, and who knew how long they'd be at it.

It'd also put Sage in a horribly vulnerable position. Not just

emotionally, but physically. Samson was right . . . What if she got
pregnant?

Sage wanted to cry. She wanted Damian so badly. It didn't help
that her entire body was pulsing now, begging for his touch.

"You are intoxicating," Sage whispered, staring at his face. God,
he was beautiful.

"I know," Damian whispered back. "And so are you, my beautiful Sage."

Sage craned her head. She trailed kisses along his jaw.

"What's wrong?" He asked again. "I can sense your distress."

Sage buried her face into his neck. She breathed in his wonderful scent, sweet with a hint of spice. It drove her insane. She was
definitely in heat. Or maybe it was Damian and this horrible effect
he had on her, the one Blackburn had warned her about.

"Can you please put a shirt on?" Sage asked.

"Only if you put a bra on."

"What's the difference? I hardly have breasts."

"But I can see your nipples."

"They're covered, Damian. Yours are not."

Damian laughed. It was robust and genuine. Sage joined him,
but the more she enjoyed it, the more her problem flared up.

She was compromised, could no longer execute any means to
kill him on behalf of justice. If they managed to capture Diamond
City, and Damian turned around and seized power for himself, who
was going to stop him? Not only that: Sage had to deal with her
sister. Wasn't that what Samson wanted?

Uncertainty seized Sage hard. It must have shown on her face
because as soon as they were done with breakfast, Damian brought
up that very dreaded conversation. Sage was washing dishes, all
ears as Damian started with news from his brother.

"He won't let us in," Damian said. "Even with you at the fore-
front, he'll chance an attack. I'd rather not fight unless we have
greater numbers on our side. So you're right: we should stay here
and gather more allies. While it sounds simple, it's anything but.
However, with you, I'm confident I'll be able to persuade most of

the Enhanced to come back. You are the Optimum. I saw how August looked at you . . . " He cleared his throat. "With that said, I must ask: was he an ex-lover of yours?"

Sage looked at him over her shoulder. "Well, someone's astute."

"I can smell these things from a mile away. It's obvious he still desired you, from the gleam in his eye."

"We went to school together and we were very close during the war, but it never fully evolved into a relationship."

"Is there a reason for that?"

"August had goals very different from mine," Sage said. "Whereas he wanted to join your rebellion, I wanted to settle down. Is there anything else you'd like to know?"

"Who's Rick?"

Sage stiffened visibly, as if someone had thrown a bucket of cold water over her. She didn't usually react this way, but she had *not* been expecting to hear Rick's name from Damian's lips. The name unearthed a lot of memories from the past, and Sage wasn't sure they were good ones when she knew she'd never see that dazzling smile again.

Damian shook his head. "I don't mean to pry if you don't feel comfortable talking about your lovers, but I'm curious. I saw the tattoo on your left wrist last night. I didn't want to ruin our sex, so I decided to wait until now to ask."

"Rick wasn't a lover," Sage said softly. "He was a friend . . . someone who did whatever it took to be happy in this life. I admire that."

Damian cleared his throat again. "I see. Do you admire me?"

In other words: *Do you admire me enough to get my name tattooed on your body?* Sage wasn't sure why it annoyed her, but it did.

Damian picked up on it right away. "And with that, I'll do the right thing and give you some space." He touched her cheek. "How about you rest for a bit? I think we all need it. Wolfeld residents are still getting sorted, and everyone is coming to terms with our previous campaign. That includes, of course, losses."

Blondie and Mohawk. Right.

"I have to check on them. But please feel free to do as you wish in the meantime. Gertrude should be back soon." He reached for a fresh shirt and coat from the closet. Any of Louis' would do. Sage remained leaning against the kitchen counter, head swollen with all her troubled thoughts. She followed Damian to the front door and jumped when he gasped.

"Oh my!" Damian gaped at the living room, the neat walls, the shiny couches, the *cleanliness* of it all. His mouth hung open for a full five minutes. Even the furniture was sparkling. "What? How?"

"Louis," Sage said curtly.

"*Louis?*" Damian rasped, still looking around. "He did this?"

Sage nodded.

"So he is good for something," Damian mused. "We could have had him renovate the rest of the building, too. Speaking of which, where is he?"

"Good question. I suppose I should go look for him."

Damian didn't suspect she had a pizza date in a few hours. He kissed her hand again. This time, before he released it, he slid a ring onto her finger. It was his signet ring from his time in the Diamond City military. He never went anywhere without it. He kissed her one last time, promising to be back tonight if he didn't see her again throughout the day. She left him to his trials and went to face hers.

The sight of a happy, peppy Louis standing in front of the Marketplace's only pizzeria didn't alter her mood one way or another. Sage had a one-track mind at this point, and it wasn't going to change until she got answers. Perhaps she was a bit rude with the way she cut off Louis' "Hey, Sage," and even more intolerable when she stepped back from his embrace.

"Have you seen Samson?" Sage asked, her mind far from recruiting his attention. This was night and day compared to her behavior at the birthday party.

"Well, last night at the apartment," Louis said uncomfortably. "He wasn't there this morning? That's strange. You know he doesn't like to wander in public."

"I know that, but we got into an argument and there's a chance he might have taken off for good."

All Louis could do was blink. Sage led him inside where there was more noise to mask their conversation. She didn't look Dough in the eye as she took a seat in the corner. A waitress came to tend to them. She let Louis order whatever pizza he wanted and clarified her situation once they were alone again.

"He wants to go after my sister," Sage said. "I think he's desperate. He came here in hopes that he'd meet a Squid. He figures my sister is his best bet."

"Oh." Louis grimaced as if someone had punched his shoulder. Was that because Sage had used the word "Squid" to insult Samson's race or was that his thinking face? "Well … maybe that's good? Maybe he'll take care of your sister. I mean—he'll defeat her so we don't have to worry about her. Or are you worried about him *joining* forces with her?"

Wow, so he was perceptive to some extent. Sage was glad that he had said that and not her. It would have sapped a lot of her energy to pronounce the words, and she was already feeling woozy. She held her head because it felt too heavy for her shoulders. She sighed.

"I wouldn't worry about that, though," Louis said. "If the two of you have been living together for a hundred years, he has to hold you in special regard. What would he gain by backstabbing you? It's not like your sister is purposefully out to get you … is she?"

"No. I don't think so."

Louis shook his head. "Then put it out of your mind. Just let him figure it out. I think you have to focus on yourself and Diamond City at this point."

"Which includes you," Sage said, looking at him. She sat back and picked up her soda. "How are you feeling about it?"

"Actually, I'm nervous as hell. Not that that's anything new, but I don't trust the Warlord."

Sage wanted to say that she didn't either, but she didn't want to plant any doubts. She had no reason not to trust Damian despite what other people said. And she had already learned not to listen to others' opinions. She was confident they'd be successful in returning to Diamond City and giving everyone a chance to come back. Enhanced would no longer be persecuted and they'd be able to live with dignity.

"So you think he'll do the right thing?" Louis asked incredulously as the waitress came with their pizza. It was cheese with pineapple and ham. Sage eyed the crust, knowing the dough could have used more water and kneading before hitting the heat.

"I do," Sage said, taking a slice.

"And then what? He'll just live a nice life?"

"I think that's what he wants. He's into his fashion and stuff."

Louis snorted a bit at that. He shook his head. "And what about you? Will you go back to your pizza restaurant?"

"That's the idea." When the pizza here wasn't that great, every fiber of Sage's being wanted to return to the legacy she had created in Cut. Her pizza was number one, stars above this shit. She gave Dough a dirty look, one that he reciprocated. Sure, Sage was the Optimum, but that didn't give her the right to be a bully . . . at least to everyone except Dough. For him, she had a special message: she stuck out the middle finger.

"I think that'd be great!" Louis said quickly. "You can go back to what you love to do. If that's still what you love to do, of course. I know you had other goals when you came to Heart that time. Sorry if I disappointed you." He puffed out his chest. "But we can always start fresh. I mean—not in that way—as friends, right?"

Sage smiled. "I'd like that."

"I think you're amazing."

"You're not such a bad kid yourself. The Warlord was certainly impressed with your apartment renovations."

Louis blinked. "Wait—the Warlord was at our place?"

"He's keeping a close eye on me. I'm doing the same to him."

"Oh." Louis was having a hard time figuring out what that meant. He just had to ask, "Are the two of you together?"

Sage glanced at the signet ring on her finger. "Yes."

"S-Stars! For real?"

"You sound like Samson now."

"But I would have never imagined you with him," Louis croaked. "Ever. I thought you didn't trust the Warlord."

"I'm willing to give him a chance."

"So you're manipulating him to do the right thing."

"Yes," Sage said honestly. "Sort of. Although I will admit I do have feelings for him."

"You mean you feel sympathy," Louis said. "You don't really know him, do you?"

Sage had to admit that Louis impressed her. She had never imagined he was this perceptive. It made talking to him easy and guilt-free because he seemed to understand her and the reasons behind her actions. Sage said, "I need to see what happens and this is the only way."

"All right," he said easily. After another slice of pizza, which Sage respectfully declined, he smiled and said, "How about we do this again tomorrow?"

"Sure." Sage eyed Dough again. "Let's pick another restaurant, though. The pizza here is not that great."

Louis chuckled. Sage grinned. It was nice to have a friend because she didn't see Samson again and Damian only came to her at night.

It wasn't always to seduce her either—sometimes he fell asleep right when his head hit the pillow. Sage knew he was working hard all day, situating all the people from Wolfeld and organizing their camp's offenses and defenses. In the quietest and darkest nights like this one, Sage took a moment just to study Damian's face. As his alleged partner, she vowed to side with him and stand by him as long as she could. She helped out as much as she could, too, doing what she did best: training.

It was hard not to think of Blondie and Mohawk, but Gertrude was there to take her mind off death with all her crazy teenage stories and quirky aspirations to become the world's fastest knitter. Indeed, Gertrude had been a handful as a kid, cross-dressing to enter women's pageants (and even winning one once) and knitting so many Wooly Socks that she had a whole damn collection in her closet. These weren't officially licensed, but they were so close to the real ones that Sage could never tell otherwise. Her heart pitter-pattered when Gertrude gave her a Star Raider one.

"I meant to give it to you on New Year's day," Gertrude said happily. "But it wasn't finished by then. Getting neon thread for Star's energy blasts wasn't easy."

As days since the Wolfeld campaign became weeks, Sage started to notice a change in the rebels. The energy was higher than it usually was around camp. At the very least, people were a bit more friendly and . . . hopeful. Sage didn't get any more dirty looks. Maybe they were afraid of her, but she also knew it was Damian.

He was no longer sitting on his throne telling people what to do—he was out there doing it himself. That included everyday tasks like cleaning, filling up water jugs, distributing food, and walking through his camp to make sure everything was in order. On top of that, he was training again. He didn't do it in hiding either—he often joined them without his shirt on, which made everyone gape at his beauty, both men and women. He wasn't huge like a bodybuilder, but he was defined enough to display each and every muscle in the human physique. While Sage rolled her eyes, Gertrude started a horrible drool. It made Little Man smack her arm.

"Hey!" she hissed. "I have the right to admire perfection!"

"Perfection?" Sage snorted. "Please."

"He's *beautiful*, Sage!"

"Seriously?" Little Man hissed at her.

"You don't understand," Gertrude snapped at him. "He's mesmerizing!"

Gertrude had a full arsenal of synonyms that described Damian. And although Sage didn't show it, she was in the same trance as everyone else. Her head was still spinning from this morning's kiss, the longing and desire to be with him astronomical. Even with Gertrude around to entertain her, Turtle to argue with, and Little Man to throw punches at during training, Sage still couldn't stop thinking of him. She had his ring on her finger to remind her there was the possibility of a future together once this campaign was over, but the road to Diamond City felt like light years away.

"Wow, I'm not used to this," Turtle said, watching the Warlord fight Justice. "It certainly makes me feel more confident." He threw a snide look Sage's way. "If we get attacked, we'd have him and the *Optimum* to defend us."

Sage glared at him. She hated when they called her that.

"Even though we're fatigued by fighting," Gertrude said, "I feel so much more comfortable with Sage around. I know we're going to be successful."

Turtle didn't look convinced. But ever since Damian's series of punishments for cornering and exploiting women, he'd learned to keep his mouth shut and avoid confrontation at all times. It certainly made him more tolerable. Unfortunately for him, it was too late to hit it off with Gertrude.

Gertrude no longer looked twice his way. She no longer blushed or giggled girlishly when she was around him. She and Sage talked about it late one night, and her reasons were very simple. "I've moved on, Sage. You've taught me that."

"Good for you." Sage bounced a fastball up and down on the court. Tonight, they were hanging out at the stadium. At long last, Sage had found a ball to play with at the Marketplace, and it was time to test it out. She had Gertrude on the other side to volley with.

"He does seem particularly mournful." Gertrude tightened up her fists and braced herself. Sage served, smacking the ball over the net dividing the court in half. It hit the floor on Gertrude's side, and then Gertrude was able to hit it back. Barely. "He cornered me in the cafeteria during breakfast and let it all out. He wanted to talk, but ... " She shook her head. She completely missed Sage's counter, but the ball was far from her mind now. "I don't think there's any mending the relationship. Not after all the horrible things he said."

"Sometimes there's no coming back from something like that," Sage agreed. "And that's up to you to decide. Besides, don't you have your eye set on Little Man?"

Gertrude blushed a horribly bright red. She was able to hide it as she ran to get the ball from the sidelines. "How do you know?"

"I'm not an idiot. He likes you, too."

And Sage had living proof because Little Man stepped into the stadium the next second.

"Hey," he chortled at the sight of them. He had a net of fastballs over his shoulder, just purchased from the Marketplace. No one was interested in playing but him, but that's not why he was here. His eyes made another obvious pass at Gertrude who clapped.

"Oh, great! You can take over. I'm horrible at this game."

And against Little Man? So was Sage. Such a simple game, but strength turned it into a marvel when two adept players stepped onto the court. True fastball was too fast for the average human—the volleys were like shooting stars, flashing back and forth, never-ending until someone pooped out or messed up. In the Color District, Sage had seen a fastball game in the dark with light-up balls and glowing uniforms, and *that* had been so cool.

Sage got all tingly thinking about it. If only she were good enough to compete. Perhaps if she practiced against worthy opponents who weren't afraid to kick her ass. Little Man had a lot to prove playing in front of Gertrude. Those huge forearms couldn't be for nothing.

"All right, Optimum," he teased, bouncing a ball next to his foot. "Let's see how good you are on the court."

Sage readied herself. Holy shit, this was going to be intense.

And golly, it was. When Little Man hit the ball, it sounded like a bullet going off. It *exploded*, blasting right onto her side of the court, and Sage had to dive to hit it back. Just one volley, and already she had a scrape and a rapid heartbeat. Little Man was a spectacle on his side, jumping over to the ball and taking precisely-timed swings to smash it right back. Sage was a little bit more prepared this time, so she made contact with more ease. She could say the same for the next few turns, until Little Man decided to end this fast. On the next hit, his backswing shot the ball to the far corner behind Sage, and unless she could teleport to the edge of the stadium, there was no way she was getting that.

"Damn!" Sage panted, watching that ball bounce away in wonder.

"Wow . . ." Gertrude gaped a bit, too. She gazed at Little Man with newfound respect. "You actually beat her?"

"Just because I'm strong doesn't mean I can beat people at sports," Sage grumbled. "It still takes skill."

"She's right, you know," Little Man said, readying another ball from his bag. "When I was a kid, my older brother taught me proper technique every day after school. He showed me the right way to hit the ball so it goes where you want when you want it, and how to best angle the body to achieve it. Novices don't have the know-how, so it's understandable they'd lose. Based on my position, Sage should have been able to anticipate where I was going to hit the ball next, but she didn't know what to look for."

"I'll show you 'what to look for'," Sage grumbled under her breath, but there was no sense in getting mad about her losing. Against Little Man, she didn't stand a chance. Two hours later, and she still hadn't won *one* volley against him. While she could appreciate that Little Man didn't gloat, she just couldn't accept that he was better, so that's why they practiced.

A lot.

Every day after training for the next month. The month of Love was supposed to be about compassion and being nice to others, but for Sage, it brought too many memories of Samson. To celebrate, they used to buy each other something small and thoughtful for twenty-eight days. Chocolate bars were cheap, but there was something about getting one at the end of the day or seeing it in the bathroom cabinet with a hand-scribbled note that lifted her mood. This year, the void in her heart was filled by Louis, who watched every practice, and Little Man's attention to her form, technique, and stances.

"Head up!" he called from across the court, swinging his fist to smash the ball right to her. "Jump back and take a back stroke!"

Got it. Sage got it.

"Get it in the corner of my side like I showed you—come on!"

She got it again—yes!

"You see where I am—the angle?" Little Man called, bending

his knees to hit the ball back to her. "You know it's going to land right in front of you—dive!"

And dive, Sage did.

"WOO!" Louis hooted. "Go, Sage!"

She was becoming a pro at this, and Sage felt it simmering in her blood. While she still hadn't won a damn volley, she was going to rest up and get him tomorrow, for sure.

"Great." Little Man high-fived her. Louis did, too. "Truly. Once you get the hang of this, I think I'll be afraid of you."

Sage laughed. "That's the idea."

"Isn't she incredible?" Louis said wondrously.

Little Man hesitated. He was probably wondering why Louis was getting so attached to Sage, but he didn't voice his thoughts. For someone his size, he was way too quiet around camp. That's why his soft-spoken nature was perfect for someone like Gertrude.

"I'll wait for you outside the showers!" Louis said happily to Sage. "Then we can start dinner."

Sure thing. Cooking was a nice distraction because too much downtime allowed Sage to think of Samson. As soon as she hit the shower, thoughts of him flooded her mind.

A month without him was too much. That's why she made the decision to go look for him next week. She couldn't get up and leave in the middle of the night because it wouldn't be fair to Damian, so she'd talk to him about it the next time they saw each other.

"Are you all right?" Little Man asked her after she left the stall. He was still in his. It took a lot of time and power to scrub down a body that big. "Usually, you're a bit more talkative after practice."

"Yeah," Sage said softly, tying a towel around her body. Then she brushed her hair in the mirror. "Just thinking of someone."

"Don't worry," Little Man said. "He won't get mad. He knows you're just friends."

Sage looked over her shoulder. Steam was floating out of Little Man's stall. "What?"

"He's flirty, too, but he won't do anything. That's the one quality I love about him."

"Wait, who are we talking about?"

"The Warlord, of course."

Sage scoffed. "Please." She went back to her hair. It was so much nicer and smoother after all the routine Suave-Suave applications. "I'm not worried about that bastard."

Little Man laughed nervously. "Just wondering. You're a tough cookie, so it's only natural for you to attract attention, especially from wimps like Louis."

"Louis and I are friends, Little Man. Why are you so worried?"

"I've just never seen the Warlord so motivated. I'm not sure what you do to this camp, but everyone's so different. I can't fucking stand Turtle, but even he's apologizing for all the shit he's given everyone. I don't want that to go away . . . you know?"

Sage understood what Little Man was talking about, and she was about to say that would happen regardless of who her partner was, when Damian strutted into the room.

"Darling, you're here!" He was in all his shirtless glory, sweat glistening off the muscular cuts in his torso. He was a living, breathing model of a man. "Did you just finish playing games with Little Man? I wanted to come by and watch, but I had an audience of my own to entertain."

"I'm sure you did."

Damian stepped up behind her. He wrapped his arms around her waist and dug his face into her neck. He took a huge inhale. "You smell delightful."

"I don't," Sage said. "The soap in here sucks."

"Then allow me to use it on your body correctly," he whispered against her ear.

"I think I know how to use soap, thanks."

"Maybe not the right way."

"I'm not getting in the shower with you," Sage stated flatly. "Little Man is right there, and a shower with you is going to lead to more than just getting clean."

Little Man coughed.

Damian chuckled. "So?"

"So I'd rather not have an audience."

"Don't be shy, darling."

Little Man coughed again. It was hard to tell if he was laughing or embarrassed.

"I'm sure you can hold out until tonight," Sage said matter-of-factly.

"I'm not sure I can. Can't you feel it, darling?" He rolled his hips against her backside.

"We all know you have problems, Damian—you're a sex fiend."

"Only with the right person," Damian admitted. "I'm sure Little Man knows what I'm talking about."

"S-Stars, sir!" Little Man croaked. It sounded like he was drowning beneath the shower. "I-I'm not sure what to say!"

"The truth would be nice so that Sage doesn't think my sexual drive is strange."

"Are you suggesting I'm sexually active?"

"Absolutely," Damian said. "Everyone sees how you and Gertrude interact with each other. I know you've shared a few nights already."

"Can't he have some privacy?" Sage snapped. "Or are you in everyone's business?"

"Gossip is my forte."

"You're worse than a woman."

Damian chuckled. "So I've been told."

"I need to talk to you about something."

"We can talk in the shower."

"No," Sage said as he sucked on her neck. "If I can't talk to you out here, there's no way it's going to happen in there. You're distracting me."

"I'm sure it can wait." Damian cupped her breasts. He drove his hips into her ass, and the only reason he wasn't inside her was because of his pants and her towel. It was too much work to take them off, so he started thrusting right through his clothes.

"Can you stop humping me for one moment?" Sage snapped at him. "I'm trying to talk!"

"We can talk later, darling."

"Later when? Tonight when you're trying to seduce me again?"

"I wasn't successful this morning, so I'll have to employ a different tactic." Damian's eyes glistened. "I'd like to see you try and resist me then."

"Stop it, Damian."

"Darling, look at me." He waved at his crotch. It was a miracle his pants hadn't torn yet. "Forgive me if I'm not exactly thinking clearly."

"How much medication are you on?" Sage asked, facing him now.

"None," Damian said honestly. "I'm sober. Now please take off that towel. How the hell did you tie it so tightly?"

"I wouldn't want any undesirables to see me naked, and I'm not talking about Little Man—I'm talking about you."

Damian chuckled. "You are a horrible tease, darling. Why does having sex with you feel like I'm climbing a mountain every time? And I don't always make it to the top."

"I think you're being dramatic," Sage said, amused. "Although I'm glad to hear you feel that way. Easy sex isn't anywhere near as good, is it?"

"You're absolutely right."

"And that's why you're going to hold your penis and listen to me, right?"

Damian breathed in and out. Little Man was awfully quiet in that stall. Coming out would mean finding his Warlord in a compromised position, so it was better to wait until all this subsided. This was perfect for Sage who could finally talk without being humped.

"Samson," Sage said, lowering her voice so only Damian could hear. "I'm worried about him."

"Isn't Samson the one who trained you?"

"Yes. I found Samson when he was a child, abandoned by his parents. He's stuck with me ever since. He was curious about his people, but I never had the courage to venture out of Diamond City. It wasn't until we came here that he became desperate. He left the camp and he never came back."

Damian furrowed his brows. "What do you mean 'he left the camp'?"

"Don't you see how nice the room is?" Sage said. "The reparations? The paint? You don't think that was all Louis, do you?"

"What the hell? There was a Squid in my camp and I didn't know it?"

"Exactly," Sage said. "I mean it: Samson sticks with me everywhere. He's very resourceful, so no one ever sees him. But now he's gone and I'm worried."

Damian rubbed his temple. It was obvious he was processing all of this.

"Where is he now?"

"He got angry with me after I told him about Wren. No idea where he went, but I'm worried about him. He's super shy because he doesn't want to be judged."

"What would he want with Wren, Sage?"

"He thinks she'll lead him to the Squids. She's been out here a while."

"Then let him interact with her," Damian said with a frown. "I doubt he'll make a move against you, if that's what you're worried about. If anything, he might take care of her for us."

Sage doubted that. That's why she continued to worry, even long after she had left Damian with the biggest erection of his life. She had no idea where Samson had gone, but she had a sneaking suspicion that he wasn't too far away. He'd be in the kitchen waiting for her, right?

He wasn't.

Louis was, though. He was at the table with a dead look on his face.

Sage furrowed her brows. "Everything all right, Louis? You look startled."

"Um." Louis tugged at his collar. His face had gone pale. "Yeah . . . I . . . uh . . ."

"What?"

Louis shook his head. "I'm sorry, Sage."

"For what?"

"I didn't know the Warlord took such offense to us going out! I really don't want to be a bother."

Sage blinked. And then it dawned on her: Louis hadn't been waiting for her outside the showers like he had said. Damian must have gotten a hold of him after training and given a very intense declaration of who was seeing who. Now there were no doubts, and Louis looked terrified at the idea of stepping on toes. His head would probably join his father's.

Sage wasn't amused. Not one bit. She barreled out of the building and headed straight for Damian's compound to give him a piece of her mind, but Fahrenheit and Celsius told her he was waiting for her in the training grounds.

They were empty at this time of night. There were a couple of Enhanced duking it out before bedtime, but other than that there was all the privacy in the world for a very heated conversation. Damian was there, swinging his sword—*her* sword—to let off some steam.

"Are you serious?" Sage spat at him, drawing her sword to clash with his and strike at him. "What the hell did you do to Louis?"

"Put him in his place." Damian scowled. He reminded Sage of a child who had to share his toys. His hands clenched into fists. His rings glinted in the dim lights of the training grounds. He kept his face straight, though, skin all white and eyes all outlined in black. He looked like a vampire ready to pounce on her. "It was something I had to do. The more I think about it, the more I don't like you sharing a room with him."

"Why?" Sage said. "Because you think I'm going to cheat on you?"

Damian didn't answer, but *yes* flashed in his eyes and the way his jaw tightened.

"Then you must think I'm some cheap slut who can't stay away from pretty boys and their beds. That shows how much you trust me."

"It's not about you," Damian said. "It's about him. I thought about our conversation last month, the one in which I proposed to you. I swore I'd put Louis and Agathe on the throne, so that's what I'm going to do once we infiltrate Diamond City."

"What does that have to do with you being a dick to Louis?"

"I did what I had to in order to ensure he understands you are mine."

"So you own me now."

"You may not appreciate it, but you are my partner and I value you greatly," Damian said steadily. "Not just in battle, but as a lover. When we love each other, we care for each other, and that's why I didn't want you to look for Samson by yourself. When it comes to Diamond City, you're right: I only stir hostility. It's the reason Ileana tried to kill me in my sleep and my daughter abandoned me like a diseased puppy."

Sage closed her eyes. She sighed in frustration. "I'm sorry. I didn't mean to be a pain in your ass, but you can't think I am anything like your ex-lovers. We have a mission to accomplish first. Our love comes later. I know you understand that."

Damian held her cheek. The metal of his rings was so cold against her skin. "I do, even if I want to abandon this. I mean it when I say I want to spend all the time I can with you. I want to get to know you, to wake up with you every morning. I want to defend you just like Commander has always defended me." He brushed his lips against hers. "I want to be your defender now, my Star."

"You mean you want to have sex twenty times a day."

Damian chuckled. "Of course. Although I have a lot to learn about seducing you. What makes you tick." He kissed her again. "And I intend to become an expert."

"I know," Sage said with a smile.

She wanted to do the same to him. And, like him, she was so sick of the fighting, the battles that never ended, and the wars that popped up way too soon. She didn't forget about Samson's mission either, his relentless quest to find the Squids. Maybe she'd take Damian's advice and bury any thought of more adventure and just return to her life at the pizza restaurant, which she craved and loved so badly. Perhaps it'd be a life in which she was pampered, by Damian—not Louis. Maybe this was what she had been looking for for so long. But before she acquired Damian ... she had to earn it. They had to finish this campaign first.

That's what she told him. Damian already knew that, so he didn't fight her anymore. He took her hand and kissed it.

"I'm throwing a party soon," he said. "Just for you. And I want you to be there."

"A party?"

"Yes, to celebrate our success. Think of it like a pep rally. I want to energize everyone and prepare them to enter Diamond City. But I also want to announce our marriage."

Damn it. Damian sure knew how to charm her. How could Sage say anything against that or the way he kissed her then, as if she were the world to him? He wasn't aggressive or nasty—he was just . . . expressive. Loving. Passionate. By the end of the kiss, Sage had all his gloss on her lips. Her head was spinning a bit, too. Even the Enhanced training in the corner were watching now.

Sage wasn't sure why, but as she and Damian sparred, face-to-face, she felt brainwashed. She swore it was the way Damian's tongue had swept her mouth and slid down her throat. He hijacked her emotions by filling her body with his presence. As a result, Sage moved like a zombie, sagging against him. She wanted nothing more than to lose herself to him, to spread her legs so he could thrust into her like he did nearly every day. Admittedly, it was getting harder and harder to resist him.

Sage shook her head. What the hell was wrong with her? She knew the answer to that.

"He is very . . . charismatic. He will seduce you until you open your legs for him and fall for his false promises of love. Once he has you wound around his finger, he'll capture you and use you as a source of power."

Isn't that what Damian was doing right now? Seducing her and using her to gather his forces? While he claimed that he didn't want her to leave and threw tantrums like a baby, what if it was all an act to *get* her to do his bidding?

No way. Sage said those words over and over again as Damian kissed her one more time, in front of the Enhanced and all.

"I love you, my Star," he said to her.

Sage wasn't sure she believed him that time.

CHAPTER 21

The Monster's Heart Returned

The rest of the week was the best of Sage's life yet. She visited all the settlements scattered throughout the eastern side of Mousafeld, meeting Enhanced she hadn't seen since the times of the Unification War. Most of them were from Wolfeld, but there were also many from the towns Sage had made recent negotiations with. By the end of the month of Love, Sage had recruited quite a number of Enhanced and allies to join in their campaign. From a measly five hundred to a whopping two thousand strong, the camp's confidence surged. They weren't necessarily all fighters either—she enlisted whatever help they offered, whether it be supplies, weapons, or their sworn loyalty. In return, if they were successful in taking back Diamond City, they'd receive automatic citizenship. For the first time in their lives, some of the Outskirts' biggest towns were allies.

For Gertrude, Little Man, and the rest of the rebels, it was an amazing change. They were no longer bribing hostile Enhanced or fighting for their lives—they were following Sage's lead and promoting their campaign. The hope was strong.

"I can't wait to see Emma and Sally again!" Gertrude sang. "Want to help me pick out some gifts?"

They went to the East-Side Marketplace for that. Winterfeld and Wolfeld residents had set up shop fast, creating a flea market that looked more like a mall. There weren't any buildings, but the tents were sturdy enough to pass for them. Sage thought of her nieces as she wandered around, keeping up with Gertrude, who was ecstatic with all the goods. The frog legs were a delicacy here, and there were plenty of them around thanks to the warm, wet weather. Even in the middle of winter, the drizzle never quite stopped in Mousafeld. Diamond City was only miles away.

Sage welcomed the distraction to keep her mind off anything having to do with war and politics. She tried to stop thinking about Damian, too, but that always failed. As Gertrude dragged her into another rack of clothes, Sage couldn't help a longing glance at the shop next door where they sold jewelry like wedding bands . . .

"What do you think, Sage?" Gertrude held up a pair of T-shirts; one couldn't go wrong with clothes.

"Yeah, sure." Sage forced a smile. She tried to feel happy for her friend, but all she got was a bunch of anxiety at the thought of returning to Diamond City . . . What had become of her pizza restaurant? And where the hell was Samson?

Samson had never returned to Mousafeld.

Sage had already vowed not to think about him. Of course, it was nearly impossible when everything she did (and didn't do) reminded her of him. She tried to focus on herself and the people around her, but little things like taking off her boots in the kitchen made tears well in her eyes. She was heartbroken until Damian paid her a visit at night. Even all the way on the east side of camp, he always found his way to her bed. Not without a gunshot to avoid, though.

"Damn it, Sage!" he cried as Sage died of laughter.

"Just in case you're an intruder."

Damian tackled her to the ground, where they wrestled for dominance. There was a knock on Sage's door from Gertrude, asking if everything was well, but the Warlord's rough grunts were enough to paint a very detailed scenario of exactly what was going down on the floor.

"He must really love you," Gertrude said the next morning while they had breakfast. Damian had taken off already, to see to "business." "I mean, he never behaved this way with Ileana. He was always so quiet and brooding by her side."

"Well," Sage said, sipping on her orange juice. "I'm glad I can make a difference."

"You're coming to the party tonight, right?"

Why did Sage keep forgetting about that? A part of her was hoping she could skip out, but no one at this table was going to let her play hooky. If they had to dress up, then she did, too. Costume parties weren't her thing, but she supposed she'd do it for the sole purpose of pleasing Damian.

Except this wasn't just any party. From the sky, she could see that every corner of Mousafeld was alight with red and gold. The dreary buildings of old looked renovated, were coated with fresh paint, and illuminated by arching lamp posts and glowing globes. Most impressive of all were the people—the rough, war-torn Enhanced—dressed in much nicer and colorful attire than usual. Sage held her breath as she came down the ramp. She nearly tripped, so she shot out a hand to take hold of Little Man who was closest to her.

There were new Enhanced to greet them, so the old ones behaved to make a good impression. They crowded around Sage as others went to unload all their equipment and supplies from those bulky boxes tucked in the storage space. They meant to help Sage to her room for a shower and some rest before the party, but there was no way Damian was going to let that happen.

He didn't care that she was unpresentable and dirty from so much traveling—he bulldozed his way through the crowd, knocking some people over, and made a spectacle in front of everyone by sweeping her into his arms and kissing her. Sage had failed to get a good look at him, but she already knew he was the star of this show, glorious in all his colors and silk. He reminded Sage of a resurrected phoenix, sweeping them all in power and life.

"Darling!" Damian held her face with one hand; the other was wrapped around her waist. "You look horrendous."

Damian did not. He was in similar wear as everyone else, flashing red and gold from his hair to his boots. He wore this long coat with ruffles like a dress and trousers that hugged his very trim waist and toned legs. He surely was a sight, if Sage could keep her eyes open. Stars, she was so tired . . .

"You would look horrendous, too," she shot back. "I haven't even had a chance to pee!"

Damian arched a brow. "Would I really look horrendous, even with a full bladder?"

Maybe not. Even at his worst, he still looked fabulous. And at his best, Damian was someone Sage no longer recognized.

He no longer carried that heaviness with him. The circles under his eyes that no amount of makeup could erase were gone. They had never had anything to do with his withdrawals either—Sage had always sensed anger and grief, but now Damian pranced around like a free man, a spirit that had been released into the sky. Or maybe he was more like a teenager who had won a kiss with his crush because he never let her go, carrying her around like a prize. If there had ever been any doubts about the Warlord's new love interest before, everyone confirmed that he definitely had someone in his clutches now.

His very creative clutches.

Sage hardly believed what she was seeing: the museum where the Enhanced had thrown his get-well party was no longer a museum. Actually, the entire building had been remodeled, replaced by one that was much more spacious and beautiful for occasions like this. With all these reparations and brand new furniture, no one doubted they'd be marching into Diamond City and taking back what was rightfully theirs. These Enhanced who had fought with Sage such a long time ago were salivating for it. And, thanks to her, they had put their differences with the Warlord aside for another chance at this conquest. That in itself was huge, earning Sage respect from the rebels who had hated and doubted her before.

But, inside this space, it was hard to tell who was who. All the faces blurred together under those incredibly bright lights. The smell of freshly baked meatballs and spicy chicken wings died down under the coppery taste of fever in Sage's mouth. She was so exhausted that she closed her eyes and dozed off on Damian's shoulder. There was high talking, but what on earth were they saying?

"...Is she all right?"

"Stars, is she asleep?"

"Why don't we get her a drink?"

"Drink? She needs the bed!"

"My lord, are you sure today is a good day?"

"Darling?" Damian lowered Sage's body onto a plush couch toward the back of the room. Here, Sage could hear the orchestra and see the red and gold banners hanging from the second floor. There were some Enhanced leaning over the railing, looking at her, whispering about her. Sage recognized all their faces... her loyal comrades...

"I'm a bit tired," Sage admitted. She felt horrible for saying it, but it was the truth. It was unusual for her in the eyes of others, but those others had no idea that she was ovulating right now and her bleeding was coming. Hybrids like her only had it once a year, a small sacrifice to make for the great amount of power she had the rest of the months. Of course, those weren't details anyone had to know

Still, she did her best to stay awake, drink, and toast with her fellow Enhanced. They were all so excited for the future, to reclaim their precious city, and she partook in that from her seat on the couch. When Damian got up to address the room and give a magnificent speech about Blackburn's imminent demise and the council's execution upon marching into Diamond City, Gertrude took his place next to her. She had Sage's personal bag over her shoulder, which she rested on the floor next to her feet. She had already showered and changed to match everyone else. Sage was the only one still in her jumpsuit.

"Hey," Gertrude said, wiping a cloth against Sage's forehead. "Are you sure you're all right? I've never seen you like this before."

"Even the great Optimum has off days." Sage snorted.

"It's good to know you're not all alien. Here, drink some soda."

"Are my eyes deceiving me?" Sage said, watching as the Warlord—the tyrant with no heart—called up Agathe and Louis to present them to the crowd. "Is he . . . honoring them?"

"And with Louis and Agathe in their rightful place in Heart," Damian called out to the listening crowd, so loud that even the people standing outside heard him, "we will make Diamond City a safe place for *all*. We will protect our citizens from any potential attacks from the Squids."

Now Sage wondered if she was dreaming. Or perhaps her fever made her delirious. Whichever one it was, those were the words in her head. She fell asleep again, waking up only when she heard her name being called.

"Sage!" Agathe approached, picking up her heavy skirts to slip through some tight spaces to reach her. Louis stayed a safe distance away, even if he was craning his head to get a good look at her. That was so ridiculous, but Damian was hovering close by, dark eyes like that of a hawk's. Sage wanted to ask him about Samson, but she wouldn't get the chance to tonight. "Oh, it's so nice to see you again!"

"Same here." Sage flashed a small smile.

"Why don't you go to bed? You look terrible."

"Two new Allseers, huh?"

Agathe shook her head. "I told you I hated Heart when my father was there. Perhaps now things will be a little different. Maybe I'll have more liberty to travel the districts, talk to the people. I want to put them at ease after so many years of persecution. At the same time, I know I can't let my guard down. I don't want to come across as weak, so I've decided to create a justice system that will serve all."

Sage arched a brow. "A justice system? That's night and day compared to what your father had."

The Allseer had had no justice system—just rulings that had been biased and harsh. It was the reason everyone had strove to gain the Allseer's favor—a friend in jeopardy was often a friend saved no matter the crime. It worked the other way around, too—non-friends, who had done nothing but wave anti-Allseer banners, had seen the chopping block just for jaywalking.

   DIAMOND CITY

Agathe nodded her head. She looked beautiful with all that red and gold entwined in her hair. Her cheeks were as plump as ever after so much pampering in Mousafeld. To Sage, it was a miracle that Agathe wanted any part in Diamond City when she had it so good here. Perhaps Agathe figured she could transfer that same comfort back to Heart, especially when she had such strong allies on her side.

"I want to join the Warlord's rebels with the Diamond City military," Agathe said. "While I'm not a proponent of creating more Enhanced, I want to honor the ones we do have."

"Respectable," Sage said.

Agathe clasped her hands in front of her. She was insecure about something. It always took her a great amount of energy to voice uncomfortable topics out loud, but what could be worse than Bram's betrayal of Sage to the Allseer? Something, in her eyes, that was a lot worse.

"I was supposed to rule with the Warlord," Agathe said quietly.

Sage blinked. That damn fever was doing a number on her head. She would have picked up on the implications of that statement in a heartbeat, but she was too slow to get it right away. Agathe had to elaborate some more.

"He broke off the engagement to me," Agathe whispered, voice lost beneath all the chatter in the room. Sage could hear her, though. "And for so long, I wondered if it was me. If I wasn't good enough, strong enough, to keep him interested. But I heard from Louis that he's with you now. Rumors, too, between the maids and people in the market. Is it true, Sage?"

"I . . ." Sage's throat closed up. Her head was pounding horribly now. It wasn't guilt—it was never guilt—it was fear. That's why she couldn't speak. She was afraid because she saw a certain curtain over the chocolate hue of Agathe's eyes, one that Sage hadn't seen before. Not in bumbling, foolish Agathe who ate pastries all day long in her plush chair. This was a different Agathe, one whose potential husband had been snatched right from under her nose. The irony. Sage had come to rescue her . . . except Agathe had had no intention of leaving.

Agathe took Sage's hand. She came to kneel in front of her, those deadened eyes like dried-up fall leaves boring right into Sage's, betraying the friendliness in her voice. "If it's true, I congratulate you, Sage," she said. "Really . . . I do. I just want you to be wary of one thing."

Sage swallowed thickly.

"He knows you're the Optimum," Agathe said. "He knows what your blood can do. If he wants you, it's because of that. He wants to create more Enhanced."

"For what? He's already getting Diamond City. In fact, if the city's what he truly wanted, then he would have married you, wouldn't he?"

Holy shit, that had come out wrong. But now that the words were in the air, they made so much more sense to Sage and put any doubts she might have had toward Damian's intentions at ease.

If Damian truly wanted the throne . . . to become an evil emperor . . . wouldn't he have married Agathe as he had planned to? Agathe didn't make any sense, but Sage figured she was hurting. This was Mega Woman 2.0, and Sage needed to get away if she was going to keep her head.

"Excuse me." Sage got up.

Manipulative Allseers. God, they were all the same. What hurt the most was categorizing Agathe as one of them, but that wasn't Agathe the Allseer talking—that was Agathe the Jealous Bitch talking. Thankfully, once this ordeal was over, Sage could go back to her restaurant. She wouldn't have to deal with royals and politics . . . she hoped.

Sage noticed a line of people coming out of a set of double doors in the back. Apparently, they were all marveling at the heads on display, and Sage remembered that's where Damian had moved them. They must have been fascinating to the crowd because Enhanced were immortal, couldn't die without Slainium, and were capable of talking if their tongues were still intact. Damian had always touted he could talk to his heads. Maybe this was stupid, but Sage had something she had to get off her chest.

When Sage reached those doors, the people inside had already cleared out. She peered in to confirm what she had suspected: all of the Warlord's conquests were perched on the wall in front of her like a collection of shoes. Most of the heads were asleep, eyes closed, but a few were looking out, horror on their faces. One of them belonged to the Allseer.

Sage stepped inside, breathing in the fumes of fresh paint and newly-constructed walls. The heads never stank of death because they weren't really dead. She wasn't sure any of these Enhanced were very good at taxidermy when they were fighting for their lives in the Outskirts.

"I can't really call you Allseer anymore, Marchello," Sage said. "Because your reign came to an end a long time ago. It sounds like your children will take your place as equals. You should be proud of them."

There was no movement from Marchello, nothing to indicate that he had heard her or cared about her words.

"What you shouldn't be proud of," Sage went on, "is what you've done. You wanted to use me without my consent, to capture me so I wouldn't be a threat to anyone, especially not to you. Your worst fear was my siding with the Warlord if we ever met. But you never found me. Not until recently. And all this time you were looking for me . . . you never bothered to determine what your brother was doing. He has Wren. Or rather . . . she has him."

The Allseer met her eyes.

"She's injecting him with all of her Cells," Sage said. "She's creating a monster."

" . . . Squids . . . "

Sage blinked. She could have sworn she'd heard him say something. It sounded more like a rasp. Then he said it again.

" . . . Squids . . . Council."

"Darling." Damian found her. He had her bag over his shoulder, retrieved from the couch where she had left it. Agathe must have walked away as soon as her person of interest had moved out of sight. He carried a smile all the way up to her, completely oblivious to Agathe's catty words.

Ultimately, though, what did it really matter? Agathe and Louis were going to become the new Allseers, and Damian was going to move on with his life. Wasn't that what Sage wanted?

Damian wrapped an arm around her waist and looked up at the Allseer, too. It was hard to tell what emotions he was feeling when cynicism toward his enemies was no longer present in his eyes. It was as if Damian had more important feats to focus on than laughing at a bunch of bumbling heads.

"Why don't we step out?" he said to Sage before the silence pressed on any further. "You need your rest. Come with me." He led her out of the room. They didn't have to cross the museum and bypass small talk—Damian took her out through another door in the back.

"So what do you think?" Damian asked as they stepped outside.

Sage froze and not because of the weather. There was a massive garden out here now, in place of that rusted playground. If only Sage were strong enough to walk through all the paths and admire flowers she didn't know the names of. She told Damian the truth.

"It's beautiful. Really. But I guess what's impressed me most of all is you."

Damian chuckled. "Please do tell."

Sage rolled her eyes. "Aside from your"—she hesitated—"*beauty*, I'm impressed with how you've treated Louis and Agathe."

"You were right about everything. I figured it'd be best—"

Sage clutched his arm, bending over as dizziness struck. Her surroundings spun as if someone had just thrown her on a carousel. She had to close her eyes or else she'd see her lunch on the ground. "Sorry . . . just give me a moment."

"I want to believe this is fatigue," Damian said, lifting her into his arms. "But I'm starting to doubt that."

"Don't worry—this happens regularly."

Damian raised both brows. "Oh."

"But it's different for me," Sage said quickly. "I don't get it once a month like humans—it's once a year. And they're horrifically painful."

"Women are such powerful creatures. I remember when Ileana gave birth, I nearly passed out."

Sage laughed. "Figures."

"But I've never heard of someone who only has their period once a year," Damian muttered thoughtfully. "Even Enhanced women are monthly. I suppose it's because you're a hybrid."

"Yes, and I'm also a warrior—I can't be going through this shit every month."

"Very true." Damian smirked at her. "There is so much to do in bed. So many positions to try."

"Damian, I look like hell," Sage said. "You can't seriously think I look attractive."

"I do," he said huskily. "Very much. With that flush in your cheeks and the swell of your breasts? I am extremely aroused."

"Is there a pill that lowers your libido? Unless there are other ways to satisfy you."

"I am over masturbation. Why would I when I have you?"

"We've only been mating a couple of months and already my vagina's destroyed."

Damian laughed. "That's not true."

"It's true," Sage said.

"I will be the one to determine the state your vagina's in, and based on its performance last time we had sex, it's in tip-top shape. With all the pounding it's been getting on a daily basis, I wouldn't be surprised if it could catch bullets in battle."

Sage laughed so hard, she started coughing. She had a stupid picture of her vagina eating bullets out of the air. So not feasible, but Damian was dumb and inappropriate. She shook her head after clearing her throat. "I can't believe we're talking about this."

"They are necessary topics, darling." He licked her nose, making Sage laugh again. "And when my penis underperforms, you let me know, all right?"

"Not sure that will ever happen. You can use that thing in swordplay. You never know when you'll run out of daggers."

Damian's laugh was hard this time, deep and genuine. It came from his gut, brightening his face and making his eyes shine with life. Sage licked his nose in turn, and then Damian caught her tongue with his. They battled out in the open until they reached his compound.

Cushion was waiting for Sage inside. She helped her into the bathroom while shooing away her son for some privacy. "How he longs for you," she commented with a shake of her head. "You should see all his designs. He has a book just for you."

And that was *extremely* impressive. After Sage cleaned up, she joined him in his study. There wasn't a single syringe in sight and no pill bottles in the cabinets—every corner was stacked with fabrics, most of them purchased from the East-Side Marketplace. The "Sage book" was made up of drawings of her in all these different outfits, from dresses to pajamas to . . . thongs . . . and . . . nothing at all.

"You've got my boobs all wrong." Sage shook her head as Damian laughed.

"No, I don't." He stared at her chest with a stupid grin. "I remember those lovelies very well. Can I see them, please?"

"I am not going to entertain your sexual fantasies tonight," Sage said. "I'd be a major disappointment. Besides"—she rubbed her abdomen—"I'm in a lot of pain right now."

"I understand. I am sorry you have to experience such difficulty. At the very least, I know there is a chance of making babies in the future."

Sage snapped her head up. She blinked. She hadn't been expecting him to say something like that. Maybe because she was reminded of Bram and the reason he had sold her to the Allseer. It made her slightly sick. While Damian's intentions were pure, Blackburn's same haunting words came back to her. And now she had Agathe's to add to that.

"He knows you're the Optimum. He knows what your blood can do. If he wants you, it's because of that. He wants to create more Enhanced."

　　　　　　　　　　　　　　　　　　　　DIAMOND CITY

"I guess that's why you don't mind the unprotected sex," Sage said softly. "In the back of your head, you want to impregnate me. Either that or you thought I was infertile."

"To be honest, I didn't really think of it."

Sage snorted. "Obviously. You were too busy humping me."

Damian chuckled wryly. "But if it did happen . . . or does happen . . . I wouldn't mind it. Would you?"

Sage said nothing.

"Wouldn't you want children, Sage?" he pressed gently.

"I . . ." Sage lowered her head. She rubbed her abdomen. "Maybe . . . yes . . . But I've never given it much thought. The idea of children was just too much of a hassle in Diamond City. I haven't been married or committed to anyone in such a long time. It's never crossed my mind."

"Is it something you would consider if you were committed to me?"

Sage played with his signet ring on her finger. "Yes. But, Damian, you must understand there is still so much for me to do. I've had the opportunity to think about us a little more, and there's something I need you to know."

She looked him in the eyes. "I love you greatly. At this point, I think I would do anything to ensure your safety and well-being. You asked me to marry you before, and the answer is yes."

Damian gasped. "Really? Oh—I have wedding gown designs, too!"

A book of them. Full of them. But Sage couldn't get distracted by what she'd look like in one of those, an explosion of white and glitter like some sort of angelic prophet.

"There are personal issues I have to take care of at home," Sage went on despite the fast beating of her heart. "Once we enter Diamond City and situate Louis and Agathe, I have to speak to Bram and ensure the safety of my nieces. Then I have to look for Samson. He set out on his own, and I . . . " Sage wiped her eyes fiercely. She hated showing weakness. "I have to find him. And when I do, I'm afraid I'll have to confront some very ugly situations. My sister is out there for a reason."

"Sage." Damian kneeled before her. He took her hands and kissed them each. "You don't have to do anything alone. We'll do it together, understand? My strength has been restored and you have accomplished what I could not: allies. Now that those trials are behind us, we can move forward."

"Damian," Sage whispered, visibly shaking now. More tears welled in her eyes. "There's ... there's one more thing ... "

She didn't know if this was stupid or offensive or both, but it was something she had to get off her chest. She already knew that the old creepy man who had painted the beastly version of Damian was David, but what she still had a hard time wrapping her head around was the preserved heart in the jar. Sage carried it with her everywhere, not because it was a keepsake, but because she was afraid something would happen to it.

"Sage?" Damian prompted.

"I went to the Art Festival shortly before I set out to find you," Sage said, eyeing her bag on the floor. "There was a man there who seemed to know a lot about you. He sounded like he was traumatized, sort of loony ... At Wolfeld, when we ran into Blackburn, he mentioned David was one of your lovers. I'm confident it was him."

Damian stood up from the floor. He looked away. If he was seizing up, then he wasn't very comfortable talking about the man who had betrayed him to Kilstrong.

"He wanted money," Damian whispered in the dimness, eyes drowning in unpleasant memories. "And fame. I'm glad he got what he deserved—he's become a worthless vendor making money off of street rats."

"He had something of yours," Sage said tentatively. "I just wasn't sure if it was legitimate ... or a hoax. That somehow, in his warped mind, he honestly believed it was yours."

Damian turned his head back to her slowly. His brows were furrowed in confusion, but before Sage showed him anything, she had to say it.

"You said your brother carved out each of your organs when he tortured you. The only one he never put back, he preserved in a jar and gave it to David as a gift. Is that true?"

"I have no idea," Damian whispered weakly. He was as tense as a board as Sage reached into her bag and zipped it open. It would have been creepy to flash a frozen heart at him, so she was glad for the covering around the jar. That way, he could look at it himself when he was ready.

Not that that was going to happen anytime soon. Damian looked like he was getting ready to handle a viper, a certain trauma surfacing in his mind like a wave, making his hands shake viciously. Even his eyes got watery. Before he exploded, Sage got to her feet and rested a hand on his shoulder. She said, "You don't have to look at it."

Maybe not, but Damian needed to. He couldn't go on without the closure, not when it was sitting right in his hands, so he did it: he peeked at it, then he dropped it, fumbling back and releasing a loud cry.

Sage grabbed it before it hit the floor. "Damian?"

"Oh, Stars, Sage!" Damian cried, clutching his head. "How is that possible?!"

"Embalming," Sage said gently. "I mean, there's no certainty that it's yours—"

"I don't want it—get it the hell away from me!"

"Why wouldn't you want it? Why wouldn't you want to find out if it's yours?"

"I don't need it!" Damian yelled. "I've lived without it for so long!"

Sage looked at him in wonder. "What the hell is wrong with you, Damian? If it's yours, I sure as hell would want it back in your chest. In fact, you should have Dr. X take a look at it."

Damian sank to his knees. Tears spilled from his eyes and sobs erupted from his throat. Sage was at a loss for what to do or say because she wasn't used to seeing Damian this wrecked. This wasn't like one of his petty temper tantrums. She thought he'd be furious with her for keeping his missing organ a secret all this time, but these cries were from old heartache. He didn't appear relieved that the only missing piece of his body was within reach. She couldn't force him to understand, so she tucked the jar back into her bag and held him until he calmed down.

"I was betrayed," Damian whispered into her bosom, "by the man I loved . . ."

"I know," Sage said against his temple. "Life can be difficult . . . and there are a lot of nasty people out there, even ones we think love us . . . but we have to carry forward."

"If it's truly mine . . . then I want you to have it."

"No, Damian—it's *yours*. I want you to take it back because it belongs to you. It would make me happy to see you . . . complete."

Damian said nothing. He was cold and shivering, and that had nothing to do with the realization that his heart was in a jar just feet away from him. Sage watched the shadows play off his face, outlining his sharp cheekbones and pale skin. She helped him stand and took him to his room. It was time to retire for the night— emotions were way too high, her own included. She was thankful to finally get some rest by his side, curled up underneath his covers that smelled like cologne.

His scent. Teakwood and lavender.

"You have done nothing but save my life since you arrived at this camp," Damian said in the darkness, holding her to his chest. "I'm not sure you're done yet, either. How do I repay you?"

"You can start by getting some sleep."

"Only if you promise you'll teach me how to make one of your favorite pizzas."

Sage raised her head. "How did you know I liked pizza?"

Damian cleared his throat. "Louis. He shouted it at me when he claimed I didn't really love you. Didn't know everything about you. Why didn't you ever tell me, darling?"

Sage's first response was, *You didn't ask.* The second was she had never brought it up simply because when they weren't talking about war strategies, they were having sex.

"I want to know all your dreams," he murmured to her. "All of them. You have a pizzeria in the Cut District? I will help you run it when we return."

Sage's eyes stung. "Really?"

"Yes. And I want you to teach me how to make the Hippo."

"Louis told you about that, too?"

"He did."

All of the toppings, including bananas. Sage smiled. "Rick came up with that one."

Damian looked at her. "Your friend?"

Sage nodded. "He said hippos were his favorite animal. They're greedy and territorial, but they don't look it. Just like no one would ever be able to tell that Rick was a Speed Star."

"Then I am very much looking forward to making the pizza he created."

"Yeah, just don't fuck it up."

"I definitely wouldn't want to do that," Damian muttered. "I value my penis too much. I wouldn't want it featured on the Friday hook-up special."

Sage laughed. "Not a bad idea, Damian. Although I think I'd rather use sausages. I've still got other plans for your penis."

"You're going to give me an erection, so can we not talk about penises or sausages? How about raisins?"

"You mean like a raisin pizza?" Sage thought about it.

"A *golden* raisin pizza," Damian amended. "And we can call it the Minefield. What do you think?"

It was a wonderful night of hopes and dreams. Sage pictured her married life by Damian's side, serving pizza all day, then watching Defenders Unite! all night. It was nice, but it certainly wasn't reality.

For now, though, Sage could pretend. And as she succumbed to sleep on Damian's chest, she heard nothing but peace.

CHAPTER 22

Fight in Diamond City

When Sage woke up, she was alone in Damian's bed. She hadn't felt or heard when he got up at all. At some point, she must have rolled onto his pillow. It was thick and warm, and it smelled like him. She would have fallen back asleep if she didn't notice the bouquet of roses and the note on his nightstand. That got her up immediately. Heart thrumming, she grabbed both, glancing at the flowers before reading his message.

Darling,

I am at the clinic. Don't worry, I'm fine. You're right: I have to do this. Even so, my heart will always belong to you.

- D

As soon as she read "heart," she knew exactly what he had done. An empty travel bag in his study confirmed it: Damian had taken his heart back.

Without hesitation, Sage showered, dressed, and rushed out of the compound. She felt bad for leaving Cushion's breakfast on the table, but she was too anxious and hyper to eat properly. She didn't pay attention to anyone on the streets, not even Preacher, who attempted to reel her into the chapel by waving his arms like a crazy man. Sage's sights were on the clinic, and her memories of it weren't very pleasant. While she had never seen Damian in a hospital bed, she remembered what it was like to bring him back to life as he lay seconds away from death.

When Sage burst into the lobby, the cold sliced her bones and the antiseptic smell made her cough. Her senses were exceptionally sensitive with her period around the corner. She didn't care about the attendant at the desk—she rushed down the hallway and slammed into Dr. X, who stumbled back in surprise.

"Damian?" Sage pushed him aside, peeking into the room.

Sage had never felt her heart twist this way before, like someone squeezing every last bit of water from a soiled towel. It hurt, making her see more stars than any punch had in her lifetime, drawing a stinging wave of tears from her eyes. That's what happened when she was looking at the unconscious form of a man who held so much conviction, power, and drive. Maybe, more so, that's what happened when she looked at the man she loved.

"Damian?" Sage stepped inside, but her movements weren't so quick this time. Dr. X held her back before she made a ruckus, fixing his glasses as he glared at her.

"Please, my lady," he said patiently. "Let's try not to disturb him, yes?"

"D-did it work?" Sage found the heart monitor next to his bed—the jumping lines, the changing numbers—so it was a success?

"I think you can see for yourself that it did," Dr. X said curtly.

Sage drew closer for a better look.

Damian was fast asleep, head turned. He had a clean medical gown on. Beneath the low neckline, Sage could see the thick white bandages around his chest. As an Enhanced, the incision was probably all healed by now. There were electrodes all over his skin, measuring every bit of electrical activity in his sternum.

Sage glanced at the monitor again. His heart rate was at a steady seventy beats per minute.

"How?" was her next question.

"How?" Dr. X frowned. "Well, it certainly wasn't easy. Even though the DNAs were a match, and chances were very likely that that heart had been his, it wasn't easy to restore something that'd been embalmed for nearly thirty years. The fluids used to preserve it were very precise, unlike anything I had ever seen before. It was as if whoever had put it away wanted to ensure that it would one day work again." He shook his head. "It took quite a number of electrical charges to get it to beat, a process that could have destroyed the Warlord's body, but due to a sheer miracle from the Squids, his heart came back to life."

Sage took a seat by Damian's bed. She brushed some of his hair back. She found his hand, an oximeter on his finger. She held it, caressing it, as she processed all this in her very fuzzy brain.

"He said you'd found it," Dr. X went on, "from an ex-lover of his. Is that so?"

"Yes. Why? Did you think it was me who'd mummified it in a jar?"

"Most certainly not. He would not hold you in such high esteem if you had."

Sage knew exactly what Dr. X was talking about. She found it on Damian's wrist, snaking its way up his arm and into his shoulder.

It was a tattoo of sage leaves entwined on a vine.

Sage held her mouth. There were tears in her eyes again. Damian hadn't bothered to tell her he'd gotten a new tattoo.

"He didn't care about the risks," Dr. X said. "He just wanted it inside him where it rightfully belongs. Truly, my lady, it still shocks me that you've had it all this time. From the bottom of my heart—no pun intended—I must thank you for returning it to him."

"Thank me? It looked like you wanted to slit my throat seconds ago."

"Apologies." Dr. X took a seat as well. When he removed his glasses to rub his face, Sage noticed the dark circles under his eyes. The guy had been in surgery since early morning, when Damian had come knocking on his door. Had the bastard slept at all? Or had he been thinking of the heart the whole night? "But I must admit I was quite nervous about the procedure. I didn't think it would work. On the other hand, I'm glad it did.

"Since the Warlord escaped from Diamond City, he's been an angry, aggressive, and depressed individual. He was nothing like the man I remembered from the frontlines of the Unification War, one with so much hope for the future. He was thrilled at the idea of bringing the districts together because it was always his dream to move to the Color District. It goes without saying that this torture at the hands of his brother played a major part in the person he turned out to be. Although he fell in love with Ileana and had a child with her, he still carried around that . . . emptiness."

"You didn't know he was missing his heart?" Sage said.

"I did," Dr. X replied. "I examined him when we first moved here. I confirmed his worst fears. Of course, as Enhanced, we are immortal. We could practically walk around without our heads. But there is something detrimental to not having your heart, isn't there? It was as if Blackburn had played a sick joke on him, one the Warlord had taken seriously. He acted like the very monster Blackburn had created, ruthless in his ways of acquiring allies or strategic vantage points.

"The Warlord was no stranger to torture and executions . . . both as a receiver and a deliverer. I suppose we can't make excuses, but I certainly wasn't surprised by his cruel behavior. We all went along with it. When Phoebe was born, he humbled himself greatly. Sadly, it wasn't enough. Ileana couldn't handle him anymore, so she planned to put him out of his misery. He killed her in self-defense, but then Phoebe ran away and you know what happened to her."

Dr. X sighed. He gazed at the Warlord's sleeping face. "I don't envy his life. But I do wish for him to live a better one. And perhaps, with you at his side, that can happen."

Sage held Damian's hand. She said nothing else to Dr. X, who stood up to tend to his other patients. Enhanced overdid it a lot during training, and ever since the new recruits had joined them, the injuries had been plentiful. A lot of them had probably seen the

Warlord here earlier, and so they were curious to know if he had overdosed again. Some came to pay him a visit in hopes of learning more about his condition, but Sage didn't speak to them. She pretended to sleep, head against the chair, until she felt a familiar foul presence by her side.

"Hey," Mega Woman said gently, a light hand on Sage's shoulder. "Are you awake?"

Sage sat up. She was pale and dehydrated now, but survival instincts took over. She gazed right into Mega Woman's eyes, ready to defend herself, but Mega Woman raised her hands in surrender. She wasn't here to fight.

"Sorry," she said, very unlike her. Her brows were always tight, a natural look to her, but her expression was softer than usual. "I don't mean to interrupt. I really don't. But there's someone here to see you, and we need you outside."

Sage's head was pounding and spinning. "Someone's here to see me?" she repeated.

"Yes. Um . . . " Mega Woman made a face. "A few people. Would you just follow me outside?"

Sage got up. She laid Damian's hand by his side and kissed his lips before leaving. A horrible feeling fluttered through her chest and spread through her veins like ice. If Mega Woman was fetching her, did that mean there was trouble? Sage didn't trust her one bit, but this couldn't be a trap in the middle of Mousafeld for all to see. There were too many witnesses. That meant there was trouble from the outside, and it could be any of the three.

Wren, Blackburn, or Samson.

It turned out to be neither. Sage had to cross the Marketplace and enter that clearing next to the Ferris wheel to see that it was Penelope and the Private Guard who were demanding to speak to her. Not just them, though—Bram, too.

Bram was here.

Sage's heart already felt like it had been torn to shreds when she saw Damian in bed. There was nothing worse than seeing a comatose person because it brought back horrid memories of the

Frasers on their deathbeds. But now her stomach felt like it was caving in on itself, alight with horrible nausea that made Sage throw up in the bushes.

"Sage!" Gertrude exclaimed, running to her. Little Man was right behind her, both of them helping Sage to her feet when she was done. Turtle, Eye Candy, and Rockstar were as still as statues. Butcher, Clara, and Sailor, who were always patrolling these parts outside of Mousafeld, were at a loss for words. This was not the sort of reaction they had been expecting from the Optimum in the face of a measly organization like the PG.

"Shit," Sage croaked, wiping her mouth.

"You're not pregnant, are you?"

Everyone gasped. They had all been thinking it, but Gertrude had said it. It sounded like a type of confirmation, and Sage had to nip that in the bud immediately.

"No." Sage got to her feet, taking deep breaths. "I'm not."

No one looked convinced, especially not Mega Woman. They used their common sense to figure out that Sage and the Warlord had been together for a while now, so pregnancy was a very real possibility. Even so, it wasn't something that was open for discussion in front of the enemy.

"All right then," Butcher said, turning his attention back to the PG. "We've got Sage. You wanted to see her. What the fuck do you want?"

"Sage!" Bram croaked; he and the PG were on their knees, restrained by Turtle, Eye Candy, and Rockstar. "Oh my Stars—it's really you! I wasn't sure I'd be able to find you!"

Sage clenched her jaw. Her fists went right along with it. She looked at Gertrude with that intense look in her eyes, making Gertrude worry.

"Sage," she whispered, "what's wrong?"

"I can't talk to him." Sage shook her head. "I can't even look him in the fucking face. You do the talking and tell me what he says—"

"SAGE!" Bram wailed, making everyone jump. "Whatever you're mad at me for—I'm sorry! But there's—"

" 'Whatever I'm mad at you for'?" Sage snapped. " 'Whatever'? You fucking know 'whatever', you little piece of shit. Is that the kind of person I raised you to be? A backstabber?"

"I was selfish—I get it. But that's not what I came out here for—Sage, they have Olivia and Candice! Blackburn took the girls because he wants you in Diamond City now!"

It was all eyes on Sage. No one knew who Olivia and Candice were, but they all surmised that the two were of dire importance to her. Mega Woman bypassed all that and spoke her mind.

"Are you kidding me?" she hissed at Bram. "You come all the way out here spewing that shit? Sage doesn't act when you tell her to—she has a plan to take Diamond City back, so you better stay the hell out of it." Mega Woman reached Sage's side and said, "Let's take these guys into custody. Once Damian wakes up, we can make a move like we planned."

Sage looked at Mega Woman. If she weren't so damn sick, she'd be able to process all this so much faster. She had to rub her temples and shove the images of her nieces out of her mind. Rushing into something was a horrible strategy, and that's not the way Sage wanted to go about doing this. But Bram wouldn't have come all the way out here if his words were false . . . would he?

"You can't wait!" Bram protested. "Or he'll kill them, Sage! Do you think Blackburn gives two shits about my daughters? Your nieces?"

"It's a trap!" Little Man exclaimed. "Diamond City knows we've got the upper hand!"

"So let's attack them now!" reasoned Turtle.

"No, dumbass! We can't rush in there like that!"

"Then what do we do?" Clara asked, looking at Sage.

Sage took a seat on the ground. The pain in her belly was killing her, but the urgency in her mind was about to burn her. There wasn't a doubt that she had to go after the council. The question was how?

"You can't leave them to die, Sage," Bram croaked. "Not for the sake of some battle strategy."

"No," Sage said quietly. "I wouldn't be like you, selling out people I love for the sake of favor or money. It makes me wonder: did you sell them out to Blackburn, too, for leverage over me?"

"What? N-no!"

"Candice said you were in hiding at Mother's old house. No one knows about it unless you got so sick of waiting for me to come back that you spoke. Or maybe you feared my return. So you sold your daughters to the council in exchange for joining the PG all the way out here to lure me out."

The Allseer's face popped into Sage's mind.

"... *Squids... Council.*"

And then what Nova had said so long ago after Sage's first campaign in Winterfeld: the missing women, all confirmed by the entries in Preacher's books. Bram had just given over his daughters to a bunch of people working for the Squids, possibly to be used as sex slaves.

Sage turned to Mega Woman. "Arrest them and take them back to camp. I want a team of ten to go with me to Heart."

Mega Woman gasped. "To go with you alone? Just the ten of you? Sage, what about our army, all the people we've gathered—"

"Listen closely," Sage said to her. "I can handle the council. It's the military I'm worried about. I need you to mobilize all our forces and stand by until I give the signal. Meet me at Heart."

Everyone froze.

This was it. The moment they had been waiting for—training for—happening right now. Some thought it was a bit too hasty, but what better opportunity was there for an attack? Sage's nieces were in trouble, and everyone already knew that she was flying to Heart tonight with or without them. They had to support her and follow through as a team.

Even if this still felt like a trap.

Sage threw up again on the way back to Mousafeld. This time, it was from fear. Candice and Olivia . . . Stars, where were they now?

"Sage, are you sure you can go like this?" Gertrude said worriedly. "Maybe you should have Dr. X take a look at you."

"Unless he has a remedy for menstrual cycles," Sage panted, "it's unlikely he'll be able to help. I'll be fine, Gertrude."

Sage wasn't worried. Not with the sheer amount of Slainium she carried in her weaponry. It wasn't so much her physical state that weighed her down—it was the outcome of this confrontation. The lives of her nieces.

Sage hated the fact she was leaving Damian so suddenly, but she didn't have a second longer to waste. She, Gertrude, Little Man, Turtle, Eye Candy, Rockstar, Butcher, Clara, Sailor, Justice, and Preacher (to bless them with luck) boarded the nearest vessel and took off to Heart, leaving Mousafeld behind. Sage's heart ached for Damian, so she sent him a text message.

Darling, I'm on my way to Heart. The Council has my nieces. Bram betrayed them, too.

Sage stopped herself there. If she said more, she'd be bombarding Damian's phone with unnecessary explanations and details. Right now, she had to concentrate on the task at hand. She took a deep breath.

Sage had never entered Diamond City through air before. She had never gotten to land at the big runway behind the palace, greeted by people who were once on her side. The Diamond City military were more than just a couple of rows—they could fill an entire city. Unlike last year, when Damian had come to take the Allseer's head, the military was much more substantial—more prepared—and eager to make a dent in their enemy. Sage didn't like the feel of this at all.

The rebels didn't either. When they got off the ship, they gravitated toward Sage, huddling around her as if she could defend them from a 360 attack. The military clutched their weapons in case Sage made any moves. It was a stupid kind of security because they probably had no idea what the council was really up to.

The looks on the five councilmen and women's faces were smug. Without an Allseer to advise, they had taken control of the city and were looking to broaden their borders. Just when Sage had thought these five wanted to keep Diamond City all to themselves, they were the ones calling for black markets and spy networks. After the fiasco with Francis and Wren, they definitely needed more leverage from somewhere. Sage knew, without a doubt, that her sister was not involved with these five. There was nothing for her to gain here.

"My Star." All five of them bowed. Then the entire military followed like one giant wave until everyone was on his or her knees.

Sage remained stoic. Not because this show bothered her in front of rebels who had hated her some months ago, but because it felt fake. As Diamond City's secret weapon, fighting to unite all the districts, a feat that should have been impossible against the Squids, she had earned a lot of respect from those who knew her. But now that Heart had matched the name with the face, this was their way of honoring what they didn't understand and hoped to acquire. Sage felt another stir of nausea.

"It is so very nice to see you again," said Gregory, the leader of the council, with his head still bowed. That man was ancient, had become an Enhanced in his later years, and he was still going strong. So much to live for . . . as if the very promise of power, money, and freedom was enough to keep him in this world. The others at his side agreed—three females and another male—all dressed in white robes with the Diamond City insignia on their chests.

"Wow," Gregory went on, lifting his head to its proper height now. He wasn't afraid to make eye contact, not with his ex-wife. "I am so very moved, my love. As Commander Blackburn reported, you are alive and well. And here I thought you had retired for good, taking to the shadows while watching us bicker about power yet again. At the very least, you were able to successfully run your pizzeria, no, Sage?"

Sage hated the way her name sounded on Gregory's lips, but she wasn't here to be dazzled. She wanted her nieces back. "I was able to," she said. "Quite peacefully, too. It's a shame this all went south, but I have my lovely nephew to blame for that. I guess I wasn't the only one bored with life."

"No." Gregory stole a glance at all the rebels behind her. "You certainly weren't the only one. These rebels have been exiled for thirty years and they're still thinking of ways to return to the city they want to destroy."

The rebels already knew to keep quiet and calm. They were experts at political deliberation because they had to be. Slicing off people's heads was appropriate only when necessary.

"I'm sorry you feel that way, Gregory," Sage said thinly. "But even I acknowledge that these rebels did quite a bit for the benefit of your power. They fought for you just like I did, but you made them do all your dirty work, too. You just had to control everything, even the Enhanced who fought with you in the war. When that didn't work out, you exiled a bunch of them from the city to protect yourself. But you didn't stop there—you sent the Private Guard to deliver deadly drugs and gather information on potential threats. And now you're kidnapping human girls because it's what the Squids want, right? What kind of power did they promise you, I wonder."

"My sweet Sage, you must understand that we are under great duress." Gregory turned serious. "We do not have the luxury of standing by while worthless rebels throw tantrums and play games with authority. Bram came to us at a very pivotal moment, when we needed the Outskirts on our side. You have done the work yet again, Star, so what other way to bring you here was there than to threaten you with your beloved nieces?"

Sage swiped her arm, but it wasn't her fist that connected—it was a wave of energy, invisible to the eye. The rebels had seen this before when August had attacked them, but they had never seen *her* do it. Gregory must have, or, at the very least, he must have been expecting it because he stepped to the side as casually as if he was avoiding a water balloon.

"Are you holding back?" Gregory asked. "Or is it that time of the year again? It's nearly spring, so you must be ovulating, ready to mate and bear children. You never did want children . . . for good reason, of course . . . but can you imagine how powerful they'd be? Enhanced don't pass down their genetics, but you certainly do."

"Shut the hell up!" Sage exclaimed. "Where are the girls?!"

"I delivered them to the Lolligo."

Sage lost her footing. Her knees gave in, unable to hold her weight any longer. Gertrude and Little Man held her, equally distressed by what they were hearing. They had already suspected that this was all planned by the Squids in an attempt to lure Sage to Heart and then to wherever they dwelled. If the rebels lost Sage, how would they take back Diamond City? Who would defend them from the Squids?

"No . . ." Sage croaked, trembling all over. Her fever was sky-high, sweat pouring down her face. She thought she was going to explode. "H-how could you do that?!"

Gregory shrugged his shoulders. "I didn't have a choice. It was either the girls or the city. The Lolligo set the rules here, Sage. We are just doing what we need to do to survive."

Sage screamed. She screamed until her voice was raw. She was losing her composure because all she could picture was Candice and Olivia in the hands of some disgusting Squid, impregnated with a hybrid baby.

"What do you think you're doing?!" Sage exclaimed at Gregory. "You're giving them women so they can reproduce! They're building an army and they're going to march their asses right into this city!"

"And how is that any different than what you're doing?"

"We're not here to overthrow anyone," Sage said clearly. "We're here to compromise."

"Does that include working with you?" Gregory's eyes made another swivel to the rebels behind her. "Or them?"

"Both."

"And since when do you side with rebels, Sage? For nearly a hundred years, you've lived a quiet life among us. You didn't even choose sides during the Warlord's Rebellion. It was the reason we divorced after so many years together, and while I respect your decision in not choosing sides, I suppose my question is: why involve yourself *now*?"

"You didn't give me a choice," Sage hissed. She finally found Blackburn among the sea of white, and she made sure to deliver a particularly nasty glare. "You forced me to chase after the Warlord when he killed the Allseer because you couldn't do it yourselves. This was all a bribe."

　　　　　　　　　　　　　　　

"That you've taken quite seriously," Gregory said politely. "To the point of even siding with the Warlord and recruiting all these fascinating individuals who are standing outside our borders, ready to invade the city. Is this what you wanted?"

"What I want is irrelevant," Sage spat. "I'm doing what I think is best for everyone. Either way, I don't have to answer to anyone, especially not to you fools, who aren't even making attempts to fight the Squids. Instead of hunting down Enhanced in the Outskirts, *you* should be the ones looking for ways to recruit them. My Stars, just what have the Squids promised you in return?"

Gregory jumped, as if Sage had just insulted him. Maybe she had by saying "Squid", since they were obviously all a bunch of ass-kissers, but Gregory ignored it and said, "Our lives."

"Oh, I get it. So you're a bunch of cowards. The Unification War meant nothing to you."

"You disappeared, Sage, when we needed you the most."

"You can't throw this on her!" Little Man finally spoke up, taking a step forward. "She can't be the answer to everything!"

"But she *is*," Gregory said icily. "Tell me, big man, would you be here if the Optimum herself wasn't standing in your presence? You'd all still be playing beer pong at your camp, shooting up drugs because you're not capable of anything else. Why do you think no one bests her? She has powers you wouldn't even dream of—she is a hybrid, far more powerful than any Enhanced, than any of you can begin to imagine. Her sister is the reason we all exist, so can you even begin to comprehend what potential she has?"

"Good," Mega Woman spoke up next. "So if she is so critical, then you'll welcome her with open arms and cooperate with our terms."

Gregory bowed his head. "Most certainly. We will welcome her—"

Sage drew her sword so quickly that she was already pointing it at Gregory's throat before the Diamond City military could raise their own weapons. The entire field held its breath, tension spiking as everyone braced themselves for the fall of yet another one of their leaders. Sage might have just reminded everyone of why people like her, Damian, and the rebels were dangerous, but that was a good thing.

"I want you to surrender the throne to Louis and Agathe Kilstrong," Sage said. "And I want you to welcome any and all rebels back into the city without repercussion. If they begin acting like heathens and destroying everything in sight as you claim they will, then I will personally take care of them."

"My lord." Blackburn finally came to life, stepping from line to make a point they should all hear. He looked like the taller, more wolfish version of Damian. His hair was groomed, his face was shaved, and his uniform had all the shiny medals, but he was itching for a fight and it was evident in his snarl. "Inviting these *heathens* into the city is not advisable. Do you not remember what my monster of a brother did to the Allseer?"

"If we are going to trust you, then you have to trust us," Sage said. "No secret meetings or anything of the like."

"You wench!" Blackburn spat. "How dare you speak to us that way as if we owe you any favors!"

"I'd say you do. You kicked all of us out and now you're facing me. As Gregory described, I'm indestructible."

Blackburn snorted. "Even with your *period?* Oh, females are all the same."

Sage threw the sword at Blackburn's head—the hilt smashed right in between his eyes—jumped over to him, grabbed her sword when it rebounded, and held it to his throat.

The entire military aimed their weapons, but Gregory was quick to act before this got out of hand. He already knew that his troops would suffer major losses against Sage and the Outskirts combined. He was all too familiar with her success on a battlefield.

"STOP!" he roared. "STOP RIGHT NOW!" He waved back Blackburn. "Don't do anything hasty! I am the one who will make the final decisions here!"

"I don't appreciate being called a wench." Sage pushed Blackburn forward with a scowl. "This son of a bitch doesn't have any idea who I am and who I sleep with. Secondly, I have been nothing but polite and fair with my terms, so I'm not sure how I warrant such an insult. You are the assholes who took *my* nieces from me!"

"Forgive him, Sage!" Gregory sputtered, composure crumbling. "He doesn't know what he's talking about! We're just so very flustered with the whole situation. You must understand that the rebels are our sworn enemies."

"I understand that completely." Sage put away her sword. "But now they are not. I already told you my terms, so we can fight or talk like civilized people. If we are all on the same side, then we should focus our attention on the Squids." She glared at Gregory. "Now tell me where the fuck my nieces went! *Right now!*"

Gregory chuckled. "My sweet Sage, you think *I* know where they went? If we knew where the Lolligo dwelled, we might be doing more to confront them."

"Then how do you take orders from them? Through text messaging?" Sage scoffed. "Give me a break, Gregory—tell me where they went right now!"

"Samson, was it?"

Sage froze. Gregory looked thoughtful.

"That's his name, I believe," Gregory said. "He's the Lolligo who took your nieces."

"What?"

"Indeed."

Sage was waiting for more, but Gregory didn't talk further. She took a step back, bumping into Little Man, who held her. Mega Woman whispered in her ear, "You know him, Sage? This Samson?"

"Oh, Stars!" Sage held her mouth.

"Why are you so shocked, my sweet?" Gregory said slyly. "Does this really take you by surprise? It was the Lolligo who controlled the districts a hundred years ago, and it's the Lolligo who continue to control them now. Samson is the Lolligo we answer to, keeping Enhanced under our thumbs and gathering them up in the Outskirts. It was *his* idea. We just followed along."

"No." Sage shook her head. "It wasn't him. Samson is my fucking roommate."

Everyone stiffened anew. Even Blackburn stopped fidgeting to listen to this.

"HE WAS MY ROOMMATE!" Sage roared. "I SAVED HIM FROM THE CLARITY DISTRICT AS A BABY!"

"He was your roommate?" Gregory rasped. "Then surely you must know—"

"NO! Samson was terrified of all of you because he didn't want to be captured!"

"A Lolligo?" Blackburn snorted. "Captured? Even with Slainium, we can't get near them with their impenetrable force fields."

"You were living with him all this time?" Gregory asked incredulously. "And you had no idea he was puppeteering the Allseer?"

"He wasn't puppeteering the Allseer—he wanted to flee the city!" Sage exclaimed. "He wanted to find the Warlord just like me!"

"I'm sure he did," Blackburn said coolly. "With my brother, he'd be able to scour the Outskirts. He'd be able to bring all of us together just like the Lolligo want. They're a manipulative bunch. What enrages me the most is that you—the Optimum everyone at Clarity prays to—allowed him to do this. We are sitting ducks out here now."

No.

No, no, no.

"Fine," Little Man said at last. "Let's say that Samson did sneaky shit behind Sage's back. He's the Squid controlling everything. Why does this change our current situation? We're together and that's a good thing—we need to be together if the Squids are going to invade, aren't they?"

"We will need to work something out," Gregory said. "And in the meanwhile, I think—" He stopped.

Sage collapsed. If Gertrude and Little Man hadn't been there to hold her, she'd be on the floor. Her fever took away her ability to talk and move. At the very least, she was still conscious and able to hear.

"Let's get her to a room!" Gregory called immediately. "She needs to rest!"

Blackburn looked horrified. Now he had to accommodate his little brother's rebel gang on his sacred grounds, the worst possible outcome of this meeting. Even death would have been preferable over this hit to his ego—submitting to his brother's forces was more lethal than any injury he could have received. Regardless, he followed Gregory's orders to the t, moving to gather the rebels and the legions outside of Diamond City.

In the meanwhile, Little Man and Gertrude carried Sage's body. They took her to the palace, a place that swam with horrible memories. Sage thought of the dinner from hell with Blackburn, but what hurt her more than that was Samson. She had talked to Samson that night, one of the few people who loved her, cared for her, and always gave her advice on what to do.

Gregory had to be lying … It couldn't be Samson working for the Squids … Not when he had spent his whole life searching for them … unless that was a lie … and he had just been using Sage all this time … but using her for what? Or maybe he wasn't using her—maybe he was biding his time, doing what his fellow Squids told him to do. But what exactly were they planning?

Little Man and Gertrude took Sage to the top floor, a suite. Gregory had maids prepare a bath and medicine. After Sage was dressed and tucked into bed, Gregory pulled up a chair next to her. Gertrude and Little Man remained in the corner to ensure her safety.

"My Sage," he said a bit more majestically than he had in the past. He looked at her a bit differently, too, as if he was seeing her in a new light. He reached out a hand to grasp hers, bony fingers kneading her own. The sincerest of looks flashed across his face. "It has been so very long. The last memory I have of you was when I left to put down the Warlord's Rebellion. We kissed in the garden next to the family of orchids I took care of."

"They all died when you left," Sage said.

Gregory sighed. "I know that plants aren't your specialty, but fighting and this city are. Do you remember that battle in Clarity, where we first met? We were down to a measly dozen soldiers … I had just sent my sister a goodbye notice … blew kisses to my little niece … and yet we survived because of you."

"It's what I was paid to do. Just like you were paid to deliver my nieces to the Squids."

"I wish you had stayed with us in politics, in leading us, my Star. We've always looked to you for answers."

"Politics isn't my specialty." Sage gazed at the ceiling, the chandelier with all of its twinkling pieces. Clarity had been the final major conquest. After that, she had fought one last battle in Cut against the Overseer, where she had seen her sister for the first time. With baby Samson in her knapsack, she had returned home to spend time with her family . . . watched them grow old and die . . . stayed hidden, for the most part, as Diamond City flourished. It had until the Enhanced had disagreed on how to rule, on how much power to distribute to its citizens. It had become a war of greed, one Sage had refused to partake in.

"I'm a warrior," she said quietly. "Not a politician. I can, however, suggest to you what is fair. It may not be something you want to hear, though."

"I suppose this is a conversation saved for another time . . . especially if the Lolligo will make their move soon."

"It isn't a wonder Francis joined forces with my sister," Sage said. "He must have sensed Heart was about to tank, too."

"You saw him?" Gregory said, astonished.

"I fought him. My sister's been taking back her Cells and implanting them into him. It was . . . a difficult battle."

Gregory called for some tea. His bony fingers thrummed against the cup, rings shining in the dim lights. Sage already knew what was ailing him, why he looked so old.

"You're worried, aren't you?" Sage said. "Your plans blew up in your face. You were hoping to capture me and use me like you did my sister. This time, perhaps, with reproductive experiments since you seem to know so much about my menstrual cycles."

"Yes," Gregory admitted. "I was. We only have so many Enhanced, and if we were going to topple the Lolligo, we needed more power. We needed more Enhanced. You and your sister were the only ones who could provide that service. But Francis hid Wren from Heart and you—well—you were at the pizzeria."

"I'm so sorry that I didn't fulfill my purpose," Sage spat. "Popping out babies for your army sounds like a great honor."

"I'm sorry you've had to carry this pressure all your life. You of all people know what you are, Sage. So if the Lolligo are out there, how do you plan on stopping them?"

Those weren't plans Sage was going to divulge to her enemy, but she already knew she was leaving as soon as Gregory turned around. She had an idea of where the Squids might be. She'd take a trip to Winterfeld and cross the Roaring Mountains. That, she suspected, was what the Squids used to pass into human lands.

Sage turned around in her bed, bringing the covers to her chest. She picked up her phone, hoping to see a message from Damian. It looked like he still wasn't awake. A new heart would certainly take a toll on his body.

"Do you trust me?" Gregory asked quietly.

"I trust the rebels," she said truthfully, making Little Man and Gertrude smile. She kept her eyes on the window and her back to Gregory. "I trust Louis and Agathe. No one else."

Gregory waved his hand. "Children, even if they are over a hundred years old. You expect them to lead like the Allseer did?"

"Yes, and I'm certain they'll do a better job. A fairer job."

"Damn it, Sage—this isn't about being fair. This is about what's best for the people."

"And what's best for the people isn't to sacrifice me and my sister like lab rats. It doesn't mean we exile Enhanced that don't agree with our policies." Sage glared at him over her shoulder. "You're right: maybe I should have stayed in politics. I certainly would have avoided a lot of heartaches and betrayals from people who I thought loved me."

She settled back on her pillow.

"I wish to get some rest now. Please leave me alone."

"We will talk about this in the morning," Gregory said. He didn't leave without kissing her cheek and showing respect.

But once he did, Sage was glad. She knew she had to get up now, tell Gertrude and Little Man her plans...but she was exhausted. And so she fell asleep just minutes later.

CHAPTER 23

Sisters

There was a pounding on the door. That's what jarred Sage from her dreams where she was making the Hippo pizza with Damian and partying all night with Candice and Olivia. The two were absolutely ecstatic to be taking part in Damian's ultra amazing fashion show, but before they got a chance to approve the designs, Sage woke up.

She jumped. Gertrude and Little Man were at her side, zeroed in on the door.

"Sage!" Gregory cried from outside. "Run! We're under attack!"

"Attack?" Sage croaked, looking around at Gertrude and Little Man. She couldn't think straight, so she couldn't figure out what was attacking them. She hoped it wasn't their comrades stationed outside the city, the Outskirts dishing out a massive betrayal at the last moment. Thankfully, from the cries echoing in the hallway, it didn't seem to be that.

But what kind of cries were those? They didn't sound human. Sage recognized them as soon as Little Man broke the window to her room for escape.

Taz.

"It's Taz!" Sage croaked to Gertrude. "Taz is here! M-my sister!" She didn't realize how much she was shaking until Gertrude held her arms steady.

"Our priority is getting you to safety," she said. "We need to move—now."

"No! If I leave, Taz will continue destroying everything! He'll kill even more people and I can't let that happen!"

"Sage, how do you know he's here for you?"

"Who else would he be here for?" Sage rasped weakly. "He wouldn't just attack unless he knew for certain I was here! Please, Gertrude, I have to go!"

"AND GET YOURSELF KILLED?!" Gertrude cried in her face. She had never looked so deranged before. "What the hell's wrong with you?!"

"I NEED TO STOP THEM!" Sage cried back, and it took all the strength she had to do so. "If I show up, fewer people will die! I'll find my own way to escape after I deal with them—please clear as many people as you can!"

And then, in her pajamas, Sage rushed out of her room. She picked up her sword on the way, but before she got to burst through the door, someone grabbed her arm.

Sage whipped around, facing Gertrude.

Gertrude looked like she had swallowed a rock.

"They'll kill you," she whispered, as if they had all the time in the world to talk about this.

"They won't," Sage assured her. "They won't."

"We can't take that risk. Don't you understand? The Warlord will go *insane* if he finds out something happened to you while he was unconscious."

"This isn't anyone's fault, Gertrude! This isn't on anyone—"

"It's on *us*, Sage. If he finds out that we let you be taken or killed, he'll hang us and torture us."

"That's ridiculous!" Sage exclaimed. "Why on earth would he do that? This isn't your fault—"

"He won't see it that way!" Gertrude yelled, desperate now. She was hyperventilating. Little Man was doing the same, completely unnerved. Not for their lives, but Sage's. Forget Taz—the Warlord would have their heads. "You just don't get it, do you, Sage? There's a reason they call him the Warlord. He's vicious and cruel, nothing like the charming man you've fallen in love with. You've distracted him, given him a new reason to live, and he's changed because of that. If you're gone, however, he'll revert back to his old self and he'll make sure to hang our heads next to the rest of them at the museum!"

"That is bullshit," Sage stated steadily. "First of all, nothing is going to happen to me. Secondly, *I* make my own decisions, and if he has a problem with that, he will face me. Thirdly, if I find out that he's hurt anyone because of a decision I made, then I won't ever forgive him. If you are that terrified of the outcome, wait for me outside. I'll handle Taz on my own. Just trust me, Gertrude!" She yelled that last part when Gertrude was about to argue. Then she burst through the door before the two could call her back.

Damian would hurt his own allies? Sage found that hard to believe. The man was childish and dramatic, but he wouldn't punish Gertrude and Little Man for something Sage did, would he?

Sage didn't have time to think about Damian right now—she was about to enter a battle, and she had a terrible feeling in her gut. Instinct was trying to tell her that Gertrude was right—she was in extreme danger—and the proof was the blood. It wasn't anywhere in this hall, but there was plenty of it downstairs where Taz was having a field day.

"Sage!" Gertrude and Little Man joined her. "We're not leaving you alone!" And it was a good thing, too, because Little Man slashed at something behind Sage that looked like a large spider. It collapsed on its back, cut in half, legs twitching in the air. It was pink and fleshy like Samson, but this wasn't a friendly creature that could think and act for itself. It seemed to be coming from a source, taking over the palace as an extension of something else.

Horror exploded in Sage's chest. The farther down she went, the more of those creatures she ran into. It was Gertrude and Little Man who were knocking them back to give her the leeway she needed to make it to the bottom floor.

That's where Sage saw all the blood. And the carcasses.

She threw her hand over her mouth.

Then there, in the middle of it all, was Taz.

He was twice as monstrous as before, standing at over seven feet tall. He looked like an oversized eel with gray wrinkly skin and bulbous lips. He was a tank acting on behalf of Wren, who was nowhere to be seen. It was apparent that he had collected even more Cells in the past couple months, and this time he didn't intend to lose against Sage or any of the fools who tried attacking him. Bullets, swords, and force fields were child's play. And here Sage thought she had gathered an indestructible army.

Actually, most of those bodies were from the Diamond City military. She knew by the stark white uniforms strewn around the floor like doves that had been shot down. For them, there was no strategy, no order, to what was happening inside the palace. This was a fight for survival, and these kinds of battles always unsettled Sage. When she didn't have a plan or know her chances of winning, her mind went into overdrive and her concentration broke. It made her grip shake around the hilt of her sword, rendering her useless.

Taz straightened, eyes on hers. His frame was long and twitchy, with tendrils coming out of everywhere, as if the Cells within him were overflowing in the shape of more limbs. There were eyes and mouths galore, saliva dribbling, blood dripping from the lips of some, still gnawing on the flesh of victims. He was much more aggressive, too, driving a talon right through Sage's chest and pinning her to the wall.

Little Man sliced through the tentacle and Gertrude yanked out the talon. She grabbed hold of Sage, steadying her, then turned to Taz, who remained unfazed. Little Man was panting. Some of the council were still hiding beneath tables, Gregory included, completely defenseless now that most of their guards were dead.

Despite the carnage, it was obvious that Taz was here for one person. He killed anyone who was in his way, and his next obstacles were Little Man and Gertrude, who weren't going to back down. With their training and weapons, they were a formidable foe, and with Sage jumping in, the fight was fairly even. Wren wasn't in sight, but Sage feared that'd change soon. If Taz was here . . . she had to be, too.

It didn't take long for Taz to quickly gain the upper hand, throwing Little Man across the room and capturing Gertrude by the throat. He squeezed tightly, keeping her down, as the lifeless eyes poured into hers. Sage used a blast of energy to knock him back, stunning him before throwing her sword into his face. With so many Cells in his body, Slainium hardly made a dent, but it allowed Gertrude to scramble away. Taz yanked the sword from his face, but he didn't use it because Wren didn't want her sister dead.

"Down, Taz," came Wren's voice from the other side of the room. "Don't hurt her. Can't you see she's about to keel over?"

Taz stopped. Sage looked over his shoulder at Wren, who manifested from the carnage, sashaying her way over to them in that long white gown she liked to wear. Her expression was significantly different than the one from the Junkyard. This attack on Heart wasn't meant to be a game—she had every intention of tracking Sage down for a reason.

"Gregory had to die," Wren said flatly. She had his head in her hand, cut at the neck. Without his Cells, he was all white and wrinkly. "The council did, too."

Sage blinked. Her head and heart were pounding too violently, and they weren't allowing her to process what Wren was saying.

"They were working with the Squids," she went on. "After all this time and effort to free this precious city, they continued taking instructions like dogs. The promises of grandeur were too great. I was completely sickened by them, so I figured out a better way: I took all my Cells back. Most of them anyway. I know the Warlord and your crew won't allow the Squids to come back, so all we have to do is disappear."

"D-disappear?" Sage croaked.

"Leave this pitiful city," Wren clarified with a scowl. "Where we'll be used as lab rats, either to make Enhanced or babies. Ultimately, that's what the Warlord wants. He's using you, sister. Don't be stupid."

"You want us to leave?" Sage clenched her fists, sweat pouring down her face. "Leave them just like that? They need us, Wren!"

Wren shook her head. "No. They need to defend themselves. We, on the other hand, have to fight the Squids." She stepped up to Taz, stroking his arm. "With Taz all nice and powerful, we'll make a dent in them."

"That's lunacy!" Little Man cried, rising to his feet. "You're saying that the two of you are going to take on an army of Squids? We need to do this together—"

Wren seized Little Man with nothing but her clenched fist. He rose in the air as if pulled by invisible ropes. Wren's eyes flashed remorselessly.

"Shut up."

"NO!" Sage screamed, lunging at her sister. She didn't even make it halfway because Taz smashed into her, throwing her across the room. It didn't take long for Wren to drain Little Man of all his Cells, too, not caring a damn for the life she was killing in the process. Wren wasn't here to win Sage's favor—she was here to take her by force. Or maybe she just didn't care, and so she didn't think Sage cared for someone so insignificant either.

Gertrude was so horrified that she didn't scream. She shuffled back, her face losing all color. Wren turned to her next, and Sage cried out to get her attention.

"ALL RIGHT!" Sage threw up her hands. "ALL RIGHT! I-I surrender! I'll go with you—just stop fucking killing people!" She gnashed her teeth to stop the screams in her chest. Veins popped out of her face from the strain. She bit her tongue and clenched her fists even harder, drawing blood from both. She tried not to look at Little Man on the floor, but his body was a white speck in her peripheral and he was impossible to ignore.

"My goodness, sister, was it that terribly difficult for you?" Wren smiled at her, eyes narrowing into slits. "I thought you'd want to spend time with me. Don't you love me?"

"I can't love someone who acts like a damn monster," Sage croaked.

"A monster? Dear sister, what about what the humans did to me? Weren't they monsters?"

"Not all of them, damn it! Enhanced had no fault in your torture—it was the Kilstrongs, and one's dead while the other is your favorite pet!"

"Well, excuse me," Wren spat. "I didn't know you were so righteous after all the people you've killed."

"I don't kill them for fun!" Sage yelled.

"And do you think I do this for fun? I am taking back what is *mine*."

There was absolutely no reasoning with Wren, so Sage just stopped. Aside from the horrible pain in her body, she had others to consider. The rebels and the rest of her allies were about to come barging in soon, and she couldn't put them in danger. While numbers were sure to overwhelm Wren and Taz, Sage didn't want to risk losing anyone else today.

Sword on the ground some feet away, Sage slowly made her way to Taz. She rested her hand on his arm and closed her eyes, refusing to look at anyone or anything as she surrendered to this beast. Even Gertrude didn't have the strength to croak out her name. Perhaps it was best if Sage left after all.

Taz wrapped an arm around her waist and hoisted her onto his shoulder. It was ironic that his movements were so careful and gentle now, as if he was afraid of hurting her. Maybe he sensed how weak she was.

"Let's go, Taz!" Wren said from his other shoulder.

Not only did Taz have monstrous strength, but he sprouted wings and took off into the sky. He smashed through the roof of the palace and burst into the cool dawn air. Sage kept her eyes closed because she didn't want to see her allies below, some of them shouting and pointing in wonder. They all had to know that the council was dead by now. Blackburn was probably scurrying around like a chicken with its head cut off, unable to function without his beloved leaders.

Agathe and Louis, Sage said in her mind over and over again. Those two gave her hope. Those two were going to do the right thing. And with Damian at their side, they'd be well protected. Sage's only regret was leaving her phone behind because she couldn't communicate with him one last time. Surely, he had to be awake, with his heart beating in his chest again. At the very least, Sage could leave Diamond City knowing she had given a man the most precious part of himself back.

I love you, darling, Sage thought to herself, fighting not to cry again. She couldn't when she still had a mission to accomplish. Now that Wren was taking her to the base of the Roaring Mountains, she had to prepare to find her nieces. She still couldn't fathom that Samson was the one who was behind this . . .

Eventually, Taz started his descent. Sage didn't even feel the temperature change. Her fever was that high, and she wondered if she'd suffer permanent brain damage because of it. Maybe she should have allowed Dr. X to examine her, but Stars, he was creepy and Sage shuddered at the thought of anyone poking and prodding her. Poor Wren must have gone through so much in that laboratory with scientists constantly extracting Cells, but that wasn't an excuse to torture others. And it certainly wasn't an excuse to steal Sage away from her family and friends.

She'll help you find your nieces, said that voice in her thoughts again.

Would she? Maybe. But Sage wasn't here to play along with her sister, who had been keeping a close eye on her in Mousafeld. How else would she have been able to pinpoint Sage? And now she was ready to deliver her to the Squids. Fight them? Wren wasn't that stupid. Wren couldn't care less about Candice and Olivia so long as she had a gift for the Squids in exchange for a place in their ranks. That's what this was about.

Sage reached into her pajama pants and whipped out her

dagger. She had always taught her nieces to be ready, and she had to follow her own advice. It was part of being a good parent. Her heart ached for them, but she'd never be able to rescue them if she was a slave.

She stabbed Taz right in the eye, making him howl. It shook the air, the very mountains—these foul sounds that left his throat—and followed her miles below into the never-ending snow.

Sage hit the ground hard. She blacked out upon impact, just as bones shattered and blood flooded her mouth. When she regained consciousness, eyes fluttering, she was amidst a bed of broken branches. She thought she could hear someone yelling in the distance.

"Stars," Sage rasped, crawling to a tree. Her right arm was broken and there were a few shattered ribs. Maybe her hip, too. These were the kinds of injuries that never lasted, but the healing process was especially slow at the moment. Her head was pounding and her heart was out of control, sending her body into shock. She was worthless and defenseless with her sister and Taz out on the prowl. She didn't even have her dagger anymore. Her sister probably had it now.

All Sage could do was rest. She closed her eyes and tried to keep as still as possible. She trembled because she was terrified and didn't know what to do. It wasn't so much for her own safety either—she couldn't stop thinking of Candice and Olivia.

Survival instincts kicked back in, and Sage pinpointed her own location. She was at the base of the mountains, so if she traveled south, she'd eventually hit Winterfeld. Winterfeld wasn't very far from here either.

Gathering her strength, Sage slowly climbed to her knees. She used the trunk of a nearby tree to stand up straight. When she took a few steps without tumbling, she inched south as planned. All she could do was focus on her breathing and keep an ear out for Wren and Taz. The forest was doing its job of concealing her, so Sage covered a couple of miles before she collapsed again.

Then, in the distance, she saw a cemetery. The tombstones

stretched on as far as the eye could see, aligned in perfect rows to honor the dead. It was a practice from the Clarity District. Claritians believed that burying the dead at the base of the Roaring Mountains was good luck, since it was the closest any human or Enhanced could get to the Squids. Or so they said. Right now, Sage believed it. Maybe that was why she had made it out of the forest alive: the Squids were smiling down at her. What luck.

Sage trudged across the clearing, perfectly aware that she was out in the open. Wren and Taz were probably in the sky, searching for her from above. Still, Sage felt a sudden need to find Phoebe's grave, as if her proximity to Damian's daughter would cure her of all of her ailments.

HERE LIES PHOEBE DAMARIS

BELOVED DAUGHTER AND FRIEND

MONTH OF LOYALTY, 22, 81 - MONTH OF FLARE, 9, 100

Damian visited every day. Nova came regularly, too. But would any of them come today when Sage needed them the most? More than likely, she'd freeze out here. Her body temperature was already starting to plummet. She was clad in her pajamas, and it wouldn't take long for her heart to stop. She just didn't have the energy to crawl to Winterfeld right now, and she much preferred lying still and falling asleep . . .

"Hello?"

Sage raised her head. She got the feeling that was directed at her.

Sure enough, some Squid must have overheard her prayers because Nova came rushing out of seemingly nowhere. She was like a beacon of light in all the white, her cheeks flushed with life, hair spilling out from beneath her beanie. Her eyes widened as soon as she recognized the body in the snow.

"Sage?!"

Sage got up. She fell right onto Nova, who grabbed her and held steady.

"Stars, you're freezing!" Nova cried. "W-what the hell happened to you? E-everyone's going crazy in Heart! I-I heard about the fight, and no one even knows if you're alive!"

"Gun," Sage breathed raggedly.

Nova blinked. "What?"

"I need . . . a gun . . . "

Nova had a lot of coats on, but she didn't have a gun in her pockets. And definitely not the kind Sage had in mind. Ignoring her request, Nova staggered back to her home, which was right along the edge of the clearing.

"Stars!" Nova croaked, bringing Sage inside. It smelled like pine, and the electric fireplace was lit up, heating the room. She grabbed a quilt, sat Sage on the couch, then made some very hot tea that Sage dribbled all over herself. Nova looked on worriedly, but at least Sage was conscious. "What happened to you, Sage?"

Sage gazed at the large shotgun in the corner of the living room. God only knew what foul beasts could potentially attack here. Her mind screamed at her to pick it up. That's what she had to do to survive. She didn't hear a single word that was leaving Nova's mouth. Eventually, she dozed off.

"Sage?" Nova snapped her fingers in her face.

Sage looked up.

"Are you with me?"

No. Sage laid down and curled up beneath the quilt. Seconds later, she was fast asleep.

The next time Sage woke up, it was dark. Night must have fallen. She was still on the couch in Nova's very cozy living room. She heard Nova talking on the phone in the bedroom. The door was ajar.

"Yes, she's safe and still asleep . . . " Nova whispered, so as not to disturb Sage. "She was so cold and wounded . . . No, she didn't say anything . . . I-I don't know—I haven't seen Wren . . . There haven't been any disturbances . . . "

Sage hugged her body because she didn't want to get up. But something kept nagging at her to open her eyes, to move. Wren wasn't going to give up looking for her—she had probably figured out that Sage was no longer in the forest and had made her way to Winterfeld...

"No, I won't move from here," Nova went on. Who was she talking to? Damian? "I will wait for you, of course..."

Sage rolled off the couch and landed on the rug with a thud. She felt every bruise on her arm and ribs. Thankfully, they were no longer fractured. That didn't make moving around any easier, though—Sage crashed into the glass table, knocking over the TV remote before making it to the gun in her line of vision.

Yes, this thing shot huge waves of energy, capable of blowing anything remotely Enhanced off their feet. When it came to weapons, Winterfeld was number one. Gavin had put so much time and energy into securing his people, and Sage thanked him for it even if an alliance with him hadn't quite worked out. The Diamond City military might have stood a better chance against Taz if the rebels had had time to jump in. The attack on the palace must have happened so quickly. Who the hell had seen Taz fly in from the sky? Certainly not anyone at the palace.

"Sage?"

Sage rushed out of the house before Nova caught her. She was in a new set of pajamas now, with thick, cozy socks, so the cold wasn't so biting on her soles. She had a hard time navigating the ankle-deep snow, but at least she was warm and much more nimble.

Then there, in the distance, was a speck with wings. Taz and Wren were on their way. Nova reached her and all Sage said was, "Call for backup!"

She made her way to the cemetery, where there was no one around. She didn't want to disturb the graves, but it was better than putting Winterfeld citizens at risk.

"Sister?!" Wren cackled from afar—she was coming in at a quick clip, about to dive right into Sage.

Sage was ready, and perhaps Wren wasn't expecting that. If she was, she certainly didn't care or didn't think that her weakened sister could cause too much damage. She had no idea what Nova's weapons were capable of, so she didn't dream that a single blast could blow Taz right out of the air.

Taz had already recovered from the dagger to the eye, but now he was missing half of his body. Wren jumped as he crashed into the snow, an explosion that alerted the whole town. Sage approached with caution, gun raised and ready for another round. She didn't let Taz regain his composure—she fired again, destroying his chest and shoulder, blood spurting like lava from a volcano.

"HOW DARE YOU!" Wren stabbed Sage in the back, plunging Sage's own dagger into a lung. Sage whipped around, smashed her sister's face with an elbow, and quickly dislodged the blade before she suffered any more damage.

Wren was just as exasperated as Sage, but she wasn't anywhere near as wounded. She danced around Sage's swipes fairly easily and even evaded a blast from the gun. Sage couldn't focus on her too much because Taz was coming around, and she needed to finish him quickly.

Sage chanced a strike from her sister and turned around to shoot him again. When Taz staggered, Sage pounced on him, thrusting the dagger straight into his heart. She did this as many times as she could, blood spraying all over her amidst his yelps of pain. Surely a being with that many Cells in his body wasn't stable and anywhere near functional in a life-or-death situation like this. There was a reason scientists never infused more than one dose—maybe two for commanders—of Cells into humans.

Of course, this was all wishful thinking. Taz wasn't that vulnerable or he wouldn't have survived this long. Thanks to Wren, who blew Sage right off of Taz, he was able to stand back up.

Sage tumbled on the snow, then hit a grave. She coughed up blood and held her side, vision going dark.

"Sister!" Wren cried, coming closer. "Just give up! You've lost!"

"N-never," Sage choked.

"You poor thing—you must be exhausted. Man . . . " Wren rubbed her abdomen. "The blood is horrible, and the pain even more so. I'm sure you're going through the exact same thing." She grabbed Sage's pants and yanked them down. She furrowed her brows when she saw no blood.

Sage raised a leg and kicked her sister square in the face. She pulled up her pants, squirming on the snow, and glared at Wren across the field.

"You're ..." Wren held her bleeding nose. "Y-you're ... not bleeding? So, wait, are you—"

Taz screamed.

Both Sage and Wren jumped and looked around. They gasped when they saw a massive Squid puncturing Taz with a flurry of tentacles.

Wren dropped to the snow, shocked. Sage couldn't believe her eyes.

Samson?

Sage had only ever seen one Squid in her lifetime, so she had no idea if this was another. But it didn't take her very long to recognize a person she had lived with for so many years. Even though Samson was in the middle of dismembering Taz like an artichoke, a look of fury on his face, one Sage only saw when she left her boots in the kitchen, Sage knew it was him.

"S-Squid?" Wren choked. "T-that's a Squid?"

Fast—so fast—Samson whacked her across the head. One was all it took to knock her out. He did it so quickly that Sage hadn't seen him move.

Sage backed up some more, utterly horrified. All those horrible things the council had said about him manipulating them and then taking the girls rained over her, bombarding her. She couldn't look at him the same way. In fact, she grew enraged.

"You lied to me," she whispered, despite the rage brewing in her chest. "You've been a spy all this time."

Samson sighed. His form slumped a bit, those sharp teeth as pronounced as ever. "Perhaps I wasn't clear about my intentions ... but that doesn't change anything, does it? That doesn't change the fact we grew up together and helped each other survive."

"BY LYING!" Sage roared, climbing to her feet. "WHERE ARE THE GIRLS?! I-is it true? Y-you took them?"

"Would you rather the council have them?" Samson asked quietly. "Or me? They're safe, Sage. I brought them here as soon as I collected them from the palace. I had no idea Bram had sold them in exchange for a bit of glory. Then again, he did that with you, so I'm not surprised."

"This is bullshit! Absolute bullshit!"

"What? That I was sent here to spy on you? Of course it's not." Samson picked up Wren from the snow. "That was my mission: to spy on the Optimum. We wanted more information regarding your physique. I gathered it, and so I am done."

Sage blinked. The air was getting colder now, cutting into her bones again. "D-done?"

"Yes, I'm done. The Lolligo want a full report on the hybrid. And so . . . " He patted Wren's behind. "I'm taking her in, going to make them believe it's you. The Lolligo don't know that the Optimum and the creator of Enhanced are two separate beings."

"W-wait—what's going to happen to her?"

"I don't know," Samson said quietly. "I imagine we'll retire her . . . for now."

"Why?!" Sage half-yelled, half-laughed. "Because the Squids have other hybrids in their military?"

Samson shook his head. "All the conceived hybrids are dead, Sage."

"W-what?"

"We've been unable to successfully birth another hybrid like you," Samson said.

"What kind of sick experiments are these?" Sage croaked. "How can you be behind this, Samson?"

"It's not me, Sage. Trust me . . . it's not."

"What are the Squids doing? Are they building some kind of army?"

Samson's silence neither confirmed nor denied that allegation. All the same, Sage crumbled beneath the implications. It was obvious the Squids were dabbling in reproduction experiments, whether it was to make themselves stronger or appease their curiosities didn't matter.

"Wren doesn't deserve this, Samson. Put her back."

"Then you'd like to go in her place?" From the look on Samson's face, this was the last thing he wanted.

No. No, absolutely not.

"SAGE!" Damian's voice boomed out of nowhere.

Sage turned her head immediately. Her heart took off when she saw Damian for the first time since his implant and then, behind him, her nieces as Samson had promised.

"Aunt Sage!" Candice was brave and she took a step, but Damian kept her back.

"Stay back!" he said to her. "Stay back!" He kicked through the snow until he reached Sage's side, sweeping her into his arms with a frazzled look on his face. Sage remembered that look from her previous fight with Wren . . . now it was turned to Samson, who remained stoic.

Samson's amber eyes flashed with affirmation. He, as well as Sage, knew that it was better for her to stay here. She had Damian, the girls—how could she possibly leave them? She couldn't. The answer was clear. Damian made it so.

"*You're not taking her!*" Damian hissed, like a rattlesnake spewing venom. He didn't have any makeup on in his rush to chase Sage, but shadows still touched all the right crevices on his face to make him look lethal. He was in an all-black coat and pants, an array of weapons strapped across his chest and waist. Most prominent was the sword—Sage's sword—and the gun. He didn't draw anything, but he was ready to. "Whatever the hell you are—you stay away from her!"

"Then I guess that means you'll take good care of her."

"No harm will ever come to her on my watch. Coincidentally, I was incapacitated yesterday when she faced the council, but that was a fluke."

"I understand," Samson said patiently.

"I'm sure you do," Damian spat. "Now fuck off."

"Damian." Sage clutched him. "That's . . . that's Samson."

Damian already knew that. Candice and Olivia must have filled him in. And while this was the Squid he supposedly looked up to, Sage's life was in danger. The defensiveness was overwhelming, as Gertrude had predicted it would be.

With nothing more to say, Samson stomped off with Wren over his shoulder.

Sage had to ask, "Will you come back?"

Samson glanced at her. "Possibly," he said in Lolligo.

Epilogue

Sage heard giggling in the living room, and it was definitely Olivia. Stars, how she had missed her little niece. That girl always captured her heart. Her boy stories and dramas would entertain the hell out of anyone. A thirteen-year-old had a lot to learn about relationships, and who better to consult with than Damian?

"Well, I did like him," Olivia said thoughtfully. "But all my friends kept telling me he was talking to other girls, too."

"That, my dear, is what we call a womanizer."

"That's what Candice says, too. But what if he's not really serious when it comes to the other girls? What if he's trying to be friendly?"

Damian snorted. "Ask your aunt what she would say if I started to be 'friendly' with other women."

"But isn't it normal for boys my age to just be friends with girls?"

"Boys are not interested in 'just being friends.' They want sex with whoever is willing to give it to them. If he is truly the one for you, then he will like you for you and not pressure you into doing something you don't want. For example, I never pressured your aunt into sex. That happened naturally because we love each other."

"Seriously?" Sage breathed to herself. Damian pressured her every chance he got!

"No wonder she likes you!" Olivia said happily. "She stabs men who make the first move."

Damian chuckled. "I learned that lesson the hard way."

Sage sighed, but she let a smile play on her lips. When she moved her head, she found Candice on the bed next to her, typing away on her phone. It was a brand-new one from Winterfeld, with features that weren't available in Diamond City yet, like holographic touch screens and area scanners for full-fledged maps of a person's surroundings. That made exploring new areas a blast. Sage didn't like so much dependence on technology, but she cut the girl some slack after a horrible six months in hiding. At long last, Candice was free and ready to celebrate.

Winterfeld was hosting a festival at Capital Square. After the incident with Taz, these people needed a night of fun. It was nearly the month of Loyalty in Diamond City, too, but honoring spring in a foot of snow wasn't very practical. That, however, didn't stop Candice, who was in a beautiful fur dress, hair in intricate ringlets that ranged from small to big, front to back. Where the hell Damian had learned to do that, Sage didn't have a clue.

"How are you feeling, Aunt Sage?" Candice sat up, getting a good look at her.

"I'm all right." Sage caressed Candice's cheek. "Well, someone looks beautiful."

Really beautiful. There wasn't a single blemish on Candice's skin. Her silver eye shadow was a perfect contrast to her light brown complexion. Her lips looked fuller and plumper, too—was that Damian's gloss?

"It's all thanks to Damian, of course," Candice said happily.

"He hasn't said anything inappropriate around you, has he?" In addition to his already sexually-charged comments.

Candice chuckled. "I think everything he says is inappropriate. But that's fine because I think he really loves you. He talked about how there's going to be this massive wedding in Diamond City, and he has all these fashion ideas for you, the guests, and some guy named Preacher who's supposedly going to perform the rites."

Sage rolled her eyes.

"Is it true, Aunt Sage? I mean, are you really going to marry him? If you do, I think that would be awesome."

"You think so?"

"Well, yes. *If* you love him . . . but how can't you? I mean, he's really handsome—"

"Please don't tell him that."

"I think he already knows." Candice held Sage's hand. "And I know what you're going to say—it's not just about looks—but Damian went crazy when we told him you were fighting a monster. He nearly attacked Samson, and that's . . . well . . . brave. Who would attack a Lolligo? It's obvious he cares a lot about you. I mean, he's even staying with you tonight when we all know he really wants to look glamorous at that festival. He's worried about you, Aunt Sage." Candice turned serious. "I kind of am, too. It's been two weeks . . . Since when do you get sick?"

"I'm pretty worn out," Sage admitted. But thanks to all her bedrest, she did feel loads better. And knowing that her nieces were safe put the cherry on top of the cake. She basked in this moment of having the girls so close to her. Candice's hand was so warm. Olivia's giggles were obnoxious. Sage's smile grew. This was the dream she had been longing for.

Sage got out of bed to appreciate it a bit more. Nova was still at work, so the four of them had the house to themselves. It was a good thing, too, because Damian had shit everywhere, from hair irons to bows to fabrics to sprays to brushes to makeup kits. They had gone shopping that morning.

"Nova's going to have a heart attack," Sage breathed, marveling at the mess.

"Don't worry, darling." Damian beamed. He was standing behind Olivia, fixing her hair. "I will clean up after myself like my mother taught me."

"*Still* teaches you."

"Then it's a good thing she's around, so I don't forget."

"You need a spanking."

"Darling," Damian purred. "Not in front of the girls."

Candice and Olivia laughed. Sage rolled her eyes, but she laughed, too.

"How do I look, Aunt Sage?" Olivia asked.

Like Candice's sidekick. The two had the exact same hairstyle and similar dresses. Because Candice was older, hers was much more furry and sparkly. Olivia's was the kiddie version.

"All right, Aunt Sage." Olivia hopped off the chair. "I think I'm ready!"

Both of the girls were ready. They flew out of the house to spend some much-needed time at the festival. After so many months of hiding, this was their chance to have fun. They got to dance, socialize, eat, drink, and go on sleigh rides. There were competitions in each category, from whoever could prance around the dance floor like a fool to whoever could control a pack of dogs and cross the finish line first. There was a How-Much-Parfait-Can-You-Eat? Challenge, too, that was sure to create an epidemic of brain freeze and stomachaches. The girls weren't shy, and they were determined to bring back a prize.

Sage leaned against one of the beams from the front porch, her thoughts shifting from the girls to Samson. Breathing in and out shakily, she glanced toward the cemetery. She wondered how Samson was doing… While she still loved him dearly, Damian didn't trust him at all. Not after so many years of lies and deception. In fact, he wanted to leave here as soon as possible.

"I worry about him." Sage looked at Damian in earnest. He was standing by the door, watching her closely. Dizzy spells were common. "Maybe he is sneaky… but I trust him. He didn't hand over the girls to the Squids."

"I don't think they would have made a difference in his grand scheme," Damian said. "To him, they're just two young girls who might not even survive childbirth."

"Yes, but they were meant to draw me in, to be used as bait."

"Sure, but he has your sister now. And based on what the Squids have been up to lately, it seems they really are strengthening their forces. They want hybrids because hybrids blend into human populations and are near indestructible. A hybrid is the reason they lost the war."

"Doesn't it sound silly looking back at it?" Sage said quietly. "The Squids retreated because of me . . . one person."

"Who they then spied on for nearly a hundred years," Damian replied. "This is all part of their experiment. They're not going to barge in and destroy us too quickly. They want to watch us first, then take us down in the swiftest way possible. One to their benefit. The why is irrelevant to us."

"Is it?"

"Of course. We are not pawns to fight in the wars of Squids, no matter the reason."

Sage hated it, but Damian was right. He was so right. And that's what made her upset. It wasn't just Samson and Wren and where they were now that kept plaguing her thoughts either—it was the fact they were sitting ducks. The unknown was too vast for Sage to feel any comfort.

Damian stepped up to her. He held her chin. "We'll figure something out. We don't have to think about it this very instant, do we? Let's just relax for a little bit."

"He knows you're the Optimum," Agathe said. "He knows what your blood can do. If he wants you, it's because of that. He wants to create more Enhanced."

No, that couldn't be Damian. Not the one standing in front of her, eyes ablaze with so much warmth and love. He wasn't Bram, looking for ways to use her.

Bram was dead now. Somehow, he had committed suicide in his cell, slit his wrists with the edge of a broken bowl. Sage's head spun thinking about it. Damian was a bit too dismissive, but that was his way of trying to move on. He wanted to return to Diamond City with her, to throw that wedding/fashion show he was organizing. He cared more about that than Louis and Agathe's coronation next weekend.

Already they were proving to be effective leaders. Even with no council, the two had taken charge of Heart and instilled some order in the after-effects of the horrible battle that had taken place there. Taz's attack had thrown the entire Diamond City military off course, and the rebels, although the majority of them hadn't fought, still needed direction. The clean-up was massive, but underway. Sage knew because Damian informed her of everything. Otherwise, she'd have no way of communicating . . . or knowing that Gertrude was stable. Somewhat.

Little Man was dead. And Sage would've had nightmares was it not for Bram, who kept worming his way into her thoughts. Something was wrong, and it felt wrong, because Bram wasn't the kind to commit suicide. If anything, he'd be trying to find his way into the rebels' good graces. He wouldn't have left the girls behind . . .

No, said the voice in Sage's head. *But he'd give them over to the council.*

"Look at me, Sage." Damian turned her face to him. His palm was so warm, soothing her. "Please don't worry. Samson is gone, and we should be glad about it. I know you raised him, but he was working for the Squids. He took your sister in your stead, and I prefer it that way. When it comes to Bram . . ." He went quiet for a moment. "Guilt plays a big factor in his actions."

"I don't understand why he'd betray me like that." Sage screwed up her face. "Did the council really promise him that much?"

"Yes," Damian said simply. "Living at the palace for some is a dream come true. And maybe it was for you at some point . . . but it was more so for him. He'd been willing to do anything to achieve it."

Sage wrapped her arms around his waist, hands sliding up his back. She tucked her head underneath his chin, cheek on his chest. She closed her eyes, listening to that steady, powerful beating in his sternum. It reminded her that she had made a very special man's dream come true, completing him in so many ways. In return, Sage swelled with happiness. Her own dreams had come true, too. Perhaps not in the way she had envisioned it many months ago, but here she was with the man she loved in a town that was remote and peaceful. It didn't have the glamor that Heart had, but did Sage really need that? Gilded utensils and lacy dresses? No, this was perfect. All this after so much fighting and loss. Somehow, through it all, she had found what she had always wanted.

Her very own fairy tale. One that had endured so much chaos. A journey with unknown outcomes, starting with her trek into the Circular Forest and ending with the battle against Wren and Taz in the cemetery.

"When I woke up," Damian started softly, holding her tighter, "I was so afraid. You had gone to Diamond City on your own … and I didn't know how you were. I couldn't reach you. And that fear was greater than any I had ever felt in my life, even when I was strapped down to a table and tortured by my own brother. With my brother, I fought for my life … but now I fight for yours."

Tears welled in Sage's eyes.

"You are pure." Damian kissed her head. "And I will let no one tarnish you. Anyone who does will pay with their life."

Even Bram.

"My brother's in containment. He won't be a bother to you anymore."

"I don't want you to be a monster," Sage whispered.

"Worry not." Damian nudged her forehead with his nose, lifting her face. "It is Agathe and Louis' call to make now. Not mine."

That horrible pressure in Sage's chest lessened. She relaxed, tucking her head back beneath his chin, and continued listening to his heartbeat. She closed her eyes and sighed with ease.

"Come inside, darling. I wouldn't want you to get sick." Damian took her back into the house. "Speaking of, how are you feeling?" He touched her forehead, feeling for a fever.

"Better." Sage smiled at his face. It looked like Olivia had been trying her hand at makeup. Damian's foundation was too dark and the blush was off. At least his eyeliner and shadow were decent.

Damian shrugged. "She insisted."

"I'm not sure"—Sage picked up a damp cloth and dabbed at his lips—"that red lipstick suits you."

"That bad?"

"Pretty bad."

They kissed. It was the first one they'd shared in a while. Damian picked her up and wrapped her legs around his waist. He deposited her on the couch, his body on top of hers. Sage held him, breathing in his scent. She ran her hands over his shoulders to his back. At least the festival wasn't over until midnight. They had plenty of time to forget that the outside world existed and that they always had each other. After suffering such betrayals at the hands of family, their loyalty to one another was unquestionable to this day. Because of it, they'd soon be married and leading peaceful lives. Sage would teach Damian how to make the Hippo . . . and Damian would make her the star of his ultra fashion show.

"Darling," Damian whispered against her lips. "You are delightful."

Sage smiled. This time it reached her eyes and pure happiness shined from them. Damian's hand in between her legs only fueled her desire. Somehow, it had wormed its way into her pants. It was enough to distract her from the lack of blood dripping from her uterus. At least, until Damian mentioned it.

"Are you not menstruating yet?" he asked, eyes lidded. "Ileana didn't like to have sex when she was. Or do you not care?"

"I haven't bled yet," Sage said softly. She closed her eyes as Damian's fingers pressed into her, confirming her words.

It was the truth. No bleeding, just a sharp pain in her womb as if a cocoon was weaving itself inside her. What that meant, Sage could only speculate. She could neither say nor do anything else until she knew for sure. Until then, she pulled Damian in for another kiss.

Desire bursting into flames, Sage embraced him wholly and heartedly. She lost herself in him and continued living the fairy tale.

She had a feeling it wasn't going to last.

Acknowledgements

Writing a book takes so much more than just sitting in front of a screen or notebook for a few hours everyday for a year (or years). Aside from plotting, world-building, and character developing, it's putting it into the hands of the reader that truly takes work and dedication.

Diamond City's first revisions came from the incredible Nathan Bransford from Nathan Bransford Books, LLC. It's never easy for an author to relinquish his or her baby to another set of eyes, but alas, it's a necessary evil. The first round of edits was a bit tough because I changed the first chapter quite drastically, but I also acknowledge how much better the story became as a result of it. Thank you, Nathan, for those harsh critiques—I learned a lot!

Additionally, I'd like to thank my editor, Emily Lawrence, for her patience, guidance, and moral support as I continued to change and better what was a manuscript I had read over a gazillion times. Rome wasn't built in a day, and neither was Diamond City. What started as an idea in 2021 took years to develop into the full-fledged story it is today. Kira and James, your beautiful cover design is matched by no other. Julie, Ryan, Mike, and Matt—wow. Emailing you on a weekly basis has become routine, and I think I'd go into withdrawals if I stopped. Cheers to many projects in the future. Thank you for your patience and amazing work!

While my publication team helped me put this book out there, there wouldn't have been one to begin with had it not been for some incredible friends and family members who pushed me (in a good way) in this amazing undertaking.

I don't think I'd be writing these acknowledgments right now if it wasn't for you, Aris, and our countless lunch and planning period meetings to discuss plots and dreams of authorship. Your light-heartedness, laughter, and sincerity helped launch this story (and so many others to come) into the sky and I have nothing but love and appreciation for you and your help.

Thank you to my dearest friend, Jonathan, who is the best co-worker I could ever have. You weren't just at the ready when we were disciplining sixth graders, but you were there to encourage me to achieve my dream by showing me that you could achieve yours through music.

To Danielle, for all your positive advice even from a state away. Your text messages always keep my head straight, and I have your glare forever imprinted in my mind to remind me to be sensible in my goals.

To Armando and Claudia, for kicking ass not only in the gym, but also in life. You guys are a bigger role model to me than you will ever know. Thanks for encouraging me whenever we talked about my career and my goals for the future.

To Bianca, for all your smiles, laughter, and bonding over TeeTurtle shirts. We spent a lot of evenings talking about the road to publication and how many gigs I should get for my iPod.

To Andrew, one of the most genuine human beings I know. You always greet me with a smile every time I see you. You and your family are beautiful souls who've helped me so much. Thank you for all your support and guidance.

To Ronald, the superman from Steelhouse. You believe I can do anything, but I don't think I told you I wrote a book.

To my best friend, Cassandra, who keeps a smile on her face no matter where life takes her. Diamond City started because of my critiques and complaints of a certain book and character (you know the one) and our endless discussions over feminism.

To my family: you guys were there the day I thought it'd be a good idea to publish a book in 2012. Eleven years later, after so much growing, improving, and persistence, here we are. Thank you, Mom, for keeping a clear head on my shoulders and teaching me about life, through good and bad times. Thank you, Dad, for believing I could do anything and for cheering me on even when I thought about giving up publishing. Thank you, Richard, for always sticking to what you love and doing it no matter what anyone says. You've inspired me so much. And thank you, Robin, the most beautiful Siberian Husky in existence, for showing me that sometimes the best thing in life is chewing a bone.

Thank you, THE READER, for your support! Writing is fun, but at the end of the day, true pleasure comes from knowing I have entertained you with a story I made up. I hope that you were able to escape from the daily grinds of life even if it was for a little bit, and that you're looking forward to the next installment of this series (coming soon).

And, lastly, I'd like to thank my Heavenly Father, Jesus Christ, and Mother Mary for giving me the inspiration, dedication, and persistence that it takes to write and publish a novel from beginning to end. Not only that, but I am forever grateful for the people they put in my life that helped me achieve this goal.

Thank you!

About the Author

Astrid Cole has a master's in English Literature from Florida International University. Although she enjoys all subjects, she started writing fiction in high school and hasn't stopped since. When she's not plotting her next novel, she's hitting the gym. A former body-builder, running and exercise are a part of her daily routine . . . and so are playing video games and watching horror movies. Diamond City is her first published novel.

You can find her on all social media platforms @astridcolebooks.